HUNG

Bᵢ

IMMORTALIꓕ ꓬ ᵁ CHAOS
(epic fantasy series)
Wreckers Gate: Book One
Landsend Plateau: Book Two
Guardians Watch: Book Three
Hunger's Reach: Book Four
Oblivion's Grasp: Book Five

ALSO BY ERIC T KNIGHT

CHAOS AND RETRIBUTION
(sequel to Immortality and Chaos)
Stone Bound: Book One
Sky Touched: Book Two
Sea Born: Book Three
(BOOK 4 SPRING OF 2018)

THE ACTION-ADVENTURE-COMEDY SERIES
Lone Wolf Howls

THE ACTION THRILLER
WATCHING THE END OF THE WORLD

All books available at Amazon.com

Follow me at:
ericTknight.com

Hunger's Reach
Book Four of
Immortality and Chaos
by
Eric T Knight

Copyright © 2018 by Eric T Knight
Version 1.1 8/2016
ISBN-13: 978-1986064514
ISBN-10: 1986064514

For Daniel

I am so proud

of the person you are growing up to be,

your gentleness, your heart, your sense of humor.

ONE

The Gur al Krin desert was quiet. No wind stirred the massive orange and red sand dunes. The night was clear. A sliver of moon hung in the eastern sky.

In a flattened area a scattered handful of huge, black stones, their angles too regular to be natural, lay scattered about the edges of a small crater, as if tossed there by an explosion from below. At the bottom of the crater the entrance to a tunnel was just visible, choked with sand and rock.

From the tunnel came a scraping sound. Stones were shifted; sand poured down. The tunnel grew wider. A hand – too large to belong to a human and the color of dark copper – emerged from the darkness and gripped the edge. Another hand appeared, and then Shorn pulled himself from the crater, Netra draped over his shoulder.

He laid her gently on the sand, then knelt beside the tunnel for a moment, listening. No sounds came from below. Nor had he heard any sounds of pursuit since fleeing the cavern with Netra.

What happened down there? He was not entirely sure. All he knew for sure was that he'd caught up to her too late to save her from it.

To save her from herself.

He'd heard the explosion and when he entered the cavern she was lying unconscious on the ground. On one side of the cavern was a huge stone wall the color of rotted ice, a gaping hole ripped in the center of it. In the shadows of the hole he'd glimpsed movement and felt the presence of something ancient and powerful. He hadn't waited to learn more, snatching her up and running.

One thing he did know: Melekath was free. His gut told him Netra was the reason. She'd been used, tricked. He'd failed her. He'd promised himself that he'd protect her. He should have found a way to stop her, but instead he'd stood aside – even though he could see what was happening to her – and said nothing until it was too late.

When he first made his vow to Netra he did so purely out of a sense of duty. But over the next few weeks as he traveled with her that vow changed, deepened. She showed him that there was still something worth living for, that maybe there was still a chance to redeem himself. Her cause had become his. But it was more than that. From her he began to glimpse the true value of life, to see that there was more to the world than fighting.

Then, seeing her head down the dead-end path that he'd spent so much of his life on, hating, killing... He knew where that path led but he didn't know how to divert her from it.

So he did nothing and this was what it led to.

He knelt beside her. "I'm sorry," he said softly. He felt for her pulse. It was thin and faint, but it was there. She had not moved since he'd picked her up. She wasn't bleeding. He ran his fingers across the contours of her skull but found no lumps. Whatever injuries she had, they were internal, which worried him. He was no healer, but he was a warrior and he had seen a great deal of injury and death, enough to know that internal injuries could be the deadliest. If she was injured inside, there was nothing he could do for her.

He sat back on his heels and took a drink from his water skin, noticing how low it was. Water would soon be a problem. With daylight would come the brutal heat. Injuries wouldn't matter if they both died of thirst. They needed to get out of this desert as soon as possible.

He scanned the horizon, wondering which way to go. Towering sand dunes surrounded them on all sides. There was nothing else to see. There were no mountains or other landmarks for him to fix on. Any tracks he had left had been wiped away by the wind. None of the sand dunes looked familiar. On the way in he had been focused only on following Netra. He had not considered what might come after. He frowned. He had no idea how big this desert was. Choosing the wrong direction would leave them at the mercy of the sun and the heat. They would not need Melekath to kill them then.

After a time, he noticed a slowly spreading glow in the sky, which told him where east was. Now he had something to go on. As best he could remember, he had traveled roughly south through the desert. Which meant that they needed to go north. He picked Netra up, cradling her in his arms instead of over his shoulder, now that he did not have to worry about striking her head on the sides of the tunnel.

Choosing a gap between two of the dunes that seemed to lead north, he set off.

He had not walked for very long when there was a fork in the path between the dunes. Neither went directly north so after a minute of pondering he chose the left one and continued on. The dunes did not run straight, but twisted side to side and a few minutes later he realized that he was walking more west than north. He cursed under his breath, but continued on. A short while later he realized he was now walking almost due south.

Cursing under his breath, he backtracked and took the right fork. This one meandered left, then right, and forked several more times, but he seemed to be proceeding more or less north, though it was hard to tell for sure. Eventually the sun rose, but it was on his left instead of his right, which meant that he was actually walking south.

He stopped and laid Netra on the sand. She was still motionless. He held the water skin to her mouth and managed to get a small amount down her throat. He looked up at the dunes that towered on all sides. He needed to get his bearings.

Leaving Netra where she was, he climbed the dune. It wasn't easy. The sand was like powder and he sank in almost to his knees with each step. He slid backwards one step for every two that he took forwards. And it was starting to get hot. It took longer than he'd thought, but finally he reached the top of the dune.

There was nothing but sand dunes in every direction as far as he could see. No sign of a way out. No sign of where he had come from. The sun was climbing and the heat was rising steadily. Frustrated, Shorn slid back down the dune to where Netra lay.

If only she would wake up. She'd know which way to go to get out of here. But she showed no signs of stirring.

He looked back the way he'd come, considering backtracking, then discarded the idea. The way the dunes twisted around, he was likely to be walking north again soon enough. If he started doubting himself and turning back, he'd never get them out of here. Best to just keep moving forward. Picking Netra up once again, he continued on.

In time the sun rose over the dunes and the last of the shade disappeared. The heat quickly became murderous, seeming to beat on him from all sides. Heat waves made everything wavery and uncertain, as if seen from underwater. The sun was so bright it hurt to look at the sand and Shorn had to squint to keep from being blinded. The air grew so hot that it burned in his chest, each breath like a searing flame. He tried to protect Netra as much as he could, pulling the hood of her cloak up to cover her face. She seemed very pale and her breathing was shallow.

He gave up trying to guess which direction would free them from this hell and concentrated on simply moving. The dunes branched over and over in a never-ending maze. It was crazy. This place didn't make any sense. On the way in it had seemed so easy. He'd known which way to go and he'd gone that way. It was as simple as that. Thinking back, he realized that it had seemed simple because he was following Netra. Now he no longer had that beacon and he was completely lost. For the first time he had to consider the very real possibility that he would fail at this, that he and Netra would simply die out here in this maddening desert.

No. Failure was not an option. He had failed Netra once already. He should have stopped her before she broke the prison. He had seen what was happening to her, as the madness for Song slowly took her over. He did not really understand what Song was, though Netra had tried a number of times to explain it to him, but he knew what happened to warriors who became addicted to *fenis* back on Themor, and he thought that something similar had happened to Netra. Warriors who took *fenis* were initially stronger and faster. But it did not take long before the downside began, before they became delusional and irrational. Eventually the drug made them psychotic. He should have seen that it was happening to Netra. He should have stopped her.

He would not fail her again.

It was late afternoon when he decided to climb another dune. Maybe he would be able to see a way out.

This time he carried Netra with him, not wanting to leave her alone in the sand. It seemed to take forever, but finally he made it to the top of the dune. By the time he got there he was shaking from the heat and the strain and his water was gone. He had to set Netra down and stand with his hands on his knees until the blackness in his vision had passed. When he straightened and looked around his heart jumped.

There was a spire to the southeast, shimmering in the heat waves. Had he reached the rocky canyons at the edge of the desert? But there was nothing else beyond the spire, only unbroken sand dunes. Dazed as he was by the heat it took him a minute to realize it was not a natural spire. It was too symmetrical. Which meant that it was

manmade. Was there a buried city out here? Netra had never
anything about there being one.

It didn't make any difference what it was. There really wer
other options. They were out of water. It would be hours still be
the sun set and the heat let up. There was nothing else but san
every direction. It was the spire or nothing.

He gathered Netra up again and started towards it. Fortunately,
dune he was on, though it bent around in a long arc, seemed to
heading generally for the spire. Walking on top of the dune, while
as easy as walking along the bottom, was many times easier th
climbing the dune had been. A breeze even came up, stirring the sa
so that it blew around his ankles. The wind was hot, but it felt goo
drying his sweat and cooling him. He felt somewhat more hopeful.

Over the next hour the spire drew closer and what looked like th
roof of a building was revealed beside it. At the same time the win
increased, so that Shorn pulled Netra's cloak tighter around her an
pulled his hood down lower to keep the sand from his eyes. His thirst
grew more intense and he could not help but think that if there was no
water to be found up ahead then he and Netra would die. The thought
brought increased determination and he set his jaw, willing himself
forward at an increased pace.

At first he did not notice the howling in the distance, focused as
he was on simply putting one foot in front of the other. Only when he
heard the same howl coming from the opposite direction did he finally
look up. Ahead and to the left was a tornado of red-orange sand. He
stared at it, surprised. Turning, he saw that there was another one
behind him to the right. They were similar to something called
hovidos that he had seen a couple times in his youth on Themor, but
much bigger and denser. As he watched, they grew even taller and
thicker.

All of a sudden a hollow boom echoed across the desert as the one
in front of him exploded into flame. Shorn's eyes widened and he
spun in time to see the other one do the same.

Then they began to converge on him.

Shorn stared at them for a moment in disbelief. What kind of
crazy place was this? Sand didn't burn. And it sure didn't chase
people down like prey.

Which didn't change the fact that they were definitely getting
closer.

"Sorry, Netra," he said, tossing her over his shoulder. It wasn't going to be a smooth ride.

He ran along the top of the dune, keeping an eye on the one that was ahead and to his left as he went. The wind was blowing harder, screaming around him, driving the sand into his exposed skin and obscuring visibility. Already only the top of the spire was visible, jutting up from the far side of the next dune over. It would be invisible in a minute. The dune he was on was veering further to the left, towards one of the fiery tornados and away from the spire. It was time to take the plunge.

Shorn half-ran, half-slid down the face of the dune, somehow managing to keep his balance and not drop Netra. The blowing sand was thicker in the trough between the dunes, so bad that he ran with his eyes nearly shut, choking. The burning tornados were dimly visible through the blowing sand, their roar growing louder with each minute.

Shorn charged up the face of the next dune, cursing the sand as he went. It was like running in glue. It pulled at him greedily, reluctant to let him go, almost actively trying to drag him under. Every breath was a battle and his limbs were made of lead, but he fought his way upward, refusing to give in to weakness. On and on he climbed, until it seemed he had been running in sand forever, chased by fiery demons. His skin was starting to blister. The roar of the tornados had turned into a shriek.

All at once he reached the top of the dune. Blinded by the sand, he lost his balance, and fell over and down, trying to shield Netra with his body. They rolled and slid until they were brought up short by contact with something hard. A stone wall. Standing, he leaned against the wall and tried to shelter Netra as best he could in his arms. He could smell her hair burning. His skin was on fire. Sun and sky were gone, replaced by sand and the glow of the burning towers of sand as they closed in. The wind was howling like a wild thing.

Shorn stumbled along the stone wall, feeling it with his free hand. If he did not find a way in soon it would be too late.

All at once there was an opening. But it was small, not even big enough for Netra and far too small for him. Setting Netra down, Shorn put his hands into the opening and grabbed one side. The wall was easily several feet thick. Placing his foot against the wall, he took hold of one side of the opening, leaned back and gave a mighty heave. At first nothing happened, then with a groan, the stone slid outwards a

little. He shifted his grip and threw everything he had into it. A stone as big as his chest pulled free and Shorn shoved it aside.

Grabbing Netra, he shoved her through the opening and then dove through after her.

TWO

Sand had blown in through the opening over the centuries, half filling the room. Otherwise the fall would have killed them. They slid down the piled sand and onto the floor. After the heat outside, the stone floor was blessedly cool. A lurid glow came from the opening far above. Shorn set Netra down as gently as he could and bent over her. In the dim light he could see that she was still unconscious, but otherwise she seemed unharmed. The room shook as first one, then the other fiery tornado slammed into it. It seemed to Shorn that the howling grew more intense then, the sound of predators deprived of their prey. Dust swirled thickly through the air.

He picked up Netra and walked to the other end of the room. It was a large room, large enough to comfortably hold several hundred people, and his footsteps echoed hollowly on the stone tiles while the wind moaned outside. At the far end of the room was a pair of closed double doors. They did not yield when he pushed on them so he stepped back and gave them a solid kick. There was a cracking noise and they flew open. On the other side was a dim room smaller than the one he had just left, the far end swallowed in darkness. The walls on either side had arches cut into them. Running down the middle of the room was the remains of a rug.

He laid Netra down on the rug and knelt beside her. He thought she looked paler than before, but that might just have been the poor light. He touched her cheek. Her skin was hot, her pulse erratic. His water was gone, but when he looked through her pack he found a water skin with a few swallows left in it. He lifted her into a sitting position and put the skin to her mouth. Water dribbled down her chin, but she swallowed some. He laid her back down.

How long could she live like this? What if she did not awaken?

They were not questions he wanted to think about. He stood and went back to the room they had entered through. The wind was still howling outside and sand blew through the opening, enlarging the pile that had been growing for uncounted years. Whatever else had been in the room was covered in sand.

He went back to where Netra lay on the floor. He didn't like the idea of leaving her alone, but they needed water badly. It seemed highly unlikely that he would find any water, but he had to at least try.

He had not gone far before he found the first body, just visible in the gloom at the far end of the room. It was lying on its face, arms thrown over its head. With the tip of his boot he turned it over.

It was a young woman. Clearly she had been dead many years, but she had not rotted. The dry air had preserved her as it dried her. Her eyes were gone, her cheeks sunken, and the skin on her face had turned to leather. Her clothing had decayed to rags that crumbled away when he rolled her over. Her face was contorted, as if she'd been screaming when she died. A deep wound cut across her torso diagonally, slicing cleanly through the rib cage.

He looked around. Ahead was another set of doors, one of them partway open. Stumbling around in the dark wasn't going to accomplish anything. Maybe there was some wooden furniture that he could break up and use as a torch.

He froze, staring at the open door. Was there a dim glow coming from the next room?

He pushed open the door and went into the next room. One of the stones in the wall to his right, about waist high, was glowing a soft yellow. Cautiously, he reached out and touched it.

A horizontal line of stones set into the wall began to glow, bathing the area in a soft, golden light and revealing a wide corridor. Shorn stared at the glowing stones, wondering. He would not have guessed that the people on this world were capable of such a thing. What powered the light? Why was it still working?

He did not ponder it for long. Once Netra was awake she could figure it out if she wanted to. He had other things to worry about. It occurred to him then that if Netra awakened while he was gone that she would be frightened and disoriented. He looked back through the open door. She hadn't moved.

In the end he continued on because he had no other real choice. For the next couple hours he wandered through a maze of rooms and corridors, his footsteps echoing hollowly in the still, dry air. There were more bodies. All had gaping wounds or missing limbs. One had tried to crawl through a narrow doorway and died halfway. Two that he found on the other side of a pair of double doors were clearly guards or soldiers, killed defending their post. The rest were civilians, wealthy ones to judge by their clothes. Some wore jewelry, and the one who died in the doorway was cradling a large gem of some kind. Whoever – or whatever – killed them had not been interested in looting. The depth and severity of the wounds made him question whether they could have been caused by a person.

The building was huge, large enough to house an entire town, and everywhere in it were signs of great wealth, from the rotting art on the walls, to intricate friezes, colored marble tiles, and faded murals. One room was semicircular, with seating on stepped tiers leading down to what looked like a stage. Another had doors on the far side that had fallen off their hinges. The doors led to a balcony that looked out over nothing but darkness.

He found more of the glowing stones on the walls as he went, all of them still working. When he came to stairways he chose down instead of up, thinking that if he could get to a bottom floor or a cellar, he might come upon a well that would, against all odds, have water in it.

Finally, a couple hours after he began searching, he entered a circular room that had what looked like a well in the middle of it. A low stone wall was built up around it and over it was a mechanism with a chain wrapped around it. A metal bucket hung off the chain. Shorn looked down into the well but couldn't see any water. He turned the crank on the mechanism and with a squeal of protesting metal it turned and the bucket began to descend.

After a time there was a splash of water and he reversed the crank. The water in the bucket was clear and cold and he drank deep. He filled his water skins and then headed back for Netra.

Netra was still unconscious when Shorn got back to her. Through the opening where they had entered the building he could see that it was dark outside and the stars were out. He had as much water as they could carry. He was tempted to leave then, push on through the darkness and see if they could make the edge of the desert before daybreak. But in the daylight he had not been able to find his way out of the desert. It seemed less likely at night. If he waited until Netra was conscious, perhaps she would know which way to go.

Shorn lifted Netra and tried again to give her some water. Most of it ran down her chin. At least he did not have to worry about conserving it.

Shorn sat down near Netra and proceeded to eat some of the food he had taken from the Crodin camp that Netra destroyed. When he was done he sat there. After a while the lights dimmed, then went out, but he did not get up to relight them. There was no need. For the first time in days there was nothing to do but sit and wait. The silence of the desert was immense. It pressed on him. He should sleep, but he didn't feel tired. He wanted to act, but there was nothing to do. Finally, he stood and started pacing.

It was still hard to believe Netra had killed all those Crodin. He remembered the bodies scattered across the stony ground like dolls with their stuffing missing. How could the woman who spent so much time speaking of her love for life do something like that? It did not seem possible. He looked at her, just visible in the darkness and realized that he needed her to wake up. He needed her to push back the darkness. If she died, there was nothing left on this world for him.

"Wake up," he said. "I do not know what to do here without you." The silence pressed down on him with stone hands. "I cannot face the emptiness again."

He sat back down and sometime in the early morning hours he finally drifted away into a restless sleep. In his dreams the tani roared out of the forest over and over, killing a young girl named Micah and dragging her small body away. When he awakened in the gray dawn his head ached and his vision was blurry. He was lying there staring at the ceiling when Netra suddenly sat bolt upright.

"Where am I?" she cried. Just as suddenly she lay back down.

Shorn crawled over to her. "It's okay," he said. "I am here."

"Why am I alive?" she moaned brokenly. "I should be dead."

In the gray dimness he could see that her eyes were closed. Her pain tore at him and he searched for something comforting to say but he found nothing. After a while her regular breathing told him she had lapsed back into unconsciousness.

Shorn knelt there for a long time. At last the pain in his knees from kneeling on the stone floor grew too great and he started to stand up. As he did, Netra moaned and her eyes opened.

"I'm thirsty," she whispered.

Shorn opened a water skin and held it to her mouth. As he did, her hands came up and grabbed his wrist. A sudden jolt went through him and for a moment his heart seemed to stop. Netra clutched his wrist with both hands, pulling it to her. He could feel something draining

11

out of him, drawn out by her, and he knew in an instant what was happening.

She was taking his Song, just as she had done to the Crodin nomads.

A terrible feeling swept through him. It wasn't pain. It was too great for that. It was a horrible, agonizing feeling, as if he was being torn open while something vital spilled away into the darkness that rushed at him from every side.

A moment later he reacted, slapping her on the side of the head with his free hand. The blow broke the contact between them. Her head flew backward and smacked on the stone floor, bringing from her a yelp of pain.

Shorn jumped to his feet and backed away. Netra rolled onto her side, then onto her knees. For a moment she remained thus, then she stood. Her hair hung in ropes around her face and blood seeped from her nose.

"Stay away from me!" she cried, and ran off into the depths of the building.

THREE

Netra did not know how far she ran. The darkness wrapped around her and she had no idea where she was. She knew only that a terrible hunger filled her, a hunger that no food could sate. It was all she could do to keep moving away. More than anything she wanted to turn and run back to Shorn. She wanted to steal every bit of Song from him.

She came to stairs leading down and managed two before her strength failed her and she collapsed. She pitched sideways, hit her shoulder and then it was a blur of falling and pain until she struck a landing and stopped. She lay there on her side, hurting everywhere, and numb to everything except the gnawing hunger. She pushed herself up so that she was leaning against the wall and tried to drive the taste of Shorn's Song from her mind. Even from here she could sense it, not so distant and drawing steadily closer. How easy it would be to reach out and take it, draw it into her, make the hurting go away.

"Stay away!" she yelled, but her voice was thin and the darkness swallowed it.

He did not come closer, but he did not leave either. Sometime later, she did not know how long, Netra lapsed back into unconsciousness.

Shorn waited, and when Netra had been quiet for over an hour, he made his way down the stairs. The realization of what she had almost done to him made him cautious, but when he saw her lying on her side, his caution abated and he hurried to her. He sat her upright and her eyes opened. Her pupils were very large, her breathing shallow. Shorn set a water skin in her lap and stepped back.

Netra picked up the skin finally and took a drink, then another one. He could see that although her eyes were open, they did not register anything. They were blank, empty. After a while she lay back down.

Shorn sat down and waited. The day crawled by and Netra lay on her side unmoving. Her eyes remained open. He couldn't tell if she even blinked. He had seen that empty stare before, in a child he had found in the wreckage of Fanos, a colony on one of the moons in Themor's solar system. Everyone else in the colony was dead. The child, a boy, had watched it all from hiding.

As afternoon turned toward evening, finally Shorn couldn't take it anymore. He stood up and approached her. "Get up. Come back to camp."

Netra turned her head and looked up at him. Shorn held out his hand. For a moment she looked at it as if it was a foreign object. Then she shook her head.

"I can't control the hunger. I won't be able to stop myself."

"Yes," he told her. "You will."

Slowly, tentatively, she took hold of his hand. Once again the feeling of being torn open hit him and he gritted his teeth, putting his other hand on the wall for support. "Fight it, Netra. You are stronger."

She cried out and her hand tightened on his, her nails biting into his skin. She shuddered and gradually the feeling began to pass. He saw tears on her face.

Shorn lifted her to her feet and together they started back up the stairs. After a few steps she pulled her hand away. She wrapped her arms around her chest, huddling in on herself.

The lights on the next floor had gone dark. Shorn touched the softly glowing stone on the wall beside the stairs and the room lit up. Netra stopped and stared. Then she slowly scanned the room and seemed to see where she was for the first time. A quizzical look crossed her face.

"Where are we?"

Shorn answered cautiously, glad to see something pierce her gloom. "Some building. Part of a city, I think. Buried in the sand."

"What?"

"I carried you out of the tunnel. When we came out I didn't know which way to go." He shrugged. "I took the wrong way."

"We're in the Gur al Krin?"

Shorn nodded. "We were almost out of water. I saw something sticking out of the sand. Then the fires started. This was the only shelter."

"A city buried in the sand," Netra mused.

"Do you know of this?"

He could see her thinking. She was like an old woman looking through someone else's memories. "Kaetria? It was swallowed by the sands after the fall of the Empire. No one has seen it since."

"Something killed the people here. There are bodies." Shorn pointed at one sprawled nearby.

Netra stared at it for a while. Slowly she approached it, stopping an arm's length away. "She didn't rot." She took a step closer and bent down to peer at it. "That poor woman." She crouched down beside the body. "She didn't deserve this." She started to cry, her body shaking. There were more tears. Once again Shorn was at a loss what to do.

After a while Netra's sobs subsided. She laid her hand on the woman's forehead, closed her eyes and was silent for a minute. Then she opened her eyes. "She was frightened," she said softly. "She was desperate." She looked up at Shorn. "She was desperate!" she said more loudly. "She would have done anything to save the city she loved. All of them would have," she cried, her gesture encompassing several other bodies sprawled a short distance away. Once again her body began to shake. "You see that, don't you? They only wanted to help. They just didn't know what else to do."

"I see that," Shorn replied, not knowing what else to say.

Suddenly Netra's face crumpled. The next words were torn from her with a cry of pain. "I freed Melekath, didn't I?" She met Shorn's eyes, willing him, begging him to deny her words.

Shorn hesitated. Time seemed to stop.

Slowly he nodded.

Netra seemed to collapse in on herself then. Her body shook and her cries were the cries of an animal in pain. When the cries subsided, Netra spoke. Her voice was listless. "I should be dead. You should have left me." She sat there with her hair hanging down around her face, shielding her.

Shorn was silent and Netra did not move or speak for some time.

Finally, she raised her head to look up at him. "Why didn't you leave me there?"

Still Shorn did not respond, though the pain in her voice struck deep into his soul.

Netra's face twisted. "Answer me!" she cried. "Tell me why!"

"How could I?"

15

She leapt to her feet suddenly and charged him, hitting him with her fists, scratching him, screaming at him. "Why didn't you leave me there?!" she yelled over and over.

Shorn made no move to defend himself. He stood like a statue while she rained blows on him. He felt her nails tear at his cheeks. Blood trickled down his face. When her strength failed her she half fell against him, trembling all over.

"I should be dead. You should have left me," she mumbled.

"I could not."

"Why? Why couldn't you? You know what I did." She tilted her head back and fixed her gaze on him. Her eyes were rimmed in red, her long brown hair snarled. The tears had traced tracks through the dust on her face. She was tall, but still she did not come up to his shoulder. "Don't you see what you've done?"

He stared at her. How could he tell her what he had no words for? How could he tell her that his life had been nothing but darkness and pain until she came along and showed him a glimmer of something else? In her fight he had found a purpose, maybe even a way to redeem himself. "You saved my life," he said. "I owe you *tenken ya.*"

"I never wanted your *tenken ya.* I told you that in the beginning. And now we're even anyway, so you don't owe me anything anymore."

Shorn could not speak. There was so much that he wanted to say, but he did not know how to let it out. She had saved far more than his life. That had been only the beginning. It was during the days they had walked together since that she had truly saved him. "You showed me that *terin'ai* is still possible." *Terin'ai* was the warrior's search for the hidden self. It was the goal of every Themorian.

"I've doomed the world," Netra said in a very small voice. "Everything will die because of me."

"You still live. You have not lost yet."

Netra pulled away and wrapped her arms around herself. "It is only a matter of time. It took eight of the most powerful gods to imprison Melekath before and at least one of those is dead. It's hopeless."

Shorn saw that she was shaking and he wanted to put his arms around her and comfort her but he did not know how. Fighting and killing were all he knew.

"I must be the stupidest person ever," Netra continued. "I believed Xochitl was trapped in the prison. I thought she had chosen me to free her." Her voice had risen again as she lashed herself with the words. "Melekath tricked me so easily. I am nothing but a fool. I should be dead." There was a hysterical edge to her voice and she was digging her fingernails into her arms deep enough to draw blood.

"Stop!" Shorn took hold of her by the shoulders and gave her a shake. "You will kill yourself with this. You made a mistake. It happens."

"This isn't just a mistake," she snapped. "Don't you understand? *I* freed Melekath. *I* did it. That can never be forgiven."

"You're right," Shorn said, seeing how she crumpled slightly at his words. "It can't ever be forgiven. But that does not mean your *velen'aa* is over. The question is what you will do now. Will you give up? That is the only true mistake."

"There's nothing I can do to fix it," she said miserably. "So what difference does it make whether I give up or not?"

"Probably none. But *velen'aa* means to continue fighting even when you cannot possibly win. It is the warrior's path."

"I am no warrior."

"There you are wrong."

She looked at him for a long moment and it seemed she would say something, but then she twisted out of his grasp and turned away.

Netra was standing at the edge of the room when she felt a sharp pain in her stomach and she doubled over suddenly. She had to put her hand on the wall to steady herself.

"What's wrong?" Shorn asked. He had been standing a ways away, giving her privacy while she thought, but now he came up to her quickly.

"Nothing," she said, though the pain seemed to be growing stronger. "I think I'm just hungry. Do you have anything to eat?"

"At the camp I do. Follow me." He started across the room and after a moment Netra followed. He led her to where their packs lay on the stone floor. From his Shorn pulled out some dried meat and a hard chunk of something whitish and held them out to her. Netra took the whitish stuff and squinted at it. "What is this?"

Shorn shrugged. "Some kind of cheese, I think."

Netra managed to break off a small piece and put it in her mouth. "I think it's goat cheese." She wondered how long it had been since she last ate and realized she couldn't remember. The last couple days before reaching the Gur al Krin were a blur. Another wave of pain passed through her and her hands shook.

She looked at the cheese in her hand, suddenly realizing where it had come from. It was bitter and chalky and she felt like she was choking on it. She dropped the cheese and stepped back. The images broke over her like a tidal wave, one after another until she was gasping. She saw a young woman, whimpering as she tried to crawl under a fallen tent and hide. A man swinging a club at her and the look on his face when his body ceased to obey him and he crumpled to the ground. An infant sitting on the ground in the midst of the chaos, screaming, then suddenly toppling over as she snatched away its life.

Shorn took hold of her arm. "What is it?"

Netra hung there in his grip and the tears were back in her eyes but she couldn't give in to them. She couldn't. If she gave in to the shame she would fall forever. *Oh, what have I done?*

"I just don't feel well," she said. She couldn't meet his eyes. Hunger and shame warred inside her. She had killed those innocent people. How many? Twenty? Thirty? How could she have done that? And yet, even as she thought that, she knew. She knew how she had murdered. Hunger rode the pain in her gut, and it was not a hunger that food could reach. She was suddenly aware of Shorn's closeness, the heat of his hand on her arm. All she had to do was reach, just a little, and the hunger would go away.

Netra jerked her arm away from his grasp. "Don't touch me." She backed away from him, breathing hard. *Never again*, she tried to tell herself. But it rang hollow in the empty places inside her. She spun away. "Stay away from me. You don't know what I am now."

FOUR

The next morning when Netra awakened, bright sunlight filled the room. She rolled over. Shorn was at the top of the pile of sand that had partially filled the room, grunting as he broke stones free from the wall, enlarging the hole they had entered through. He felt her looking at him and stopped, gazing down at her. Then he pulled one more stone free and slid down the sand. He walked over to her.

"Before we leave, I will refill our water," he said.

Netra looked up at him. In the morning light his skin was a deep, coppery hue and the faint tracings of the numerous scars that crossed his cheeks were visible. His eyes were yellow-gold and deep set below a thick brow, his nose broad and flat. He was hairless, his scalp smooth except for some old scars. He looked fierce, savage. And yet she trusted him completely. She came to a sudden decision.

"We're not leaving. Not yet."

One eyebrow rose in his blunt face, but Shorn said nothing.

"I don't feel well enough. Not yet." That wasn't exactly the truth. While it was true she didn't feel well – she felt hollow and there seemed to be bugs crawling inside her skin – that wasn't the reason she wanted to stay. In truth, she didn't think she'd ever feel well again. What was the truth then? She wasn't ready to face the world. Not just yet. What could she do out there anyway, except die with the rest? At the thought, a terrible lassitude settled over her. She felt herself standing at the edge of a vast abyss and knew how close she was to falling into it. She had to move, to do something, before it reached up and claimed her.

"I want to look around this place more. There's something here. I want to learn more about it."

"Another day will not hurt," he answered. "But we do not have much food left."

Netra stood and looked around. In the back corner of the room was a closed door, sand piled knee-high in front of it. "I wonder where that goes," she said.

Shorn walked over and began digging. In a few minutes he had moved enough sand that he was able to pull the door open. The hallway on the other side was dark, but there was a glowing stone on the wall and when Netra pushed on it the lights came on. She considered the lights briefly, her fingertips resting on the stone, still cool in the morning. There was a thrum of energy under her fingers, but it was unlike any she had felt before. She frowned. What kind of energy could flow through stone?

The hallway had a high, arched ceiling decorated with a mosaic, though many of the small, colored stones had fallen out and lay scattered underfoot. The walls were a dark stone veined with rose quartz. There was a body sprawled on the floor. It looked like the man was clawing at the wall when he died. Netra stepped over him without slowing. Ghosts of dead Crodin clamored after her.

At the far end of the hallway a set of stairs led upwards. At the top of them was a landing that led through a pair of open, double doors. Beyond them Netra found herself in a round room at the base of a tower. Stairs wound upwards into darkness. Shorn touched the light control and looked up. "This must be the spire I saw," he said.

"Let's go up," Netra said. "Maybe we'll be able to see a way out of the desert."

Netra felt weak and her skin itched all over, but she pushed herself hard climbing the stairs, and soon the sweat ran freely and the dizziness was enough to cause spots in her vision. She welcomed the pain. It was only what she deserved. She bit her lip, forcing herself to push on. When at last her limbs failed her, she was shaking and would have fallen had Shorn not taken hold of her arm. At the contact she felt the jolt as her hunger took hold of him. Shorn's eyes widened. She pulled away with an effort, her heart pounding. For some time then she couldn't even look at him.

When she felt better, Netra continued on, although she found that she tired quickly and had to rest often. The morning was old by the time she reached the top of the stairs. Where the stairs ended, iron rungs were set into the stone, leading up to a trap door. When she took hold of the first rung Shorn stopped her and went up first. The trap door opened with a screech of rusted metal. He stuck his head through and looked around. Then he came back down and looked at her.

"I'm going to carry you. Can you control it?"

She hesitated. She wanted to say no. Instead she nodded.

She closed her eyes when he put his arm around her. She was freezing cold and his LifeSong was a blissful, roaring fire. She shivered and bit her lip until it bled, but she managed to resist the hunger.

The spire had a small platform at the top, barely large enough for the two of them. There was no railing. In the center of the platform was a stone column about waist high. Protruding from the top of it was an oddly-shaped piece of metal a couple of feet long. At its top it was rounded and had a number of holes in it.

"That's odd," Netra said. "I wonder what it's for."

Shorn did not reply. He was staring off into the distance. Netra followed his gaze. The view was impressive, revealing unbroken ranks of dunes stretching into the distance in every direction except to the east where the glimmer of the sun on the ocean was visible.

"I didn't realize we were so close to the sea," Netra said.

"Tomorrow we can walk out," Shorn replied.

Leaving meant going to Qarath. And going to Qarath meant facing the women she grew up with. They would know what she did. They would look at her and they would judge her. "Maybe not tomorrow."

Shorn gave her a sharp look.

"I don't think I'm strong enough," she said.

"I will carry you."

"I said I'm not ready!" she snapped. "Just give me time."

A gust of wind pushed her and she grabbed onto the stone column to steady herself, suddenly conscious of how far it was to the ground below. With the wind came a strange wailing sound and it took a moment for Netra to realize that the sound was caused by the wind blowing through the holes in the metal thing that stuck out of the stone column.

The wind grew stronger and the strange wail grew louder, varying in pitch as the wind shifted. "I've heard something like this before," Netra said. She frowned, trying to remember. Then it hit her. "Dorn."

Shorn gave her a quizzical look. "He's a Windcaller. I met him when Siena and I – " She broke off, remembering Siena, crushed along with Brelisha at Rane Haven. "When I was on my way to Nelton, where I saw the Guardian Gulagh. He had this piece of bone with holes in it and when he swung it around his head it made a sound kind of like this." Her eyes widened. "Oh. I wonder if…" She listened some more. "Dorn used the bone thing to call the wind, well, not the wind, but things that live in the wind. He called them *aranti*. Maybe this was used for the same purpose."

"Maybe it still is," Shorn said, pointing.

Out across the dunes a whirlwind of blowing sand had arisen. It grew larger by the second.

Netra took hold of the metal thing and when she did her vision flickered. She rubbed her eyes. There was something in the whirlwind, something ethereal and wispy.

"It's time to leave," Shorn said.

"In a moment," Netra replied. She felt as if she was on the verge of uncovering something important.

All at once there was something else in the whirlwind. A pair of eyes, staring at her. They flared red and what looked like a mouth gaped open below them.

There was an explosion and the whirlwind burst into flame.

"Now!" Shorn yelled.

There was another thump and another whirlwind of sand, this one behind them, burst into flame. Both were growing larger and converging on the tower. Netra felt a sense of malice, strong enough that it was almost a physical blow, and then Shorn was lifting her bodily and carrying her down into the spire. He slammed the trap door shut and a few seconds later the spire shook as the pillars of flame struck it. A tiny bit of sand wafted down through the trap door, but otherwise the spire was unaffected.

"Those are not like the *aranti* Dorn showed me," Netra said, remembering the wild, free creatures that had cavorted through the desert night while she watched. Those others had seemed playful, even friendly. She turned to Shorn. "Those things out there hate us."

"This is no normal desert," he growled.

"I wonder what the Kaetrians were doing?" she mused. "They must have put that thing there on purpose. Which is odd, because Calling the Wind is forbidden under Tender law, and the Tenders were as powerful as the Emperor by the end."

"They did not try to hide this," Shorn said.

"No, they didn't." Netra started down the stairs. The wind was growling and hissing outside the tower and she couldn't shake the image of a wild animal trying to get at them. "When you were looking around did you see a library by any chance?" she asked Shorn.

"I did not. But there were doors I did not try."

"Because maybe I could find some more information there. Or maybe what I'm looking for would be in the office of whoever was in charge here."

They descended the stairs and made their way back to the room where their camp was while the wind raged outside. Then they went through the building carefully, focusing on the rooms that Shorn had skipped before. Netra tried not to look at the bodies they found sprawled here and there, all of them with large, gaping wounds. Looking at them made the bleakness yawn inside her all over again, as if she was to blame for their deaths also.

They discovered that there was another floor above theirs. There were fewer bodies and the rooms were larger, more opulently furnished. In one room there were two bodies lying on the floor. They were elderly, a man and a woman. Both had been torn nearly in half, yet had somehow managed to crawl together and embrace before dying. Whatever death had come for them, they had chosen to meet it together. Netra looked down on them while tears began to flow. All at once the abyss stretched wide under her feet and she felt herself falling into it again. Wiping her eyes, she turned and nearly ran from the room, leaving Shorn to check the room's other door.

When he reemerged they continued on down the corridor. Some of these rooms had windows and those they found choked with sand, so that simply opening the door was a struggle. Whatever was in them was buried and lost.

Netra reached the end of the corridor and was about to turn back when something caught her eye. The remains of a wooden cabinet leaned at an awkward angle against the wall. "Help me move this, Shorn. I think there's something behind here." When Shorn dragged the cabinet out of the way it promptly fell into pieces.

"I think there's a hidden door here," she said, pointing to the faint outlines just visible in the stone wall. Netra pushed on the edges of the door, but it didn't budge. There was no handle that she could see. "There's probably a hidden catch," she said, feeling around the edge of the door. One of the stones she tried moved. When she pushed it harder there was a soft click and the door swung inward.

Netra triggered the lights and saw that the room was filled with books. "I think this is what we were looking for," Netra said, looking around. "Whatever they were doing, there should be some record of it here." She pulled a random book off the shelf and opened it. The ink was faded, but the book was in surprisingly good shape. It was hard to read at first, the diction being different from what she was used to and interspersed with words she did not know the meaning of, but she was able to figure out most of it. "It seems to be a book comparing the unique qualities of Song in plants to Song in animals. Interesting, but not helpful."

She put the book back and took another one from the shelf. "This is going to take a while. You may want to find something else to do." Shorn nodded, but did not move. Netra opened the book, but she found it hard to concentrate and stopped reading after a few lines. She could feel Shorn looming over her, staring at her. "Don't you have something else to do?" she said finally. He shook his head. "Well, find something," she snapped.

After he left, Netra went back to the books. The next book she found was a history that was very different than what she had been taught. It said that Xochitl was not a god, any more than Bereth or Melekath or Sententu, but something called a Nipashanti. The Nipashanti came from three different Spheres, Stone, Sea, and Sky. From the Spheres, the Circle was created, and Life given form. Life was allowed to continue because what it took from the Spheres was returned at death. All that changed when Melekath created the Gift for his Children –

Netra hissed in frustration. She could not read further. The ink had faded too badly. Maybe if she could look at it in the sunlight. She set it down, thinking. The Book of Xochitl mentioned Melekath's Gift and said that somehow the Gift had turned his followers into abominations, but it was very sparse on details and the truth was she'd never cared much about it before. But now she found herself wondering what this Gift was. Could it be some power that made his followers a threat to the other Nipashanti?

The Book of Xochitl claimed that Melekath had perverted the humans who came to be known as his Children, and led them away from the true faith. It was because of this that Xochitl led the Eight to besiege Durag'otal. It also claimed that Xochitl was a god, the most powerful of all the gods. She shook her head. What was the truth? It was hard to imagine, with what she knew now, that she had once believed every word of the Tenders' sacred text. She looked at the shelves full of books. No wonder this room was hidden. The words contained in this book would have been considered heretical by her order, and back then they had the power to imprison or execute anyone they wanted to.

She set the book aside and went back to the shelves. Over the next hours she looked at hundreds of books. A handful she was able to read, but the ink in many of them was too faded to be legible. Others were written in a language she didn't understand – or were written in code – she couldn't tell which. It didn't really matter. They were useless to her. There probably wasn't a single person left in the world who could make sense of them.

She found a slim volume bound in cracked leather. The title on the first page said simply, *Stone Force.* That sounded promising. According to the book, there was power contained within the stone, power that was very different from Song. The Kaetrians had learned to tap into it in a limited way. Stone force was the basis of their lighting.

Netra looked at the glowing stones in the ceiling, their light still strong after all these centuries. She was right. She *had* felt power in the stone.

Unfortunately, their understanding of Stone force was very limited. They had made almost no progress in that area until they were able to get a hold of one of the *ronhym*. The *ronhym* were a race who dwelt underground in the Truebane Mountains, home to the Takare city of Ankha del'Ath. According to the book, they were able to burrow through stone like badgers burrowed through soil. But the *ronhym* died – Netra got the feeling, though the writer did not say it explicitly, that the *ronhym* was tortured to reveal its secrets – and the Kaetrians had not been able to get their hands on another one.

Netra put the book back, pondering this new information. What kind of creatures were the *ronhym*? Why were the Kaetrians so desperate to learn about Stone force?

As she was sliding the book back into place she glimpsed something behind it. She pulled out a couple more books and reached into the back of the shelf. It was several sheets of parchment, rolled up. It seemed to be a letter, though there was no name at the top. She sat down and leaned against a wall to read.

The sands draw closer every day. Already there are dunes spilling into the river and the west fields were not planted at all this year. It is clear to any intelligent person that this is the hand of Melekath. The sands were born above his prison. Surely no proof besides that is needed. But open discussion of the problem is forbidden by the Tender hierarchy. Even here, where we have the backing of the Emperor himself, we must work in secret. Only days ago Uded was arrested and taken to the Temple. We have heard nothing of him since.

Netra paused and sighed. How could her order have been so blind? The Kaetrians had known of the prison's weakness even then. But the Tenders had not allowed anyone to investigate it.

It is not just the sand I fear either. There are things *in the sand. I have seen one with my own eyes. I was on top of the spire, using the longsight glass, when it appeared. It was taller than a man, a gaunt, withered creature, with empty holes where its eyes should be and running sores over much of its body.*

Netra stopped reading. *Gulagh.* He was describing the Guardian known as the Voice, the one she and Siena saw in Nelton.

It raised its face to me and I dropped the glass. My eyes burned and I could not see for a day. Its hatred for us still burns in my heart. Nor is it the only thing trapped in the sands. Before he disappeared, Uded spoke of seeing a tall, white-skinned creature out on the sand. I fear what will become of us when they are free to enter our city. The Tenders say the web of Life-force they have spun around the city will protect us, but I do not believe it will.

We continue our work, pushing as hard as we can. There is so little time and so much we do not know. We have made no more progress with Stone force. I wish we knew how the ronhym *was able to control the crystal. We can see Stone force, and even touch it at times, but it is terribly dangerous. Only last month Burin was studying the crystal, he accidentally touched it and...I shudder at what happened to him. There was not enough left of him to identify.*

Our study of Sky force appears to be at a dead end as well. We made a summoner, as the old Windcaller taught us, and planted it on the top of the spire. It works. The creatures come, but they are brainless and uncontrollable. We should destroy the device while we can. I think the creatures that come each time are the same ones. I believe our device has trapped them somehow and they are not happy. At first they played around us like puppies, but lately they are darker and a sudden gust from them almost threw me to my death. But the others will not listen to me.

So the thing on top of the spire *was* similar to what Dorn showed her.

At least we know now that the underground pool empties into the sea, as we theorized. Sea force is our last hope. It is not as alien as the Stone and not as unpredictable as the Sky. But I do not see how it will help us, even if we master it. Sententu, the Shaper who made of himself the door to the prison, came from the Sphere of Stone. If we are to strengthen him, and thus the prison, it seems that we should do so with Stone force.

The letter ended there.

More searching revealed a journal that gave more information about the *ronhym*. Netra was studying it when Shorn returned.

"It is late."

Netra jumped. She'd been so engrossed in the reading that she hadn't heard Shorn's approach. "Is it?" She blinked a few times, having trouble focusing after reading for so long.

"You need to eat."

Netra realized then that she was hungry, and it was an actual hunger for food, not the taut, stretched hunger for Song.

"You will eat?"

Netra thought of the dried meat and the chalky cheese and grimaced. "I guess I have to."

Shorn turned and left the room and Netra followed. She didn't see much as they made their way down the silent corridors, past the blank doorways and the torn, desiccated husks that used to be people. Her mind was full of all that she'd learned. Power within the stone? The water? The wind? It seemed crazy, and yet why not? Why would life be the only thing containing energy?

On the staircase leading down was the dried body of a woman. Netra paused and looked at it. The woman's legs had been torn completely off, but it looked like she had made it up several more stairs before dying. Whatever had killed her had been so terrifying that she had kept trying to get away, even after receiving such terrible wounds. This woman had known the sands were coming, that the Guardians would come into her city and kill everyone. All the dead in here had known. They'd done everything they could. They'd had the might of an Empire behind them and knowledge far beyond anything that was present in the world today.

Yet still they died and the sand owned all that was once theirs.

It hit her again, the futility of what they faced. Melekath was free. He could not be stopped.

I freed him.

Her knees buckled and she almost fell. Shorn turned back, concern on his face, but she waved him off, trying to keep what she felt from showing on her face.

Shorn had gathered pieces of furniture and he soon had a fire going. It was too warm for a fire, really, but Netra was glad for it anyway. It felt comforting. Through the opening high in the wall that Shorn had made she could see a piece of the night sky and there were stars. It was difficult, but she forced herself to eat some of the food Shorn handed her.

"We do not have that much food left," he said. "We will have to leave soon."

"Just a couple more days, I promise. I know it sounds crazy, but I feel like I'm on the verge of learning something important. I just need some more time."

Shorn grunted noncommittally. After a time, he said, "I found something today."

"What?"

"A room with a stone in it."

"So?"

"There is something different about this stone."

Now he had her attention. Netra stood up. "Show me."

"Now?"

"Of course now. You said yourself we couldn't stay here very long. There's no time to waste."

Shorn shrugged and stood up. He led her through a room she hadn't seen before and down two flights of stairs. Partway along a corridor was a door that he had clearly kicked in. Shorn stopped outside it and motioned for her to enter.

Inside, on a metal stand, was a large, yellowish crystal, about as long as a man's arm and pointed on both ends. Curious, Netra walked closer. As she did the color of the crystal changed, first becoming more orange, and then growing darker until it was a deep red color.

"I think I know what this is," she said. "I read about it in one of the books in the library. The Kaetrians brought a *ronhym* here. They were trying to learn how to harness Stone force, to stop the sands that were getting closer and closer to the city. The *ronhym* burrowed underground and found a crystal that it said could be used to create an opening into the heart of Stone force.

"But it refused to do so. It said the power which would be unleashed would be uncontrollable, that only one of the Nipashanti of the First Ring would even have a chance to do so." She trailed off. There was a sensation of massive pressure in her chest. The room seemed to have grown a great deal warmer. She realized that sweat was running down her back and her hands felt clammy. Her arms itched and she glanced at them, almost expecting to see red welts there, but there was nothing. She felt a moment of dizziness and a moment later she blinked and realized she had gone – or been pushed – *beyond*.

Shorn was looking at her.

"I'm all right," she said. "It's just…so strong." The crystal was a dark orange and red shape, all harsh, sharp angles. It hurt to look at it and she knew without a doubt that if she was to touch it that she would be torn apart. The power within the crystal was not something that could be wielded by humans. It was too remote, too inaccessible. It did not feel hostile to her, merely alien. It was a power that moved at glacial speeds and yet relentlessly crushed. Life was simply too fast-moving, too fragile, for the crushing weight of Stone.

Netra stepped back and with an effort of will managed to claw her way out of *beyond*. That felt better. She could still feel the roaring furnace that was the crystal, but it was as if the door of the furnace had been closed. The barrier of unawareness that protects people from the vaster world that surrounds them was helping her.

"What happened to the creature?" Shorn asked.

Netra took another step back and looked up at him. He seemed genuinely untouched by the crystal's presence. Was his alien physiology really so different? "They tortured the creature, tried to force it to open the doorway. They were desperate. Their city was dying. They thought it could help." Saying the words brought up painful memories of the dying Crodin, people that she killed. She understood all too well what desperation could drive a person to.

"They killed it."

Netra nodded. "After that they tried to access the power themselves. It…didn't go well. Everyone who tried died. They were torn apart." She scratched her arms. Nausea roiled inside her.

Shorn grabbed her arm. "Promise me you will not touch it," he growled.

Netra's hunger reawakened at the contact with his skin but she controlled it and pulled her arm away. She shook her head fiercely. "I'm not crazy. I'd have more chance of surviving a jump into a volcano."

"We should leave this room."

"I agree." It was a relief to get away from the thing. It still seemed impossible to Netra that power like that could be part of LifeSong, yet the Kaetrians had been quite sure of it. They speculated that there was some point where power from the Spheres of Stone, Sea and Sky was drawn out and combined, becoming the source of the River that fed LifeSong to every living thing. Part of their studies had been aimed at finding that spot, believing they might find answers there. But they had had no luck. Their best chance of finding it lay in following the River back upstream to its source and the only people capable of that were the Tenders. The same Tenders that would not hesitate to imprison and probably execute them for carrying out the studies they were involved in. How could her order have been so blind? Netra wondered. They were facing the destruction of the Empire and yet they refused to even consider those ideas which might save them. It was beyond blindness; it was insanity.

"I do not understand something," Shorn said when they reached their camp. "If the sands were coming closer every day, why not leave? It is only a city."

"I've wondered that too," Netra said. "There must have been something here, something compelling them to stay. Maybe it was sacred to them. The tomb of Hame Terinoth, the Tender who stood with Xochitl at the siege of Durag'otal is supposed to be here."

"Thousands die for the bones of a woman long dead?"

"I don't know, Shorn," she admitted. "I'm just guessing. I know that thousands of people did flee the city, though most stayed. I think maybe they stayed because they trusted that the Tenders would save them. The Tenders were very powerful back then. Although their abilities had been declining for several centuries, the average person wouldn't have known anything about that. I'm sure they kept it hidden. As for the people in this building, maybe they thought they'd be able to figure out an answer in time. They had certainly accomplished a lot. They knew about the power within the Spheres of Stone, Sea and Sky, massive amounts of power, if only they could figure out how to tap into it and control it. By the end they'd decided that the power in the air and the stone was out of their reach and were focusing most of their efforts on the power within the Sea. It makes sense, Shorn, if you think about it. Water is the basis of all life. Without water, nothing lives. It's part of us."

"So is air."

"Yes, but it comes and goes. It's never really part of us. And the stone isn't the answer." She thought of the crystal and shuddered. She still felt faintly sick to her stomach and the itching wasn't completely gone. "Only water is truly a part of us."

"It did not save them," he said.

Netra was awake when Shorn climbed back through the opening high up in the wall the next morning. He'd climbed up the pile of sand that filled most of the room and gone out to look around before the sun came up. Now he slid back down the sand and walked over to where Netra was sitting, a water skin in her hand.

"There is no wind yet," he said. "The wind seems to come in the afternoon. If we leave soon, we can reach the sea before the wind starts."

"I don't know, Shorn," Netra said. "I'm not sure I'm ready. I don't think I'm strong enough yet."

Shorn hesitated, knowing he needed to choose his words carefully, and also knowing it probably wouldn't matter. But he had to try. "Melekath will be moving. If we wait too long, we might not be able to get to Qarath before him."

"I said I'm not ready!" Netra snapped. "Can't you hear? What difference does it make anyway if I get to Qarath? There's nothing I can do. The whole world would be better off if I'd just done nothing."

"Your family…"

"Is dead. I've killed them. I've killed them all." The heat was gone from Netra's voice and she had her head down. She was shaking slightly.

"They aren't dead yet."

"No, but they will be. Melekath's going to kill everything and everybody, just like he killed everybody in this city. They were close to learning something here; I'm certain of it. Out there, there's nothing I can do to help. But here…I may be able to learn something. I may be able to atone for what I've done. I know it's a long shot, but I don't have anything else."

Shorn stared down at her, wishing there was something he could do to help and knowing there wasn't. "We will stay as long as you want," he said at last.

"Thank you," she said. She stood up, still not meeting his eye. "I'm going to go to the library."

We have found a pool underground. It is no normal pool. It glows green and all of us can sense the power coming from it. The glow is caused by Sea force, we are sure of it. The pool must connect to the Sea by a flooded tunnel or passage.

This could be the answer we are looking for. We could not control either the power of Sky or Stone, but perhaps we can the Sea. It is a terrible risk but we have to take it. The sands have choked the river and threaten Kaetria itself. In answer the Tenders have created a barrier woven of LifeSong along the west side of around the city. It is holding for now, but the Guardians prowl the edge of the sands and their hunger is palpable. Many of Kaetria's citizens have already evacuated, including some of our own people.

We have hidden the entrance to the cavern where the pool lies. The Tenders have become more and more paranoid and irrational as the days go by. They have all but forbidden our research, though we have the backing of the Emperor himself. They say that Xochitl will come and save the city if only we are faithful. I think they are delusional. If something is going to be done it must be us.

There was a blank page and then the final entry.

Marah says I am crazy, but we have no choice. No matter how dangerous, I have to try.

I am going to drink from the pool.

The rest of the book was blank. Netra sat there thinking for a minute. This was the second reference to the pool she had come across. She hurried from the room.

She found Shorn in the room where their camp was, staring up at the opening high in the wall. Sand was drifting through it and the sound of the moaning wind was clear. From the color of the light it appeared to be late afternoon. Another day had slipped by while she was in the library reading.

"I need your help."

He turned to her, fixing his almond eyes on her unblinking.

"There's an underground cavern with a pool in it. The entrance is hidden. I need your help to find it."

His eyes narrowed slightly. "What is in this pool?"

"The Sea." At his confused look, she added, "Sea force."

"You read about it in that?" he said, gesturing at the book, which she realized she was still holding. Netra nodded. "What are you going to do?"

"Can you just not question me?" Netra asked, exasperated. "We don't have all day."

In answer, Shorn crossed his arms.

"Okay, okay," Netra grumbled. "The man who wrote this believed that Sea force held the answer to the threat his city faced."

Shorn looked around him. "He was wrong."

Netra fought her frustration. "Okay. He was wrong. Or maybe he just didn't have enough time. But I have to see it for myself." She took a deep breath. "I might be able to do what he couldn't. I...I've changed since..." She drew a hand across her face and gathered herself. "All that Song I stole from the Crodin camp. It changed me. I can feel things I never could before. The flows of Song around me, in me, in *you*, I can feel them all. They are perfectly clear to me. I...it's easy to take hold of them now." She thought back to the trunk line she had used to break the prison. It seemed like something done by another person, a bizarre, impossible dream. She recoiled from the memory and the guilt it carried.

"I have to find this pool, Shorn. Maybe there's nothing I can do, but I have to try."

He stared at her for several long moments, then said, "I believe I know where it is."

Netra blinked. "You do? Why didn't you say anything?"

He shrugged. "It is a hole in the earth. I did not think it important."

"Will you take me there?"

Without replying, Shorn walked past her and headed for the door. Netra followed, excitement building within her. He led her to a stairway she had not been down before and they descended flight after flight of stairs until she lost count. The stairs ended in a large room carved out of the earth, the walls raw, unfinished. It was filled with crumbling crates and barrels. On the far side of the room was the mouth of a rough tunnel. The twisted remains of a metal door lay nearby, along with numerous shards of rock.

"You just can't help breaking things, can you, Shorn?" Netra said when she saw the wreckage.

"I did not do this," he said gruffly. "Look closer. It was broken from the other side."

He was right. The door had burst into the room. Something had struck it very hard from the other side.

"What did that?" Netra asked.

Shorn shrugged. "We will need a torch," he said, scanning the room. He tore a couple pieces of wood off a nearby crate and set about lighting one of them with his flint and steel. The wood, being very dry, burned well, and he gathered a few more pieces, then led the way into the tunnel.

Beyond the broken door was a roughly circular tunnel cut through raw stone, leading down. The tunnel was not high enough for Shorn to stand upright. It veered right and left only slightly as it led steadily downwards. For some time they made their way through it, silent except for the sound of their breathing echoing off the walls. The torch Shorn was carrying wavered and died down and he lit another one from it. When the second torch began to die down Netra grabbed his arm and pointed down the tunnel.

"I see light," she said.

A green glow reflected off the walls of the tunnel. It grew stronger as they continued on. The tunnel ended and they stepped out into a large, natural cavern. The floor of the cavern was covered in white sand. Against the wall to the right was a pool of water. The pool was contained in a waist-high wall of natural stone. The green glow was coming from the water.

"This is it," Netra said, hurrying past Shorn. "This is the place the book spoke of."

"Wait," Shorn said, taking hold of her arm and pointing. "There are bodies."

FIVE

There were three of them, sprawled on their backs on the sand. Two had been cut nearly in half; the third had his chest torn completely open.

"We've seen lots of bodies," Netra said, exasperated, trying to pull her arm away. "So what?"

"Look at how they lie. They were killed by something that came from the pool."

"Even if they were – "

"That is why the door was broken outwards. What killed all these people came from here."

"I *know* what killed these people, Shorn. It was the Guardians. The books make that very clear."

"You said this pool is connected to the sea." Netra nodded. "Why would the Guardians come from the sea?"

Netra sighed. "I don't know, Shorn. Maybe this is how they got around the Tenders' defenses."

"Or it was not the Guardians who killed them."

"What difference does it make, really? This happened centuries ago. Let go of me."

Reluctantly Shorn did so, but he preceded her to the pool and scanned its depths intently. The water was milky and he could not see much, but there didn't seem to be anything moving in the water. Which did nothing to calm the ugly feeling in his gut. "This…feels bad to me," he said. "Why does the water glow like that?"

"There is power here. A great deal of power. This is no ordinary water." Netra held her hands out over the pool, her palms down. A trace of excitement had crept into her voice. "They believed that the answers they sought could be found within the water, if only they could tap into it. If only they could control it."

Shorn looked down at the bodies. "Power did not kill these people. I have been thinking on this. I do not believe they were killed with a weapon. I believe their wounds were made by the claws of some creature. A very large creature."

Netra wasn't listening. She was pressed up against the wall around the edge of the pool and was holding her hands very close to the water. "I can feel it. I can feel the power."

"Do not stand so close to the water, Netra."

She ignored him and when he took hold of her shoulder to pull her back she turned on him angrily. "Stop babying me! If you are so frightened of a little water, then leave."

Shorn let go of her and she turned back to the water. He began to walk along the edge of the pool, his eyes moving constantly.

"I'm sorry, Shorn," she said a minute later. "I didn't mean to snap at you. I know you're only trying to keep me safe. But can't you see that maybe I could learn something here that could really help against Melekath? Maybe there's nothing I can do, and maybe I will get myself killed trying, but I have to do *something*. I'm not a child. You said it yourself: this is war. Let me fight this war in the only way I know how."

Shorn considered her words, then nodded. She was right. She wasn't a child. He could not deny her the right to fight for the lives of those she loved. He felt the pain and emptiness inside him at the thought of those he loved, and his utter helplessness where they were concerned.

"I think this is some kind of a source," Netra said, waving her hand at the pool. "Like the River is to LifeSong, a place where the power in water is concentrated. See how the water bubbles up from below? This water isn't coming from the sea. It is going out to the sea."

She dipped her hands in the water and then pulled them out and looked at them. Shorn tensed as she did so, but nothing happened. Perhaps it was as she said: all this happened so long ago.

Netra was staring at her hands, her eyes unfocused, her breathing very regular and slow. Shorn realized then that she had gone *beyond*. She had told him of that other place outside the normal realm. He didn't really understand what she meant by *beyond*, but somehow she was able to *see* energies while she was there, energies that flowed in the essence of things.

"It's beautiful," Netra said softly, awe in her voice. "It sparkles with blue and green. Its power is older and deeper than Song. With this power I could do anything."

Shorn moved closer to her, not knowing if there was anything he could do, but not liking where this was going.

Netra put her hands in the water and swirled them around, her face lit with joy. "If only you could *see* what I can, Shorn. You'd know there is nothing to fear here. LifeSong draws its vitality from the water. It is part of who and what we are."

"I think that is enough for now," Shorn said. "Maybe you should learn more from the books first."

"It's so close," she said, ignoring Shorn. "I can almost touch it. There's so much power. It wouldn't be like what I did before. No one would get hurt. No matter how much I took."

"It is late. We can come back tomorrow." Reluctantly, Netra let him pull her away from the pool.

That night, Netra had difficulty sleeping. She kept thinking of the last entry in the book. Did the writer carry through with his decision to drink from the pool? What happened? What did he learn? Whatever he learned, it hadn't been enough to save the people of Kaetria. But maybe that was because the writer waited too long and there wasn't enough time to take advantage of the Sea power. There was also the fact that the writer wasn't a Tender and so did not have the understanding of, or ability to, manipulate Song. As a Tender, she would have a better chance of harnessing that power.

Nor was she an ordinary Tender any longer. The huge quantities of Song she'd taken when she destroyed that Crodin village had changed her in a fundamental way. She was no longer the same person. Some inner barrier had been shredded. She was more open to the hidden, interior world of Song than any Tender had been in hundreds or even thousands of years. Maybe something good could still come of the mistakes she had made. Maybe she could still put this all right.

The risks were high. It frightened her to think of what might happen. Drinking that water might kill her as surely as any poison. Even if drinking it allowed her to touch the power contained therein, it might be too much for her. She might be torn apart.

In the end her decision was a foregone one. What choice did she really have? She had freed Melekath. What difference did it make

37

what happened to her? If there was even a chance she could put it all right, she had to take it.

She resolved not to tell Shorn of her decision. He would resist. He might even physically stop her.

The next morning Netra was tired and jittery over her decision, but excited at the same time. She avoided meeting Shorn's eyes while she ate from their dwindling supply of food, afraid he would see there the decision she had made.

"Are you going back to the library today?" he asked.

"Yes. Later. First I want to go back down to the pool. I had some ideas during the night and I want to look into them."

She could feel the weight of his gaze on her, the question he wanted to ask.

"I have an idea how I might be able to touch the power in the water." Still he gazed at her. "It's just a thought. It's probably nothing, but I want to try it."

"We have only enough food for one more day."

"Well, then, I better get started," she said, stuffing the last bit of cheese in her mouth and standing up. She half hoped he wouldn't come with her – then she wouldn't have to worry about him trying to stop her – but she was relieved when he stood and began to follow her. She didn't relish the thought of going down there alone. With Shorn protecting her, she didn't have to fear anything that came out of the pool. Whatever happened, he'd be able to take care of it.

Netra could feel the power coming off the pool before she even made it into the cavern. It was like a steady background hum that seemed to vibrate in her veins and center in her heart. It was faint, but it was unmistakably there and she found herself wondering how come she had never noticed it before. It was like the drone of insects in the desert night, so much a part of the normal background that she never heard it until she started listening for it.

Her excitement increased as she drew nearer to the pool. Slipping into *beyond*, she could *see* the currents of Sea power, ephemeral webs of energy in constant motion. The currents joined together and split apart constantly. The currents sparkled with green and here and there were flecks of blue and gold. It really was beautiful. Unlike the power she had sensed coming off the yellow crystal, this power felt welcoming, almost familiar. If there were answers to be found, they would be found here.

For a time she simply stood at the edge of the pool, gazing into it, enraptured by the beauty. She wondered what she would be able to *see* in normal water after this. Surely it was not so dense with power as this was, but there must still be power in it.

She waited until Shorn had moved away along the edge of the pool a few steps and then she cupped her hand in the water and brought some to her mouth.

"What are you doing?" Shorn demanded. He ran to her and grabbed her wrist but it was too late.

"It's okay, Shorn."

He pulled her away from the pool and then leaned over her. "You do not know what is in that," he growled.

"Actually, I think I do. It is power. Power that I am not yet able to touch. But maybe now I will."

"You should sit down."

"No. I feel fine. Just give me a minute. Stop talking and let me concentrate."

Something was definitely happening. She could feel it spreading outward from her stomach. It was a heady feeling. She'd only had wine twice in her life, and neither time did she have more than a cup of it, but it was similar to that. She felt strong and confident and slightly dizzy, though the dizziness did not seem to be a bad thing. She held out her arms and looked at them. They appeared no different, but they certainly felt different.

"What's wrong?" Shorn asked.

"Nothing's wrong. I'm okay." She cocked her head suddenly. "Did you hear that?"

"What?"

"I think it came from the pool." She pushed her way past him and walked to the edge of the pool. "It sounded like something splashing in the water."

Shorn scanned the pool. "I see nothing. We should leave."

"Not yet." Netra leaned against the edge of the pool and held her hands out, palms down, just above the surface of the water. She calmed her thoughts, calmed her breathing, and sank deeper into *beyond*. From there the currents in the water were so bright they nearly blinded her. She *saw* intricacies in their movement beyond anything she could have dreamed. It was so beautiful, so complex. It felt right. The power here was hers for the taking. She need only reach out and grab hold of it.

39

She put her hands into the water, letting it flow over her skin. The power was so close. She reached out with her will for the closest current.

And found herself holding nothing. It flowed through her grasp like the wind. She tried again, and again, with the same results. It was frustrating. The power was so close. With it she could solve all her problems. She was sure of it. If only she could take hold of it.

She pulled back, the effort starting to wear on her. "Maybe if I drink more of the water," she mused.

Shorn grabbed her arm and pulled her back. "No. I will not let you do this."

"Let go of me, Shorn."

"No. Later, if you are well, you may take more. But first I will see that you are not harmed by what you have taken so far."

Netra pulled against his grip, but of course it did no good. Then she nodded. "Fair enough. I'll wait until the end of the day. In the meantime, I'll go to the library and see if I can learn anything else."

She spent the rest of the day in the library but learned nothing more about the pool or Sea force. Finally, she grew frustrated. What she needed to know clearly wasn't in here. She needed to go drink from the pool again.

But when she left the hidden library she discovered that Shorn was waiting outside. Before she could say anything, he said, "In the morning."

"But I feel fine."

He looked closely into her eyes. "In the morning."

"Okay," Netra said irritably. "I guess it can wait until then."

Shorn knew she wasn't going to wait. And so he lay down and only pretended to sleep after they had eaten and the fire had died down. When she stood up and began to slip stealthily away he got up as well.

"Don't try to stop me," she warned. "I feel fine."

He simply waited. She frustrated him, with her willfulness and her stubbornness, but at the same time he loved those things about her. She had a strong will. She wouldn't lie down and give up. She was a fighter.

They made their way down to the pool. It seemed to glow more brightly than it had before, but Shorn assumed that was only his imagination, caused by his concern for her. "Not too much," he said when she reached for the water.

Netra cupped and brought water to her mouth two times before he stopped her. Then she stood and stared into the water, her gaze unfocused. She held her hands out, palms down. She grew very still.

For a time, nothing happened. Then the water under her hands began to move sluggishly. It swirled slowly and directly beneath her hands it began to rise. Netra had her eyes closed. Her jaw muscles were bunched and her forehead was creased. The water rose higher.

Shorn felt something. His eyes flicked to the pool. There was movement in the murky depths.

Suddenly a creature burst from the pool. It was shaped like a man, but completely hairless, its skin an ancient yellow color. It was shorter than Shorn, and built slightly, with a wide, lipless mouth, two slits for a nose and bulbous, wide-set eyes. Gills lined both sides of its neck.

Shorn reached for his sword, but before he could even get the weapon free the creature was upon Netra. Shorn shouted, but it was too late. With eerie, inhuman grace and speed it lunged forward and struck Netra once in the forehead and she dropped bonelessly to the floor.

Shorn roared and threw himself at the creature, the sword carving a wicked arc. Had it landed, the creature would have been cut in half. But it slipped inside his attack, moving with the same inhuman speed, and almost casually slapped him on the forehead. Shorn fell back a step, blinking hard. His vision blurred and he shook his head, swinging wildly with the sword as he did so.

The thing struck him twice more and he fell into unconsciousness.

The creature stood looking down at the two bodies at its feet. Its face showed no expression. There was movement in the pool and it looked up.

Rising from the pool was a monstrous, shark-like thing. It lifted its head from the water and began to change. The powerful fins on either side of its body shifted, becoming arm-like appendages that ended in what looked like wide, short blades, but formed of bone rather than steel. From its tail sprouted two thick legs. The eyes slid forward and down. Its mouth opened to reveal rows of triangular teeth.

It moved forward, black, pupilless eyes fixing on the two motionless figures. One bladed arm raised.

The yellow-skinned creature moved in front of it and held up one hand. "I have taken care of the threat," it said. "Return to the deeps."

The shark thing stared down at the yellow-skinned creature unblinking. Its mouth opened and a harsh tangle of sound cut the cavern's stillness. It gestured at the bodies on the floor as it did so, making a cutting motion with its bladed arm.

"I am aware that you are sent by Golgath, Master of the Deeps."

More harsh sounds and more arm waving from the creature. It took a step forward. The yellow-skinned creature moved to stay between it and the motionless figures.

"Perhaps you have forgotten who *I* am," the yellow-skinned creature said calmly.

The shark thing stopped. It was twice as tall as the one who thwarted it and many times greater in bulk. But all at once it stepped back. The eyes slid back up and to the outside. The bladed arms wavered, then slid back to fins. The thick, stump-like legs folded back into its body and it slid down into the water. With a thrust from its powerful tail it submerged and swam away.

The yellow-skinned creature bent over Shorn. It held one hand to its mouth and blew. A bubble formed around its fingers. It pressed the bubble to Shorn's face and the bubble clung there without breaking, covering his mouth and nose. Then it did the same for Netra.

One at a time it picked them up and dropped them into the water, seemingly having no trouble even with Shorn's bulk.

It gave one last look around the cavern, hopped into the pool, grabbed hold of Shorn and Netra and swam away.

In seconds the cavern was empty once again.

Six

Wulf Rome stood on the battlefield, the enemy dead littering the ground around him, the remains of the enemy army in flight, and knew he had just lost the war. He was staring south – nearly everyone was – and though there was nothing to see, no plume of smoke or anything, still he knew they had lost.

Melekath was free.

He could feel it in his chest, as if he had just breathed in something poisonous. A feeling of dread, a terrible foreboding. Melekath was free. The thing he had feared, but somehow never quite believed would happen, had happened. He wanted to throw down his weapon and walk away from the battlefield. Just give up. An enraged god was loose and he was coming for them. For all of them. What could he or any of them possibly hope to do against that?

Gritting his teeth, Rome fought to master himself, to wipe the doom from his face, knowing how it would infect his army if he let them see it. All around him men were turning toward him, the same sick realization in all their eyes. They felt it just as he did. Exhilaration and courage were evaporating. They looked to their leader to change that, to show them they were wrong.

To give them hope.

Hope he didn't have. So he fell back on the first lesson any commander learns: keep the soldiers busy. Rome rubbed sweat and hair out of his eyes and faced his men.

"All right, you know what to do," he yelled at them. Standing nearby was a sergeant, his mouth open, the sword in his hand barely hanging from his nerveless fingers. "Sergeant! Get some men together and start carrying the wounded up to the stitchers. Now!" He didn't know if it would work. His words sounded faint and small in his own ears. But then the sergeant shook himself like a man coming out of a nightmare. He stared at Rome for a moment, and in his eyes Rome

43

saw that the man knew what he was doing and why. Then he nodded slightly, saluted, and started barking orders.

Just then Nicandro, Rome's aide, came hurrying up. He was a short, bald, sinewy man, dark skinned and muscular. The smile he seemed to always wear was gone and desperation lurked in his eyes. "Orders, sir?" he asked.

"Put a team together and start gathering our dead." Rome looked around. Looming over the battlefield on the north was the shattered bulk of the Landsend Plateau. Uphill from him, crossing the width of the pass between the northern reaches of the Firkath Mountains and the Plateau, was the ancient stone wall his army had fought to defend, now with two gaping holes in it from where the Guardian Tharn tore through it. On the south side of the pass stood the ruins of a stone tower, all that remained of the fortress that was once Guardians Watch. The battlefield on this side of the pass was steep. Chunks of rock poked through the thin soil everywhere. The other side of the pass was no better, even if the slope was gentler.

Rome knew they couldn't just leave their dead lying here. The men wouldn't stand for it and he didn't blame them. No soldier wanted his body left lying for the carrion eaters that were already starting to circle. Taking the dead with them was out of the question, which meant they needed to be buried. And quickly. Rome wanted out of this place. He wanted to get back to Qarath as fast as possible. He knew in his gut Melekath would go there first, and he wasn't leaving his home undefended. But digging a mass grave in this soil would take days and he meant to leave at first light tomorrow. He made a decision and lowered his gaze to Nicandro.

"Lay them out in that ruined tower. When they're all in there, knock it down. That will be their monument."

Nicandro saluted and hurried away, calling to men as he went. Rome's next thought was to talk to Quyloc. He felt lost, unsure what to do next. What orders did one give when the end of the world had come? Quyloc would know what to do next. He always did.

He looked to where he'd last seen Quyloc, near the south end of the wall, but there was no sign of his old friend. Alarm rose in him. Had Kasai killed Quyloc right before fleeing? Or somehow taken Quyloc prisoner?

He turned to look at the huge block of stone on the north end of the pass that he'd been commanding from before leaping off to attack Tharn, and what he saw stunned him.

Quyloc was up there, standing beside Tairus. Rome turned around to the opposite side of the pass, where he'd last seen Quyloc, then slowly turned back to look at him. How in the world did he get up there so quickly? For that matter, how did he manage to get clear across an active battlefield and attack Kasai like he did? Thank the gods the *rendspear* worked as well as they'd hoped. But it seemed he was going to need a lot of answers.

Feeling terribly weary, Rome trudged up the slope to one of the holes in the wall. As he got close, he looked up and saw the FirstMother standing on top of the wall, looking down at him. Her white robe was covered in dirt and splashed with blood. It looked too big for her, as if she had shrunk recently. What little hair had grown back on her bald head seemed to have turned completely gray. Her *sulbit* lay limply across her shoulders. It looked more yellow than usual. The eyes in its blunt face were closed. Around her, the other Tenders seemed mostly to be in shock, faces pale, not speaking.

"Melekath is free," she said, her voice filled with doom. "We were supposed to be there, at the prison. Not here."

"Lowellin said we had months before Melekath got out." It was a silly thing to say. What difference did it make what Lowellin said now? But he didn't like the accusation in her words.

She sagged a little at his words and he realized then how much she had put her faith in Lowellin.

"We have to get back to Qarath," she said.

"We will," he replied, turning away from her.

T'sim emerged from the hole in the wall as he drew near. In the midst of the carnage, with blood everywhere and the cries of the wounded and dying filling the air, T'sim looked as placid as ever. His coat was freshly brushed, the silver buttons gleaming. His hair was neat, his features calm. He might have been back at the palace, rather than in the middle of a battlefield. He stopped and waited for Rome, his hands folded before him.

"I need to talk to Lowellin."

"Lowellin is gone, Macht," T'sim said. "I can find him, but it will take time and I may not be able to bring him back here in a timely fashion."

Rome's face twisted. "He ran away."

"He did not expect the prison to break when it did. I confess I was surprised too." His brow furrowed slightly.

"What happened?"

T'sim held his hands out, palms up. His hands were small and somewhat pink. "Sententu finally broke."

"Who's Sententu?"

"A Shaper. Of the First Ring. He made of himself the door to the prison, after Xochitl allowed the flaw." He frowned. "I would like to see her one day, and ask her if it was deliberate, if she wanted them to be able to escape someday. She was ever soft-hearted."

"I don't care about Xochitl right now," Rome growled. "Tell me something I can use. How did Melekath break Sententu?"

T'sim gazed off to the south for long moments before replying. As he did a breeze rose up, gusting around him. He seemed to be listening to it. Rome realized that this wind only blew right around them. Nearby trees were unmoving. After a minute, he gazed at Rome once again. "Melekath did not break Sententu."

"So you think one of the Guardians helped him? Was it Gulagh? We didn't see him here." Quyloc came walking up right then, Tairus behind him.

"Not a Guardian," T'sim replied. "A human. A woman." He pointed at the Tender camp. "One of them."

"One of the *Tenders* helped Melekath?"

T'sim nodded. "For all your strengths, you are easily misled. You have a way of only hearing what you want to hear, and ignoring the rest."

"You're saying one woman had the power to break a prison that held Melekath for thousands of years?" Quyloc asked. "That's impossible. Where would she even get that much power?"

"She used a trunk line," T'sim said.

Quyloc was visibly staggered. "It's not possible," he gasped. "Not even a Tender of old…"

"She killed a number of Crodin," T'sim said matter-of-factly. "She drained them. Their Songs gave her the strength, and Melekath gave her the reason." He shook his head. His soft face showed genuine surprise. "She thought she was rescuing her god. She was so sure she was right that she ignored all the signs. She *wanted* to be right." He looked over his shoulder at the Tender camp. "There are many who would like to know what became of Xochitl. Alone of the Eight, she has disappeared completely. Even the *aranti* have had no sign of her. She is the only one we have not found."

Rome stared at the little man, surprised. Never had he said so much before. He didn't seem to be talking to them. It was more as if he was musing aloud.

"Who and why don't really matter all that much now," Rome said. "The only important question is: What do we do now?"

T'sim raised one eyebrow, as if he had never considered the question before, and Rome was struck by the realization that this being before him was vastly different from them. He was an observer. Why he had helped them at all, Rome didn't know. But it was not because he cared what happened to them.

"I don't think it matters," T'sim said at last. "Melekath's Children have changed. More than even he realizes." He paused, a realization striking him. "In this way he is not so different from your kind. He sees what he wants to see, and denies the truth before his eyes. His Children are not what they once were. They will not heal as he hopes. Their hunger for Song is very great. That is what you feel here: the flows are beginning to bend toward them. Nothing will sate this hunger." He stopped, seeming to realize that they were staring at him, horrified.

"You can run, I suppose. It will keep you alive for a time."

"There has to be some way we can kill these things," Rome said, thinking of the black axe.

"Kill them?" T'sim gave Rome a quizzical look. "Oh, you do not know about the Gift, the nature of it. The reason for the siege of Durag'otal. The Gift is immortality.

"The Children cannot die."

SEVEN

Quyloc was looking at Rome as T'sim's words registered on the big man. They seemed to hit him like a physical blow and he almost visibly reeled. For some reason Quyloc was reminded of the bear their squad had tracked and killed years ago. The animal had been raiding nearby farms and had killed two men on its latest raid so their squad had been dispatched to bring it down. The hunting dogs cornered the bear in a small canyon, up against a wooded bluff. The thing was huge and they shot arrow after arrow into it, seemingly without effect, while the dogs snapped at its hamstrings. But then one of the soldiers hit it with one more arrow, right in the throat. As soon as the arrow landed, Quyloc knew that was the final blow. The animal rocked backwards and it seemed to Quyloc that something desperate flashed in its eyes. Rome was that bear and T'sim's words were the final arrow.

"They can't *die*?" Rome croaked. "What do you mean by that?"

"Why, it means exactly what I said," T'sim replied, putting his hands in his coat pockets. "They can't die. It must have once seemed a great blessing, though I doubt they think so now. I do not think their time in the prison went well. Sometimes dying can seem like a good thing." He sounded wistful when he said it. "You have such short lives and you long for more. But you don't know what it is like to live on, when there is nothing left to hope for, nothing to want. It is why Melekath and Lowellin are so sharp. In a way, their hatred for each other gives their lives meaning."

"Hold on," Rome interrupted, holding out his hands as if to stem the flow of words.

T'sim paused and regarded him.

"So we not only have a mad god on our hands, but we have a bunch of his children as well. How many are we talking about?" Rome looked like he was having trouble breathing.

Quyloc stared at him, aghast and awed. Was this Wulf Rome he was looking at? The irrepressible Wulf Rome? Had something finally shaken him? It was something Quyloc had secretly longed to see for many years, yet now that it was here it was, frankly, appalling.

"It is hard to say. Durag'otal held tens of thousands. But it has been many years, as you reckon time, and how many will emerge is hard to say."

"Tens of thousands?" Rome seemed to be shrinking before Quyloc's eyes.

"Why wouldn't they emerge?" Quyloc asked. "You said they can't die."

T'sim rocked back and forth on his small feet while he chose his words. "Some of them may be...broken."

Rome looked at Quyloc. There was something pleading in his gaze that pierced Quyloc deeper than he could have imagined. Quyloc looked away. Rome shifted his gaze back to T'sim. "Is there no way to stop them?"

T'sim shrugged. "Anything is possible, I suppose."

"But how?" Rome's voice was little more than a whisper.

T'sim looked startled, then shook his head. "It is not for me to become involved in this." He turned and walked quickly away.

Quyloc was watching Rome from the corner of his eye and saw what happened next, but it was still hard to believe.

Rome stared after T'sim's departing figure. He was bent over as if he was being slowly crushed by the weight of the world on his shoulders. Then, he simply changed. A transformation came over him. He straightened. The despair on his face smoothed away as if it were never there. He turned to Quyloc.

"We have a seriously pissed off god on our hands and with him is a bunch of people who can't die." He made a wry face. "Is that about right? Did I miss anything?"

Quyloc just stared at him.

"I know it looks bad right now, Quyloc, but we'll figure it out. Just like we always have, you and me." Rome clapped him on the shoulder. "We won today when we should have lost. We'll win next time too."

Then he turned and walked back to his army, shouting at men who were moving too slowly, calling encouragement to others. Quyloc could not miss the impact Rome had on his men. Where he passed even the wounded seemed to straighten. Where he passed the dark cloud over the men lifted. Men set to their duties with new purpose. Just like that the day changed.

Quyloc could only stare and wonder.

Nalene walked back to the Tender camp in a daze, only vaguely aware of people and voices around her. She had felt the breaking of the prison like something tearing open inside her. It was as if she'd lived her whole life huddled by a tiny candle and something had just blown the candle out; ugly, frightening things were drawing closer in the darkness.

She'd gotten down off the wall and was near enough to hear what T'sim said about Melekath's Children and what she heard terrified her. What did he mean by their hunger for Song? Were they really immortal?

She felt movement on the back of her neck as her *sulbit* burrowed deeper into her robe. She could feel how frightened it was. It wanted only to hide. Not so long ago her *sulbit* had made her feel so powerful. Now she just felt helpless. What could they possibly do against a foe that could not die?

Slowly Nalene became aware that someone was walking beside her, talking to her. She shook her head and turned away, but the voice did not stop. Now there was a hand on her arm. Finally, she turned. The woman standing there was young and tall, with a stubble of dark brown hair emerging on her scalp. It took Nalene a moment to remember her name. Bronwyn. "What do you want, Bronwyn?" she snapped, yanking her arm away.

To her credit the young woman did not flinch before the harshness of Nalene's tone. "FirstMother, you can't go over there like this."

"What?"

"You can't go back to the camp like this."

"What are you talking about?" Had the woman been hit on the head? Was she simple?

"They need you, FirstMother," Bronwyn said. "*I* need you. You can't go over there like this."

Nalene felt a spark of anger inside her. Who was this woman to tell her what she could and couldn't do? She was the *FirstMother*. She would be treated with respect. "I will not stand here and be spoken to like this – " she started, and then broke off as she realized what Bronwyn was saying. She looked over at the camp. Even from here

50

she could see the white faces, the looks of loss and confusion. She turned back to Bronwyn and took a deep breath.

"Thank you." She put a hand on Bronwyn's arm. "How much do you know of what just happened?"

Bronwyn's face grew grave. "I don't know what just happened. But it feels bad." She looked like she would say more but didn't.

"What is it? Speak your mind, Tender."

"Is it Melekath? Is he really free?" There was dirt on Bronwyn's face and blood as well, though it didn't look like hers. But Nalene could see that she was having a hard time. With the heightened awareness given to her by her connection with her *sulbit* she could *feel* it. This woman who faced her so bravely was close to breaking, very close.

"Go on ahead and gather the others," Nalene said, her voice quieter now. "I would speak to you all at once, but I want a moment to gather my thoughts."

Bronwyn looked relieved. She ducked her head and hurried off.

Nalene watched her go. What would she say to them? she wondered. All at once the burden of leadership seemed unbearable. They were looking to her for guidance. How could she provide it when she felt like lying down and crying? She turned, and in the distance she saw Rome, standing with several soldiers around him. He looked like he was giving orders, though she couldn't hear him. He stood tall and confident, as if it was only another day. She knew he was upset, but it didn't show.

She turned back and faced the Tender camp. A new truth came into her: it didn't matter how she felt. She was the FirstMother. She had to show the others that she was not afraid. It didn't matter what the truth was. All that mattered right now was that. She squared her shoulders and continued on.

"I'm going to talk to the troops," Rome said. He and Tairus were watching as soldiers heaved on ropes tied to stones on top of the ruined tower. Their dead – Kasai's dead were still strewn over the battlefield – were piled within the tower and now they were bringing it down. The soldiers gave another heave and a row of stones fell inward with a crash.

"Figured you would," Tairus said. The stout man had washed the blood from his face and hands, but the rest of him was still spattered with it. "Otherwise we're going to lose a lot of them during the night."

"We may anyway." Rome's confidence and attitude had helped bring the soldiers through the initial shock at the end of the battle, but they were clearly wilting again. Men spoke in low voices as they worked and there were long looks to the east and south, where their homes lay.

"I can't say that I blame them," Tairus said. "When the end of the world comes, a man's got a right to be with his family."

"You're not saying what it sounds like you're saying," Rome said. "I hope not anyway."

"No, I'm not suggesting we let them go. I'm just saying in their shoes I'd feel the same."

Rome turned to his aide. "Spread the word to the captains to muster the men over in that flat area on the east side of the pass. I'm going to speak to them." Nicandro saluted and hurried off. Just then there was a loud rumbling, crashing sound and most of the rest of the ruined tower collapsed, raising a cloud of dust. Rome turned to another aide. "Tell the cooks to throw it all in for dinner tonight. Don't hold anything back." He'd gotten word that the first of the supply wagons sent from Karthije were closing in. They should be able to meet up with them by the end of the day tomorrow.

Rome was sitting on his horse, waiting, as the men began to gather. He still had his armor on, with its fresh gashes and splattered blood. After a moment of thought, he reached for the black axe, which was strapped to his back. He'd sheathed it after attacking Tharn and used his battle axe for the rest of the battle, somehow not wanting to know what it might do to a human being.

As his fingers touched the haft, the axe buzzed. Just for an instant he found himself looking on a world other than his own. It was dark, barely lit by a dim glow, and there was water dripping from above.

He jerked his hand away and the image was gone. Tentatively, he touched the axe again. Nothing. He pulled the axe free and held it up to the light. It looked the same as ever. Didn't it? He turned it side to side. Did the eyes carved into the sides of the head look different?

Quyloc came riding up. "What's wrong?"

"What isn't wrong?"

Quyloc shrugged.

"When I touched it, just for a second I thought I was somewhere else, somewhere dark."

"Didn't you say Lowellin said it might be alive?"

Rome shivered slightly. He'd tried to forget that. "How could stone be alive?"

"How could stone turn into an axe when you pull it out of a stone wall?"

"That doesn't make me feel any better."

"It's not supposed to."

Rome didn't want to talk about the axe anymore. He didn't want to think about what it might or might not be. "How did you do that?" Quyloc gave him an inquiring look. "Travel from one side of the battlefield to the other and attack Kasai. How did you do it?"

"I went into the borderland between our world and the *Pente Akka*. Then I came out in a different place."

"I didn't know you could do that."

"Neither did I."

"If you hadn't though…"

Quyloc had the *rendspear* across his saddle, once again in its leather wrappings. "Lowellin was right about how powerful it is."

"Think you can do the same thing when we come up against Melekath?"

"I think so. But I think our problems are bigger than that."

"What do you mean?"

"You heard what T'sim said, about the Children. How do we fight thousands of people who can't die?"

"Can they fly? Can they burrow through stone walls? Maybe the question is how can they get past Qarath's wall? They're just people, aren't they?"

Quyloc shrugged again. "I don't know." He looked at the assembling soldiers. "How much are you going to tell them?"

"All of it, I guess. I hadn't really thought about it."

Quyloc drew in a sharp breath. "Is that a good idea?"

"You don't think they deserve the truth?"

Quyloc shook his head and frowned. "I don't think they can handle it."

"You might be surprised."

The look Quyloc flashed him was angry. "But probably I won't be. Probably they'll react just as I know they will." He was biting off his words, though he turned away and did not meet Rome's eyes. "This is bigger than you think, Rome. I know how you are. I know how much you believe in the common soldier, but this time you're wrong. We're looking at the end, Rome. *The end.* If you tell them that, you'll lose them completely. I don't care how much *confidence* you have in them, you'll lose them. They'll break. You'll be in command of a ghost army. Then we really *will* have no chance."

Rome stared at him, surprised. Then he said, "Well, I never thought of it that way. I just thought – "

"That's the point, Rome. You don't think. You just do. Then you leave other people to clean up the mess."

"Where's this coming from, Quyloc?" Rome asked, genuinely puzzled. "What are you so mad about?"

"Why do you even have an adviser when you never take advice?" Quyloc asked, and this time he did meet Rome's eyes for a few seconds. Then he jerked his horse's head around and started away. "Just do what you were planning to do, Rome. Like you always do."

Rome stared after him, wondering. Was it true? Did he never listen to his adviser? Maybe Quyloc was right this time. Maybe he shouldn't tell the men what T'sim had said about the Children being immortal or about their hunger. It might be too much for them.

Then he realized some of the nearby soldiers had grown very still and were looking at him. They must have overheard at least some of what went on. He gave them a look and they quickly turned their heads away. He hoped they hadn't heard enough to really know what was going on. Things were bad enough. They didn't need to think there was a rift at the top of the command as well.

The sun was almost to the horizon. A chilly wind blew up the slope from the west. Far overhead a flock of geese flew over, their honking just barely audible. It was time to tell the men whatever he was going to tell them.

"You all felt it, I guess," Rome said, using what he thought of as his sergeant's voice. His words cut clearly through the air and as a man the gathered soldiers went still, all of them straining to hear him. "That empty feeling, like you're just about to fall over a cliff. Right after the battle ended."

There were murmurs of agreement from the men. Rome saw that Dargent had his mounted troops pulled close off to the right. In their glitter and finery they stood in clear contrast to the common soldiers. They had been surprisingly useful in the battle. To the left he saw the small knot of Tenders. They looked worn out and more than one seemed to be upright only with the help of her guard, but they were listening closely as well. It seemed everyone wanted to hear what he had to say.

"That was Melekath's prison breaking."

If he had been expecting some kind of outcry or panic, it didn't happen. Surely the possibility that the worst had finally happened had been the subject of nearly every rumor all afternoon. Instead the gathered soldiers let out something almost like a collective sigh. Somehow fearing the worst was worse than actually having it confirmed.

"So it's happened. The thing we were hoping wouldn't happen, finally did. Sooner than we thought, too." Rome raked his fingers through his hair, tugging at some of the snarls he found there. How long since he'd had anything resembling a bath? "I won't lie to you. It's bad. It's real bad."

They stared at him in riveted, horrified fascination.

"Right now a lot of you are thinking about running." Rome paused, let that sink in. "I don't blame you. I feel like running too."

They blinked at him, surprised.

"After all, it's the end, right? What kind of man wouldn't want to run back to his family, to anyone he loves, and spend whatever time he can with them? You wouldn't be much of a man if you didn't feel that."

Rome took a deep breath and leaned forward on his saddle horn. "But you won't. I know you won't. You want to know why?" He waited, letting them think about it for a while. "The reason you won't run is because of your families, your loved ones. Because if you run you might as well just cut their throats when you see them. Kill them and get it over with. Because if you run, if this army falls apart, then Melekath has already won. You'll get some time with them, sure, but it won't be long and when Melekath shows up, you'll be defenseless. There'll be nothing you can do."

Rome held up the black axe. "I stopped Tharn with this. Quyloc…" He turned, looking for Quyloc, but didn't see him anywhere. "Quyloc stopped Kasai with his spear. But we could never have done that without all of you." His gesture encompassed all of them. "Together we beat Melekath's top two generals and their army. It shouldn't have happened. They should have beaten us. But they didn't. And you know what that means?"

They waited, watching him.

"It means we're not done yet. It means no matter how black it looks we can still win this. But only...only if we stay together."

They stood and stared at him when he was done talking. They didn't cheer and Rome didn't expect them to. But he could see in their eyes that they were thinking, and that was all he could hope for. A man caught in a panic doesn't think; he acts. Rome wanted them to think.

Tairus walked up to Rome. He was on foot. The short stout man loathed horses and only rode when he had to. "I don't know if that was brilliant or idiotic," he said, spitting on the ground. After a battle he always had the taste of blood in his mouth and he couldn't seem to get rid of it. Had he bitten his tongue?

"We'll know in the morning."

"Oh, I think we'll be fine in the morning. It's on the long walk home I'm worried about. A man gets a lot of time to think, marching. Every day we'll get closer to their homes and they'll think more and more about running to them."

"Am I doing the right thing?" Rome asked suddenly.

Tairus looked up in surprise, shading his eyes against the last rays of the sun. Rome wasn't a man given to self-doubt. It was his unshakeable confidence that was a big part of how devoted his troops were to him. "A little late to wonder that, don't you think? You already told them."

"No, not that," Rome said, sliding the black axe into its sheath on his back. "I'm talking about trying to hold them. Maybe I should let them all go home. What good's a sword or an axe going to be against a mad god and his immortal followers?"

Now Tairus was really surprised. This didn't sound like Rome at all. If the troops heard this, they'd really get in a lather. He looked around to make sure no soldiers were close enough to hear. "I don't know, Rome. Maybe no good at all. But I'm thinking it's better to have an army and have no use for it than have no army and need it. What if Kasai rallies and comes back at us with a new army?"

"You're probably right. I hope so, anyway." Rome picked up his reins and gave his horse a tap with his heels.

Tairus watched his king and commander walk away and swore to himself. There was a coldness in his heart that had nothing to do with the approaching darkness. He looked to the south. Were Melekath and his Children even then heading for Qarath? How fast would they move? Qarath suddenly seemed very far away and the coming night seemed very long.

EIGHT

Nalene lay on the hard ground that night and barely slept. There seemed to be fearful whispers on the wind. The world recoiled from Melekath's presence.

Her *sulbit* made it worse. All night long it scurried back and forth over her, quivering. Its body was slick and cool. She tried stroking it, but it was not calmed by her touch. It made tiny, anxious sounds as it moved, upset by events it could not explain to her.

When the gray light of morning crept over the horizon Nalene sat up with the weight of doom on her shoulders. Her neck was stiff and her back ached. Her *sulbit* crawled up onto her shoulder and stood up on its hind legs, staring off to the south. Its blunt head swiveled toward her and the black, pupil-less eyes fixed on her. It chittered, showing its fine, needle-like teeth.

"I know," she said. "I feel it too." It felt as if everything was bending to the south. There was something there pulling at her, pulling at every living thing. Was it the Children? Could they really be that strong? How much worse would it get?

Wearily, she got to her feet, suppressing a groan as she did so. By then the army was beginning to stir. She felt old and used up. She hurt everywhere. Nearby she saw Bronwyn get up and roll up her blanket. The woman was less than half her age and though she was clearly tired, she didn't look nearly as bad as Nalene felt. What she wouldn't give to have that woman's youth and vitality. She was going to need it before this was all over.

She opened her mouth to tell Bronwyn to get the rest of the Tenders up, but before she could get the words out Bronwyn was already nodding and moving to do it, as if she'd expected Nalene's command. She seemed to do that a lot. She was a complete contrast to Velma, who needed even simple tasks explained to her slowly. Nalene made a mental note to raise Bronwyn up and give her more authority.

Nalene had her women ready before the army was. She wanted them out in front. She didn't ask Rome for permission, just got her women mounted up and onto the meager trail first. She saw him looking at her, but he didn't say anything. She wanted to get to Qarath as fast as she could and she was prepared to leave the army behind if she could.

They had not been moving long when a horsefly, its body as big as her thumb, its wings iridescent green, flew up and landed on the back of her hand. Nalene jumped and the insect flew away, but it was back soon, landing on her hand again. Again Nalene waved it off and again it returned. She slapped at it, but it was too fast. Irritated, she watched for it to return, planning to crush it this time.

It landed on her arm this time, but as she raised her other hand to strike it she had an odd feeling and she looked around, for some reason expecting to see Ricarn, though of course she wasn't.

Nalene frowned. Could this bug somehow be connected to her? She resisted the urge to slap it and waited.

Hurry back. The city ignites. They need hope.

The bug flew away and Nalene stared after it. The feeling of Ricarn's presence was gone. A minute later she turned her horse and made her way back along the army until she found Rome. He was talking to an old, bearded man, with scars everywhere and equally scarred weapons. The man nodded, hitched his belt, then rejoined the mass of soldiers. Rome looked at Nalene and waited.

"My Tenders and I will – " Nalene began, then checked herself. "I want permission to go on ahead." All the Tenders were mounted. Only a few of the soldiers were and they could not go as fast.

"Why?"

"Qarath is…" She hesitated, not sure what she really did know. "Things in the city are bad since the prison broke. I think we can help calm things down."

"How do you know this?" Rome asked.

Nalene took a breath. "Ricarn."

Rome thought on his, his brow furrowing. "The Insect Tender?" he said at last.

Nalene was surprised, but she got over it quickly. He was the macht. It made sense that he had spies watching her. "Yes."

"How did she tell you this?"

"A horsefly." It sounded impossible as soon as she said it, but Rome only nodded.

"I've been thinking about going on ahead myself," he said. "They must have felt what we did. We may arrive at Qarath and find only a smoking ruin." He looked out over the mass of troops and his face grew somber. "But if I leave, I think this army will fall apart. I think I'm the only thing holding it together."

Nalene said nothing, only waited.

"Go ahead," he told her. "But I'm sending Quyloc with you. One of us should be there."

Quyloc came trotting up and reined in beside Nalene. Behind him, also mounted, were four soldiers. He gestured and they spurred their horses and moved on ahead.

"Where are they going?" Nalene asked.

"The *sulbits* need food."

He was right. Already Nalene could feel her *sulbit*'s hunger. It wasn't too strong yet – the *sulbits* had all fed on the last few shatren last night – but it would get worse. "We should meet up with the supply wagons by the end of the day. Tomorrow at the latest."

"No, we won't. We're going to leave the trail in a few hours and turn south. It will be shorter. There's no need to go by way of Karthije like we did on the way here."

That made sense. Karthije was further east than they needed to go. If they headed directly for Qarath, they could cut a day or two off their trip. "So you sent them ahead to find some shatren for the *sulbits* to feed on?"

"Shatren. Pigs. Goats. Whatever they can find." Quyloc turned to look at Nalene's *sulbit*, crouched on her shoulder. "I don't want those things feeding on *us*."

NINE

Rome and Tairus were sitting on their horses, watching the army pull out, when they heard a familiar drawl.

"Leavin' so soon?"

Rome turned. Sitting on a rock to his right was one of the Telinar brothers, the young one with the twin braids. His leathers were as worn and disreputable as ever, stained with grease and dirt. His moccasins looked like they would fall apart any second. Rome exchanged a look with Tairus. There was no cover nearby, only some spindly bushes and scattered rocks. How could the man have gotten there without being seen? And yet there he was, slouched on the rock as if he'd been there all day. He was working at his teeth with a long knife.

"What are you doing here?" Tairus asked.

"Hold on," the brother said. "Almost got it." He screwed up his face, digging around with the knife in a way that made Rome's mouth hurt to watch. The knife slipped through and the young man reached into his mouth. He pulled out something black that might have been a tooth once, looked at it critically for a moment, then tossed it away. "You were saying?" he said.

"What are you doing here?" Tairus asked again.

"Just watching. Nothing else to do."

Another one of the brothers came walking up right then. Rome and Tairus stared at him openmouthed. He didn't seem to come from anywhere. It was as if one second he wasn't there, and the next he was.

"Don't play with them, Lem," he said, scratching at his beard. It was a long beard, reaching halfway down his chest. A great deal of dirt came out of it when he scratched. He was older than Lem. "Say what we came to say."

"Okay," Lem said. "Wasn't causing trouble."

The older brother sat down on the ground and leaned against the rock Lem was sitting on.

"Wondered if you might like some help," Lem said.

"We're going home," Tairus said. "We don't need your help anymore."

"Hmm," another voice said. Rome and Tairus started as another brother walked up. He was the heavyset one with the red hair. "Thought I heard Melekath was out and about again."

"Quit doing that, would you?" Tairus asked.

All three brothers gave him a blank look.

"What kind of help are you offering?" Rome asked, cutting off Tairus before he could speak again.

"We thought…" The youngest one looked to the other two, and when they nodded he continued. "We thought you might like to know what he is up to."

"Could be helpful," the bearded one said.

"Could be worth some growl," the heavy one said. "Liquor. Happy water. Snuff stuff." The bearded brother gave him a dark look.

"You can tell us what Melekath is doing?" Rome asked.

"How are you going to do that?" Tairus demanded. "He's hundreds of miles away."

"We have ways," another voice said. It was the brother with gray hair. He pushed the youngest one off the rock and took his place, sighing as he sat down.

"If you can tell me what Melekath is up to…" Rome said. At his words, all the brothers perked up, each leaving off the other minor tasks he was involved in and sitting up. "I will give you each a barrel of liquor big enough to drown yourselves in."

"Ain't no such thing," the oldest one scoffed.

"But we like your words," the heavyset one added.

"We'd like to try," the young one said.

"You'd drown straight off," the bearded one said to the young one. "You can't even swim."

"Nor you!" the young one said. His words came out loud, but he didn't rise from his position, lying on his side, propped up on one elbow. The bearded one didn't bother to respond.

"It's as Tairus says, though," Rome said. "He's hundreds of miles away. How can you tell us what he's doing?"

"There's ways and there's ways," the gray-haired one said sagely. For some reason the other brothers found this funny and there was much slapping knees and wiping eyes.

"We can crawl up his ass if you like," the heavyset one said, setting off another round of laughter.

"Do you know what he's doing now?" Rome asked.

"Ain't looked, and you ain't paid," the young one said.

"We need what you call an advance," the old one added. "Otherwise, we're kinda busy."

"Tairus," Rome said.

"It's all right," T'sim said, just then approaching. "Perhaps this will help." The little man had a jug in each hand.

TEN

"**Where** are they?" Donae whined. Quyloc and the Tenders had just stopped to make camp beside a small spring. The sun was already down. "I thought the FirstMother said the soldiers would bring animals for us today. Even some goats would help," Donae said, climbing wearily down off her horse. "You'd think they could at least find some goats." The horse, jittery from a day spent with a hungry *sulbit* on its back, sidestepped as she dismounted and she lost her balance and fell. The horse would have run off, but one of the guards caught hold of its reins.

From her seat on the ground, Donae glared at the horse. "I hate that horse. It hates me too."

"She never said they would make it back today," Karyn said irritably, giving Owina a look and rolling her eyes. She climbed down off her horse holding her blanket and started looking for a place to sleep. "She said they *might* get back today. Obviously they won't. Complaining about it isn't going to make anything any better."

Owina knew how she felt. Donae had complained most of the day and it was getting on her nerves too. She prided herself on her ability to remain calm and upbeat even during trying times, but it was difficult with Donae.

"I don't understand what's taking them so long," Donae continued, putting her head in her hands. A new worry occurred to her then and she raised her head to look at Owina. "You *do* think they're coming back, don't you?"

"Why wouldn't they?"

"Maybe they deserted. Maybe they just ran off and abandoned us out here."

"I'm sure they didn't do that," Owina replied, though she wasn't actually sure and the thought of it gave her a chill. "They were handpicked by Advisor Quyloc and I'm sure they're all very reliable."

"That doesn't mean anything," Donae shrilled. "I heard some soldiers talking before we rode out this morning, and they said a whole lot of soldiers deserted during the night, that they ran home to be with their families."

"I'm with Owina on this," Karyn said. "A much more likely conclusion is that they simply haven't found a farm yet where they could buy animals, or they found the farm too late in the day to make it back so soon. Look around. This isn't exactly farm country, is it?"

"Maybe you're right," Donae said doubtfully, peering at the surrounding landscape as if just noticing it for the first time. They were still in the foothills of the Landsend Plateau and the countryside was fairly steep, with lots of narrow canyons and thickly wooded hillsides. Her *sulbit* popped up out of the sleeve of her robe then, stood up on its hind legs and chittered at her.

"Be quiet," she snapped at it. "I know you're hungry. You don't have to keep reminding me." She looked back at Owina. "Honestly, I don't know if I'm more tired from the long ride, or from wrestling with this thing. All day long it was trying to feed on my horse."

"I know how you feel," Owina replied. She'd spent all day wrestling with her *sulbit* too.

"Maybe we could let them feed on one of the horses," Donae said. "Maybe someone should ask the FirstMother." The FirstMother and Quyloc were off by themselves, talking in low voices.

"And then how would the person whose horse it was keep up?" Karyn asked. "Are you going to volunteer your horse?"

"Of course not. Don't be ridiculous. I'm thinking one of the guard's horses. I mean, do we really need them all that much now?"

"We have a great deal of ground to cover between here and Qarath," Karyn said. "Who knows what we're going to run into? I, for one, would like to keep the guards if we can."

"I'm not saying we should do it," Donae said querulously. "I'm just saying it's a possibility, one we should consider."

"Let's wait to consider it until it becomes a necessity," Owina said. "Until then, try to think of it as practice in controlling your *sulbit*."

"You *can* still control your *sulbit*, can't you?" Karyn asked.

"Of course I can. I made it through the whole day, didn't I?"

Karyn exchanged a look with Owina and she knew the other woman was thinking about what happened when they stopped for a break at midday. As Donae was dismounting, her *sulbit* suddenly lunged for her horse. It missed because the horse bolted, but it took a while before one of the guards was able to catch the animal and after that it wouldn't let Donae anywhere near it. She'd had to switch to another horse.

"Let's just try to get some rest," Owina said. "Things will look better in the morning. I'm sure the soldiers will have some animals for us before it becomes a real problem."

Rome looked at the sleeping army that night and wondered how long he could hold them. The supply wagons had helped. Full stomachs settled men who had been too long hungry. And he'd doubled the ale and rum rations. He had doubled the patrols too, and made sure they were all Qarathians, but he knew that even as he watched there were men sneaking away into the darkness, that come morning the army would be somewhat smaller, and that some of those gone would be the men assigned to make sure the others did not leave. Most would be from Thrikyl, he knew that. Their families were closest to Melekath, probably would be the first to feel his touch. Telling them that he would send orders to evacuate their city to Qarath had not helped, and he had not really expected it to. Why should they flee the city whose walls had never fallen, except before his axe? Why should they think Qarath would be safer?

The truth was that Rome did not think Qarath was safer, but it was further. Further meant they had more time to plan, to figure out something that would work against Melekath and his Children. The truth was that Rome did not blame those who slipped away during the night. Part of him wanted to let them all go, tell them to run to their families and find what time they could with them before it was too late. They faced a god whose strength was such that it took the strongest of the old gods to contain him. Now those were gone, and they had to deal with his Children as well. What chance did they have against such might?

But he did not because he knew that once they scattered any hope mankind had was lost, and he was too stubborn to give up on hope just yet. They might still find a way out of this. Help might still arrive at the end. Anything could happen in war, this much he knew. So he held them together as best he could, tried to will them to hope while not letting his fear show.

He looked to the south, as he found himself doing over and over, as if he would see something there that would shed light on what was happening. Knowing what Melekath was doing, what he *could* do, would help. Even knowing it was worse than he feared would still help, for then he would at least know.

Would the brothers return with information? It seemed impossible that they could travel such distances, that they could spy on Melekath and return intact. But he had nothing left but the impossible. Only the impossible could save them now. So it was in the impossible that he must believe, even if it made more sense that the brothers had taken what they could in drink and would never return, like a man stealing the boots off a dying man. The dead had no need of boots, nor of liquor.

ELEVEN

"Hey! What's wrong with my horse?"

Owina lay there, suspended between sleep and wakefulness, wishing the guards would shut up. The sun hadn't risen yet and the morning was cold. She felt as if she'd hardly slept at all. The whole night her *sulbit* had been restless, walking back and forth across her, even stepping on her face.

"It's dead," said another voice. "That's what's wrong with it."

Some of the pieces fell into place for Owina then. The voices belonged to two of the guards. Owina didn't know their names, but one of them, a big, burly man, was assigned to Donae. She opened her eyes a tiny bit. The two men were nearby, looking down on a horse that was lying on the ground.

"You sure it's not just sleeping?" It was the big, burly guard.

"I know you're not that dumb, Larin," the other guard said. "Horses don't lie like that."

"But what happened to him? He was fine last night."

"It's not a him," the other corrected. "You grew up on a farm, didn't you? Didn't you learn anything?"

"Don't twitch me, Haris. You don't know what I learned and what I didn't. It looks skinnier, don't you think?"

"They're all skinnier," Haris replied. "So are we. Marching halfway to hell and back will do that to a body."

"It ain't that. Look closer. The thing looks kind of shrunken."

All at once the sleep fog cleared from her brain and Owina knew what had happened to the horse. She sat up. Two more guards came walking up to look at the dead horse, blocking her view of it. Feeling a chill inside her that had nothing to do with the temperature, Owina nudged Donae, who was lying beside her. The small woman was curled up tight in her blanket, only a little bit of the top of her head showing. She didn't respond.

Owina gave her a shake. "Wake up, Donae." When Donae didn't respond, Owina became alarmed and shook her harder.

"What?" came the muffled reply. Donae poked her head out of the blanket, her eyes bleary. "What is it?" she asked querulously.

"Where's your *sulbit*?"

"Why? What's wrong?" Donae sat up, her eyes wide.

As if summoned, her *sulbit* scurried up her arm and perched on her shoulder, peering at Owina. Owina blinked. Was the thing larger than she remembered? Owina pointed to the guards gathered around the dead horse.

"What are they looking at? Is that a horse? What does that have to do with...oh." Donae seemed to shrink suddenly. She looked around her to see if anyone was listening. "Do you think my *sulbit* did that?" she whispered hoarsely.

"I don't know. But you said last night – "

"What are you two talking about? What's happening?" Karyn sat up. She'd been sleeping on the other side of Donae. She peered from one woman to the other.

Owina said, "We think Donae's *sulbit* might have killed that horse."

"*I* don't think that!" Donae shrilled. "*You* said that. There's no way my *sulbit* did that. It's been with me the whole time."

"We need to tell the FirstMother," Karyn said.

"No!" Donae cried. "Don't tell the FirstMother!" She clamped her hand over her mouth, afraid she'd been too loud. "She already hates me. She'll blame me for it. Probably the horse just died from tiredness. I don't think we should tell the FirstMother anything."

"I think it's too late for that," Owina said.

The FirstMother was approaching from one direction, Quyloc from another. Other guards were getting up, awakened by the commotion. Tenders were sitting up and looking around.

"What's happening over here?" the FirstMother asked.

"One of the horses is dead," Haris said. "Something doesn't look right. I don't think it died naturally."

The FirstMother knelt to examine the animal just as Quyloc arrived. He was carrying his spear, wrapped in leather. "One of your *sulbits* did this," he said.

"You don't know that for sure," the FirstMother replied.

"Then what do you think happened to it?"

69

The FirstMother stood up. "I don't know. I just don't think we should jump to conclusions."

"Did anyone see anything?" Quyloc asked, looking around at the gathering Tenders and guards. There was a general shaking of heads.

The FirstMother was eyeing the Tenders. Her gaze fell on Donae and she said, "Was it yours?"

Donae wilted. "No, FirstMother. I'm sure it wasn't."

The FirstMother came closer, a skeptical look on her face. "Is its hunger less this morning?"

Donae shook her head. "It seems as hungry as ever."

The FirstMother studied Donae's *sulbit*. Donae stared at the ground. The FirstMother looked around at the other Tenders. "We're riding out in ten minutes."

She turned and walked back to where her bed lay, Quyloc following her.

"It had to have been one of the *sulbits*," Quyloc said.

"I know," she replied irritably. "What do you want me to do about it?"

"I thought the women you brought could be counted on to control those creatures. If that one is too weak to do so, why did you bring her?"

"Because we're desperate!" the FirstMother snapped, then looked around, making sure no one else had heard. When she continued, her voice was lower. "Rome's orders were to bring every Tender I could. I brought every woman I thought had a chance to be useful. I didn't have a lot of options. But that doesn't matter now. All that matters is getting these things fed. Where are those men you sent out? When are they going to show up?"

Quyloc looked off to the south. There was no sign of movement, no dust in the air to indicate moving livestock. "They'll be here as soon as they can. They know how important this is."

"Unless they deserted."

He gave her a sharp look. "They didn't desert. I don't want to hear you say that again."

"Then maybe something else happened to them. Whatever it is, if we don't get some livestock here soon, we're going to have some real problems."

It was near midday and Rome was riding alongside the army, lost in thought, Tairus behind him, when Sem appeared. One moment there was only the dust and the rocks, and the next the heavyset brother was there in his dusty, worn leathers, walking beside Rome's horse as if he'd never been anywhere else. This time, at least, Rome managed not to be startled, as if it was normal to have people appear out of nowhere beside him.

But something was different this time.

Sem's eyes were wide, his face pale under his beard.

"What is it?" Rome said, checking to make sure none were close enough to overhear. "What did you learn?"

"Pardon," the man said. His voice was low and shaken. "A sip first if you would. I'm not...that wasn't what I thought it would be."

At least Rome was ready this time. He had a skin of rum hanging from his saddle horn and he handed it to the brother, who took a long drink and handed it back. For a time he said nothing, simply walking beside the horse, and Rome thought he would scream at him to hurry with his information, but he sensed the need to wait. At last the man took a deep breath and spoke.

"We found him, the one you want. In the desert."

"Where's he headed? What's he doing?"

The man held up his hand. Rome held his words and tried to wait once more.

"He crawled out of a hole in the ground," Sem said.

Rome caught a motion from the corner of his eye and looked up to see three more brothers up ahead, waiting by a stunted tree. They were not sitting or lying around as they usually did, but were on their feet in a tight group, their stances tense.

"There's them that come with him," the heavyset brother continued. "Close to a hundred of them."

"Forget about them," Rome said, though it was good to know there were only a hundred of them, instead of the thousands he'd feared. "I want to know about Melekath. What does he look like? What can he do? Where is he going?"

"You see them, you'll want to forget about them," a new voice chimed in. It was the oldest brother, the one with the gray hair. Without asking he snatched the skin from Rome's saddle and took a long drink.

"They're...broken," the heavyset one said. "Gray and broken. There's signs they were once human, but not much. They don't move good either."

71

"It hurts to look at them," the oldest one said. "Not what I want to see when I close my eyes."

"Tell me about Melekath? Did you learn anything about him? Where is he going? Did he see you?"

"Oh, he saw us all right," the oldest said, and there was disbelief in his tone. This was not something he had thought possible. "But he didn't care. His eyes are for them that follow him, like his children they are."

"They saw Rem," the heavyset one said suddenly, and grabbed the older brother's arm. "They saw Rem."

"Rem'll get away," the other replied. "He knows what he's about."

"What about Melekath?" Rome repeated.

"Nothing to see," the oldest replied. "Looks like any man."

"He's tired," the other added. "And angry."

"They're moving east, but they're going slow."

"Hard to move when you're broken."

Rome stared at them as they passed the flask around. When it didn't look like they had anything to add, he said, "I need more information. I want you boys to shadow Melekath and his Children, let me know where they are, what their power is."

"Not going to happen," the gray-haired brother said.

"Not for all the liquor in the world," another one chimed in.

"I'll pay you well. More than that, I'll make you rich."

"Coin just weighs a body down," the gray-haired brother said. "Men like us can't do what we do weighed down."

"Can't spend coin when you're dead," the heavyset one added.

"There must be something I can offer you to get you to change your minds," Rome said, starting to feel somewhat desperate. "I need that information."

"Have to get it on your own then," the gray-haired one said. "Our time here is done." He gestured to the others and they began to walk away.

"What about your liquor?" Rome called after them, wanting just to slow them down, to give himself a chance to try and change their minds.

"Keep it. You're going to need it more than us."

Rome and Tairus watched while the men dwindled from sight.

"At least there's only a hundred of the Children," Tairus said. "That's something."

72

Rome looked over at him, his expression dour. "I hope it's enough."

TWELVE

"It's getting worse out there." Terk closed the window and barred it. He was a big man, tall and broad, with a nose that looked like it had been mashed with a rock too many times. He had his club in his hand and he kept shifting it from one hand to another, as if he couldn't decide where it fit best. He was wearing a short sword and a brace of daggers as well, stuck in a broad leather belt over ring mail, and he had a leather helmet on his head.

Arls, the other bouncer at the Grinning Pig tavern, grunted from his spot on a stool by the door. He wasn't as tall as Terk, but he was wider and there was something in his eyes that made men fear him more. Most men, no matter how drunk they were, took one look into those eyes and left quietly. Bonnie had never heard him raise his voice before.

Bonnie looked around the room, seeing the same tension in all of them. Gelbert was behind the bar, wiping glasses furiously over and over, something he only did when he was nervous. A scowl was fixed on his fat face and his eyes were constantly moving, to the door, checking the bar, then to the two windows, checking the heavy wooden shutters, then back to the heavy sword that lay on the bar before him.

Lita was sitting at a table near the back of the room, by the stairs leading to the upper floors. Two brightly polished knives lay on the table before her and she was staring at them as if they were snakes that might bite at any moment. Sereh sat on the stairs; the thin, hollow-eyed woman had her hand over her mouth. A tic periodically seized one side of her face. Talind sat alone at a table, drumming her fingers anxiously. Now and then she reached to touch the short sword that lay across her lap. Bonnie had never figured out where she got the thing. It looked like something a soldier might carry, badly nicked and with a fair share of rust to it. Only Rowena seemed calm. The dark-skinned woman sat on one of the stools at the bar, rhythmically

74

brushing her long, black hair over and over. Bonnie didn't believe she was as calm as she looked, but she wasn't about to call her on it.

They all jumped just a little, even Rowena, when Tomy came running in from the door leading to the kitchen. "Door's still secure," he called to Gelbert. He was skinny, with eyes too big for his face. He was probably about ten, though it was hard to tell. He slept on the floor by the fireplace at night, and had for the last two years, since he'd tried to nick Bonnie's purse and she hit him over the ear so hard blood ran. He'd tried to run but she'd grabbed his arm and gave him a quick kick in the rear just to settle him. He was only one more street urchin among hundreds, but she'd taken pity on him and talked Gelbert into taking him on. He was carrying a blade, a long dagger stuck awkwardly through the bit of rope that served as his belt.

They were all armed, even Bonnie. A body had to be now, ever since *it* happened, a couple days ago. It had been late afternoon, the Grinning Pig busy as usual, drunks yelling and laughing, and then it was like something heavy and important just ripped in half. That was the way it felt to Bonnie. Everyone in the tavern just stopped what they were doing then, looking as one to the south, drinks forgotten, mouths hanging open. It was *him*. Melekath. No one needed to say the name. They all knew it was him. Just as they knew their lives would never be the same again.

Since then the city seemed to get meaner and crazier by the hour. There were fires, riots, people running crazy in the streets. Finally, this afternoon, Gelbert couldn't take it anymore. He'd ordered the last of their customers out of the tavern – except for Burk, who was passed out cold under one of the tables – and barred the door. Something bad was coming. Maybe the walls of the Grinning Pig wouldn't hold it out, but they were solid stone and it was sure enough worth a try. The place wouldn't burn like a lot of its neighbors – though if the adjoining buildings burned it wouldn't matter because those inside would cook like pigs in an oven – and its door would hold up short of a battering ram. With a little luck they just might ride it out.

There came the sound of running feet outside the door. Scores of them. Something struck the door hard enough that the thud echoed through the room. Some shouting. It all receded down the street and the people in the tavern relaxed slightly, exchanging half smiles, almost sheepish. Maybe it wouldn't be so bad.

More people ran by the door. There was more shouting. Lots of it, punctuated by screams. Bonnie thought she smelled smoke, but she couldn't be sure. She looked at the fireplace. Surely no one would try and come down the chimney? She heaved herself up out of her chair and threw some more wood on the fire, just to be sure. Gelbert opened his mouth to chew on her – he was a cheap one, rich as he was, didn't like spending a copper if it could be held back – but she pointed up at the roof. He closed his mouth and nodded. Not every day was a good time to be cheap. She was struck by the fact that neither of them said a word during the exchange. No one was talking, or if they did, it was in a whisper. It was as though collectively they believed that if they were quiet enough and didn't draw any attention, the craziness outside would pass them by.

Which Bonnie knew to be flat out untrue. Rome told her a story once, about being trapped in a fort somewhere – she couldn't remember where – and the numbers outside the fort were overwhelming. There was no way they could hold out. The attackers were drawn tight around the fort and the only thing keeping the defenders alive was the fact that it was dark. Every one of them knew that the moment it grew light outside the enemy was coming over the wall and that would be that. What struck her about the story, and made her think of it now, was that Rome said he'd had to triple the guard on the storeroom where the fort's alcohol was kept. He said once the men believed they were going to die, a number of them headed straight for that room, ready to meet their deaths with a gut full of booze. They'd had to kill two of their own before the rest gave up.

There'd be those in Qarath who felt the same way. Bonnie was sure of it.

Gelbert kept a cellar that was full to the ceiling. He didn't like spending money he didn't have to, but he understood business. When the market was flush, when ale, wine and liquor were easy to come by, he bought and stored the stuff until the place fairly creaked with it. When the market was tight, he sold. He never ran out and the drinking folk of the city knew it.

Which was why they were in trouble.

She shot a look at Gelbert. His shirt was open halfway to his waist and the fat around his neck merged with the fat rolling up from his gut. Some might think the way to stay alive was to open the cellar, push the liquor out into the street and bar the doors after it. Let them have what they wanted and rebuild tomorrow. Gelbert could afford it. Bonnie knew for a fact he was a wealthy man.

But she also knew he'd rather die than lose his inventory. Literally. Which meant they might all die for it. She supposed she should feel ticked at him for this. Her life was rather precious to her after all, and the life of her unborn child doubly so. But she wasn't angry at him and she didn't think anyone else in the room was either. This was Gelbert's place. He made no secrets about where his priorities lay and they all knew it when they signed on. If he said fight and die for the alcohol, then that was what they would do.

Bonnie shook her head. People never ceased to amaze her, and that included herself.

More running footsteps. Just one person this time. Banging on the door and then a voice, a familiar voice.

"Lemme in! It's Keryl! Lemme in! They're coming for me!" He banged on the door a few more times for emphasis.

Arls grunted and looked to Gelbert. They all did. Gelbert scratched his thick neck and shook his head. Arls nodded and slumped back on his stool.

"C'mon! You know it's me! I come in there every day! Gorim's tail, I spent half my life and all my money in your place. Lemme in, Gelbert, you fat blister!"

Arls didn't even look at Gelbert this time. He seemed to be staring at a spot on the floor. The boss had made his decision and that was that. Arls didn't need any more.

The banging went on and the voice turned pleading. Bonnie looked around the room. Everyone was doing their best to avoid looking at the door. Tomy had turned completely around and was staring at the stairs, shaking just a little bit. Keryl had always given the boy an extra copper to look after his horse. Gelbert had his rag in hand and was wiping the bar again.

"Gelbert," Bonnie finally said. "Surely…"

Her voice trailed off as the banging ceased and Keryl's footsteps took off, fading into the distance. Other footsteps pounded by, along with hoarse shouts. All activity in the tavern stopped, and Bonnie realized they were all listening as intently as she was. There was nothing for a few moments, and the tension dissipated, just a bit.

A scream echoed from down the street.

Bonnie touched her stomach and said a silent prayer.

More banging on the door. They all froze.

"We know what you got," a voice called. "You open the door and let us have it and there won't be no blood. It's easy as that."

Bonnie didn't even look at Gelbert. Nor did either Terk or Arls. All knew the answer to that.

"You're being stupid, fat man!" the voice called. "No need to die over a little rum."

Now Bonnie did look at Gelbert. If anything, he was more relaxed now. This was a game he knew. The thing with Keryl was hard. This wasn't. He leaned back on his stool, his hands laced over his substantial gut.

The door shook a few more times and then the man called out again. "That's on you, then. You'll die and you got only yourself to blame. Boys!" he yelled. "Let 'er burn!"

Now Bonnie did smell smoke. She heard the greedy crackle of fire and scratching sounds through the door that told her torches were being piled against the wooden door. The building was stone, but the doors were wood. Whoever it was meant to burn the door down and then come in a rush.

The tension inside the tavern lowered a notch and Terk even smiled.

They waited and it wasn't long before there were curses from the other side of the door. Now even Bonnie smiled. Gelbert was a cheap bastard; there was no denying that. But if there was one thing he wasn't cheap about, it was protecting what he'd spent money on. All the doors and shutters on this place were ironwood. It was terribly expensive, coming from someplace west of Fanethrin, but right now it was worth every copper.

Besides being hard as iron and just about as tough to break through, ironwood had one other important quality. It wouldn't burn. Well, it would, but only if it was chopped into little pieces. Even a door made of it would burn eventually, if it was put in a bonfire, and that bonfire was kept going for a while. The people outside the door would have to build quite a fire, and keep it going for quite a long time, if they were coming in that way.

Burk rolled over on the floor and groaned, but didn't wake up.

"Bring me a sandwich, Tomy," Gelbert said. "Turkey. I got a feeling I don't like."

Now they all smiled. That "feeling" was Gelbert's word for hunger. If Gelbert was hungry, then they were in good shape. They were going to make it. Bonnie started to walk over to the bar.

More banging on the door. The voice again. "Have it that way, then," it snarled. "But we'll find a way in. There's no doubt about that."

"Sure you will. And I'll be king of Qarath come morning," Gelbert replied. That brought laughter from the people in the room. Even Arls smiled somewhat. They were people who had looked into death and walked away. What could feel better than that? Conversations broke out and Gelbert poured himself a drink.

"A silver says they will try to break it down next," Terk said. "Use a ram."

"What kind of fool bet is that?" Arls responded. He didn't even look up, just kept staring at the floor.

"There's other ways. They could try the back door," Terk said.

"Also ironwood. No room to get a ram there. Alley's too tight."

"Roof?"

"Sure. One or two maybe. Mobs ain't too smart." Arls voice was lazy. It sounded like the two were repeating an old argument between them.

"Okay, okay," Terk grumbled, subsiding. "Just trying to pass the time with a friendly wager."

"A fool's wager," Arls said. One of the women giggled, sounding more nervous than anything.

There were voices and then a new pounding on the door. Everyone froze. The sound was erratic at first, punctuated by cries of pain and curses as those manning the ram smashed fingers. After a few thuds there was a crash and numerous cries as the ram was dropped on the ground.

But a few minutes later they had it back up and the thudding resumed. They were getting better at it and the pounding settled into a rhythmic, almost hypnotic sound. It was like being inside a giant heart.

The door was well-built and strong. But even the strongest doors have their limits. Everything fails eventually. Those in the tavern knew that eventually the door would break. Their hope lay in time. If it took long enough, maybe the attackers would grow tired or frustrated. Maybe they would give up and leave in search of easier prey. Maybe the city watch would come, though there was scant chance of that happening. There was smoke in the air and fire in the sky. If the city watch ventured out of the safety of their barracks at all, they had far bigger messes to clean up.

So they waited. They avoided each other's eyes, staring into the distance or at the floor. Time passed and Gelbert's face slowly reddened. He sat behind the bar, his thick, fleshy head nearly sunk into his equally thick, fleshy shoulders. Finally, he stood up, his stool tipping over with a crash. Lita jumped at the sound. He snatched up the heavy sword on the bar and stomped over to the door.

"Leave off!" he yelled, his face and neck mottled. "Go on and burn someone else out!"

The thudding continued without pause, though Bonnie heard mocking laughter outside. The effect on Gelbert was immediate. He began kicking the door, screaming the whole time. One kick landed badly and he howled in pain, staggering back. But in a moment he had recovered and he started striking the door with the hilt of the sword. Small dents appeared in the door. It was very hard wood. The rest of the people in the tavern stared at him, aghast.

All of a sudden there was a loud crack.

Gelbert stopped in mid-blow and stared stupidly at the sword in his hand, as if unable to comprehend what had just happened.

Arls had no such problem. During Gelbert's outburst he had remained on his stool by the door. Now he stood and shoved Gelbert back, just a moment before a spear jabbed through the finger-wide crack that split the door top to bottom. Gelbert staggered back and Terk stepped up, chopping the spear in half before it could withdraw.

There was a roar from outside and the ram resumed its attack. The bar across the door was intact, but the crack in the door was widening with each blow. It wouldn't be long now. Arls picked his helm up off the floor, clamped it onto his head and rolled his shoulders. The rest picked up their weapons.

Bonnie looked around the room. There was within her the thought that she was a damned fool. She should have taken Rome's offer and gone to the palace. But at the same time she felt oddly proud of them. Ugly and misbegotten they undoubtedly were, but they were the closest she'd had to family since her mother died when she was young and her older sister ran off with a soldier. There were worse people to die with. She touched her stomach, sorry for the little one there. She wished she could meet him, hold him, just one time.

Shortly before he'd left, she'd almost told Rome about the child, but at the last moment her nerve failed her. Instead she'd told him that if they ever had a child she hoped she could give him a son. What Rome said next surprised her.

"I don't. I hope it's a girl. A son will want to pick up weapons and fight. I don't want my child dying on a battlefield."

With a final crack the door gave way. Wild howls filled the night and the defenders hefted their weapons.

But no one charged the broken door and suddenly the howling sounded different. Not triumphant anymore. Scared.

Something slammed against the splintered door and a body sprawled across the threshold, blood spraying from it.

The night was filled with screams of pain now. The light from the tavern spilled out through the shattered door, giving them glimpses of what was happening outside. Bodies were being flung like rag dolls. Others lay scattered in the street, torsos torn open, limbs ripped completely off. People ran in screaming confusion.

There was a heavy thud, then another, as if a giant strode toward the tavern. The people in the tavern edged back from the door. Tomy ran back into the kitchen with a cry. A huge, scaly leg, the toes tipped with curved claws, appeared in the doorway and then the thing, whatever it was, roared. Lita and Sereh bolted up the stairs.

A massive, mottled-green hand curled around the last of the door and tore it away like paper. Terk and Arls flanked Gelbert, who stood gaping and unmoving, as if his mind could not accept what was happening. The swords the men held looked like toothpicks.

The thing crouched and part of a twisted, horribly scarred face appeared in the doorway –

Suddenly there was a new sound. A screeching, discordant cacophony filled the air. Bonnie stumbled backwards and saw others around her doing the same. Terrible, primeval images filled her mind and she thought she might be screaming but she couldn't hear herself over the noise.

The thing at the door roared again and clapped its huge hands to the sides of its head. It stood and lurched away down the street.

The discordant music stopped and Bonnie opened her eyes. She was sitting on the floor, pushed up against the wall. Her head pounded with a terrible headache. Rowena lay nearby, curled into the fetal position. Gelbert grunted and sat up, looking around.

"What in the bloody black night was that?" Terk said, sitting up. The big man's face was pale.

"I don't know," Gelbert replied. "I don't want to know."

A short, nondescript man came up to the doorway and peered in. He wore the clothes of a common laborer, with a shapeless hat on his head. In his hand was what Bonnie at first thought was a flute of some kind, but when she blinked she saw that it was only a piece of wood.

"Everyone okay in here?" he asked cheerfully. He smiled and nodded. "Can't stay. I need to make sure that thing leaves the city. Ta!" he cried. He spun the length of wood in his fingers with a flourish and walked down the street after the monster.

"Who was *that*?" Terk asked.

"Quit asking stupid questions," Gelbert growled. He wiped the sweat from his face and levered himself to his feet. "You two nail some tables across the door," he said to Arls and Terk. "I got a feeling this night ain't over yet."

THIRTEEN

Ricarn stood in the darkness in the trees at the back of the Tender estate, a cloud of moths swirling around her. There were hundreds of them of all different kinds, from tiny white moths smaller than a fingernail, to the massive wood moth, bigger than her hand and striped with black. Ricarn's eyes were open, but she did not see the trees or the moths. Her eyes had rolled back in her head so that only the whites showed and a thin, piercing cry came from her, almost too high for the human ear to register. The moths swirled faster and faster and in the dance of their movements a window gradually opened.

Even as dry and desolate as the lands around the Gur al Krin desert were, there were still moths. Between them and all the moths that lived between here and there existed a web of sorts, a collective awareness, dim though it was. Now Ricarn tapped into that awareness, her mind traveling through it, her eyes seeing through it. She narrowed her focus down to a single, nondescript gray moth that fluttered erratically at the edge of the Krin.

Through its eyes she saw sandstone cliffs, bleached of color and oddly distorted by the moth's vision so that they seemed to curve forward over her. Beyond the cliffs were the sand dunes of the Gur al Krin. Nothing moved on the dunes. She pushed gently on the moth's mind – if she pushed too hard its mind would crumble instantly – and the moth fluttered closer to the dunes. At the edge of the sand it resisted, dimly aware that it could not live in that place, but then it flew out over the sand.

Ricarn guided it upwards, weaving through the tiny updrafts of air, its field of vision expanding as it gained altitude. The dunes spread out before her, ghostly in the moonlight. Still she saw nothing moving. The desert seemed as dead as always. It had been the same at the dozen or so places along the northern edge of the Krin that she had tried this night. If Melekath was moving, he had not made it to the edge of the desert yet. Or he was leaving the desert in a different direction, but she did not think that was likely. She thought it most likely he would head north from the Krin, toward Qarath.

For a few more minutes she pushed the moth deeper into the Gur al Krin, scanning as much of the empty desert as she could. Slowly the insect lost altitude and finally it fell to the sand. The connection between them broke and her vision went dark.

Ricarn blinked and returned to the estate grounds. She lowered her arms, releasing the moths surrounding her. They began to flutter away. In moments the night was once again still.

One of the other Insect Tenders approached then, seeming to glide across the ground, her yellow robe a beacon in the darkness. When she got close she said, "A mob has gathered at the gates of the palace. It is larger than the others. I think we have a problem."

The FirstMother had left Velma, her second-in-command, in charge of the Tenders, but once the FirstMother was gone it was like all the air went out of her. She spoke very little and then usually in a low voice while turning her eyes away. She'd only carried on the morning services for a couple of days after the FirstMother left, but she spoke so quietly that the crowd couldn't hear her and then she'd abruptly canceled them altogether.

There were only a few Tenders left on the estate and they were either so green as to barely be worthy of the name, or nearly hopeless with their *sulbits*, to the point where they didn't try to do anything with them for fear of hurting themselves and others. These days the estate was nearly deserted. Workmen still came and went, of course, but they walked differently with the FirstMother gone, like men will, with their shoulders back and confidence in their manner, as if the estate was theirs and not the property of the few women who remained. That all changed whenever they encountered Ricarn or one of the other Insect Tenders, but they were not around very often, busy with something on their own.

Cara stood on one of the balconies of the Tender estate house. Ever since the prison broke she spent a great deal of time up here, looking out over the city. Everything had changed in Qarath since that day. People fought violently over nothing. Mobs sprang up out of nowhere. Refugees streamed in from the countryside, jostling other refugees who fled the city. On top of that, there'd been a surge of bizarre creatures roaming through the city, killing people. Some came out of the ocean; others seemed to crawl up out of the sewers. Just a few nights before a huge, scaled creature had stormed through the city, killing dozens before it was driven off, apparently by a Musician, though no one knew if that was just a rumor.

Naills, the castellan and ruler of the city in Rome's and Quyloc's absence, had doubled the city watch and then doubled it again, further straining men who were already working too many shifts and whose numbers were heavily depleted by the army, but it did no good. Most of the time Cara could see the smoke from at least three different fires burning in different areas of the city. The city was a volcano waiting to blow. It was only a matter of time.

Today she'd been drawn up here by a nagging sense that the time for the explosion had come. When she looked down and saw Ricarn and the other two Insect Tenders heading for the front gates of the estate she knew the time had come. They had sensed it and that was where they were heading.

Then she surprised herself. Instead of waiting, wringing her hands and worrying, she found herself running down the stairs, across the grounds, after the women. She heard Adira call out to her – Cara often noticed the strange, hungry-eyed Tender nearby, watching her from a distance in that unnerving way she had – but she ignored her. The sound of running footsteps behind her told her Adira was following. The two guards working the gates were just pulling them shut and she had to call to them to wait and let her out. For a moment she thought they were going to deny her and close the gates anyway, but they paused while one motioned her impatiently to go through. Clearly they didn't want the gates open any longer than they had to be.

Cara hesitated on the other side of the gates for a moment until she saw the Insect Tenders to the right, heading uphill toward the palace. The street was mostly empty and she felt terribly exposed. The few other people on the street all seemed to be heavily armed and moving in groups, scanning the area warily as they went. Nearby was an ornate carriage on its side, the doors ripped off. A dead horse lay in the harness, flies buzzing around it.

Cara caught up to the three Insect Tenders and slowed to match their pace, glad for the safety of their company. What was she thinking, leaving the safety of the estate? What had become of her? This was more like something Netra would have done. Ricarn looked over at her when she caught up and gave her a nod that seemed to say she approved. The look she gave Adira, who caught up a few moments later, was not approving, but Adira didn't seem to notice.

Adira was looking at Cara somewhat accusingly, as if she was to blame for the troubles.

Cara settled in beside the three Insect Tenders. They seemed for all the world to be simply walking briskly, but she had to jog periodically to keep up.

Cara had spoken with Ricarn a number of times since the strange woman had taken notice of her predicament, back when Cara had refused the *sulbit* and the FirstMother ostracized her. For some reason Ricarn seemed to take an interest in her, though Cara couldn't imagine why. What was she but just a girl from nowhere? Whatever the reason, Ricarn sought her out on occasion, continuing to teach her ways to open herself to the flow of Song. Under her direction, Cara had progressed rapidly. Going *beyond* was easy now and felt completely natural to her. She was sensitive to Song, hearing its melody, feeling it flowing over her skin. And all this without even a *sonkrill*. It never ceased to amaze her. She liked to imagine the day when she would see Netra again – and she *would* see Netra again; Netra was okay, she was always okay – and show her what she had learned. Netra would be so surprised. And it would be nice to be able to show her that her old friend Cara wasn't so much the bumbling idiot anymore. Netra would be proud of her.

As they walked, more than once she saw hard-faced men with swords find a reason to cross to the other side of the street rather than come too close to the eerily calm woman in red and her two companions in yellow.

As they drew closer to the palace Cara became increasingly aware of the crowd gathered there. Crowds, like people, have an *akirma*, a sort of collective aura made up of the participants' combined energies. The crowd's *akirma* seethed with anger and hate and, most of all, fear. The anger and hate were only outgrowths of the fear, the public expressions of that much deeper and more primal emotion.

She opened herself to a deeper awareness and soon realized that the anger and fear were rapidly building to a point beyond which there would be no pulling back, only a rapidly escalating violence that would sweep the city like a wildfire. The mobs and fires Qarath had suffered in the past few days to this point were only the prelude. This was the one that would leave the city a charred husk. This would be the one they would never recover from.

Now Cara could see the walls of the palace. Soldiers swarmed the top of the wall. Most were armed with swords and spears but a number held bows. The mob was huge. It roiled and swarmed around the big double gates like a living thing. The people held old swords, clubs, farm implements, pitchforks. There were even torches, as if they could burn the stone walls through the sheer force of their wrath. Voices were raised in anger, screaming questions for which there could be no answer, and the soldiers on the walls screamed their rage and confusion back, each side like a diseased animal whose reason is gone and only the thirst for blood remains.

On the wall above the gates Cara could see a familiar figure. It was Naills, the castellan. She had only seen him once before, from a distance when Rome stopped by the estate to speak to the FirstMother, but her impression of him – aided by her newly awakening inner senses – had been of a solid, yet unimaginative man. He could be counted on to follow orders to the letter, but he would not know what to do when the situation went beyond those orders. As the mob seethed and roiled beneath the walls, Cara realized that he was close to ordering his soldiers to fire on the mob. She sensed the soldiers massed behind the double gates and knew that once the arrows started to fly, those gates would open and they would sally forth and into the mob. They would kill and be killed in return. They were better armed and organized, but they were outnumbered by far. Both sides fought from a position of madness. When it was done, Qarath would be in flames and they would not need Melekath to bring the city down.

Cara looked to her right to see how Ricarn was reacting. The woman's expression was calm. She seemed almost to be watching a curious interaction between unusual species she had never encountered. Cara had the impression that Ricarn had already decided what needed to be done and was only delaying while she absorbed the impact of this strange behavior she saw before her, as if her time amongst the insects had made her own species unusual to her.

Ricarn looked at the women who flanked her and something unspoken passed between them. The three women spread out so they were about an arm's length from each other. They closed their eyes and spread their arms, palms down. Slowly they brought their arms upward, hands closing, and a strange humming, buzzing sound came from them.

"What are they doing?" Adira demanded. Her *sulbit* was slithering up one arm, across her shoulders, and down the other, a nervous chittering coming from it.

Cara looked at her, startled. She'd forgotten she was there. "I don't know," she said. "But I think we better stand back." She began edging backwards, and Adira followed, still asking questions Cara no longer heard.

Cara looked around, confused. The buzzing was growing louder, far louder than three women should have been capable of, and it was coming from all around. Then Adira cried out and pointed. Cara turned, following the gesture, and fear rose within her.

Strange clouds were coming, converging fast on their location. She blinked, and saw that they were not clouds at all, but swarms of flying insects. She shrank away, even as she knew there was nowhere she could run to. The swarms were on them in seconds, bees and wasps and hornets of every kind. But they flew past her without slowing, arrowing in on the mob and the soldiers on the wall. Moments later people were running, flailing their arms, screaming, while the flying insects swarmed over them, stinging. Soldiers on the wall threw down their weapons and ran. The mob broke in a thousand directions. The violence was forgotten in a deeper need to escape this attack from the sky.

In a remarkably short span of time the square before the gates was empty except for the five Tenders. Cara stood there stunned. Ricarn turned to her.

"I believe it is time to begin the morning services again," she said. Her tone was calm, as if she was only making a passing remark to a woman she saw on the street.

"What?" Cara said, still trying to absorb what she had just seen.

"The people need the morning service to give them hope. You are the one to do this."

Cara took a step back. "But I can't. I'm not even supposed to wear a Tender's robe. What can I do?"

"The robe doesn't matter. What matters is the message."

"What message is that?"

"They need hope. You have to give them hope."

FOURTEEN

Cara awakened early the next morning, while the gray of predawn was just making its appearance. She walked out of the little hut near the back of the estate that she slept in – even though she could have slept anywhere these days she felt somehow comfortable in the hut – and looked at the sky. Clouds hung low and forbidding over Qarath and the air was thick and tepid. There had been no new fires during the night, no fresh explosions of violence. She knew because twice she had gone up to the top floor of the estate and looked out into the darkness, unable to sleep. The city was calm, but it was the calm before a storm. Ricarn had broken the last storm before it could peak, but the emotions still seethed underneath in the city's heart. Qarath would explode, one way or another. It was only a matter of when.

"Ready to lead the morning service?"

Cara jumped at the words and Ricarn moved soundlessly out of the trees. She carried a white robe draped over one arm and in her other hand something glittered.

"I can't do that," Cara said, putting up her hands as if to fend the other woman off.

"Someone has to," Ricarn said reasonably. "I don't see anyone more qualified." She shook out the robe and held it up.

Cara eyed the thing like it was a snake. "I don't know if I'm actually even a Tender anymore. The FirstMother said – "

"Forget what the FirstMother said. What does she know anyway? You are more a Tender than she is."

"Is that a Reminder in your hand?"

"It is." Ricarn held it up. The many-pointed star set within the circle was made of gold and gems were set in it. "Gaudy, I know, but I think you need to make an impression."

"Where did you get it?" Cara asked, fighting for time, fighting against a feeling that she had no real choice in this matter.

"Oh, it was tucked away. It doesn't matter." Ricarn's eyes glittered in the dim light. "We don't have time to waste. The sun is still rising, I believe."

"But I still don't think…"

"Don't think at all. Just *do*." Ricarn leaned in close. "You can feel it just like I can. I know you can. Your inner senses are awake now. The people need something to hold onto or they will fall over the cliff and they will take the whole city with them."

"Velma…"

"I have spoken to her already. She agrees. Even now men move through the city announcing the morning services have resumed."

As if it belonged to someone else, Cara saw her hand reach out to take the robe. "You'll come with me, won't you?" she whispered. "I don't know what to do."

"You don't need to. Just give them hope."

"Is there hope?"

Ricarn shrugged. "I don't know. But it will probably help if they don't kill each other before they have a chance to find out." She slipped the Reminder over Cara's head. "Come now. Velma will have the other Tenders waiting for you by now."

Cara struggled into the robe, still feeling like this must be something that was happening to someone else. She was *Cara*, for Xochitl's sake! She went along and kept quiet. Others did the important things. Not her. All she wanted was to live her life quietly in the shade of others. Words came to her unbidden as Ricarn straightened the robe and started to turn away.

"Why me?" Ricarn turned back. "Ever since you got here you have…? Why me?"

Ricarn gave her an odd look. "You really don't know, do you?" Cara shook her head. "Because you are a *Tender*." She said the last word almost fiercely, her teeth flashing. "A *real* Tender, and those are very rare now."

"I…I don't see that."

"It doesn't matter," Ricarn said, turning to go. "I see it for you."

It was only a few minutes later that Cara was leading them through the streets of Qarath. It was not the procession as Nalene FirstMother led it. There were only a handful of Tenders, two were little more than peasant girls with clumsy feet, and one was quite old and had to lean on another to stay upright. Of them, only about a third had their *sulbits*, but the creatures were still quite small and somnolent. They were the ones Nalene had left behind, too raw or hopeless to be useful.

Velma walked behind Cara, her head down in thought. Cara had expected her to be resentful at having her place usurped – the FirstMother had left her in charge after all – but instead she seemed grateful and had patted Cara more than once while they were assembling for the procession. Beside Velma was Adira. She walked very close to Cara, almost stepping on her heels. Cara could feel her breath on her neck. Cara had the oddest feeling that Adira was feeling protective of her, though that made no sense to her.

Behind the pathetic group of Tenders marched an equally sad group of guards. They were clearly uneasy at being out of the protective embrace of the estate's walls and appeared to be trying to look every direction at once, as if the attack would come at any moment. Behind them came Ricarn and the two other Insect Tenders. Cara wondered if they were there to keep the guards from fleeing at the first opportunity.

At first the streets were silent and empty, though Cara could feel the people who watched from behind shutters and peepholes in doors. Some dogs barked and a drunk leaned against a wall, singing unintelligibly. But as they continued, people began to emerge from their homes in ones and twos, slinking furtively behind the ragged procession like strays, sniffing the air cautiously, ready to bolt at the first sign of danger. Their numbers grew with each passing block and by the time Cara saw Seafast Square ahead in the growing light there must have been a hundred of them, and their numbers were increasing rapidly.

Cara crossed the square and it seemed to her that surely someone would notice then. The sun was near the horizon. She could not hide in the shadows any longer. Someone would call out at any moment, exposing her as a fraud. They would yell and she would have no answer.

But no one did. Nor did they as she climbed up the stairs fronting the shell of the new Temple that was rising on the far side of the square. They gathered quietly as she mounted the last stair and looked down on them. She felt her knees grow weak then and thought she might faint, but all at once Ricarn was beside her. Cara felt relief flood her. Surely Ricarn would speak. Surely the crowd that had gathered – and was still gathering – would look to her. She was a rock. They could cling to her.

But to her dismay the crowd was looking at her, not Ricarn.

"I don't know what to say," she whispered to Ricarn. The sun was very close to rising out of the sea. The clouds to the east had parted slightly.

"You are a Tender," Ricarn said. "Speak from your heart. Let your words come from the Mother."

Cara took a deep breath and was suddenly afraid she would begin to cry. Just at that moment the first rays of the sun broke the horizon, catching her eye and entrancing her so that she turned and stared. For a long minute she was held thus, amazed as always. She had always loved sunrises, the promise of a new day and all that it held. She stared at the sun until it blinded her, then she turned to the crowd and let the words come.

"It was beautiful. It was beautiful," Velma kept saying. The long-faced woman was walking beside Cara as they made their way back to the estate. She couldn't seem to stop herself. It was the most animated Cara had ever seen her.

Cara felt a hand on her shoulder and arm and realized Adira was furtively stroking it once again. "Adira, please," she said, turning and looking at the other woman. "I asked you to stop doing that." Adira scowled darkly and pulled her hand back.

"What you said was perfect," Velma added, seemingly oblivious to anything else. "It made me cry."

Cara gave her a sidelong glance as she continued walking but said nothing. In truth, she wanted to get back to her hut and lie down before she collapsed.

"How did you know?" Velma said wonderingly.

What did I say? Cara wanted to ask her. The truth was that she didn't know. The sunlight had filled her. Or Xochitl had spoken through her. Or the lack of sleep and the fear had made her giddy. But whatever she'd said seemed to have made a difference. Qarath's *akirma* felt different. There was still tension, still fear, but the sense of impending explosion was gone. Somehow she had given them something to hold onto. She'd caught one look at Ricarn as she was walking back down the steps, and the Insect Tender had given her a nod, as if she had done exactly as Ricarn had expected her to.

Cara sighed. She had a feeling she wouldn't be getting back to her hut right away. She had a feeling that things had changed too much for that. Once again she felt Adira's hand stroking her arm.

FIFTEEN

It was late afternoon, the wind was rising and clouds were building up overhead. Owina was riding along in a daze, so tired she was nearly delirious. Wrestling with her *sulbit* was wearing her out. The thing kept trying to feed on her horse and she had to stay constantly vigilant to keep that from happening. The horse spent most of the time with its neck bent to one side or the other, trying to keep an eye on the danger it could sense.

Owina raised her eyes and scanned ahead. They were winding down out of the foothills of the Plateau and she could see for several miles, but there was no sign of riders coming toward them. Where were the soldiers with the animals? Were they coming back? Had they all just deserted?

She glanced over at Donae, riding beside her. The small woman hadn't spoken in hours and that worried Owina much more than her constant complaining. She rode hunched over, her eyes squeezed tightly shut. Her lips moved, but if she spoke, Owina couldn't hear her.

Owina lapsed back into her daze, her mind wandering. At some point she found herself staring at the back of the guard riding just ahead of her, a young man with long, blonde hair. She found herself thinking how badly she wanted to be closer to him. As if in a dream she saw herself riding up behind him and grabbing hold of him…

Draining him.

With a start she jerked out of her reverie, her hand coming up to wipe her mouth, her eyes darting guiltily to see who had noticed.

But no one had noticed because she hadn't done anything. It had all been in her mind.

She pulled back on the horse's reins, increasing the distance between them.

Owina's sleep was restless and unpleasant that night. Somewhere in the depths of the night she had a vivid, frightening dream of sneaking through the sleeping camp to where the young guard with the long, blonde hair was sleeping. In the dream, she crouched over him, then placed her lips on his throat. What followed then was pure ecstasy, as his Selfsong rushed into her, filling her.

When she awakened in the morning it all came rushing back to her and she lay there, feeling completely sick at heart. Worst of all was the truth that she could not deny to herself: that she'd enjoyed it. That she wanted to do it again.

The only thing that brought her any solace was the fact that it was only a dream.

Then she heard voices raised in alarm and she knew right away what they'd found.

"He's dead! Just like the horse. I'm telling you, it was one of them *sulbits*."

Owina sat up. Two of the guards were standing over a figure on the ground. The looks they gave her were fearful and suspicious and Owina quailed. You don't understand, she wanted to tell them. I'm not like that! I wouldn't hurt anyone!

She felt movement on her lap and looked down at her *sulbit*. Did it look different this morning? As if it had fed?

All over the camp people began to get up. Owina did too, following the general movement toward where the body lay. The sickness in her heart increased when she saw that it was the young blonde guard who was dead. She looked around in alarm, sure everyone would be looking at her suspiciously, but no one seemed to be paying any attention to her.

In fact, most of the Tenders were looking at Donae. Donae looked up from the body, saw their eyes on her and began shaking her head.

The FirstMother started to speak when she noticed the look Quyloc was giving her. "Why are you looking at me like that?" she demanded.

"Why do you think?" he snapped.

"Are you thinking this is my fault? That I'm to blame for not controlling them?"

"It was a *sulbit* that killed him, wasn't it?"

"No!" she snapped. "You're not pinning this on me. If anything, this is your fault. If the soldiers you'd sent to get animals hadn't deserted, this wouldn't have happened."

His face darkened. "You don't know that they deserted."

"Of course not," she hissed. "I'm sure they'll show up any minute now."

"Anything could have happened—"

"We shouldn't have left the trail. We would have run into the supply wagons yesterday and there would be plenty for the *sulbits*." By then her *sulbit* was crouched on her shoulder, its back arched, dark eyes fixed on Quyloc. Quyloc had the *rendspear* in both hands and had dropped into a crouch. The others had begun edging back.

There was no telling how far it would have gone if Bronwyn hadn't spoken up right then. She took a step forward, subtly interposing herself between the two of them. "This isn't helping," she said softly. "If we want to fix this, we need to get started and try to find a farm or a town. The sooner the better."

Quyloc and the FirstMother glared at each other for a few more seconds, then they backed down. "Pack up," Quyloc ordered. "We're riding out in five minutes."

"What about Keven?" one of the guards asked, gesturing to the man on the ground.

"Pile some rocks over him," Quyloc said. "There's no time for anything more." Then he strode away to get his horse.

When he was gone, the FirstMother turned on Donae. "Did your *sulbit* do this?" she asked fiercely.

"No!" Donae cried. "It was with me all night!"

The look on the FirstMother's face indicated how little she believed Donae. None of the other Tenders looked very believing either. "Let me see it."

Donae's *sulbit* was cowering in the hood of her robe and it took her a minute to coax the creature out. With shaking hands, she held it out to the FirstMother, who peered at it. "It's just as hungry as always," Donae insisted.

"It looks like it has fed recently," the FirstMother said.

Owina almost spoke up right then and confessed, but she just couldn't make herself. Besides, Donae's *sulbit* did look like it had recently fed. When the *sulbits* hadn't fed in a while they tended to turn more yellow and hers was more of an off-white.

Owina looked down at her *sulbit*, which had climbed down and was clinging to her forcarm. It was yellower than Donae's, and she could sense the intensity of its hunger. Maybe it wasn't hers that killed that man. Maybe it was all just a dream after all.

When they were mounting up to leave a few minutes later the next problem cropped up. Four of the guards were sitting on their horses, clustered together in a group and when the FirstMother gave the order to move out, they stayed where they were.

"We're not going," one of them said. He was a lean man with a perpetual frown. Owina thought his name was Terens.

"What are you talking about?" the FirstMother demanded. "I gave you an order."

"Well, it don't apply, because we quit."

"We didn't sign up for this," one of the others said. "Being eaten by one of those things wasn't in the job description."

The FirstMother's eyes took on a dangerous glint and some of the men paled. Owina could feel the FirstMother starting to draw in Song from around her and she looked at Karyn, who looked back at her with wide eyes, both of them thinking the same thing. Would the FirstMother really attack them?

Quyloc rode up just then. "Leave them be," he told her.

"I do not tell you what to do with your people," she retorted, without looking at him. "Don't presume to tell me what to do with mine."

"Don't you see? This is actually a good thing."

The four guards gave him puzzled looks. Gradually the FirstMother turned to face him, her eyes narrow.

"These men, and any others who don't want to continue on with us, are free to go." Quyloc sounded very calm, almost conversational, but something about his tone frightened Owina. She decided then and there that he was a man she never wanted to cross. "There's just one little thing. You leave the horses behind."

"You can't do that!" Terens exclaimed. "We're in the middle of nowhere. We need them."

"Not as much as we do," the FirstMother put in, suddenly seeing where Quyloc was going with this. The horses could be used to feed the *sulbits*.

"Go east," Quyloc said. "You'll cut across the trail eventually. With luck you'll intercept the army. You can march home with them."

"No," Terens said stubbornly. "We need them and we're taking them." He started to spur his horse forward, but Quyloc cut him off.

"I won't tell you again," Quyloc said. He had the spear in one hand. The leather cover was off.

The men's eyes went to the spear. All of them knew what he'd done to Kasai with it. They exchanged looks.

"We changed our minds," Terens said sullenly. "We'll stay with you. Just...keep those things away from us."

They came across no towns that morning and only one farm, but it was abandoned, the roof of the farmhouse fallen in, the barn little more than rubble.

Quyloc rode far in the front, alone. After him came the FirstMother, also alone. Any Tenders who rode too close to her received a dark look and soon pulled back.

After her came the Tenders. The few who spoke made it clear they blamed Donae for what had happened. Once Owina tried to defend her, but the others glared at her and she soon gave up. Donae gave her a grateful smile when she did so, which made her feel guiltier than ever.

The guards rode in the rear in a tight clump and Owina felt as if she could feel their hostile, frightened gazes on her back. She didn't blame them. They had no real idea what the creatures were, only that they were dangerous and they were stuck in close proximity to them. In their place, she would feel the same way.

By midday the *sulbits* were so desperately hungry that it was all the Tenders could do to restrain them. Most of them had to physically restrain the creatures, trying to keep the squirming things from leaping onto the horses' necks.

Finally, the FirstMother called a halt. "It's no use. Some of the horses have to be sacrificed." When some of the guards began complaining, she silenced them with a scowl. "Some of you will just have to double up," she told them. "It's the only way."

"I agree," Quyloc said. He picked out four guards at random and told them to get off their horses.

Ten minutes later they were on their way again, four dead horses lying on the ground, their riders sitting on the back of other horses. It helped and it was a lot better than nothing, Owina thought. But her *sulbit* was a long way from satisfied. There was a time when one horse would have been plenty for two dozen *sulbits*, but that time had long since passed. The *sulbits* were much bigger now. Each of them could have easily drained a horse by itself.

When they made camp that night Donae came over to sit by Owina. Her eyes were red and it looked like she'd been crying.

"I don't know what to do," she moaned. "Everyone hates me now."

"That's not true," Owina said, but could find no conviction in her words.

"They all blame me," Donae said miserably, "and I suppose they're right. Oh, I never should have taken a *sulbit*. I should have said no like Cara did. I'm not cut out for this."

"You're stronger than you think. The FirstMother wouldn't have chosen you to come along if she didn't think you could handle it."

"She only brought me because she was desperate and there was no one else to choose from. The others she left behind were even more pathetic than I am, if that's even possible."

Owina had to agree with her there. The women the FirstMother had left behind either had *sulbits* so young as to be useless, or they had so little control they were a danger to themselves and those around them. She'd made sure that the women in the latter group were only allowed to feed their *sulbits* tiny amounts of Song every day, to keep them from getting large enough to be a real danger. They weren't even allowed near the goats or the shatren that the others fed theirs on, but only chickens.

"It might not have been your *sulbit* that killed that guard," Owina said. "It could have been anyone's."

"But it probably was mine. And now I have to live with the knowledge that I killed him. I'm supposed to be a Tender. We're supposed to save lives, not end them. What am I going to do? I must be the worst Tender ever."

Owina started to tell her then, about the dream, about her own fears, but Karyn came walking over and she lost the opportunity.

"Can I talk to you for a minute alone?" Karyn asked.

"Of course," Owina said.

Karyn stared at Donae, who at first just stared blankly back at her. Then she got the point that Karyn wanted her to leave and with an exaggerated sigh she stood up and moved off.

"What is it?" Owina asked her.

Karyn sat down and put her head in her hands. "I had these terrible dreams last night and…" She looked around to make sure no one could hear her. "I'm afraid it might have been my *sulbit* that killed that man," she whispered.

Normally Quyloc preferred to camp off by himself, but that didn't seem like a good idea this night. The guards set up their camp several hundred yards from the Tenders and he helped them gather firewood until they had a large pile, enough to keep a good blaze going throughout the night. Then he organized them into watches, making sure the guards who'd threatened to desert that morning were all on different watches. He put himself on the last watch, knowing that was the time when it was hardest to avoid falling asleep.

The horses were hobbled nearby. It seemed likely that they would lose at least some of them to the *sulbits* during the night, but he couldn't see any way to completely protect them without risking human lives. Perhaps it would be better this way. Sacrificing a few horses to the *sulbits* might ease their hunger enough that they would leave the men alone.

He spread out his blanket and lay down, wondering what he was going to do tomorrow. How long until the Tenders completely lost control of those things? How many horses would have to be fed to them? Why did he decide on taking this route? If they'd stayed on the trail, none of this would be happening. With all this and more running through his mind, he fell asleep.

He awakened hours later with the feeling that something was wrong. From the position of the stars he knew it was late, past the time when he should have been awakened for his watch. The fire had died down to embers.

Suddenly he felt tiny feet running across his chest and he bolted upright, slapping at the thing, his heart pounding.

Grabbing up a handful of dried grasses, he threw it on the fire and what he saw in the firelight made his blood run cold.

Perched on the guard sleeping next to him was a *sulbit*, its mouth clamped on the man's neck. At least three other nearby guards had *sulbits* on them as well.

Snatching up his spear, Quyloc leapt to his feet and stabbed at the nearest *sulbit*. But he had to hold back out of fear of cutting the man and the *sulbit* easily avoided his attack and ran off into the darkness.

He turned on the next one, but this one didn't flee right away. Like a predator defending its kill it hissed at him, showing needle-fine teeth. He jabbed at it and it backed off unwillingly, giving a last hiss before disappearing into the darkness.

When Quyloc turned to the others, he saw that they'd run off. Throwing more wood onto the fire, he began yelling at the guards to get up.

Not all of them did. Five remained on the ground, four of them unmoving, the other stirring weakly.

Quyloc did a quick head count and realized that eight of the men were gone. They'd deserted, left the rest of them there to die.

Quyloc pointed to a big man. "Go get the FirstMother," he ordered.

The man began shaking his head and backed up. "There's no way I'm going out into the dark with those things. I'm staying here."

"I gave you an order," Quyloc said.

"I don't care. You can stab me if you want. I ain't going."

"I'm with Larin on this," another guard said. "Why don't we yell for her instead?"

Shouting produced no results. "You don't think they're all dead, do you, Haris?" the big guard asked. Haris didn't answer.

Quyloc took a burning stick out of the fire. Holding it in his left hand and the spear in his right, he started for the Tender camp. As he left the nervous circle of guards, he veered off to check on the horses and received another unpleasant surprise. A number were missing, obviously taken by the deserters. The rest were dead. He swore under this breath. Without horses it was going to be a whole lot harder to find food for the *sulbits*.

Cautiously, he made his way toward the Tender camp, the impromptu torch held high, listening intently, eyes constantly moving, watching for movement in the darkness. A couple times he thought he saw an ivory shape in the gloom, but when he tried to get a better look there was never anything there.

Halfway there the stick began to go out. Blowing on it didn't help. He speeded up, sure that at any moment he was going to be attacked.

He reached the Tender camp and threw some more wood onto their fire. When the flames built up he could see the FirstMother, asleep under her blanket and he went over to her and kicked her in the side.

"Get up!" he snapped at her.

Mumbling, she sat up, rubbing her eyes.

"They've killed again," he said through gritted teeth. "I want to know which ones did it." When she didn't respond, he rapped her on top of the head with the shaft of the spear. "Show me your *sulbit*!"

That got through to her. "It's right here!" she shot back at him. "It's been with me the whole time."

He could see it then, peering out of her hood. Turning around, he began shouting at the others to get up and show him their *sulbits*. The FirstMother got up and pushed her way in front of him.

"What are you doing?"

"I'm going to find the ones that did this and I'm going to kill them."

"No, you won't."

"Are you going to stop me?" He raised the spear.

The FirstMother didn't back down. "Have you lost your mind? Whatever they've done, you can't kill them. We *need* them. You know that."

For a long moment he stared at her, knowing she was right but hating it. The things were dangerous. How many more would they kill? He lowered the spear.

"At least four more guards are dead. All the horses too."

The FirstMother whispered something under her breath, prayer or curse he couldn't tell, then, "What are we going to do?" She was looking away when she spoke and it wasn't clear if she was talking to him or to herself.

"We have to keep moving. There has to be a village out here somewhere."

"We should turn east, try to cut across the trail, catch up with the army."

Quyloc shook his head, dismissing the idea. "It's too far. It will take us at least two days on foot to make it to the trail and then who knows how long before we actually catch up to the army. If they've already passed, we might not catch them at all. Our best hope is to keep going the way we are. There has to be someone out here."

It was starting to get light then and Quyloc went back to the guards' camp. When he got there, one look at their faces told him what they were going to say before they said a word.

"We're out," Haris said. "Before nightfall we want to be as far from those things as we can."

Quyloc didn't try to argue with them. What was the point? He didn't want to be near them either.

102

It was late in the day when Quyloc saw the village in the distance. He stopped and stared at it, wondering if he'd ever been so happy to see a village in his entire life.

The FirstMother caught up to him a couple of minutes later, started to ask him why he'd stopped, squinted, then said, "Thank the Mother. We're saved."

They continued on. Two men were working in a field and looked up to see the strange sight of one man and a couple dozen women approaching on foot. The men stared curiously until they got close enough that they could see the *sulbits* on the women's shoulders. When they saw that they dropped their tools and ran for safety.

"Maybe you should have gone ahead without us," the FirstMother said.

"It makes no difference," Quyloc replied. He was thinking how glad he was that he wasn't going to have to spend all night alone near those creatures. He might actually survive this.

From a distance they saw people hurriedly moving a small herd of goats into the safety of the palisade.

The gate was shut when they got to the village near sunset. Up close it wasn't much of a village. It couldn't have held more than a hundred people. Instead of a stone wall, it had a wooden palisade, the logs sharpened at the ends. The homes were little more than huts, the fields around it poor in the rocky soil. A shallow stream ran by it. The few trees that had grown near it were all long since chopped down.

A number of men were visible on the palisade. They held a motley assortment of weapons, including pitchforks and clubs. A few had scraps of armor. Three held bows.

Quyloc and the FirstMother approached the gates, leaving the rest of the Tenders back out of bowshot. "You don't need those things," Quyloc told them. "We're not here to attack you."

"Go on your way and we won't have to," a man near the middle said grimly.

Quyloc stared at the man and realized suddenly that it wasn't a man at all, but an exceptionally fierce-looking woman with thick shoulders, her hair cropped short. From the way she was holding her sword, it looked like she wasn't afraid to use it. Quyloc sighed. Why did they have to complicate things?

"We can't do that," he told her. "We have to have food and we're not moving on without it."

"You don't look too hungry to me. Better move on without your food. You can't eat with an arrow in your gut anyway."

"It's not for us. It's for them." Quyloc gestured at the FirstMother's *sulbit*, which was standing very rigidly on her shoulder, its eyes moving over the villagers.

"I'd ask what those things are, but I don't care. We've seen too much that ain't natural lately. Just go on your way. We won't warn you again."

"We need that herd of goats. Horses too," Quyloc said.

"Ain't you listening, stranger? Move on or we'll shoot. I mean it."

"I don't want trouble with you. I don't want anyone to get hurt." Quyloc meant it too. He'd seen far too much violence lately. There had to be other ways of doing things. "We'll pay you well."

The thick-shouldered woman's manner changed slightly when he said that. "In gold?"

"Whatever you want."

"Let's see it."

Quyloc winced. He'd known this part would come. "There's a small problem. I don't have any coin on me right now. But I am the representative, the chief advisor really, of King Wulf Rome of Qarath." There was no point in mentioning the whole macht thing right then. "We're trying to get back there right now. Once we do, I'll send someone to bring you the money."

The woman started chuckling when he said that. She turned to the man standing next to her. "Can you believe this, Henry? Is this our lucky day or what?"

Quyloc looked at the FirstMother. "How long will it take you to bring down that gate?" he asked her softly.

"Just say the word," she replied without looking at him. Her jaw was tight, her eyes narrowed.

"Try not to hurt anyone," he added.

She shrugged.

"Does that mean no?" Quyloc said to the thick-shouldered woman.

"I don't know who you are, stranger, or how they do things where you come from. I don't know what in the world you're doing out here with these women and those *things*, but I give you my word that you won't get a single goat from us. Not a scrap of nothing. Now get out of here. I don't want to waste good arrows on you."

"Go ahead," Quyloc told the FirstMother tiredly.

She raised her arms and he felt her drawing Song in from flows all around her, his as well, judging by the sudden weakness in his legs. Two of the bowmen bent their bows back.

The Song bolt she released looked more like a ball of energy than a bolt. It struck the gate and the gate exploded in a cloud of splinters. Part of the palisade was torn away as well and the concussion was such that a number of the defenders were thrown down off the catwalk and disappeared from sight. The thick-shouldered woman managed to stay on the catwalk only by throwing an arm around one of the pointed logs, though she lost hold of her sword when she did so.

"Are we done now?" Quyloc called.

The thick-shouldered woman straightened. Her face was pale, her eyes very big and round. "What the…?"

"We don't want to fight you," Quyloc said. "And we'll still pay for the livestock, but we're not leaving without the animals. So I'll ask you again: are we going to have trouble?"

"N-no," she said. "Put your weapons down!" she called out to her people.

"I don't trust her," the FirstMother said.

"That's because you're not a very trusting person," Quyloc replied. He knew the look in the woman's eyes. He'd seen it before in opponents. She was beaten, the fight gone out of her.

The villagers stared in awe and fear as the *sulbits* fed on the goats, killing them all.

"What are those things?" a man called out from their midst.

"They're Xochitl's weapons," the FirstMother called back. "They're how we're going to defeat Melekath."

The village didn't have enough horses. Most of the Tenders had to double up and a few ended up on donkeys, but there was a road now and they were assured that the next village was less than a day away. As they rode away, Quyloc thought how close they'd come to complete disaster. Their only hope against Melekath could have ended right here and all because of one wrong decision to take a short cut. More than ever he was glad that Rome was macht and not him.

SIXTEEN

Velma walked up to the palace in a light rain, two guards accompanying her, though she'd told them they could stay at the estate. She didn't really need an escort. It was daytime and the city had been much calmer since Ricarn dispatched the mob with a swarm of bugs and Cara started doing the morning services. But they came with her anyway. They went with her whenever she left the estate. She supposed the FirstMother had given them instructions to protect her and she supposed she needed protecting, on account of being the temporary FirstMother and all – although she still couldn't think of herself as the FirstMother, temporary or not. She didn't even like to think of such a thing. She had no real idea what she was doing and she knew she never would. She just wanted the real FirstMother to return quickly so she could go back to her own position. Until then all she wanted to do was keep her head down and stay unnoticed.

Unfortunately, she wasn't going to be able to do that today. Today she had to find out everything she could about the *Pente Akka* and a weapon called a *rendspear*. The Insect Tender had come to her this morning and told her to gather all the information on them she could come up with. Velma had wanted to ask her why she needed this information, but frankly the woman terrified her. Velma could barely speak when she was around. So instead of asking questions, she'd done what she always did when she had to deal with Ricarn: she just stared at the ground, mumbled whatever seemed appropriate, and fled as soon as she could.

At first Velma had no idea how she was going to get the information. It wasn't like she could go to one of the book sellers and buy a book about those things. They'd just look at her like she was crazy. Besides that, she could barely read. It would take her forever to get through a book.

But then she remembered an old man she'd spoken to some years before. He'd stopped her in one of the city markets, somehow knowing she was a Tender, though she displayed no outward sign of it. He'd assured her that he meant no harm; he only wanted information for clarification purposes only. He said he was the palace librarian and he was writing up some history on the Tenders and wanted to know if she could help him fill some holes in his knowledge. Since he'd offered to pay, she'd helped him as much as she could.

She'd never seen him since then, but it seemed to her that if he was still alive, he'd be the one to talk to. Velma concentrated, trying to remember what his name was. Pomegranate or something like that.

There were four guards at the gates of the palace. They eyed her, their eyes noting the white robe and the Reminder around her neck, but said nothing.

"I am here to see Pomegranate," Velma said, then immediately felt foolish when they looked at her blankly. "Maybe that's not his name," she ventured weakly. "He is the librarian. Or at least he used to be?"

To her great relief one of them nodded and spoke to the one who was clearly the captain, who also nodded. "You mean Perganon," he said.

"Yes. That's it." Why couldn't she stand tall and proud like the FirstMother? she asked herself. She was a *Tender*, not a mouse.

"He has not gone out today. You will find him in the library probably." The captain noticed her blank look and said, "Hari here will show you the way."

Velma followed the guard, still vaguely surprised that they even allowed her entrance to the palace. Part of her had expected to be refused or, worse yet, run off with curses and threats. The old fears did not go away overnight, it seemed.

She was led up and down stairways and hallways until she was utterly confused, then left outside a door. She knocked softly. After a bit she heard a voice from within, but she couldn't tell what it said. Taking a deep breath, she turned the handle and entered.

She walked into a room that was filled with books. An old man sat at a desk in the middle of the room. He was wrinkled and bent and the sparse yellow whiskers on his jaw were mostly white. He took off his spectacles and regarded her without comment.

"I..." Velma began. She swallowed and started again. "I came to ask you...some questions." Her voice was barely above a whisper.

"I'm old," he said, not unkindly. "I don't see well," he waggled the spectacles at her, "and I hear even worse."

"I'm sorry," Velma mumbled.

"If you would be so kind as to come over here. Getting up isn't as easy as it used to be." Velma timidly took two steps closer. He shook his head. "Not close enough." She took a few more steps. He squinted up at her.

"Oh," he said. "I remember you. You shared some valuable information with me a few years back."

"Yes, yes I did." Velma found herself nodding idiotically, sadly gratified to find he remembered her.

"Now it seems the coin has flipped." He smiled at her. "You did fair for me. I can only do the same for you. What is it you wish to know? You do wish to know something, don't you? No one comes to see the old librarian unless they wish to know something."

"Ricarn wants me to find out what you know about *rendspears* and the *Pente Akka*."

His eyes widened. "How do you know about those?"

She shrugged. "I don't. Not really. I never even heard about either of them until this morning."

He gave her a long look, as if gauging the truth of her words, and Velma's discomfort grew. "Pull up a chair and sit down," he said at last. "This will take some time."

"So you do know about them?" Velma asked hopefully. It was hard to believe her luck. She'd expected him to say he didn't know anything and then she'd have to go back and tell the Insect Tender that she'd failed. That was something she very much wanted to avoid.

"I just finished deciphering this yesterday," he said, pulling a slim leather volume out of a drawer. "It was found recently when that wall was torn out to expand the library. I don't know who put it there or how long it's been there, though I would guess at least several centuries. It dates to about a hundred years after the Banishment. No doubt your FirstMother will want it once she learns it's here."

He seemed to be waiting for an answer, so Velma finally nodded. She had no real idea what the FirstMother would or wouldn't want. She just didn't want the FirstMother angry with her.

"One more thing: the Tender who wrote this did so against the direct orders of her FirstMother. This is an account that was never meant to be told. It is possible that I am the first person to know about these events since they occurred." He smiled. "Now you'll be the second."

Seventeen

Tel'al's Tale

Tel'al stopped, puzzled. She was a tall, gangly, somewhat awkward, middle-aged woman. Above all else, she didn't like surprises. Calm and predictable was the way she liked it. Yet here the day had barely started and already it was clear her day wasn't going to go that way.

She approached the sand dune cautiously. She could see that there was something on the side of it, something that didn't look quite right. This place, the site of the Banishment, always made her feel uneasy. It was on this spot where the cursed city of Durag'otal had stood, on this spot where Xochitl and the rest of the Eight had waged war on Melekath. When she came here, it always seemed like she could feel Melekath's presence, just a little bit. Several times she'd thought she heard a voice in the wind here, calling to her.

But nothing ever happened. The place was as quiet as a grave. Just one solitary sand dune to mark the spot of the most important event in the history of the human race.

Until today.

She squinted. It looked like there was a big blob of amber on the side of the dune, but it was too cloudy for amber, and far more than could ever come out of one tree. Not that there were any trees nearby anyway. All the trees in the area had died during the siege of Durag'otal and they'd never grown back. The only things that grew in the area were a few scraggly weeds, and those didn't look too healthy.

Unlike the local plant life, the sand dune was visibly growing. When she'd first started coming out here two years ago it was hardly more than chest high and about two dozen feet long. Now it was twice the height of a man and a stone's throw long. Which was why she was out here. The Tenders wanted to know what was happening here. They *had* to know. Was Melekath weakening the prison? Was his poison leaking out into the world? Would this dune just keep growing until it covered everything?

What made the Tenders especially nervous was they could no longer ask the Mother for guidance. Xochitl had disappeared more than twenty years ago, just walked out of the city of Qarath and never came back. For a while they'd been able to hear her voice in the mists of *beyond*, but then even that faded away.

The Tenders, the Chosen of Xochitl, were alone. That the followers of several of the false gods had also lost their deities since the Banishment was little consolation. Their god was gone and she did not answer their cries.

So the Tenders waited. They argued amongst themselves. They began to splinter. Some, like Tel'al, traveled to the young city of Kaetria when word arrived that a sand dune was forming over the site of the Banishment. Some began collecting the stories and knowledge of Xochitl into a single book that would be called the Book of Xochitl. Others tended to the people, or the animals, or the plants. But all of them waited for Xochitl to return.

The "amber" looked like it had spilled out of the side of the dune. It was a lumpy, misshapen mass about three or four feet across. She stopped a few feet away from it and slipped into the heightened awareness of *beyond*. From that nether region the amber appeared to have a faint, purplish hue.

And there seemed to be something moving within its depths.

When she leaned closer she could see something inside with her normal vision as well. Nothing specific, more like shadows sliding across her vision than anything. Carefully, she raised her hand and directed a tiny stream of Selfsong at the amber, hoping to pierce it and learn more.

The stream sliced off cleanly. Sharply. It stung.

Tel'al stepped back, her eyes widening. *What in the world could do that?* Nothing that she had ever encountered or heard of could slice through Song like that.

She turned and hurried away. It was time to talk to the others.

Grissam took a deep breath and approached the amber, while Tel'al and the other three Tenders in attendance watched anxiously. In the ten days since Tel'al first found the stuff it had changed a great deal. It had spread out across the face of the dune, still amorphous, but roughly circular. Raised ribs crossed its smooth surface, some radiating outwards from the center, while others formed concentric circles. To Tel'al it looked disturbingly like a giant spider web, but she kept this observation to herself.

Grissam was a thin, intense woman, with a fine, pointed nose and a sharp chin. She was not the sort to entertain unasked-for comments, and she had a sharp tongue. Berndin had suggested they send word to Qarath and wait to see what the FirstMother said about this new discovery before doing anything, and her ears were probably still ringing from the scolding Grissam had given her. Tel'al didn't want to suffer the same fate. So she kept quiet.

All four Tenders watched as Grissam reached out and touched the amber –

And immediately fell over in a boneless heap.

They hurried forward. Sliane was the first to reach Grissam, but she hesitated, afraid to touch her. With a disgusted noise Valerin pushed her aside and knelt beside Grissam. Her gaze unfocused and she laid her hands gently on Grissam's chest.

"What's wrong with her?" Sliane asked.

"Nothing…that I can find," Valerin said, looking puzzled. "She's just *gone*."

"Gone?" Sliane echoed. "But how? Where did she go?"

"I don't know," Valerin said.

"She's gone into the amber," Tel'al said, surprising herself.

"That doesn't make any sense," Sliane said, but Valerin put up a hand to stop her.

"What makes you say that?" she asked Tel'al.

"I don't know. It's just a feeling. When I was first out here, I thought I saw something moving inside the amber."

The four women all peered into the shining mass, as if they would see Grissam herself in there. It was certainly a possibility. Tenders had an ability to step out of their bodies and travel on the winds that blew steadily *beyond*. They called it spirit walking. It was one of the many gifts of the Mother. While in that form they could travel long distances quickly and pass through solid objects.

They saw nothing.

"What do we do?" Yurim asked.

Valerin and Sliane exchanged looks. "For now we just wait," Valerin said. "Maybe she will return on her own. She seems stable enough. I for one don't want to try to venture in there after her."

Tel'al sat down beside Grissam and stroked her hair gently. She wished she'd spoken up before Grissam touched the amber mass. She'd known nothing good could come from it. If the woman died, she was going to feel responsible.

The Tenders waited. An hour later Grissam surprised them all by suddenly sitting up and looking around, as if emerging from a deep sleep.

"You're all right," Sliane said.

"What happened?" Valerin asked.

Grissam turned to look at the mass on the dune. "I think I went in there."

"What?"

"It's a…it's like a shadow world. It's kind of like our world, but different. Like someone made a copy, but then twisted it somehow."

"There's a world in there?" Valerin breathed.

Grissam shook her head. "I don't think it's in there. Not really. I think…" She frowned, thinking. "I think this is just an entryway. What I saw is too big to be held in there." She rubbed her temples as if her head hurt. "And it's growing."

Tel'al sat by Grissam's motionless form. Grissam was in the shadow world. It was her third time. She had gone in there every day since the first time. Over Grissam's objections word had been sent to the FirstMother and she suspected Grissam wanted to learn as much as she could before the FirstMother intervened. The other Tenders in Kaetria no longer came with Grissam when she went to the shadow world. Somehow that job had fallen to Tel'al.

Tel'al stretched and yawned. She didn't mind. She, Yurim and Sliane were working on putting together the Book of Xochitl, compiling the stories and early writings of the old Tenders, and truth be told it was dull work. It was a relief to get outside and the spring weather was pleasant. Sitting here, waiting for Grissam to return, gave her plenty of time to think about what this shadow world was and where it came from. The other Tenders had argued about it for a while, then come to the conclusion that this shadow world was somehow caused by Melekath, perhaps as a physical manifestation of his malice. Tel'al didn't think she agreed with them. She had a feeling that Melekath wasn't behind this. But she didn't have any proof, nothing to go on besides a feeling, so she kept her mouth shut and nodded along with the rest of them.

Grissam stirred and sat up a moment later, rubbing her eyes. "How long was I gone?" she asked.

Tel'al looked at the sky. "Two hours?"

"Time is not the same in there. It felt like a great deal longer." She stood up and that's when Tel'al saw it. Grissam was wearing a flowing, sleeveless dress that left her shoulders bare and there on her right shoulder was a mark, like a scratch, only purplish.

"You didn't have that earlier," Tel'al said, pointing.

Grissam craned her neck to look at it and frowned. "No. I didn't."

"Where did it come from? Did you get it in there?"

"There was..." Grissam broke off, holding back whatever she'd been about to say. "I remember now. I scratched myself this morning at the temple. That's where I got it."

Tel'al said nothing. It didn't look like an ordinary scratch, but why would Grissam lie to her?

Grissam started to walk away and stumbled. "Do you feel okay?" Tel'al asked, catching her arm.

"I'm fine," Grissam said, perhaps a little harshly, pulling her arm away. "You don't have to baby me."

"You look pale."

"I said I'm *fine*. Let's go."

Tel'al followed her to the waiting horses, not liking the feeling of foreboding that had settled in her gut.

"Are you sure you want to go back in there today?" Tel'al asked Grissam the next morning. "Maybe you should take a day off."

"The FirstMother will be here tomorrow," Grissam replied, hurrying toward the dune. The strange amber mass had not gotten any bigger, but it seemed thicker, more substantial. Tel'al imagined it as a malignant creature poised to leap on them both. "Once she gets here she'll take over and I won't have another chance. She's never liked me. She'll want all the recognition for the discovery for herself."

Tel'al wondered what recognition Grissam was talking about, but decided not to ask.

Grissam stopped and turned on her. "I guess there's no reason not to tell you. It's too late for you to tell anyone."

"Tell me what?" Tel'al replied dubiously.

Grissam leaned close. "I think I found *her*."

"Her? You mean Xochitl?" Grissam's eyes were very bright but her face was very pale. There were dark circles around her eyes and her hair was unkempt, which would not have been unusual for Yurim, but was alarming for Grissam. She was normally very fussy about her appearance.

"Yes, I mean Xochitl," Grissam replied, almost whispering. She looked around as if fearing she would be overheard, though of course there was no one for miles around. Who would come clear out here to stare at a pile of sand? Most of the Kaetrians were completely unaware of its presence. "I think she went into the shadow world. *I'm* going to be the one who finds her. That's why I have to go back before the FirstMother gets here."

Tel'al nodded. Not because she agreed – the idea that Xochitl was in *there* seemed crazy to her – but because she didn't know what else to do. Grissam hurried on. When she reached the amber mass she stood before it with her eyes closed, her hands held up, palms outward, as if savoring the warmth off a fire. Tel'al waited, shifting from one foot to the other uncomfortably.

Without opening her eyes, Grissam lay down on the sandy ground. Tel'al dutifully sat down beside her. Grissam reached out and touched the mass and then she was gone.

As the hours went by Tel'al became more and more alarmed. Grissam had never been in the shadow world for so long before. In the early afternoon, while she was sitting there, staring off into the distance, from the corner of her eye it looked like Grissam just flickered out. For the briefest moment she seemed to disappear. But when she turned her head, Grissam looked normal. Her heart started to beat faster and she reached over to touch the thin Tender on the shoulder, wanting to reassure herself that Grissam was still there.

She felt the fabric of Grissam's robe under her fingertips, and under that the flesh and bone of her body, but something was missing. She couldn't have said what it was exactly, but something was definitely missing.

It was late in the afternoon when Grissam finally returned. Her eyes opened and she moaned softly. Tel'al helped her to sit up. Her head wobbled and she did not answer when Tel'al spoke to her, though she did peer at her strangely as if she had never seen her before. Tel'al had to help her to her feet and then practically carry her to her horse. But it was when Tel'al was helping Grissam onto her horse that she got the biggest shock.

There was something running from Grissam's shoulder to the amber mass on the dune. Like a thread, but purple and very faint.

Tel'al blinked and it was gone. *What was that thing?*

"I couldn't find her," Grissam moaned, slumping forward in the saddle. "I looked and looked."

"It's okay," Tel'al said, not sure what else to say. "You'll find her next time." She touched Grissam's hand again, reassuring herself that the other Tender was still there. She looked pale and there was a translucent quality to her. What was happening to her?

Tel'al was awake early the next morning, sitting on the balcony off her room drinking a cup of tea, when FirstMother Koreen's carriage arrived, a team of six massive horses harnessed to it. Though they had no doubt traveled nonstop from Qarath, the horses did not appear tired. They didn't appear to feel much of anything at all. Koreen was FirstMother for a reason. No Tender had greater control of the flows of Song than she did. She could keep that team of horses going until they quite literally fell apart if she chose. The carriage had no driver. There was no need. The horses were under Koreen's complete control.

When Tel'al saw the carriage she set her cup of tea down so fast it spilled. She hurried through her room and into the hall, grabbing the first servant she saw and sending her running for Valerin. By the time she got down to the entry hall, the FirstMother and the four Tenders accompanying her had already entered.

The FirstMother was a tall, powerfully built woman with graying hair and stern lines drawn into her face. She wore a crimson robe and a white sash, as befitted her status. Her hair was cut very short and her eyes were penetrating. To Tel'al the four Tenders with her looked like bodyguards, each dressed in an identical yellow robe with red sashes around their waists. All of them had their hair pulled back in severe buns and their grim faces showed no expression.

"Where is she? I want to talk to her," Koreen demanded.

"She's still in her room. We didn't expect you so early, FirstMother," Valerin replied, just then entering, with the servant trailing her and trying to look as small as possible. Valerin was clutching her thin sleeping robe to her with hands that shook just slightly and she avoided meeting Koreen's eyes. She had come so quickly her feet were still bare. Keeping the FirstMother waiting was far worse than cold feet.

"Bring her. Make it quick."

Valerin turned to Tel'al, but Tel'al was already on her way. She wanted only to get away from Koreen before that frightening woman noticed her; suddenly the boredom of digging through endless dusty scrolls didn't seem all that bad.

But Grissam's room was empty. It didn't look like her bed had even been slept in. Tel'al fairly ran back to the others.

"She's gone?" Koreen demanded, intuiting what had happened from the look on Tel'al's face. "Come with me," she said to Valerin, already striding for the door, the four Tenders she'd brought with her following her. "You can tell me everything you've learned so far on the way out there."

"FirstMother, if I might," Valerin ventured. "Tel'al is the one who found it. She has been out there every day with Grissam."

Koreen didn't slow or look back. "Both of you, then. And hurry."

Tel'al hesitated, looking at Valerin. Why had Valerin dragged her into this? Valerin was looking down at her bare feet. Valerin turned as if she would go to her room – grab what she was missing – but abruptly gave it up as a bad idea. Moments later she and Tel'al were hurrying after the FirstMother, Valerin wearing the servant's sandals.

The seven Tenders arrived at the dune and found Grissam lying sprawled on the ground a dozen paces from it. She was lying face down, one hand flung out toward the dune. A look *beyond* showed Tel'al that she had not imagined the thin purple line she had seen yesterday. But today there were more. Hundreds, thousands of them spewed out from the amber mass on the face of the dune and wrapped around Grissam, cocooning her so that her *akirma* was barely visible. Tel'al was suddenly very glad the FirstMother was with them. Whatever was happening here was far beyond Tel'al. Without realizing it, she moved a half step closer to the FirstMother.

"It is as the Mother warned," the FirstMother said, looking from Grissam to the amber mass. Her face had gone slightly pale. The four Tender bodyguards spread out in an arc facing the mass, two on each side of Koreen. "This whole area stinks of chaos power."

"What is it, FirstMother?" Valerin asked. "What are all those purple lines?"

"I don't know," the FirstMother admitted. "I only know that they are draining Grissam. It won't be long before she'll be gone."

Valerin gasped softly and laid a hand on Tel'al's arm. The four Tender bodyguards showed no emotion. Tel'al had stolen peeks at them from *beyond* on the way out here. Their *akirmas* glowed nearly as brightly as Koreen's. LifeSong swirled around them. They were powerful women: the FirstMother had come expecting trouble.

Koreen looked at the two women, measuring them. Her next words were stern. "What I am about to tell you is a secret known only to a handful. You are never to speak of it to anyone. Am I clear?" Both women nodded. "To create a prison that would hold Melekath, Xochitl was forced to open the abyss, which is sealed away at the heart of the world. From the abyss she took chaos power, which she used to imprison Melekath."

"The prison is made of chaos power?" Valerin said weakly.

"And some of it is leaking through into our world from the abyss. Xochitl feared that this might happen someday so she left a warning, to be passed down from one FirstMother to the next."

"What's it doing to Grissam?"

"It's using her to siphon off LifeSong from our world."

"Why?"

"To breach the barrier between our worlds," Koreen said grimly.

Tel'al's mouth suddenly was very dry. This was so much worse than she'd feared.

"Can you save Grissam?" Valerin asked.

Koreen shrugged. "I don't know. I hope so. But that is not what is important here. What's important is that the creatures which live in the abyss are not able to use her to get into our world."

Koreen drew something from a pocket on her robe. It was a knife, but it was clearly not made of metal. It was yellowed, and looked to be made of old bone.

"What's that?" Tel'al asked, suddenly afraid that the FirstMother meant to stab Grissam with it.

"A weapon Xochitl left with us for this purpose. No more questions." Koreen looked to the Tenders flanking her. "Are you ready?" As one they nodded. To Valerin and Tel'al she said, "You should back up." The two women hastily complied, though Tel'al didn't move back as far as Valerin did. For some reason she had to see what happened. She had to *know*.

Koreen held out the bone knife and let it go. It hovered there in the air before her, held aloft by a flow of Song. Channeling more Song into it, Koreen set the knife to spinning, faster and faster until it was a circular blur in the morning air. Tel'al felt the hair on the backs of her arms stand up as the four Tender bodyguards began to channel flows as well. The air around all five of them glowed with power. Sand swirled around their ankles.

Koreen gestured and the knife moved until it hovered over the seething mass of purple lines. To Tel'al it seemed that the mass of lines was aware of the coming attack, that its motion became more frenzied, more chaotic. Another gesture from Koreen and the knife shot down, biting into the mass of tangled lines.

There was a series of small, fierce concussions. From *beyond* Tel'al could see that it was working. The bone knife was cutting through the lines. The severed lines whipped around in the air frantically, aimlessly, like snakes cut in half.

Koreen brought both hands together and the knife bit deeper. A strange cry, felt rather than heard, rose up.

Suddenly, Grissam's eyes opened and she sat up, her head turning side to side. Tel'al started forward, reaching out to help, when something she saw made her hesitate.

Grissam's eyes fixed on Koreen, then blazed a feral yellow. With an eerie grace she came to her feet and charged at Koreen with a soundless snarl.

Tel'al cried out a warning. Koreen half-turned just as Grissam slammed into her. She staggered sideways. The knife stopped spinning and fell to the ground.

The four Tender bodyguards turned toward Koreen, uncertainty on their faces. The Song they held at the ready crackled in the air around them.

At that moment, a hole opened in the amber mass, right where the lines emerged, and something began to emerge, pulling itself out of the hole using the lines. It was hunched and misshapen, a grim parody of a person, as if someone had made a statue out of wax and left it in the sun to melt. It balanced there, clinging to the mass of lines with one gnarled hand, blinking in the light. From its back a rubbery appendage sprouted. The appendage swiveled toward one of the Tenders on Koreen's right.

An opening appeared in the end of the appendage and a purple line shot out, piercing the Tender through the chest. The line burst out of her back and then wrapped around her torso several times. The woman shrieked, her head snapping back, a bloody froth spraying out of her open mouth. Her face darkened and she began to shrink, as if the air was leaking from her. The line glowed brighter, so bright that it hurt the eyes, as the Song stolen from the Tender rushed down it and into the misshapen creature.

The creature swelled and grew larger. Another rubbery appendage sprouted from between its shoulders and another line shot from it, striking the other Tender on the right.

All this happened in mere seconds, while Koreen struggled with Grissam and the other two Tenders froze in indecision.

With a blaze of power, Koreen threw Grissam off, the burst strong enough that Grissam's hair was mostly singed away as she was thrown backward. "Hold her!" Koreen yelled to Tel'al and Valerin and turned back to face the thing on the dune. Song built around her in a sparking cloud.

"Don't!" Tel'al yelled – while fighting with Grissam, Koreen hadn't seen what happened, how the thing drank in Song and grew stronger – but Koreen either didn't hear her or ignored her because the Song around the FirstMother continued to build and then she howled as she released it.

"Help me!" Valerin yelled. One of the bands of Song that she had wrapped around Grissam had already snapped and the others would not hold for long. "I can't hold her!"

Tel'al hesitated. The wave of Song released by Koreen had knocked the creature back, but instantly it recovered and was now clinging to the Song, using it to become stronger. Koreen's eyes bulged as she fought futilely to shut down the Song.

Another rubbery appendage sprouted from the creature's back and turned toward another Tender bodyguard.

Tel'al's eyes fell on the bone knife, lying forgotten on the ground.

She ran forward, snatched it up, and threw herself at the remaining lines leading from the amber mass to Grissam.

When the knife made contact with the first line a shock went through Tel'al, knocking her back a step.

Grissam howled and redoubled her efforts. Another of the slim flows holding her snapped. There was only one left. Valerin's face was white with the strain.

The creature that had crawled out of the mass was huge now, twice the size of a man. It pulled itself the rest of the way from the hole, its eyes now fixed on Tel'al. The rubbery appendage turned toward her.

Tel'al threw herself back on the lines and began sawing furiously at them. This time when she made contact she had an image form in her mind, a massive, horned creature sitting on top of what looked like a volcano, in the midst of a smoking, primordial world. Its heavy gaze fell on her and her heart went cold.

She cut through several lines. There was only one left.

The thing on the volcano reached out and Tel'al felt hot fingers close around her heart. Her vision began to go black. Her fingers went numb and the knife began to slip from her grasp. Gritting her teeth, she clamped her free hand on the handle of the knife, steadying her grip.

The last line parted.

There was an earsplitting crack and the amber mass split in half.

With a hoarse cry, the misshapen creature lost its footing and toppled backward. It flung out both arms, trying to get a hold on the amber pieces, but they crumbled under its touch.

With a last, furious roar it fell into the hole and disappeared from sight.

Tel'al dropped the knife and straightened. Grissam lay nearby, unmoving. Tel'al felt the hole where her Selfsong had been and knew she was dead. Valerin was on her knees, sobbing. Two of the Tender bodyguards were lying dead, their bodies blackened as if they'd been through a fire. The other two were helping Koreen to her feet. Her hair had turned gray and her face was lined with new wrinkles.

"I can stand on my own," Koreen told the women and they let go. She tottered over to Tel'al, then bent and picked up the bone knife, slipping it back into her robe. For a moment she stared into Tel'al's eyes. "Thank you," she said softly.

Turning back to the other Tenders she said, "Bury it. Bury it deep." While they complied, using Song to carve out a deep shaft near the shattered pieces of the amber mass and then pushing them into the shaft, Koreen spoke to Tel'al and Valerin.

"What you saw here today did not happen. You will never tell a soul of this. Do you understand me?" Both women nodded. "We nearly lost here today. That thing was only the beginning. If it had defeated us..." she glanced at Tel'al "...if you hadn't acted as you did, it would have been free in our world and others of its kind would have followed. A doorway to the abyss would have been opened and its denizens would have overrun our world. This knowledge is too dangerous. None can ever know of it, until we can figure a way to seal it away forever."

Two days later, mostly recovered from the ordeal, Tel'al sat in her room with a stack of parchments on the table before her. The FirstMother had left the day before and life at the temple had returned to a semblance of normality. But she knew it would never truly be normal again.

Before Koreen left, she had repeated her orders to Tel'al and Valerin: they were never to tell anyone what had happened out in the desert. They were to take that information to their graves, or they would be driven from the order. Both women had dutifully agreed.

But now Tel'al dipped her quill into ink and pressed the tip to the first sheet of parchment. What she was doing was foolish and dangerous. She knew that. Yet the historian in her nature would not let what had happened just die. What she had experienced might help some future Tender. She began to write.

There is another world, dwelling beneath our own…

Perganon set the book down and looked at Velma.

"I…I…" Velma stammered. Her eyes were very wide.

Perganon opened a drawer in his desk and took out a bottle of yellow liquor and two small glasses. "Would you like a drink?"

"The FirstMother has forbidden us to drink," Velma said. "Of course I want one." She swallowed what he gave her quickly and gripped the empty glass tightly in both hands.

"It's a lot to take in, isn't it?" Perganon said gently.

"I don't think I understand."

"I'm not sure anyone does."

"What do I tell Ricarn? She wanted to know about the *rendspear* but I still don't know anything."

"That world, the place where Grissam went, is called the *Pente Akka*. The *rendspear* came from there."

"But…the FirstMother destroyed it, didn't she?"

Perganon shook his head. "She destroyed an opening to it, that's all. I suspect the *Pente Akka* has been growing all this time."

Velma paled. "It's *bigger*?"

"Consider how big the Gur al Krin desert is."

Now she was having trouble breathing. "Are you saying that the sand dunes in the Krin are the same as the one in the story?"

"I am."

"How did Quyloc get in there?"

"Lowellin showed him how."

"The *Protector*? But…why?"

"For the *rendspear*. My guess is that chaos power is as deadly to the gods as it is to us."

Velma just sat there then, staring at the glass in her lap. She wished Ricarn hadn't sent her here. She didn't want to know any of this. She was much happier knowing nothing. Why did everything have to be so confusing?

EIGHTEEN

The Takare all felt it when the prison broke, like something tearing open deep inside. Shakre knew right away what it was and she immediately went to Youlin to talk to her about it, but the young Pastwalker from Mad River Shelter simply turned away without replying and went to the small hut back in the trees that the Takare had built for her. Since then she rarely emerged from the hut and when she did she spoke to no one and kept her face hidden within the depths of her hood.

The Takare needed leadership but since the near-disaster when the Takare warriors were nearly wiped out in Kasai's trap, Rehobim had retreated within himself, and rarely spoke. He spent his time savagely training with his weapons, his intensity and fury such that several other warriors had been wounded while sparring with him, one seriously.

Elihu did what he could, but he was not the type of man to provide the kind of leadership the Takare needed now. They were a lost people, their homeland taken from them and no plan for the future.

Nor was there much that Shakre could do. The things she had done to aid the Takare had earned her a great deal of respect and gratitude, but she was still an outsider.

Shakre looked up as Lize and Ekna approached the fire, Intyr between them. The old women each held one of Intyr's elbows, guiding her. They helped her sit on a stump near the fire pit. The Dreamwalker sat straight, unwavering. She looked tiny, insubstantial. Most of the blue dye in her frowsy hair had faded leaving gray in its place. She had not spoken, had barely even opened her eyes, since leaving the Plateau. She ate and drank when it was given to her, but other than that she was completely unresponsive. The old women had taken to caring for Intyr, bathing her, brushing her hair. Lize sat down beside her while Ekna went to get her some food.

Intyr lived now full time in the dream world she had walked for her people for so many years. Shakre wished the woman would open her eyes, step forward and guide her people. But even before she drifted away she had never been that kind of person.

The sun set and darkness began to fill the remaining spaces. More wood was added to the fire and the Takare people gathered, sitting silently, everyone waiting. There were probably a thousand of them now, all of them hardened and seasoned by the trials of life on the Landsend Plateau. Most carried a weapon. Except for the very young or the very old every Takare sat with Youlin after they showed up at the camp, and Youlin opened their eyes to past lives and warrior skills long forgotten. Daily they honed those skills in practice against one another. The Takare who had forsworn violence after the tragedy at Wreckers Gate were long gone. The warriors the world had once feared were returning.

The hide door of Youlin's hut was pulled back and she emerged. Though her hut was back in the trees, barely within the fringes of the firelight, every eye turned to her and everyone went still. It was as though they had all been waiting for her to emerge, watching her hut surreptitiously.

Youlin made her way through the Takare, her face hidden within the depths of her hood. They moved aside as she approached, making a path for her. She walked up to Rehobim. The tall, muscular young warrior was sitting on a stump, his face down, the only one not looking at Youlin. It looked as if he were unaware of her approach, but Shakre could see the tension in his muscles that said otherwise.

Youlin stopped before him. Still he did not look up.

"It is time," she said, her voice utterly cold.

Rehobim shuddered but kept his face turned down.

"I told you when I gave you your past name, Tarnin, that if you failed, you would answer for it. Do you remember?"

Nothing at first. Then he gave the slightest nod.

"Are you prepared to answer to your people, to pay for your failure?"

Rehobim looked up for the first time. There was doom in his eyes. But there was also relief, as the moment he had dreaded so much finally arrived. At least the waiting was over. He nodded again.

"Stand," Youlin ordered.

Rehobim stood. Around his neck hung his necklace of teeth from the animals he had killed. In the center was the tooth from the tani

Shorn had killed. The new scars on his face showed red in the firelight. Shakre remembered when he gave himself the first one, after Shorn saved the village. She remembered how he looked when Shorn turned away and rejected him. He had something of the same look in his eyes now. Desperate. Haunted. She did not have to go *beyond* to sense his terrible, self-imposed isolation. Since the day the outsiders killed the hunting party with fire and Rehobim did nothing to stop them he had lived with a stain on his heart. Everything he had done since then, every thought, every breath, had carried with it the desperate plea to be forgiven for his cowardice. Shakre's heart went out to him. She had never really liked the abrasive, arrogant young man, but it hurt to see him suffer.

"I have failed you," he said, drawing himself up and looking over his people. To Youlin he said, "I accept your judgment."

Youlin held out her hand. "Give me your knife."

Rehobim drew one of his knives from its sheath and handed it to her.

"Kneel. Bow your head."

Rehobim took a look around before obeying, as if to have one last look at the world. Then he knelt and bowed his head.

"She's going to kill him. We have to stop this," Shakre said, starting to stand.

To her surprise, Elihu pulled her back down beside him. "Wait. I do not believe it is what you think."

Youlin moved Rehobim's long braid aside, leaving his neck bare. He tensed, but did not move. The Takare stared, utterly speechless. Youlin raised the blade. Shakre averted her gaze, unable to look.

Youlin slashed across the back of Rehobim's neck. Blood began to flow.

"It is not a deep cut," Elihu whispered. Shakre looked up.

Youlin pressed her hands against the cut, then held them up. Blood dripped down her forearms. She walked to the edge of the clearing and raised her arms over her head. Tilting her head back, she called out. "Old spirits, it is time! Return to your people!"

Almost immediately there was an answering cry from the darkness. The Takare were like people entranced. Not a sound rose from them even as they instinctively pressed closer together.

The hair rose on the back of Shakre's neck. "What was that?" she whispered.

"I have no idea."

126

Again Youlin called, and again the answering cry came from the darkness. It was wordless, but it carried within it an ancient rage and a terrible eagerness. And it was closer.

"This is not right," Shakre muttered. "Whatever she's doing, it's not right. We have to do something." But Elihu did not respond, nor did he release his tight grip on her arm.

Youlin called again and now Shakre could see something coalescing out there at the edge of the light. It was formless, wraithlike. Within the wraith were twin glowing points, like embers of a dying fire.

It floated out of the trees, coming to a stop before Youlin.

Youlin flung droplets of Rehobim's blood into it. With each drop the wraith seemed to grow thicker, more substantial. "Come, old spirit!" she cried. "Taste the life that was once your life!"

Youlin threw her hood back. Her dark hair had been cropped short. The bones in her face were sharp underneath her deathly pale skin. She had blackened around her eyes with soot from the fire. She did not flinch before the wraith, but pointed at Rehobim, who was still kneeling, staring at the wraith with wide eyes. "Go. There waits your willing vessel. Take the first step toward restoring our people."

The wraith moved away from Youlin toward Rehobim. The unearthly cry came from it again. Rehobim stared up at it in fear and awe, his muscles twitching as he fought the urge to flee.

"Elihu…" Shakre said.

The wraith engulfed Rehobim, swirling madly around him. It grew denser until no part of Rehobim could be seen. Shakre waited for the scream. She had forgotten how to breathe.

Gradually Rehobim started to become visible. His body was contorted, his head thrown back, mouth stretched in a silent scream, eyes rolled back in his head.

Elihu pulled Shakre close and wrapped his arms around her.

The wraith faded more but now it was clear that it was not fading away, but was instead entering Rehobim through the wound on the back of his neck.

A minute later the wraith was completely gone. Rehobim sagged forward, his eyes closed, keeping himself from falling over by putting his hands on the ground. Shakre could see that the wound on his neck had closed, leaving a livid bluish mark where it had been.

She tore herself away from Elihu and hurried over to Rehobim. Dropping to her knees beside him she touched his neck. His pulse was wild, out of control. His skin was hot to the touch. She looked up at Youlin.

"What did you do to him?"

"I made him more," Youlin said. "I made him fearful to our enemies."

"You may have killed him."

"He won't die," Youlin said confidently. "He is strong. The process will be over soon."

"What did you do to him?"

"I called in one of the old spirits of our people. One of them now dwells within him."

"An old spirit? What are you talking about?"

Instead of answering her, Youlin looked at the gathered people and raised her voice to address them.

"Not everyone made the same choice we did after the slaughter at Wreckers Gate. Some refused to throw down their weapons. They saw the guilt where it properly lay, not in the Takare, but in those who we served. They wanted to turn on the Empire and drench it in blood, kill thousands for every one of ours who died that day. They vowed never to be reborn among us until we saw the error of our decision.

"That time is now. The Takare have returned to the world. But our numbers are few and we need their help if we are to have any hope."

She bent, took hold of Rehobim's arm, and raised him to his feet.

"Rehobim now houses the spirit of Tarnin," Youlin said. Confused looks met her words. "I see your confusion," she continued. "You do not remember the name, though he was our last, and greatest leader. This is because the Pastwalkers hid him from you. They hid from you all those who refused to go into exile."

Shakre looked at Rekus. The old Pastwalker had his face hidden in his hands.

"But that time is past. No longer will the names of our heroes be lost to us. In the days to come I will summon the old spirits to find new homes in you. With their help we will once again reclaim our rightful place." She paused while they stared at her uneasily. Their world had just changed again, veering off in a direction they had never considered. What would happen now?

"In a few days we will leave this place. It is time to go home. Time to return to Ankha del'Ath."

Afterward, Shakre and Elihu stood apart, near the edge of the clearing.

"Did that just happen?" Shakre asked, still shaken.

"If you mean did our Pastwalker just call in an old spirit and put it into Rehobim, then yes, I think it did."

"How is such a thing possible?"

"Over the past few months I have asked myself that many times about many things. I have come to realize that it is a pointless question."

"What's going to happen to him?"

"I don't think anyone knows that, not even Youlin. I fear for our young Pastwalker. In her zeal to preserve her people she may instead cause our ruin." He took hold of Shakre's chin and turned her face to his. "You're going to talk to her now, aren't you?"

"Is it that obvious?"

He stroked her cheek. "With you it is. Do you want me to come with you?"

"No. I think I should talk to her alone. If it's both of us she may get defensive."

"Then I will talk to Rekus. Find out if any Pastwalker has ever done something like this before."

Shakre walked over to Youlin, passing Intyr as she did. The Dreamwalker had not moved during everything that had happened. She was as oblivious as always. Youlin had pulled her hood up once again and she did not look up as Shakre approached, did not seem to even notice her presence. The bowl of food that had been brought for her sat untouched on the ground beside her.

Shakre sat down beside Youlin. For a moment she wished she didn't have to do this. She was tired of always being the lone voice of dissent. Taking a deep breath, she said, "With the greatest respect, Pastwalker, I am concerned about what you did to Rehobim."

Youlin did not respond.

Shakre swallowed. This was not going to go well. "Perhaps it would be best if we did not rush into repeating this with others until we know more about what it really means."

Youlin stiffened. Slowly her head turned and Shakre found herself looking into the depths of her hood, where just the faintest glitter of her eyes was visible.

"There is no 'we' *outsider*. 'We' are Takare. *You* are not." Her voice was cold.

"She is not an outsider," Intyr said suddenly.

Surprised, both Shakre and Youlin turned towards the old woman. She was not looking at them. Her eyes were still closed.

"What did you say?" Youlin asked in a low voice.

"She is Merat reborn," Intyr said.

"She is *who*?"

"I am the Dreamwalker. I have spoken." Still Intyr's eyes were closed. She might not have been there at all, but her voice was firm and sure.

Youlin started to respond, then changed her mind. There was nothing, really, that she could say. When it came to matters concerning the rebirth of Takare spirits the Dreamwalker was the final voice. Takare custom was clear on this. Youlin swung back to Shakre. In a loud, clear voice she said, "The Windrider is Merat reborn. Dreamwalker Intyr has spoken."

Nearby Takare heard her and turned from their conversations to listen.

"But we will proceed as I have planned, Windrider-who-was-Merat," Youlin said in a lower voice to Shakre, again fixing her with that eerie stare. "Tomorrow night I will call more of our old spirits to us. Do not speak to me of this again. It is decided."

NINETEEN

A handful of days had passed since Youlin transformed Rehobim. And he was transformed in more ways than one. The moping and guilt were gone and his swagger had returned. Daily he led the Takare in hard training, recovering the deadly skills that had long lain dormant in them. Every night Youlin called in the old spirits and found new homes for them. Now there were almost two dozen warriors who had gone through the transformation. The Takare people were growing more dangerous by the day.

It was morning and the Takare were preparing to leave their makeshift camp and journey to their ancestral home. The anticipation was palpable. What would Ankha del'Ath be like after all these years? What would they find when they got there? It was all anyone had talked about at night around the fires. They journeyed into their future and into their past simultaneously.

Shakre gathered the herbs she used for healing and the other few items she possessed and put them in her pack. Since speaking to Youlin that first night, Shakre had said nothing more to try and dissuade her. The truth was there was nothing to say. She was no more than a leaf and strong winds were blowing through the Takare people. Who was she to say what was best for them? The world had changed. Everything had changed. The prison was broken. Melekath was free. She did not see how any warriors, regardless of how powerful they were, could make a difference in what was coming, but she would not deny them any weapon they might lay their hands on.

She looked up from her thoughts as Elihu stiffened, then faced north. Those around them broke off their conversations and stared. Shakre took hold of his arm. She started to ask what was wrong, and then all at once she knew.

"The Mistress," Elihu said.

It was a nightmare apparition which burst into the clearing from the north. She stood on two legs. Short, twisted horns sprouted from her head and long fangs protruded from her mouth. Curved claws the length of daggers extended from her fingers. It was Azrael, she who was known as the Mistress of the Plateau. She was Tu Sinar's enforcer, the claws and teeth that the Takare feared most. She had nearly destroyed the Takare when first they came to the Plateau, and all knew that to offend her was to risk destruction at her hands. It was clear she had suffered in the destruction of the Plateau. Partially healed wounds marked her whole left side. She drew herself to her full height.

"Betrayers!" she hissed. "You let the outsiders in! You killed Tu Sinar!"

With a snarl, she charged them. She was blindingly fast and two Takare – both elderly – fell to her claws without a sound.

But she had badly misjudged her prey. These were not the same Takare.

Even as she charged into their midst, the Takare were reacting, drawing weapons, melting out of her path to strike at her sides. Still, despite their deadly skills, a great many would have died that morning if not for Rehobim and the others who, like him, carried the spirits of long-dead Takare within them.

Azrael had not made it halfway across the clearing before Rehobim was in her path, flanked loosely by a half dozen of the other spirit-kin – as they had taken to calling themselves – all waiting in a half-crouch. She hesitated, uncertainty showing on her bestial visage. They stood motionless, watching her.

She charged them, all teeth and flashing claws.

The warriors sprang into action. Weapons flashed, too fast for the eye to follow.

A heartbeat later Azrael lay on the ground in a crumpled heap, one leg kicking weakly. Her head was nearly severed, one eye glaring fiercely up at them. The eye dulled and became empty. The trees around the clearing began shaking. The body twitched, and then was ripped apart from within. A cloud of patchy darkness poured forth from the body and drifted out of the clearing.

Rehobim kicked the body in the ribs. Hone bent and retrieved one of her knives, buried in the creature's side. Pinlir wiped the blade of his axe clean on her tattered fur. The Takare turned away and a short while later they left the clearing, leaving the Plateau and their lives there behind forever.

TWENTY

The break in the wall was not large. Certainly not as large as the consequences that break would have on the world. It was about twice the width of a man and half again as high. The stone that lined the edges of the break was curiously discolored along its edge, as if it had gone through a fire.

Two pale hands appeared. Pieces of rock that would have taken several strong men to move were picked up and tossed out of the break as if they were pebbles. As the opening was cleared, strange, wordless cries came from the darkness behind him. They were cries of eagerness and cries of fear.

The one who emerged from the break was of medium height and slight build. He was stooped, as if he carried huge, invisible burdens. The clothes he wore were little more than rags, stained and torn. His hair was gray and wispy and there was a slight limp in his stride. The lines in his face were etched deep, like a mountain scarred by the weather over the eons. His eyes were tired.

He kicked the last pieces of stone out of the way and looked on a world he had not seen for three thousand years. He scanned the massive cavern, saw that it was empty and frowned. There was a sound of receding footsteps in the tunnel that led from the cavern. He turned back to the prison. Several figures stood back in the shadows, trembling.

"Come," Melekath said. "As I promised, you are free now."

The figures looked at him with wide eyes, but they did not move. When he reached they fell back, but he caught hold of one of them before he could flee.

"It is time to leave the prison, Heram," he said gently. "You are free now." The one called Heram resisted him, but his struggles were feeble and Melekath pulled him easily into the cavern.

Heram was only barely recognizable as human. His skin was gray and he was completely hairless. He was bent over like an old man and one leg dragged behind him. A cut ran down the side of his head, through his ear and down to his neck. The cut looked old. No blood ran from it. There was no scarring, no sign that his body had attempted to heal itself at all. A scrap of cloth was wrapped around his waist, but beyond that he was naked. Just beyond the wall he stopped and swung his head to the side to peer up at Melekath with one eye.

"Too long," he croaked. His voice was dusty and disused. No teeth showed in his mouth. "It was too long, Father."

Something that might have been a wince crossed Melekath's face but he did not respond, instead resting his hand briefly on the man's shoulder.

The next one he caught a hold of was a woman, as gray-skinned and hairless as Heram. One arm hung uselessly by her side, the hand twisted into a claw. A deep wound showed in her upper chest, revealing cracked, gray ribs. Again there was no blood, no scarring or closure of the wound. She stopped just beyond the break, breathing hard, and looked up at the cavern ceiling.

"What happened to the sky? Where is the sky?" she cried, her voice rising shrilly.

"We are underground still, Reyna," Melekath answered. "Once the others emerge I will lead you back to the world."

She looked at him suspiciously and frowned. She moved reluctantly when he pulled her out of the way so that he could get to the others.

The next one he caught hold of was also gray-skinned. His head was flattened along one side, as if had been crushed by a large stone. One eye dangled uselessly. He wore no clothing at all and his belly was bloated, like a corpse found floating in the river. "Where is the Song? Where is it?" he whined. He lifted his misshapen head and sniffed the air. "I smell one, but it is leaving. Catch it, Father! Give it to me!"

"In time, Dubron," Melekath assured him. "I will give you all the LifeSong you need, all that has been stolen from you and so much more. Only be patient awhile longer."

Reyna laughed harshly, her laugh turning into a cough. "'Be patient.' Always he says, 'be patient.'" The others cackled along with her. Melekath gave them a look, but said nothing.

With his help the Children staggered, lurched and crawled from their prison of three thousand years. Every one of them was mangled and broken, some horribly so. Limbs were crushed and sometimes missing altogether. On some the gray skin was peeling away, revealing withered muscle and gray bone underneath. Old wounds gaped on their bodies. All were hairless. If they wore clothing at all it was mere rags. Some cried in delight when they stepped out. Others were silent, watchful. Some appeared to have lost the power of speech, expressing themselves with wordless grunts, cries and shrieks.

A half-dozen of them were children, ranging in age from six to twelve, their normal growth suspended when the prison was sealed. They looked like children, but in their eyes was a terrible knowledge beyond anything any child had ever known.

They gathered in the huge cavern, standing about, staring at the floor or up at the ceiling in awe. When the last emerged, blinking, from the lightless prison, there were no more than a hundred of them, a mere fraction of the number of inhabitants of the city of Durag'otal at the time of the Banishment. Piteous cries could be heard issuing from the blackness of the prison, but they drew no closer. Many of those still within the prison were unable to leave, their bodies too broken to carry them forth. But there were others who were unwilling to leave. They had dwelled in their prison for too long. As much as they hated it, it had become all they knew and they could not leave it now.

"They will not be forgotten," Melekath told his Children. "I will return for them. This, I promise you all." He surveyed them. "We face a threatening world outside. There are those who hate and fear you, who will stop at nothing to seal you back in there." A collective groan arose from them at his words.

"I promise you they will never imprison you again."

"Never again," moaned several. The words were taken up by the others and they echoed around the cavern until Melekath silenced them.

"Time to leave," he said.

"Feed me first, Father," Reyna whined, pressing close and wrapping her toothless mouth around one of his fingers. "I'm so hungry."

Melekath's face twisted with revulsion and he jerked his hand away. "We are free now. There is no more need for that." Countless times he had fed them during their millennia in the prison. The Gift made them immortal, but the prison had cut them off from the flows of LifeSong completely. Had he not sustained them with his own energy, they would have fallen still long ago, still aware but unable to die, lost and drifting within themselves.

"But there is no Song here, Father," another whined.

"There will be soon. When we get outside. Be patient."

There were unhappy murmurings at this and they pressed closer around him, trying to feed anyway. Instant scuffles broke out as they punched and scratched each other, jostling for position around him. One of the children, little more than waist high on the others, was knocked down and the others surged over him.

"Enough!" Melekath yelled, knocking them back. "It is time to leave." He forced his way through them to the tunnel leading out. With a new chorus of whimpers and outraged cries they surged after him, fighting to be first, tripping and shoving.

The sun was rising when they reached the surface. The trip through the tunnel had been arduous and painfully slow, but Melekath would not leave the slower ones behind, though the stronger ones hissed in frustration when he held them back.

At its end the tunnel became a crater, the sides steep and loose, far too treacherous for most of the Children to navigate. Melekath was forced to pull down rocks and earth along one side, until he had a rough ramp that the Children could make their way up. Once he could have shaped stairs from raw stone with only the slightest flexing of his will, his connection to the power within the Stone as natural and automatic as breathing. But he was far weaker now. Creating the shield which had protected the city of Durag'otal from the besieging Shapers had torn something inside him. Three thousand years cut off from Stone power – the chaos power which formed the prison was impenetrable to all flows of energy, not just those of Life – had made his weakness exponentially worse.

But they were free now. Everything would be made right again. He and his Children would grow strong and the world would be theirs.

He made his way out onto the sands of the Gur al Krin, where he stopped and turned back, frowning. The Children were still huddled in the depths of the crater, peering up at him fearfully. Melekath gestured impatiently.

"I'm afraid, Father," one said. The others whined their agreement. Nothing he said would dislodge them.

Finally, he went back down into the tunnel and took hold of Reyna's arm, pulling her behind him out into the open. She cringed and squeezed her eyes shut when the sunlight hit her. "The light hurts," she whimpered.

"You're free," he told her fiercely. "At last, what we talked about so many times. You have returned to the world and it is yours."

She peered out from between her fingers. "The sky!" she gasped. "It's…I forgot how big it is." Her words trailed off.

"You will get used to it. You will remember who you are." She nodded uncertainly at his words and as soon as he released her arm she hurried to one of the stones scattered about the crater's mouth and cowered within its shade, pressing tight to the stone.

Melekath muttered and went back down into the crater. They scattered at his approach, but he grabbed two of them and dragged them up into the light. "You are free and this is your world," he told them. "Embrace it. Savor it." But as soon as he let go of them they hurried to hide near Reyna against the boulder. He shook his head and went back for more.

It took several hours to bring them all out. Some had to be brought out more than once, fleeing back into the crater as soon as he walked away. They huddled against the nearby stones, shoving each other and fighting over the meager shade.

Melekath turned his back on them and surveyed the desert. The dunes were empty. Where were the Guardians? Where were the armies of faithful he had told them to raise, the armies that would protect his Children until they grew stronger?

He could sense the Guardians out there, somewhere, could even tell what direction and roughly how far away. One thing he knew for sure: they were not close, nor did they seem to be drawing closer. He frowned. He had made his orders very clear.

He walked to one of the stones and laid both hands on it. The stone would provide a conduit allowing him to communicate with, or at least see, the Guardians. Closing his eyes, he sent the power within him into the stone, reaching for the power that lay within it.

The stone moved under his hands, becoming soft and pliable, like wet clay. He pressed his hands into it past his wrists, concentrating.

Nothing. He could not reach deep enough.

He pulled his hands out of the stone in disgust. Once such a feat would have been simple for him. Yet more evidence of what he had lost during his time in prison.

TWENTY-ONE

Their progress across the Gur al Krin was painfully slow. It was afternoon before Melekath was able to coax all of them out of the shelter of the boulders and into the dunes. They walked with their hands over their heads to shield themselves from the sun, crying and whining piteously at the heat and the brightness. There was no question of leading them up and over any of the dunes; some could barely walk. So they were forced to follow the winding paths between the dunes. The sand was soft and difficult to walk in. At most they traveled for a few minutes before some would fall and refuse to get up or a new squabble would break out, with two or more tearing into each other with savage fury while the others crowded close in excitement or simply joined in.

Conflict had been a part of life in the prison almost from the beginning. The terrible emptiness that all of them experienced once the flow of LifeSong was cut off – compounded by the unending darkness – had driven most of them mad within the first hundred years. As they fell into madness and despair they turned on each other with increasing frequency. Nothing Melekath had ever tried to do to reduce the conflict, from threatening to mediating, had ever worked and he had for the most part given up involving himself in their power struggles long ago, taking instead a policy of watching from a distance and trying to keep the damage from getting too great.

Numerous would-be leaders and factions had risen and fallen over the millennia in prison, but in the last few hundred years Reyna and Heram had gradually become the strongest, each attracting their own followers, constantly battling each other for supremacy. Part of what made them successful was their willingness to work together to take down a challenger, before turning on each other once again.

As the day went by Melekath watched them as they jostled for position, each trying to lead the broken band, but neither strong enough to actually stay in front for long. He knew the blow up was coming, but saw nothing he could do to prevent it.

Finally, near sundown, Reyna simply kicked Heram in the back of the knee, and when he fell, jumped on his back and began pounding on his head with a rock she'd picked up some time earlier.

Heram cursed and twisted under her, trying to get his hands up to fend off her blows. One of his followers lurched forward and tackled Reyna around the shoulders, knocking her sprawling. Two of her followers jumped on him, and in a few moments the lot of them had devolved into a seething, cursing mass.

Melekath simply watched them. He knew they did not have the strength to keep it up for long and sure enough within a couple of minutes combatants began to disengage from the melee, staggering away and falling down. Soon all of them were lying on the sand, panting, cursing weakly, crying. There were no tears. Those had dried up long ago. Melekath's Children were as dry as the desert they wandered in.

When the last of the Children had stopped moving, Melekath spoke. "We will rest here for the night."

Reyna raised her head and her eyes fixed on him. There was something unnerving about her gaze. Her eyes were sunken and dried. Everyone's eyes were the same. Melekath had often wondered just how – and what – they saw, but he'd never asked. He didn't want to know.

"Father, please," she croaked. "Feed me." The others stirred at her words and a few more heads were raised hopefully.

"No."

"Just a little."

"Only be patient," he replied. "Tomorrow. Or the next. We will be out of this desert and there will be Song enough for all of you." He hoped they would be out of the desert by then. The truth was that he had no real idea how big the desert was, but he sensed there was Song waiting in the distance, and they were gradually drawing closer to it.

"I hate that word, 'patient,'" she said. "I hate you."

"Hate," echoed the others. Melekath flinched.

"Tomorrow," he said, and walked away from them. None followed him and he stood alone as the day ended and the sky slowly filled with stars. When it was dark he said, "It will be better soon."

There was no answer.

TWENTY-TWO

It took several days, but finally Melekath rounded a bend in the dunes and saw stark stone ridges and canyons visible in the distance. At last they would be free of the Gur al Krin. He squinted, trying to see through the heat waves. At the edge of the dunes several dozen Crodin nomads waited on their knees. They were clad in loose-flowing, knee-length robes, hoods pulled up to shield them from the sun. They were a mix of people, from the very old to a woman with a baby in her arms. All of them but one had their faces pressed to the ground.

Melekath turned to look behind him. The Children were some distance back – he had moved on ahead to distance himself from their unceasing complaining and conflict – and they could not yet see the nomads. He started to call to them, then changed his mind and walked forward alone.

When he neared the waiting Crodin a collective moan arose from them and they pressed their faces harder into the ground. All except their leader, a squat, barrel-chested man. His shaved head revealed a ragged scar across the top of his skull. His eyes were very dark and he stared unblinking at Melekath.

"Gomen nai," he said. "You have returned."

"As I promised," Melekath replied.

"I am Trakar Kurnash."

"You do not seem awed at my presence."

Kurnash spat to the side before answering. "I do not believe as they do, that you are our god. I do not believe you are worthy of my awe. They believe you have come to redeem us after all this time, to relent in your millennia of torment."

"And you do not believe?"

Kurnash's eyes narrowed. "I *know* what you bring."

His gaze flicked to a spot behind Melekath. Melekath turned, saw that the Children had caught wind of the waiting nomads. Faint, eager cries came from them as they hurried forward. He turned back to find Kurnash staring steadily at him once again.

"I know that you bring only death."

"Then why are you here?" Melekath asked, genuinely curious. "Why do you not run?"

Kurnash gestured to the people kneeling behind him. "They are my people. I am their leader. If they choose to die, I will die with them. What is a leader without his people?"

Melekath turned, saw that the Children were getting close. Back to Kurnash. "The world has changed since I left."

"It has," Kurnash agreed. "But in no way important. We are born. We die." He shrugged. It was a shrug that conveyed defiance and acceptance at the same time.

"My Gift can change that. Bind yourselves to me in loyalty and I will bestow it on you. You and your people need never die."

"It is done, then," Kurnash replied. "For them, I accept. It has been all they could speak of since you broke your prison."

"But not for you?"

Kurnash shook his head. "It is not for me. I want only the years I can claw from this world. Nothing more."

Melekath nodded. "Always the Gift was a choice." He heard the first of the Children behind him and turned around, raising his arms. "Hear me!" he cried. "They have chosen to join you, to become your brothers and sisters. Welcome them."

They ignored him. If anything, their cries became more plaintive.

"Stop!" Melekath yelled.

Still they did not stop. Melekath yelled again, but it made no difference. He grabbed Heram and Reyna as they tried to run by him. Reyna screamed her rage and clawed futilely at him. Heram gibbered and tried to bite him, but his teeth were all gone. The next ones to arrive parted around him and charged at the nomads.

With a roar, Kurnash came to his feet, drawing his heavy sword in the same motion. He struck the first one to reach him – a man who ran with a curious, bent-over gait, as if his spine had broken badly – right at the juncture of neck and torso. Blade met flesh with a sound like chopping wood. The blade bit deep, so that the man's head flopped to the side, but then the blade stuck.

142

Kurnash brought up a moccasined foot and kicked the man in the chest, while trying to wrench his sword free.

With a whining, eager sound, the man grabbed Kurnash's calf, pulled, and managed to bite down on exposed skin just above the moccasin.

Kurnash stiffened, his mouth stretching very wide. But no sound came out, only a curious sort of choking, gagging. His face drained of color and he tried to jerk his foot free but his effort was a feeble one.

Then the man – still making the strange whining sound – got another hand on him and Kurnash collapsed in a heap. The man jumped on him and Kurnash got his hands up, but there was nothing he could do.

Dubron hit the kneeling nomads next. He threw himself on a young woman holding the hand of a small girl. She looked up at the last second, saw Dubron's ruined face and flattened skull, toothless mouth gaping wide, and knew the promise of eternal life was a lie. She twisted, trying to pull the girl with her, but it was too late. He wrapped himself around her in a grim parody of a lover's embrace and bit down on her arm. She screamed and began to spasm. The girl wailed and began to run, but another of the Children fell on her.

Seeing what was happening, Reyna and Heram went berserk, twisting and fighting Melekath's hold. Finally, he just let them go. They darted in amongst the writhing nomads, raging at the other Children, kicking and tearing at them.

Two nomads – a young man and woman – near the back realized what was happening and ran. Reyna howled when she saw them and took off in pursuit. They were faster than she was, and they would have both made it, except that the man looked back over his shoulder and tripped. Before he could rise, Reyna had a hold of his ankle. He kicked her in the face and tried to twist away. She almost lost her grip, then managed to get another hand on his foot. With a lunge she was on him, closing her toothless mouth on his leg. He screamed and redoubled his efforts, but in only a few seconds he had begun to weaken. His struggles grew more and more feeble and then stopped altogether.

In a couple of minutes it was over. Only three of the Crodin had escaped. The rest lay sprawled and twisted on the ground, faces stretched in horror, eyes cloudy in death. They looked withered, desiccated. Limbs had bowed and in some places the skin had split, showing bone and muscle. There was no blood, no fluids of any kind.

The bodies looked as if they had been left for centuries in a dry cave to mummify.

Amongst the bodies the Children crawled, like newborn pups, eyes squeezed tightly shut, clutching their bellies, crying out. Here and there one was still wrapped around a corpse, trying to glean one final drop of Song, but most were already crawling away, seeking shelter, a place to sleep and absorb. The Crodin encampment was nearby, a disorderly grouping of hide tents huddled up against a cliff face, in the bottom of a dry riverbed. Many of the Children went there, crawling into the tents, pulling them down on top of themselves. Further up the dry riverbed was a pile of jumbled boulders that had rolled down from the heights in the distant past and some of the Children crawled amongst the boulders, hiding in crevices and overhangs.

Reyna was one of the last to seek shelter. She stood up, looking for Melekath, shielding her eyes from the afternoon sun. She spotted him and walked closer. Through cracked lips she said just three words: "I'm still hungry." Then she turned away and sought shelter too.

Melekath stared down at the dead Crodin nomads. His shoulders slumped slightly. "It was not supposed to be this way," he said softly.

As the day slowly rolled into night, Melekath walked among the Children and witnessed the changes, lifting boulders or pulling back hide tents to see what was happening. As the stolen Song raced through withered flesh, rejuvenating it, it looked as if insects crawled under their skin. Before his eyes they were filling out.

The expression on his face softened. They were his children, and like children everywhere they were sometimes fractious, sometimes cruel. But they were free now and the future he had promised them would be theirs.

While he was standing on the edge of the Krin, staring into the shifting sands, Melekath's attention was drawn by a small cloud of moths that seemed to come out of nowhere and fluttered madly around him before dispersing. He stopped, pondering this. There was something unusual about them, but he could not put his finger on what it was. Why were there so many, and why here?

TWENTY-THREE

Reyna was the first to rise the next morning. On the side of her face a large patch of gray skin was peeling away. She took hold of it and pulled it off. Underneath, new, pink skin was visible. She ran her hand across her scalp, feeling the short, bristling clumps of red hair that had sprouted. Her bent, useless arm was nearly straight, and when she flexed that hand the fingers opened and closed stiffly. The deep wound in her upper chest had partially closed, and the flesh still visible was reddish.

"How do you feel?" Melekath asked her.

She looked up from her self-examination. She licked her lips. Her tongue was only slightly gray. Her eyes, while still sunken, had a glisten to them and some of the color had returned. "I am still hungry."

"I meant, how do you *feel*? *Do* you feel?" During their time in prison the Children had mostly lost the ability to feel pain. They had complained to him over and over that their bodies were like wood.

"I feel," she replied. She picked at a piece of gray skin that was peeling on her arm, then turned her arm this way and that, looking at it. "Not good, though. It hurts."

"You are still healing. Give it time."

Her lip twisted. One tooth had grown in. "Don't talk to me about time." She turned away. "Don't talk to me."

Heram emerged from the hide tent he had wrapped himself in. His back had straightened and he drew himself upright for the first time in a thousand years. The gash running down the side of his head had closed partway and the skull underneath was only visible in one spot. His twisted leg had straightened too, so that he could nearly walk normally. Like Reyna, pieces of gray skin were peeling off everywhere, showing new skin underneath. The hair on his head and patches of his beard were regrowing as well. He had been a strong,

145

broad-shouldered man, and that strength was beginning to return; his arms and legs were noticeably thicker and he grunted in satisfaction as he looked down at himself.

After him was Dubron. The dent in his skull had filled in somewhat and his left eye no longer dangled from its socket. In the next hour the rest of the Children awakened and pulled themselves into the light. All of them showed signs of healing.

"You should not have killed them," Melekath said when they were gathered about him. He gestured toward the fresh mound of sand in the middle of the dry riverbed. During the night he had dragged the dead nomads there and buried them in a mass grave. "They were faithful all these years. They waited by this desert. They suffered for it."

"They are shatren," Heram said.

"We are hungry," Dubron added. "So, so hungry."

"Next time you will listen to me," Melekath said.

"We have listened to you for a long time," Reyna said, a dark look on her face. "I am tired of it."

"You think what I have to say is meaningless?" Melekath asked. He pointed off into the tangled canyons and towering sandstone cliffs of the Crodin homeland. "Go, then. Make your own way. I will not stop you. What I have offered has always been your choice."

Reyna scowled, but did not reply. None of the Children made a move to leave.

"You are all looking better," Melekath said.

"Better," Dubron grunted. "But not *better*. I want more." He scratched at his face. Pieces of gray skin peeled away and fell to the ground. "More. More."

Around him a number of others began to pick it up and it became a chant.

Moremoremoremore…

Their words whispered off the dunes and rose into the morning sky. A chant. A prayer. A plea. And finally…

A demand.

"Go too fast and you may injure yourselves. You need time to absorb what you have taken, before you take more," Melekath replied. His gray hair blew around his face in a sudden breeze. He pushed it out of his eyes with a weary gesture.

"I don't care," Dubron said. "I want only what they stole from me."

Melekath swung on him, his face darkening. "These did not steal from you. They were faithful. They were *mine*."

"Look at me!" Dubron cried, pointing to his face. "The wall fell on me and crushed my skull!" His good eye gleamed in the light as he stuck his face up close to Melekath's. "I lost everything. They *stole* it from me. Do not speak to me of faith." He turned his back on Melekath and crossed his arms.

Melekath stared at his back. There was nothing to say.

A short while later the broken rabble left the Gur al Krin for good. They followed the dry riverbed along the bottom of a steep-sided canyon that led roughly east.

TWENTY-FOUR

It was early, the morning services only recently completed, and Cara was walking across the estate grounds when she saw Ricarn and reflexively altered her course to intercept her. As unbelievable as it would have seemed just a short time ago, Cara had actually learned to like Ricarn. "Like" wasn't exactly the right word, being something you felt for a friend, and no one would call Ricarn a friend. The Insect Tender was a cold woman, almost alien. But Cara felt comforted being around her. The Insect Tender was a rock in a wild sea.

As Cara altered her course, Ricarn stopped and waited for her. She waited calmly, as if she had all the time in the world. She did not tap her foot or cross her arms. She simply waited, completely still.

"The morning services are making a difference," Ricarn said as Cara drew near.

Cara nodded. "It frightens me," she admitted. "But I can see how badly people need it."

"It comes naturally to you."

Ricarn's words were not meant as a compliment. Cara did not believe Ricarn was capable of such a thing. Ricarn's words were simply a statement of fact. Nevertheless, Cara felt herself blush. Perhaps Ricarn's absolute frankness was what made the statement such a compliment.

The truth was that Cara *was* good at it. She realized the first morning that she could not lead the service as the FirstMother did. The FirstMother was fire and fury, burning righteously against Melekath's evil. The FirstMother spoke of Xochitl casting down her enemies and smiting the wicked.

That first morning, not knowing what else to do, Cara spoke from her heart. She shared her faith with the people of Qarath, telling them about Xochitl and her love for her children. She shared stories from the Book of Xochitl – as the FirstMother did – but she told the stories that showed Xochitl's kindness. She also told stories about Tenders from the past, powerful women who fed the hungry and healed the sick.

As Cara's initial fear faded somewhat – and she was terrified before every service – she realized that she enjoyed talking about her faith. Her words seemed to be helping too. There were more people at every service. They arrived frightened and angry, and when they left their hearts were calmer. There were still big problems in Qarath – Cara wasn't naïve enough to believe she was the cure for everything – but the place no longer had the feel of a pressure cooker about to explode.

"You are aware that the words you give them are infused with Song, are you not?"

Startled out of her thoughts, Cara gave Ricarn a confused look.

"I see you are not."

"My words have Song in them?"

"Indeed. It is what gives them much of their power. It is similar to what the Musicians do. The power in your words can change hearts."

"I had no idea…"

"Why?"

"Well, I knew that the Tenders of old infused their words with Song, but I just never dreamed I'd be capable of doing the same thing."

"That is because you still believe that when it comes to Song, some people are special, blessed with more power than others."

"That's not true?"

"Have you not been listening to me?" The words were uttered mildly, but the rebuke stung anyway. "All people, all living things, have the same connection to Song. By virtue of this connection, all have the same capabilities. The only difference is that most are convinced they are incapable."

Cara nodded. She'd heard Ricarn say that a number of times, but she still found it hard to believe. She was just plain old Cara. She'd never believed she was anything else. "I just don't understand how it is that I'm doing that, putting Song into my words. I never meant to."

"You have been practicing the lessons I gave you."

"Yes." They were strange lessons and to Cara it didn't feel like she was actually learning anything or even doing anything. A lot of them seemed to be just sitting and listening, trying to keep her mind as empty of thoughts as she could. Still, she practiced them faithfully.

"The lessons are opening you to Song. You're learning to let go of the barriers you have erected between yourself and the power that flows through all life. As those barriers fall, Song will flow naturally into more and more of your daily life."

One of the other Insect Tenders came up then, surprising Cara. She hadn't seen the woman approaching, which was odd because she and Ricarn were standing in the middle of a large, open lawn, and the other Tender was wearing a bright yellow robe.

Cara remembered Ricarn calling her Yelvin. It seemed she called both of her followers Yelvin, which Cara found confusing. They both looked the same, with flowing black hair and strangely white skin, which made it even more confusing. She'd spoken to one of them once, but the woman did not reply, only gave her an odd look.

"We have found Lenda," Yelvin said.

Cara's interest was piqued. She had heard about Lenda, the young, simple-minded Tender whose journey to receive her *sulbit* had gone terribly wrong. Lenda went crazy and ran off afterwards. Two of the other Tenders tracked her down near the Pits, but she escaped, nearly killing them in the process. Apparently she had emerged from her trip to the River with two *sulbits* instead of one.

"She is unaware of you?" Ricarn said.

Yelvin went still for a moment, her eyes losing their focus. Then she nodded.

"We will bring her in tonight. Collect what we need and wait for my call."

Yelvin walked away, but not toward the front gate. Instead she walked to the back of the property. Cara was watching, and as the woman reached the edge of the trees, Cara could have sworn that the color of her cloak ran, as if she walked through a hard rain and the color just leached away like a poor dye job. A moment later Cara could no longer see her.

Cara turned back to see Ricarn staring at her. The Insect Tender's eyes were expressionless, but not cold as Cara had thought when she first met her. Despite the lack of expression on Ricarn's face, Cara knew that Ricarn knew she had a question and the Insect Tender was giving Cara tacit approval to ask it.

"The city is in an uproar," Cara said. "The world is falling apart. Yet still you spend this effort to find and bring in a woman you do not even know." Out of nervous habit Cara reached to pull on her braid, remembered it was no longer there and pulled her hand back. "I don't understand."

"It is I who do not understand," Ricarn replied, though she certainly didn't look confused.

"Why? Why just one when so many are in danger?"

"They are the same," Ricarn replied.

"What?"

"There is no difference between the one and the many."

Cara stared at her, feeling like the slow child who couldn't understand a basic lesson. She wanted to act like she understood and just leave the question be, but she knew Ricarn would see right through her. "I still don't get it," she finally admitted.

"You are too focused on the forms. Learn to look past them."

"Okay," Cara said, still lost.

"You are right. One does not matter." Cara had the feeling that Ricarn was enjoying this. "Neither do the many matter. We can do whichever we want. Or we can do nothing. It doesn't matter." Cara just gaped at her. "It is something we learned from our insect friends," Ricarn added. "It is a lesson that brings great freedom. I do not expect you to understand it. Not yet."

Abruptly Ricarn turned away and looked south.

"What is it?" Cara asked.

"I believe it is finally happening." She went utterly still. Cara had a feeling that if the wind started blowing right then, that nothing on Ricarn would move, not her hair, not her clothing. Her stillness was perfect.

Time passed and the sun rose higher. Cara was thinking that maybe she should leave Ricarn alone when the Insect Tender broke her stillness.

"Come with me." She turned and headed for the estate house. She did not appear to be hurrying, but Cara found that she had to hurry to keep up.

Ricarn led her to the balcony that encircled the upper floor of the estate house and again faced south. After standing there for a few more minutes, wondering what was going on, Cara finally asked. To her surprise, Ricarn turned to her, focusing her attention on Cara, as if completely dismissing whatever had enraptured her just moments before.

"I believe Melekath and his Children are about to emerge from the desert."

"How do you know that?"

"A short while ago a band of Crodin nomads walked into the Gur al Krin. Now I am waiting to see if I am correct."

"How does some Crodin walking into the desert mean Melekath is coming out? And how do you know all this anyway?"

"One question at a time. The Crodin nomads *never* go into the Gur al Krin, though they often pray at its edge. Their god, Gomen nai, dwells in that desert and they both hate and fear him. Yet a short while ago a band of them entered the desert. From that I conclude that Melekath is close to leaving the desert."

"Gomen nai and Melekath are the same god?"

Ricarn nodded slightly. "They tarried when their god called and they arrived too late. The Banishment had already happened. Their god and his faithful followers had already been sealed deep underground. So they settled nearby and founded the city of Kaetria, which became the capital of the Empire. After the Empire fell, those who had secretly remained devoted to Melekath remained, living on the fringes of the ever-growing desert, always fearing their god's wrath when he should return and judge them."

"Those poor people," Cara said.

"Now a band of them have gone into the Krin. Why else but to greet their god?"

"But that's hundreds of miles away," Cara protested. "How do you know all this?"

Ricarn smiled slightly. "The flies told me."

"What?"

"The flies. The gnats too, but their awareness is so tiny that even in the thousands any information I get from them is next to useless. Other insects too. The stink beetles that feed on dung. The centipedes, the scorpions, the spiders."

"They *tell* you things?"

"Not really. It is more a matter of tuning my awareness to theirs and then perceiving what they perceive. Mind you, the awareness of something as primitive as a fly or a gnat is so limited that I must draw hundreds or thousands of them together and read them as one. In the days since Melekath's escape I have built up a network, a web if you will, that stretches across the northern face of the Krin. Since then I have been waiting for the web to twitch so I would know where to focus my attention." She stared at Cara as if waiting for her to ask a question. When Cara said nothing, she continued.

"I have spent most of my energy on the flies. Their numbers are great and they are very focused on what any humans in their area are doing. Living near people as they have for so long has conditioned them so that there is some sense among them of what constitutes normal and abnormal behavior amongst humans. So when the entire Crodin band entered the Krin a short while ago, the flies felt it. Rather, it registered in their primitive awareness as an unusual event. That twitch in their awareness was the tug on my web I have been waiting for."

"Can you see what he is doing now?"

Ricarn shook her head. "Even flies will not enter that place. But I believe he will emerge soon and I will be waiting."

"The flies will tell you when he comes out?"

"They will. Or some other insects will."

"I don't...it's all hard to believe."

"I know," Ricarn replied. "You think of the distances involved and you wonder how. You doubt it is possible. It is too far, you think." She waited, staring at Cara in that direct, unblinking way she had. "You do not realize that distance is meaningless."

"No. I don't. It seems..." Cara spread her hands helplessly. "I feel like it should make sense, but I can't get it. I'm sorry. I feel stupid."

Ricarn frowned slightly. "Not stupid. Just normal. Life is all part of the same web. The actions of each creature reverberate down that web, regardless of distance. I just know how to feel those reverberations, mostly because I was not raised to believe in limits like you were. But I think you will. I think – "

She broke off and turned south again.

Cara waited for several long minutes while Ricarn stared into the distance. Then, out of nowhere, Ricarn staggered and Cara reached out to steady her. Her skin was very cool. Ricarn straightened and rubbed her temple.

"They hunger," she said.

"Who does?" Cara asked, and then felt dumb for the question. Who else would she be talking about?

"The ones from the prison. Melekath's Children. They're people, you know. Just people. Or at least they were once." She looked around her as if she had forgotten where she was. "Three thousand years was not so long for him. No more than a single breath when you have lived as long as he has. But it is a very long time for the rest of us."

"Wait. You're saying that the same people who were imprisoned with Melekath are still *alive*?"

"You thought perhaps they had children while trapped in there? That they lived normal lives and now it is their descendants who emerge?"

"I never really thought about it."

"You do not know what the Gift was, do you?"

"The Book is not very clear on it," Cara admitted. The Book of Xochitl said only that Melekath gave his Children a forbidden Gift and for that he and they were banished. It never said what the Gift was.

"No wonder you are all so lost," Ricarn murmured. "They hid so much from you. The Gift is immortality."

The words hit Cara like a stone. She actually fell back a step. "Melekath gave them *immortality*?" she said weakly.

Ricarn simply stared at her, waiting.

"That was Melekath's crime? Giving his followers immortality?"

"It was."

"But why? What's so bad about that? To never die. To live forever and never grow old. That seems like a good thing."

"The Shapers, those beings you call gods, are jealous of their immortality. It is not something they like to share."

"But how does it hurt them?"

"You do not know the stories of the beginning. Life is made by taking from the Spheres of Stone, Sea and Sky. Life *takes* from them. They allowed it only because Life dies, and what it has taken is returned to the Spheres."

A light went on for Cara. "Life that does not die will never give back."

Ricarn nodded. "For this they were imprisoned. Just now I saw them. I saw what they have become." For the first time she sounded shaken. She visibly gathered herself. "They hunger. It is a vast, insatiable hunger. All the Song in the entire Circle of Life will not be enough for them. They will consume it all and still wish for more. Word needs to be sent to Thrikyl."

"Why Thrikyl?"

Ricarn didn't answer at first. She seemed to be studying a cricket that was moving along the balcony railing. It hopped onto her hand and she lifted it up.

"They should evacuate the city. The Children are going there next. They will drain every human being in the city." The cricket began to chirp. "They won't listen, of course. But it would still do to tell them."

"I will talk to Velma. She can talk to Castellan Naills."

"They hate us," Ricarn said. "They hate us for having what was taken from them, for being free while they were imprisoned. Right now their hunger is stronger than their hate. In time they will remember their hatred."

TWENTY-FIVE

Velma was going to the palace once again, this time to see Naills. Except that this time she was riding in a carriage with four guards and a driver. She'd tried to go on foot, like the last time, but there was a new guy in charge of the guards at the gate of the Tender estate – she thought his name was Ralp or something like that – and he had insisted that the leading Tender in Qarath should not show up on foot like some peasant. She'd tried to tell him that he didn't need to worry, she was just temporarily doing this until the real FirstMother returned, but he'd ignored her and so she had no choice but to give in.

Riding in the carriage made her feel obvious, exposed. On foot people tended not to notice her. That was impossible in the carriage. Even though no one made any effort to impede their progress, she kept feeling like someone was going to run up and stop the carriage. Demand she get out and just who did she think she was riding around all high and mighty anyway? She sat lower in her seat, trying to be invisible. How long until the FirstMother returned? She wasn't made for stuff like this. She just wanted to do what she was told and go to bed at a reasonable time. Being in charge was too confusing.

On the way she tried to remember what she knew about Castellan Naills. It wasn't much. Once she went to the palace with the FirstMother to meet with Macht Rome and Quyloc. It was when the army was getting ready to march to Guardians Watch. Naills was at the meeting too. He stood by the wall and nodded whenever Velma looked at him, as if reassuring her about something, though she couldn't imagine what.

They got to the palace gates and Velma was wondering if she ought to stick her head out the door and tell the guards who she was and why she was there when Ralp boomed out: "Acting FirstMother to see Castellan Naills. Let us pass."

Velma shrank further into her seat. *Acting FirstMother* indeed. Why did he say that? If Nalene caught wind of people using that title she'd blister Velma's ears. Why couldn't the man at least have said it quietly?

Surprisingly, the guards at the gate waved the carriage through without delay and just like that Velma was coming up on the palace itself. The carriage stopped. Ralp opened the door and Velma, taking a deep breath, got out. She stumbled a little bit and Ralp caught her arm. She felt her cheeks burn and timidly looked up to find them all staring at her. The palace guards. Her guards. The stable boy holding the horses' reins. Velma froze. She wasn't sure she was even breathing. Sweat was trickling down her back. She opened her mouth, but nothing came out.

Two soldiers in black and white livery with a wolf's head sewn to their breasts stood at the top of the steps before the huge, double doors and some kind of page or servant was hurrying down the steps to her. He wore black and white livery with the wolf's head on it also. His hair and beard were trimmed very short and neat and oiled down. He was a short man, but his posture was ramrod straight and he carried himself like a general.

"Chief Steward Opus at your service, Acting FirstMother," he said, bowing.

Velma cringed. There was that title again. "I really don't think that's necessary," she said weakly.

"Of course it is, Acting FirstMother," he replied. "At this time, you are the ranking Tender in Qarath. Now, I understand you are here to see Castellan Naills?"

"Yes," she managed to gasp out.

"Allow me to escort you," he said smoothly. He motioned up the steps and, when she didn't move, he took her arm and began to guide her. The guards and the stable boy were still gawking at Velma but Opus gave them a look and all of them suddenly realized they either had something else to do or somewhere else to look.

"Thank you," Velma managed, as they passed through the open double doors into the palace.

"You do me too much honor, Acting FirstMother," he replied, ducking his head. "It is only my job."

Velma squeezed his arm and tried not to trip over her feet. The entrance hall was very large and she was very small. "Is he busy, do you think? Castellan Naills, I mean."

"Not too busy to meet with the Acting FirstMother," he said.

Opus led her through seemingly endless halls and up a broad set of curving stairs. Velma grew uncomfortable with the silence and finally said, "How did you know who I was? I mean, I've only been here a couple of times and I never met you before and, well, not a lot of people know the FirstMother left me in charge while she's gone." Her words trailed off. She suddenly wished she could have them back.

"It is my job to know," he replied. She thought she saw a slight smile tugging at the corner of his mouth. "More than my job, really. It is my life." He led her to a tall, ornate door, a waiting servant swung it open, and then he bowed her through, saying, "Acting FirstMother Velma to see you, Castellan Naills."

Velma hesitated. The castellan was standing on the other side of a large room, looking at something on a table. He hadn't looked up. She looked questioningly at Opus. He gestured her forward and after she had passed through the door he backed out of the room, pulling the door shut behind him.

The castellan turned and looked at her then. He was somewhat short, with a barrel chest, an ample stomach, a bald head and a red beard shot through with gray. His face was lined by the years but when he walked toward her Velma could see that he was a long way from being feeble. He moved like a soldier, powerful, but quiet about it.

"What brings you here, Acting FirstMother?" He took her hand and bowed his head. His hands were large and heavily calloused.

"A rider must be sent to Thrikyl at once," she said, and then felt surprised at herself for speaking so confidently. She was reasonably sure she hadn't even stuttered. But there was something about Naills that put her at ease. He was not a man who cared for superficial forms.

"Please, sit," he said, pulling a chair out from the table. The table was covered with a large map of the city and a plate of half-eaten food.

"They have to evacuate the city," she said, taking the chair.

Naills sat down in another chair and digested this information for a moment before replying. "Can I ask why?" he said at last.

Velma sighed and leaned on the table, suddenly very tired. "It's Melekath. He and his Children are heading for the city."

"They are?" Naills said, his bushy eyebrows rising. "How do you know?"

"Cara told me," Velma said simply. Naills gave her a blank look and she added, "She's a Tender. Well, maybe not anymore. She didn't take a *sulbit*." She touched her *sulbit* under her sleeve. It was quiet today. "But she has been leading the morning services and she's really good."

Naills frowned. "How does she know?"

"She said Ricarn, the Insect Tender, told her." Velma looked down at her feet, wishing she'd found a better way to say it.

"The woman in the red robe?"

Velma nodded.

"How does she know?"

Velma shrugged. She should have practiced what she was going to say. He was never going to believe her. Cara should have found someone else to deliver the message. "Something about some flies," she said in a tiny voice.

"That's all? You want me to order the evacuation of a whole city because of some flies?"

Velma thought about this for a moment. "No. I want you to evacuate the city because Ricarn said so."

"Oh." That quieted him.

"Do you want to talk to her? She could probably explain it all better than I can."

Naills stood and walked over to a small table against the wall. A pitcher of water and a large basin sat on it. He scooped out a handful of water and splashed it on his face, before turning back to face Velma. "I met her once," he said. "She came up to the palace with the FirstMother. That was enough for me. If she says the city needs to be evacuated, then it needs to be evacuated. I will send a rider immediately."

"She scares me too," Velma said. "I can't even talk when she's around."

Naills frowned, his bushy eyebrows drawing together. "I didn't say she scares me."

"Oh." Why didn't she think before she spoke?

Naills resumed his seat then leaned close. "I didn't say she *doesn't* scare me either."

Velma blinked. She really wasn't good at this sort of thing. "Do you think they will? Evacuate the city, I mean. They don't know Ricarn."

"No. They believe in their wall." The Thrikylians had rebuilt the section of wall Rome had brought down with his axe. "But it won't stop Melekath, will it?"

Velma shook her head. "I don't think so. Next to Xochitl, he's the most powerful of the old gods."

Naills' expression grew grim. "Then the gods help those poor bastards," he said.

TWENTY-SIX

A woman crouched on a tiled rooftop overlooking a square. It was a market square, one of dozens scattered around the city, crowded with merchants and shoppers during the day, but deserted this late at night. The woman was filthy and dressed in the tatters of what had once been a white robe. She was emaciated, the bones in her face standing out in sharp relief. Her blonde hair was very short and patchy, like a moth-eaten doll. Her eyes were vacant.

There were things perched on her shoulders. They were hard to see, as if the moonlight couldn't quite get purchase on them, instead slipping off and getting lost in the shadows. They had long, multi-segmented legs, and too many of them. The bodies on top of those legs were smooth, wax-like, with beaked heads and sharp, black eyes. From the body of each trailed a tendril, though those tendrils would only have been visible to one who was in the heightened awareness of *beyond*, where Song and power become visible. The tendrils extended through her *akirma* and pierced her Heartglow.

On the far side of the square, from the mouth of a darkened street, two women emerged, the sounds of their steps echoing off the cobblestones. They wore nondescript gray cloaks with the hoods pulled over their heads. They were close together and hurrying, two women caught out too late and trying to get home without being noticed.

The beaked heads turned in the direction of the two women, the black eyes glittering. The tendrils contracted and the woman came to her feet, swaying slightly as if drunk. She turned and began making her way toward the street the women were heading for, her steps wooden and slow, her head down. The things on her shoulders shifted eagerly, hissing softly to each other, beaked mouths opening and closing. The woman's foot struck a loose tile which slid across the roof noisily, but the two women down below did not seem to notice, intent only on crossing the square and getting home quickly.

161

The woman on the rooftop reached the corner overlooking the side street and knelt, staring vacantly at the ground below her. The things on her shoulders focused on the two cloaked women as they drew closer, readying themselves for the leap.

Neither noticed another woman, dressed in a red robe, behind them on the rooftops, hidden in the shadow of a chimney. She stepped out of the shadow and hurried forward.

When the cloaked women were directly below, the creatures leapt off their perch toward their unsuspecting victims.

At which point several things happened at once.

The cloaked women ducked and rolled away, just avoiding the attacks by the beaked things. As the women moved, their cloaks swirled around them and changed colors, from gray to blinding yellow.

The red-robed woman reached the kneeling woman. Grabbing her shoulder with one hand, she brought the blade of the other hand down at her back in a slashing motion. As she did, power blazed along the length of her arm and all at once it was encased in what appeared to be a chitinous shell, sharp along the leading edge.

The cloaked women came out of their rolls and back onto their feet. The beaked creatures hit the ground hard and staggered, momentarily stunned.

The red-robed woman struck the tendrils connecting the beaked things to the kneeling woman, slicing cleanly through them. The beaked things screamed in pain.

Before they could recover, the two cloaked women leapt forward, each stabbing down at the things with an index finger that suddenly looked like a barbed stinger. The stingers bit deep, the beaked things twitched once, then toppled over and went still.

Just like that it was over. Ricarn stood on the rooftop, holding onto Lenda, who was unconscious. The other two Insect Tenders stood over the unmoving forms of Lenda's two *sulbits*.

"Their paralysis will not last long," Ricarn said. "Take them to the crack from where they came and throw them in. Maybe they will return to the River and remember what they are."

The two Insect Tenders nodded and each picked up a *sulbit*. Within moments they were gone.

Ricarn picked up Lenda, laying her over one shoulder. "Time to go home," she said. She climbed down the wall and it seemed wherever her free hand or a foot contacted the wall it changed, becoming momentarily something clawed and insect-like. Then she was down and carrying Lenda to the Tender estate.

TWENTY-SEVEN

Melekath and his Children had left the Gur al Krin behind only hours before. They were following the bottom of a canyon that twisted and turned but led roughly east. Melekath sensed a city in that direction, though still days away. He could think of no city in that direction and guessed that it must be a new one, built since he had been imprisoned. Qarath was to the north and the east and that was where he would have liked to go, but he did not know what enemies he might find there – Lowellin at least could be counted on to be actively working against him – and he wanted to wait until the Children were stronger before challenging them.

Again and again that first day he placed his hands on cliff faces and sent out the call to the Guardians. It troubled him that they had not been waiting in the Krin when he finally broke the prison. Where were the armies he had tasked them with raising, the armies that would protect his Children until they had healed? Their absence could only mean that they had been defeated.

He badly needed information. The prison had almost completely cut him off from the outside world. He'd been able to send out the call that lured in the one he had tricked into breaking Sententu's hold on the prison, but he hadn't even known if anyone was heeding his call until she actually entered the Gur al Krin. The fact that one solitary woman had been strong enough to break Sententu made him nervous. He had been gone for a millennium; he could only imagine how much Xochitl and Lowellin had taught people about controlling Song in that time. An army of them might appear over the horizon at any moment and crush his Children before they even had a chance.

Again and again he cursed his weakness. His time in the prison, cut off from Stone power, the personal cost of raising the shield around Durag'otal during the siege, feeding his Children for all those years, had all conspired to make him a shell of himself. He could feel Stone power all around him. When he laid his hands on stone,

164

especially large cliff faces or other unbroken expanses of rock, he could feel it thrumming slowly and powerfully within. But he was only able to draw small quantities at a time and it was difficult lifting it free, as if he drew a heavy weight from the bottom of a well.

Though the Children were in much better shape since feeding on the Crodin, the going was still painfully slow. Partly it was because of the difficulty of the terrain. Tangled piles of boulders choked the bottom of the canyon periodically, forcing Melekath to have to physically carry some of the weaker and more broken Children through the worst spots. Further slowing them down was the constant conflict between the Children. They quarreled over imagined slights at seemingly every opportunity and often the quarrels turned violent. They took up dead limbs and used them as clubs. Rocks were used to beat others over the head. Limbs that had only recently knit were rebroken and one man had his eye torn out in a melee.

Most of the conflicts were over Song. Now that they were out of the Krin there was life, and Song, around them once again. The problem was that there was so little of it. The animals, sensing what was coming, fled from the Children before they even got close. The plants weren't so lucky. Though the amount of Song they contained was miniscule compared to animals and especially humans, they were still better than nothing. The Children swarmed the rare trees they found growing in the canyon, draining them until they turned gray and split open. They tore into the tough grasses and hardy shrubs also. When they came upon the first clump of cactus growing in the canyon several of the Children surged toward it. In their haste they ignored Melekath's shouted warnings and their initial cries of joy quickly turned to cries of pain as they got faces, arms and hands filled with cactus spines.

"As you heal, feeling returns," Melekath told them as he pulled the worst of the thorns from them. "You can feel pain again. You need to be careful."

But they paid him no heed and within a few minutes there were more coming to him for help with cactus thorns stuck all over them.

Distracted as he was by mitigating fights, comforting Children who were hurt, and trying to contact the Guardians, it wasn't until afternoon that Melekath noticed something troubling.

He was standing at the bottom of a deadfall, lifting the weakest Children over it one by one, when he finally looked closely at the one he was helping and realized that there was no flow of LifeSong attached to her. The flows sustaining the Children had been severed when the prison was created, but he had assumed that once they were back in the normal world, new flows would attach to the Children. Frowning, he looked around. None of the Children were connected. He let his perception sink deeper, where the flows were more clearly visible and what he *saw* troubled him even more. Not only did none of the flows attach to the Children, but they actually *moved away* from them whenever the Children drew close.

What did this mean? He lifted another one over the dead fall, thinking. Still blind to Song, none of the Children had yet noticed this. He decided to say nothing for now. It would be best to avoid upsetting them until he could figure out why it was happening and how to fix it.

The Song the Children had bled from the Crodin faded over the next couple of days and as it did, their cries grew louder, more insistent.

"Father!" they cried. "Feed us! Feed us!"

Melekath did what he could. He reached out with his will and snared what animals and birds he could, dragging them struggling back to his Children. But their numbers were few and the meager quantities of Song he could scavenge for his Children were never enough.

More and more the Children turned to cannibalism, the stronger stealing Song from the weaker, until Melekath noticed and made them stop. They did, but only until his attention was diverted. Then they resumed in secret. Two would join together and gang up on a third, then turn on each other when that one had no more they could take. Melekath was forced to ride herd on them constantly and his temper grew short.

"Where are they, Father? You promised us more. You promised us the hunger would go away," Reyna said. The patches of new skin on her face were losing color, fading to white. Her lips were cracked and dried. The hair that had begun to regrow had fallen out and there was a split in the skin of her scalp that showed bone underneath. There was blood on her face from an antelope Melekath had brought in for them. Behind her a half dozen of the Children fought over the bloody scraps, though there was nothing left there for them.

Melekath thought of the flows of Song, bending away from the Children whenever they approached, and said nothing.

Reyna interpreted his silence for what it was and her disfigured face twisted in a snarl. "This promise is of no more use than all the others, is it?"

Melekath started to turn away, but she grabbed his arm with surprising strength. "Don't turn away from me! Look at me. Look at what your broken promises have wrought."

Melekath stared at her, not knowing what to say. With a disgusted noise she pushed away from him and walked away.

That morning they had passed out of the canyon and climbed onto a small plateau sliced by short, steep ridges and deep, powdery sand. Sagebrush covered much of the land, broken here and there by juniper trees and clumps of cholla cactus.

Heram took hold of a small juniper tree, draining it of Song. He growled at one who came too close to him, what looked to have once been a woman, though so bent and torn that it was impossible to tell for sure. She ignored his warning and reached for the tree. Heram struck her a hammer blow on the side of the head and she went sprawling with a cry.

In a heartbeat, two others – one who could barely stand upright, the other with a ruined face – fell on her, toothless mouths closing on her arms as they sought to suck what they could from her. She cried out, a high, hopeless sound.

With a sigh, Melekath started over to break it up, when all at once he sensed something and drew up. Dubron noticed the change and called out, "What is it, Father? Is it Song?"

"Wait," he replied, trying to focus. Something in his tone got through to those within earshot. They stopped what they were doing – even the three who were fighting – and turned toward him expectantly. Melekath turned to the east, casting out with his inner senses. Then he looked on them and smiled.

"There is a town ahead," he said, raising his voice so all could hear. "Only a few hours."

Reyna, Heram, Dubron and some of the stronger ones began to run, ignoring Melekath's shouted order. Angrily he summoned forth some of the precious Stone power he had painstakingly gathered. Lances of dark energy shot out from his hands, each one striking one of the fleeing Children and taking hold. Grimly, he dragged them back. "We will go together," he told them when they were at his feet. "All will share."

The others ceased their struggles then and he let them go, but Dubron continued to fight, clawing and biting at the power. Melekath picked him up and shook him until Dubron looked at him.

"Enough."

Dubron glared at him a moment longer, then lowered his head and went still.

"We will wait until darkness," he told them, dropping Dubron on the ground. The slower ones were catching up now, some still dragging themselves over the ground, their legs useless and dead. "That way all of them will be there. We will surround the town so they cannot escape. Then, at last, each will have enough." *Then this madness will end*, he told himself.

TWENTY-EIGHT

It was dark when they approached Ferien. The small plateau they had spent the day crossing sloped upwards at its eastern end, sagebrush and juniper giving way to hardy pines, yellowed grasses and tall, spiky agave. The town of Ferien sat in a corner formed by two low hills that came together at an angle. A shallow stream flowed sluggishly down from between the two hills and wound around the town before sinking into the ground. Irrigation canals led from the stream to fields of wheat and corn. There was a stone wall around Ferien, twice as tall as a man, a testament to Ferien's proximity to Crodin lands.

When the Children saw the walls they surged forward and it was all Melekath could do to restrain them once again. "Listen to me!" he snapped, shaking several of the more stubborn ones until they settled down and turned their misshapen faces toward him. "If you charge in wildly, you will lose most of them. These are not Crodin, who will lie down for you to feed. They will run and you will not catch them."

"Catch them for us, Father!" they cried.

He thought about this, and an idea came to him. "Wait here. I will make it so they cannot leave."

But as soon as he turned away, two ran forward once again, unable to resist the maddening hunger that drove them. Melekath snatched them before they could get by him, then looked back at the others.

"I will hold them," Heram said. "Make sure they stay put." He stumped forward and wrapped his thick hands around their necks. He squeezed and they yelped.

"Don't hurt them," Melekath said.

Instead of replying, Heram shrugged.

Melekath approached the town carefully, staying to the shadows to avoid being seen. He sensed a sentry on the other side of the gate, but he seemed to be asleep. Once at the wall, he hesitated, uncertain if he had regained sufficient strength to do this. He laid his hands on the wall, summoned his reserves of power, then pushed. His hands sank into the stone. Now he could feel the low, deep hum of Stone force, waiting, coiled within the stones of the wall. Since the stones had been cut from the earth, cut from their source, there was not as much power as there would have been if they were raw, but there was still sufficient for his needs. Drawing forth the Stone force was like drawing water from the bottom of a deep well – it kept slipping from his grasp – but at last it pulsed within his hands.

He began to circle the town, dragging the power with him, awakening more as he went, a chain that stretched out behind him. He pulled the power to the surface and spilled it across the face of the wall. When he had completed his circuit of the town he stopped. To his heightened sight the Stone force appeared as liquid silver splashed unevenly across the wall. He scratched the wall, releasing a tiny amount of his personal power as he did so.

There was an almost inaudible *whoosh* and a colorless flame leapt up under his hands. He spread his arms and the flame quickly spread to engulf the entire wall.

Melekath turned to his Children to wave them forward, but their meager self-control had already broken and they were surging forward with eager cries. Melekath took hold of the top iron band that bound the thick wooden gates – the iron, being of the Stone, had colorless flames dancing along its surface as well – and pulled. The iron peeled away easily and he tossed it aside, then bent and did the same with the lower band. After that it was a simple matter to pull the gates down.

On the other side of the gates was a small lean-to, and a guard, sitting on a stool, asleep. He came to his feet as the gate fell. His helmet clattered to the ground and he nearly dropped his spear as he struggled to make sense of what he saw coming. Then he turned and ran, bellowing the alarm as he went.

The folk of Ferien had dealt with raiders many times before and they were quick to respond. They came running out of their homes, men and women alike brandishing a variety of weapons, swords, pitchforks, hammers and pikes. They formed up in a line blocking the main street into the heart of the town and held up torches to see what danger they faced.

What they saw had not occurred to them in their worst nightmares.

Scores of gray-skinned, misshapen figures surged towards them. A few ran upright. The rest staggered, limped or even crawled. Every face was lit by savage, unreasoning need. Their mouths were stretched wide and whining, hungry noises came from them.

A few of the people broke and ran at the sight, but the town of Ferien had not survived this long in hostile territory without grit, and most held, closing up the gaps in the line to cover for those who ran, weapons held up defiantly.

It made no difference.

Heram hit them first. A tall, bearded man with a spear held the middle of the line. As Heram ran forward the man plunged the spear into his chest. The spear passed all the way through Heram and such was the strength of the man's thrust that Heram was knocked backwards and went down onto his side.

But Heram quickly recovered. He snarled and forced his way upright. The bearded man was still holding onto the spear and his eyes bulged as Heram gripped the shaft of the spear and pulled himself forward, the weapon sliding through his body. As Heram drew near and the bearded man saw what he faced more clearly, his nerve broke. He let go of the spear and turned to run, but one of Heram's thick hands closed on his arm. The bearded man whirled, a long knife appearing in his hand. He stabbed Heram in the neck, pulled the weapon free, and stabbed him in the side of the face. The blade went through Heram's cheek, tore through and out his mouth.

Heram jerked the man closer, wrapping him in a bear hug and biting down on his shoulder. The man screamed. He stabbed wildly at the monstrous thing which attacked him, tearing through flesh and tendons to no effect. One of the blows bit deep into Heram's skull and the knife became lodged there.

All at once the bearded man slumped forward. A stricken look came into his eyes and his mouth worked but no sound came out. He let go of the knife hilt and struck Heram on the side of the face with his fist, but his strength had gone. His legs folded and he went down in a heap, Heram landing on top of him. The light faded from his eyes. He spasmed once, then went still.

Reyna was only steps behind Heram. The man she attacked had not stopped to put on a shirt, his feet were bare and his leather breeches were untied. His big belly swung with his movements. But there was no panic in his eyes. He stood with his feet braced wide and when she closed with him he swung his heavy-bladed sword with both hands. The blade missed one outstretched arm and bit deep into her side. Reyna was knocked sideways by the force of the blow and staggered, screaming with pain and anger. He wrenched the sword free and hit her again, cutting deep into her shoulder. Reyna fell and he stepped forward, bringing the sword around in an arc that would have severed her head from her shoulders if it had landed.

But at that moment one of his fellow defenders, fleeing in a panic, barreled into him, knocking him off balance and causing the blow to miss. As he fought to get upright, Reyna crabbed forward on her hands and knees and threw both her arms around one of his legs. He was able to land one solid blow on her back – there was a dry wood sound of cracking ribs and a bloodless gash appeared over her ribcage – then Reyna got her mouth on his leg and began to drink.

The man stiffened, his eyes growing very wide. He tried to raise the blade and watched in disbelief as it fell from his nerveless fingers. Then he folded over and went down.

Along the line two more of the defenders went down, Children wrapped around them. And that was when the rest broke. They threw down their weapons and ran blindly. Only a few of the Children were quick enough to catch their prey before it got away and of those who did, most were too weak to hold onto it. The mass of defenders fled and the Children lurched and crawled brokenly after them, crying and wailing piteously.

A tall man wearing a long robe made it to his home, a stone, two-story building with a stout wooden door and heavy shutters over the windows. With the haft of the axe he carried he banged on the door, yelling for his wife to open it, casting frightened looks over his shoulder as he waited. Two of the Children closed on him, but just before they got there the door swung open. The man lunged through, then slammed and barred the door behind him.

The two Children were Karrl and Linde, a married couple who had been among the first to follow Melekath and accept the Gift. Karrl's face was a ruined mess, one eye gone in a huge gash that had torn most of his cheek away. One leg had broken badly hundreds of years ago. The Song he had bled from the Crodin had allowed his leg to knit, but it did so at an awkward angle so that he lurched when he walked. His wife was in worse shape. One arm had been completely torn off in one of the worst of the riots that had swept through Durag'otal like recurring plagues. A long gash received during the same riot had allowed some of her entrails to spill out. Karrl had put them back and roughly stitched the wound closed, but of course it had never healed.

Another one of the Children stumbled up to the house, reaching for the door, but Linde turned on him, hissing, and Karrl picked up a stone from the ground and raised it threateningly, so that the latecomer backed off and went to find other prey.

Karrl banged on the door with the stone while Linde clawed at it with her remaining hand. But the door was stout and they did not have the strength needed to break it down.

Melekath had entered the town after the last of his Children and stood watching the melee, his expression somber. Karrl saw him standing there and began to shout for help. At first Melekath did not respond and Linde added her voice to her husband's. Then he made up his mind and walked toward them, skirting Reyna and Heram sprawled on the ground on top of their victims.

"Hurry!" Linde whined. "I'm so hungry."

Melekath struck the door with the flat of his hand, releasing a small amount of Stone force as he did so, and it exploded inwards. Both Karrl and Linde tried to run in at the same time and they ran into each other. Instantly they fell to blows, hitting and scratching each other while screaming incoherently. Melekath yanked them apart and shook them fiercely until he had their attention.

"Stop it!" he snapped. "There are four of them, enough for both of you!" He could sense the man, his wife and two children cowering in the house. When he let Karrl and Linde go they ran into the darkness. There were screams and Melekath left the house.

Over and over he had to do the same thing. The Children were mostly too slow to catch their prey, too weak to break down the doors and get to them in their homes. When they found their hunger frustrated, more often than not they turned on each other, fighting as they had fought so many times over the centuries in the darkness.

Some of the townsfolk had the sense to run for the back wall, hoping to scale it and flee to the countryside. The first to reach it was a young couple, pulling along two children by the hands. The father threw a ladder against the wall, picked up one of the children and began to climb the ladder. Before he could make it to the top the ladder was burning fiercely as the wood ignited from the colorless flames cloaking the wall. Ignoring the flames, the father made it to the top of the ladder and reached out with his free hand for the top of the stone wall. As his hand touched the stone there was a loud sizzling noise, like meat dropped into boiling fat. He screamed. His head snapped back and he dropped the child. He tried to jerk away but it was as if his hand was fused to the wall. The flesh began to melt from his arm like wax. Just then the ladder collapsed and he fell against the wall. He was immediately engulfed in the colorless flames, twitching until he died.

The slaughter went on for hours. The townspeople had no chance. Those who hid – in cellars, in hay lofts, even in barrels – only managed to live longer. The Children could smell their Song and they were relentless in their hunger, ferreting out every last one of them and ruthlessly draining their Song.

The sun was showing in the east before the last of the townspeople died. By then the stone wall, built to keep the townspeople safe, had burned out. The stone was blackened, made brittle by the blaze. Several sections had simply collapsed into thousands of charred fragments. Those buildings within the town that were made of wood, mostly storehouses or barns, had burned as well, and the smoke from them still curled into the sky. The Children staggered around the ruined town in a daze, sniffing at bloody doorways hopefully. Temporarily sated, they were sleepy and slow, their bellies distended, their faces puffy with stolen Song. Like snakes after swallowing a large rat, they needed time to process what they had taken in, and they began looking for places to lie up.

A few hid in houses as the sun's rays flooded the town, but for most, being enclosed in stone was still too frightening, too reminiscent of their time in the prison, and they crawled under wagons and carts or burrowed into the soft soil of gardens.

TWENTY-NINE

When Quyloc rode up to the palace, exhausted, stinking of horse and sweat, he found Naills there, waiting for him.

"It's good to see you back," Naills said.

Quyloc nodded, climbed down off his horse and handed the reins to a stable boy. He stretched and felt the bones in his spine pop. "You have a report for me." Without waiting for an answer he headed for the doors, Naills hurrying to match his stride.

"There were some problems in your absence," Naills said. "Lots of them, actually. It got worse after the...after the prison broke. We had a mob at the gates. If it wasn't for the Insect Tenders a lot of people would have died."

Quyloc gave him a look, surprised. Through Nalene he'd learned that Qarath was restless, but he'd had no details and when he rode through the city he'd been surprised at how quiet the place was.

Naills filled Quyloc in as they walked to Quyloc's quarters in the palace. While Naills talked, Quyloc stripped off the shirt he was wearing and began cleaning up at the wash basin in his room. He got the worst of the dirt off and put on a new shirt.

"When you sent a rider to Thrikyl to tell them to evacuate, did you also send some scouts to spy on Melekath directly?"

"I did. It's too early to hear anything yet, of course. They've only been gone a few days."

"What else has Ricarn learned of Melekath and his Children?"

"I don't know. I haven't spoken to her."

Quyloc ran a comb through his thin, blonde hair and turned to Naills with a frown. "You didn't think that would be a good idea?"

Naills hitched up his pants, taking time to choose his words. He and Quyloc had known each other for years. For a time he'd even been Quyloc's commanding officer. But they had never been friendly. "Thought she'd let me know if she had anything to tell me," he said at last.

Quyloc shook his head in disgust. Naills was loyal and he would carry out any order given to him to the best of his ability. But he lacked any real ability to think for himself. It was why he'd advised Rome to appoint someone else as castellan. But of course Rome had ignored his advice.

"Go find her. Send her here."

Naills' face darkened at the rebuke in his tone, but he drew himself straight, saluted, and left the room without a word.

When he was gone, Quyloc wearily sank down in a chair. He needed to gather himself, figure out what to do next. He'd had days to plan what he would do when he returned to Qarath, yet still he felt lost. The same questions tormented him night and day. How were they going to defend the city? Should they march out and attack Melekath or wait here? What was Melekath capable of? How would they fight the Children?

He wondered how many days it would be until Rome arrived, then felt angry at himself for thinking that. For once he had a chance to do things the way he thought they should be done instead of having his advice ignored by Rome. He needed to take advantage of it.

Without meaning to, he fell asleep.

He found himself in the borderland, standing on the sand in the purple darkness. Cutting across the darkness, slicing the world in half, was the Veil, like a vast, glistening spider web. For a panicked instant the thought the hunter had found a new way to draw him in and he looked down, saw with relief that the *rendspear* was in his hand. Keeping hold of the weapon had become almost second nature to him. He'd learned not to take any chances.

There was no sign of the hunter on the other side of the Veil. Nothing seemed to be attached to him. He breathed a sigh of relief.

But then, why was he here?

He sensed a presence behind him and turned. The cloaked, hooded figure stood there on the sand. Though he couldn't tell for sure, he assumed it was the same cloaked figure that had helped him before, telling him where to find water in the *Pente Akka*, to give him the power to cut the hunter's bonds.

Water that almost killed him. This figure was no more to be trusted than Lowellin.

Why did you bring me here?

I want to know what you will do against Melekath.

I don't know.

176

You'll need a better answer than that if you hope to survive what is coming.

Quyloc was tired. He was tired from the long march to Guardians Watch and back. He was tired from the strain of all that was going on.

And he was tired of enigmatic beings who offered help with one hand, while manipulating with the other. So he spoke without thinking.

Why are you here? What do you want from me?

I'm here to help you.

That's a lie and we both know it. Just tell me the truth or get away from me.

The cloaked figure went very still. *You would do well to consider carefully how you speak to me.*

But Quyloc was angry now. He was sick of this figure, sick of Lowellin, sick of being pushed around as if he was nothing. He was done with it. *You're no better than Lowellin. You only help me because you're afraid of Melekath just like he is.*

The cloaked figure reached for him, fingers curled into claws. *I could kill you in a heartbeat.*

So what? If you want to kill me, get in line. Melekath and his immortal Children are coming. I doubt any of us will survive that. Then there's the hunter waiting in the Pente Akka. *I don't think it's done trying to kill me. Its master is trying to tear open the Veil and come into our world, at which point it no doubt plans to kill us all in some horrible way. Finally, there's Lowellin. I'm pretty sure when all this is over, if I somehow survive it all, he's planning on killing me. As you can see, it's quite a line. So spare me your threats. They just don't work on me anymore. I'm done talking to you. I'm leaving.* He reached for the edges of his world and began to pull them around him.

Wait.

Quyloc paused. He could feel the figure's gaze boring into him. Then, slowly, the figure raised its hands and pulled its hood back, revealing features that were very fine, almost feline, with a feral edge that was heightened by the tilted, almond eyes. She smiled and there were too many teeth in the smile. *I see now why Lowellin wants so badly to kill you,* she said.

Maybe I'm just not a very likable person.

Lower the spear.

Quyloc looked down and realized that he was pointing the spear at her. *I don't think so. Not until I feel like it.*

177

Her eyes narrowed. They glowed softly in the eerie light. *I have showed you who I am.*

So? You're another Shaper, right? I assume that means you can shape yourself into anything you want. Otherwise that's a dumb name. What you're showing me tells me nothing. What is your name?

You wouldn't really try and poke me with that thing would you? she said, pointing at the spear.

Try me.

You really are ungrateful. After all I've done for you.

You've done nothing for me, Quyloc snarled. *Your kind never do. You care only for yourself. You use me as it suits you. You'd step on me, on everyone on this world, without even thinking of it.*

The smile she gave in response was truly chilling, cold and inhuman. *You know, I think I like you. You see clearly, at least for a human, and you're not afraid to speak what you see.*

That's great, Quyloc replied. *You like me. That makes everything better.* He saw her stiffen and knew he was pushing her too far but frankly he just didn't care anymore. No matter where he turned something or someone was waiting to kill him in some new and horrible way. There was no possible way he could survive all this. The realization gave him a sort of terrible freedom. If he was going to die, at least he could do it on his terms. *I'm tired of waiting. Tell me who you are, or I'm leaving.*

She began to circle him. He was reminded of a hunting cat circling its prey. He didn't even bother to turn around when she got behind him.

Are you really this brave? she asked. *Or just really stupid?*

Mostly, I just don't care anymore. But also I'm thinking you need me. Why else would you waste your time on me?

She came up behind him and put a cold hand around his throat. He felt her nails pierce the skin ever so slightly. He held himself very still. *Are you sure about that?*

Am I sure? Lady, I'm not sure about anything anymore.

She released his throat and circled back around in front of him.

You still haven't told me who you are.

You don't need to know.

Are you so worried Lowellin will find out? Or is it Melekath you're more afraid of? What is the point of all this hiding?

She went very still. One sharp tooth showed over her lip. *Some habits are as old as this world. But you are right. There is no real point in hiding any longer. Very well. I am Khanewal.*

Quyloc searched his memory. Then the name came to him. *One of the Eight. You were there at the Banishment. That explains a lot.*

Explains what?

Of course Melekath is going to hate you and the others the most. You're the ones who put him in there.

It is possible that his time in there has made him unreasonable.

All at once Quyloc understood. *You're still hoping he won't come after you, aren't you? That's why you don't want anyone knowing you're helping us to defeat him.*

She cocked her head. The way she did it looked very inhuman. He had a sudden image of a large bird of prey standing before him.

My, you are very clever, aren't you? You know so much. Or you think you do.

It's not going to work, you know. Melekath isn't going to just forgive and forget. You're in this as deep as we are.

Now it was her turn to ponder his words. At length she said, *I suppose you are right. I guess I knew it all along. I suppose it was only old habit that made me carry on like this. I have always loved my secrets and my plans.* She looked around, at the purple sky, the glistening web. *Let's leave this place now. It is very tiresome and I confess I do not like being so close to the Veil.*

A moment later she was gone. Quyloc reached for the normal world and pulled it around himself. His vision shifted and he found himself back in his rooms in the palace. Khanewal was already there. The cloak lay in a puddle on the floor. She was standing there naked, her arms crossed beneath her breasts, staring at him with those feline eyes.

Quyloc noted her nudity, but did not dwell on it. He went and poured himself a glass of water from the pitcher that stood on a table.

"Does this form interest you so little, then?" she asked, a peevish edge to her voice.

"You mean, shouldn't I be staring at the naked woman in my room?" Quyloc scoffed. "First off, you're no woman. You're some kind of...thing. Second, I'm far too tired to be distracted by something I could easily purchase at a number of establishments in this city."

There was red in her cat's eyes and danger in her voice when she replied. "I am not the patient type. In fact, I am known to be quite rash and impulsive. Quick to anger. Be careful with your insults or you will find this out first hand."

Quyloc shrugged and sat back down. Gods, but he was tired. It would be nice to lie down and sleep without someone or something dragging him off for its own needs. "What do you want from me?"

"I want you to attack Melekath. Hit him now, before he recovers his strength."

"You want me to what, march out there by myself and stab him with my spear? Is that it?"

"Don't make it sound so infantile. March with an army. They will occupy the Children while you attack Melekath."

"You might not have noticed, but the army isn't here yet."

"There are still soldiers here in this city. Take the Tenders too."

"So, leave the city undefended and throw everything into a blind attack on the enemy."

"It's not a blind attack."

"I don't know anything about Melekath or his Children or what they are capable of. I don't even know where they are. That's what I call a blind attack."

"Now is not the time to be timid."

"And will you attack with us?"

"I will do what I can."

"Which means no."

She hissed in frustration. "Why are you being so difficult?"

"Maybe because rushing out to attack an enemy I know nothing about is the purest definition of idiocy I know and I like to consider myself not an idiot."

"They will grow stronger every day. Can't you see that you need to attack them as soon as possible?"

"What I see is you trying to force me into a foolish decision. One that could get me and all the Tenders killed, assuming I could even get the FirstMother to go along with such a mad plan, which I doubt. Then we really would have no chance."

Her hands curled into fists and her eyes grew very dark. "You are not listening to me!"

"Actually, I think I am. In fact, I'm starting to wonder if maybe you have a deeper motive. Maybe you want us to attack too soon. Maybe you want us to fail."

"Why would I want that?"

He shrugged. "How should I know? Who knows what a thing like you wants?"

At his words, Khanewal screamed in frustration and slammed her fist down on the table, which promptly cracked in half. Quyloc tensed, waiting for her to turn on him and wondering if he would be able to get the spear around fast enough.

She spun on him, teeth bared. "You are the most maddening creatures," she snapped. "Why did Melekath ever create you? Why couldn't he be happy with the dumb, mindless brutes?"

Quyloc sat forward. "What was that? Did you just say that Melekath created humans? Wasn't it Xochitl?"

"Of course it wasn't Xochitl," she scoffed. "She never had the insight or the power to do such a thing. Melekath created life, but that wasn't enough for him. He had to have more. So he created humans, which was easily the greatest mistake in the history of this pathetic world."

"Melekath created humans," Quyloc mused. "That's sure going to anger the FirstMother when she finds out."

"It is not important," she seethed.

"But I think it is. It puts things in a new light. Melekath created humans and he then came up with a way to make them immortal. But only a few chose immortality. Why?"

"How do I know? Humans are silly, brainless creatures."

"What I don't understand is how this led to war. Why would the Shapers care if Melekath made some of his creations immortal?"

"Because immortality is ours! It is not for the likes of you. The only reason we tolerated you at all was because you die and when you do what you have stolen from us is returned to us."

Quyloc nodded. This all fit with what he'd read in the old text by the Sounder. "Why does Lowellin hate Melekath so much?"

She waved off his words as if they were no more than flies. "He has hated him for ages. He is jealous of him. Melekath is First Ring, Lowellin is second. But also because of Xochitl. She and Lowellin were companions for a long time, but after Melekath created humans she became fascinated with the creatures and spent all her time with them."

Quyloc's eyes widened. "He hates us too." The implications were staggering. "If he can, he'll see us destroyed at the same time he destroys Melekath."

"You're really just figuring that out?"

Quyloc ignored her. Suddenly everything made a lot more sense. Were they on the wrong side of this conflict? It seemed like the only Shaper in this who didn't hate humans was Melekath.

"Why did Melekath create the Gift?"

"Because he's soft on you, that's why. He hated seeing you die, couldn't stand it."

There was his confirmation. "We're on the wrong side." As soon as he said the words, he wished he hadn't.

"What did you say?" Her voice was very low and dangerous.

"Forget it."

"No. You're thinking that this war only concerns the Nipashanti." Her eyes had narrowed and she was staring at him very intently. "You're thinking that maybe you can stay out of this war or perhaps side with Melekath."

"I never said that."

"I will show you why that will never happen." So saying, she stepped closer and, before he could react, grabbed him by the shoulder with a grip of iron. "Come with me."

Power suddenly rippled out from her. Quyloc looked down and realized they were sinking into the stone floor. Already he was up to his shins. He began to fight but she shook him.

"Don't be an idiot," she hissed. "If you fight, it will only hurt more. It's too late already."

The pain hit then. He felt like he was being crushed under a mountain of stone. The pain was so great he couldn't think.

"Just hold still. We are going to travel through the Stone. The only thing that will keep you alive is my hold on you. If you struggle, I may lose that hold."

Quyloc forced himself to be still, even as the pain mounted. He was up to his waist now and still sliding down. His chest, his neck, and then the stone closed over him.

What followed was a brief time of intense pain, though it felt like hours. But at length the pressure began to ease and he realized he could see again, though everything was hazy.

Then a new pain started, not the crushing pain of the Stone, but the pain of burning. From Khanewal he heard a cry of pain and anger.

The burning pain receded and the crushing pain and darkness returned as Khanewal drew them back into the Stone. Moments later they returned to the surface, only this time there was no burning.

"He lit the stone on fire," Khanewal said, sounding surprised. "I didn't know he could do that."

They were standing outside a town with a stone wall around it. Except that the wall looked strange, hazy. Quyloc rubbed his eyes.

"The wall is on fire?"

"Shhh. I don't want him to know we're here." Still holding onto his shoulder in her vise-like grip, she pulled him toward the town. The gate was open, scraps of wood scattered everywhere. They crept up to it and peeked around the edge of the wall. Khanewal pointed.

What Quyloc saw made him feel sick. Hunched, gray-skinned things that might have once been human were crouched over bodies in the street, eager, whining noises coming from them. Down the street two more were fighting over the limp form of a woman, snarling at each other.

"Have you seen enough?" Khanewal whispered. Quyloc nodded and she led him back away from the town, to the place where they'd emerged from the stone, a rock outcropping. As they reached the outcropping she made a swirling gesture with her hand and the stone began to glow. Then she stepped into it, pulling him in after her.

After a time of crushing pain and darkness they rose up out of the floor in Quyloc's quarters. When she let go of him he staggered and fell to his knees. He felt raw, his limbs clumsy and stiff, as if they no longer belonged to him.

"Traveling through Stone isn't for living things," Khanewal said. "I probably should have told you that."

Quyloc was gasping, still trying to recover himself. Her voice sounded distant and muffled. He wasn't sure if he was still breathing.

"That was the town of Ferien. Now do you see why your hopes of allying with Melekath are foolish? There was a band of Crodin who thought as you did. Their corpses are in a shallow grave at the edge of the desert."

"Those were the Children?" Quyloc gasped.

"The very same. They're quite insane, you know. Like starving animals near any living creatures, especially other people. If the whole situation wasn't personally threatening, I'd find it hilarious. In his desperate zeal to save his precious humans Melekath may have doomed you all. It's all too perfect, really."

She bent over Quyloc and looked him over. "You are going to live, aren't you? I'd hate to think I'd have to take someone else through all that." She waited for him to respond, then shook her head.

"Pathetic creatures. I never understood what he saw in you. Anyway, you see now why you need to act. Every time those abominations feed, they get stronger. They're headed for Thrikyl. Once they devour that city I expect they'll be stronger even than we Nipashanti. But they're moving slow, so there's still hope. If you ride out tomorrow, you should be able to intercept them."

She finished and stared at him again. After a moment, Quyloc nodded.

"I guess that will have to do. Goodbye. It's been fun." She rubbed her foot on the floor in a circle and the stone began to glow. Then she slid down into it and was gone.

With an effort, Quyloc managed to make it to his bed. He collapsed onto it and fell asleep immediately.

THIRTY

Quyloc was awakened by pounding on the door. At first he couldn't figure out what the noise was and he just lay there. Where was he? *Who* was he? Then pieces began to come back to him. Khanewal. The Children. Traveling through the Stone. The lantern was still burning, providing light. So he hadn't been asleep too long. He stumbled to the door and opened it. "What?"

Opus stood there, Ricarn behind him. "The Tender Ricarn to see you, Adviser."

Quyloc had a terrible headache. He felt like someone had torn him into little pieces and then left a few of them out when putting him back together. More than anything he just wanted to sleep.

"Come on in," he said.

Ricarn entered and walked over to look down at the remains of the table. As Quyloc approached she switched her cold, almost inhuman gaze to him. Her eyes moved back to the broken table, then back to him.

"Where did you go?" she asked.

Quyloc gaped at her, not sure he heard her correctly. "I just got back," he said, then wondered why he'd said that.

Ricarn's gaze moved around the room, then traveled back to him. "Where did you go?" she repeated.

"I saw the town of Ferien. Khanewal took me."

"You traveled through the Stone."

"How do you know that?"

"I have seen it done," she said, as if that explained everything. "What did you see in Ferien?"

"Melekath is there. His Children killed everyone."

Ricarn's eyes glittered in the lamplight. "Their hunger cannot be sated."

"Is that why you told Naills to evacuate Thrikyl?"

"What did Khanewal want?"

185

"She wants us to attack Melekath before the Children get too powerful."

"Will you?"

He shook his head. "We'd never get there in time. Everyone's exhausted. We nearly killed ourselves just getting back here." He yawned. His eyes seemed to be full of sand. "I don't think it would work anyway. I don't know how we're going to fight them."

"The Children grow stronger with every living thing they drain of Song. If they are allowed to feed on Thrikyl, by the time they arrive here no resistance we offer will matter. We will be no more than insects to them."

Quyloc sat down, the last of his strength gone. "The Thrikylians won't evacuate. They won't abandon their city. I'd need an army to push them out."

"This is true."

"So is it hopeless then? Should we just give up?"

"Probably," she replied. Then something like a smile crossed her face, a smile that made Quyloc even more uncomfortable. "It is what I would advise."

"You advise that we just give up?" Quyloc's voice had risen slightly.

"I do."

"That's...what kind of person are you?"

"One who sees clearly. Because I gave up long ago. I accept that my life means nothing. It is really quite freeing."

Quyloc shook his head. "You're crazy, you know that?"

She inclined her head ever so slightly, as if he had done her a great honor.

"It *is* hopeless," she said. "But we may yet find an answer."

She left the room and Quyloc sat there, wondering what had just happened.

THIRTY-ONE

It was late in the day when Nalene and her small band of ragged, exhausted Tenders entered the gates to the Tender estate. When Velma saw them return she was so happy she almost started crying. She ran to greet them, pulling up short as she got near enough to see them properly.

Her first thought was that they all looked awful. Their robes were filthy, their faces drawn and hollow. They climbed down off their horses like elderly women, and more than one fell down when she hit the ground.

Her next thought was that their *sulbits* had grown tremendously. Compared to hers, which was still quite small, theirs were huge, some as large as cats. They seemed much more menacing too, staring at the people who milled around with intense, hungry looks.

"Welcome back, FirstMother," Velma said.

The FirstMother handed the reins of her horse to one of the stable boys and glanced briefly at Velma without replying. "Have shatren brought to feed the *sulbits*," she ordered. "Come with me," she told Velma, and headed for the estate house.

Velma hurried to keep up with her. "Shall I draw a bath for you, FirstMother?" she inquired.

"That can wait. First I want a full report. I want to know everything."

Hesitantly, Velma began. She told her about the mob that gathered at the palace and how the Insect Tenders had dispersed it. When she told her how much calmer the city was since Cara started leading the morning services, the FirstMother turned a sharp look on her and she winced, suddenly sure she was about to be soundly chewed out.

"I'm sorry, FirstMother. I was no good at it," she said, hanging her head. "People didn't listen. Then they just stopped showing up. When Ricarn said to have Cara lead them I thought it couldn't hurt."

"Cara is the girl who refused her *sulbit?*" Velma nodded, unable to meet her gaze. "Ricarn told you to have her do it?" Velma nodded again and hoped she wouldn't start crying when the FirstMother yelled at her. The FirstMother hated when she cried.

Surprisingly, the FirstMother said no more about it. When they reached her quarters she sat down behind her desk and motioned Velma to take a seat as well. When Velma told her about what Ricarn had learned about the Children and how she'd said the city of Thrikyl needed to be evacuated, the FirstMother's expression grew grim.

"It's that bad, then?"

Velma nodded. The FirstMother put her head in her hands and for a terrible moment Velma thought she was going to cry. She wasn't sure what she would do if that happened. The FirstMother was the strongest person she knew. Desperate to keep it from happening, she started talking.

"But you defeated Kasai and the *sulbits* are much stronger now. Surely the Protector has a plan. Surely he knows what to do."

"I have not seen the Protector since Guardians Watch."

"But...*why?*"

"I don't know."

"But he said Melekath wouldn't be free for months yet! We were supposed to be there when it happened to stop him."

"I know. I think...I think he's gone. I think we're on our own now." The FirstMother looked very lost and vulnerable at that moment and suddenly Velma was the most frightened she'd been since the prison broke. Somehow she'd been holding onto the belief that once the FirstMother returned everything would be all right. She'd know what to do. She and the Protector would have a plan. Now all that hope shattered into a million pieces.

"He *can't* be gone!" Velma cried. "He's the *Protector*! He's supposed to tell us what to do." She wiped at the tears that were streaming down her face. "What are we going to do now?"

The FirstMother straightened herself. She closed her eyes for a moment. When she opened them again the woman Velma knew so well was back.

"We're going to fight. That's what we're going to do. We're not helpless. We'll figure out some way to defeat them."

THIRTY-TWO

"You summoned me?" Cara asked. She stood at the door to the FirstMother's quarters, looking in. The door was halfway open and she could see the FirstMother sitting at her desk. The FirstMother had returned to Qarath only hours before and it was clear she had not taken the time to clean up: her robe was more brown than white, her head sported a ragged gray and brown stubble, and her face was dirty.

"Come in," the FirstMother said curtly without looking up from the stack of parchments on the desk before her. "Sit down."

Cara approached the desk cautiously and sat at the sole chair in front of it, noticing as she did so that the chair was unsteady. One of the legs seemed to be too short. She carefully adjusted her weight so as not to tip over.

The FirstMother was reading something, now and then picking up her quill to write on the parchment. Cara sat there uneasily for some minutes, her anxiety growing. Was she going to be punished for leading the morning services? She wished that Ricarn was there to speak for her. She hadn't wanted to lead the services. She didn't want to cause any problems.

At length the FirstMother set the parchment aside and looked at Cara. Her eyes were red with exhaustion and there was a tremor in her hands.

"You have been conducting the morning services," she said without preamble.

Cara nodded. "I have. I know I'm not a real Tender but Ricarn asked me to and Velma said okay – " She cut off before she could apologize. Ricarn was often after her about her excessive apologizing.

The FirstMother made no reply, but simply sat there and stared at her, as if taking her measure. The expression on her face – anger mixed with uncertainty? – confused Cara. At last she spoke.

"You have done well in this."

Cara's eyes widened. "I only tried to serve as best I could," she said softly. "But now that you are back – "

The FirstMother cut her off. "You will continue in your present duties," she said gruffly. The words seemed to pain her. She picked up another parchment and began to read it.

After a time Cara realized she had been dismissed and she headed for the door. Before she left the room, the FirstMother surprised her once again.

"You are a credit to the Mother," she said. "A Tender she would be proud of."

Cara stopped and turned back. *Does this mean I am a Tender once again?* she wanted to ask.

"Close the door when you leave," the FirstMother said.

Later that night Cara was sitting in her little shed in the trees at the back of the estate, warming her hands over the small fire in the stone-lined fire pit she'd built in the center of the room, waiting for her evening meal to be brought to her. The smoke curled lazily up to the ceiling, escaping the shed through a large gap in the roof. When Cara had first been exiled to the shed she'd hated it. But now she found she liked the privacy, something she'd never really had that much of, living at Rane Haven where there were always other Tenders around. She'd cleaned the little place up, managed to acquire a few items like a washbasin and a proper chair, and it was starting to feel like a home to her. She added another stick to the fire and looked up as Adira suddenly opened the door. She was carrying a folded white robe.

Cara looked at the robe and her heart lifted. She said nothing, as if fearing that what she saw was only a dream, and speaking would cause her to wake up. For a long moment Adira simply stood there and stared at her with her strange, intense eyes, saying nothing. She had a crooked nose that looked like it had been broken badly and never set, and she tilted her head to the left as she stared. She seemed to be trying to discern some deep secret that Cara was hiding. Cara stood up.

Finally, feeling uncomfortable under Adira's stare, Cara said, "Yes?"

Adira bit her lip. "Who are you?"

"What? I'm...I'm Cara. You know me."

Adira's eyes narrowed slightly. "Do I?"

Cara tried to laugh it off, as if Adira was only making a joke, but the laugh died quickly. "I see you every day."

"That doesn't mean I know who you are."

"No. I suppose not." Cara was bewildered. Was Adira angry with her? There was a dark look on her face, but it was hard to tell. The strange Tender made no sense to Cara.

Adira looked down at the robe she carried, as if surprised to see it there. "Velma said to give this to you." She held it out and Cara took it, her heart pounding. "I guess you should have this, too," she added, reaching into the pocket of her robe and pulling out a Reminder, a many-pointed star enclosed in a circle.

Cara stared down at the items. Every morning after the service she gave back the robe and Reminder she'd worn and every time it hurt to do so. Her hands were shaking so that she thought she might drop them. With her heart in her mouth she asked, "Are they mine to keep?"

Adira shrugged. "I guess so. No one said to take them from you, just to give them to you."

Cara clutched them to her chest. "Thank you. Thank you so much."

Adira squinted at her. "What for?"

Cara wiped at her eyes. "For bringing these to me."

"I was told to, wasn't I?"

"Still, I am grateful."

An awkward silence ensued during which Adira stared at Cara. Finally, Cara said, "Is there something else?"

Adira frowned. "Why would there be something else?"

"I don't know. I just thought…"

"Well there is. You're to get dressed and come to the evening meal with the rest of us."

Cara gaped at her, not sure she heard correctly. "In the estate house?"

"Of course the estate house. Do you think we eat in the stables?"

Then she stood there staring at Cara again until Cara finally said, "Now?"

Adira gave her a look that implied she must be simple. "I'm waiting, aren't I?"

Cara set the robe on her chair. She wanted some privacy to change, but Adira was standing in the open door, staring at her. Cara put her hand on the door and closed it slightly. "Do you mind?" she asked gently.

"I didn't," Adira grumbled, "but I'm starting to. Hurry up. I want to eat."

THIRTY-THREE

It was more than a day before the first of the Children began to stir and clamber from their hiding places. Again, Reyna was first. Reyna had been a famous beauty, tall, with masses of red hair, flawless skin and full, red lips. Her whole life she had been sought after by rich, powerful men, and hated and envied by other women. She had used that beauty as a warrior used his sword, carving her way through the ranks of men who fawned over her, manipulating them, wringing them dry, becoming ever richer and more powerful herself. More than one man killed himself in despair after being carved open by her sharp-edged tongue. The first signs of autumn – faint lines around her eyes and mouth, the smallest sag in her breasts – had begun to appear when Melekath appeared with his Gift. Without hesitation she walked away from her palatial estate in Qarath. She who had never knelt to a man in her life, knelt to Melekath to receive immortality. She would have done anything, paid any price, to maintain her beauty and the power that came with it. When Melekath appeared with his Gift it had seemed too good to be true. Little had she dreamed of the price she would eventually pay.

All over Reyna's body the dead, gray skin was peeling away in large patches and new, pink skin was showing underneath. Her twisted, broken arm had knit the rest of the way, repaired by the stolen Song. The gaping wound in her chest had closed. Curves were returning to her emaciated frame, breasts and buttocks filling out. Patches of red hair were beginning to sprout from her skull. Her face was still a ruined mess, badly pock marked, the eyebrows gone, the eyes sunken and dull. Strangely, her lips were mostly restored. They were full and incongruously red, startling against so much else that was wrong with her face.

She stretched and looked around her like a queen surveying her realm. She saw Melekath watching her and walked to him, a hint of the sultry sway that had once been hers returning to her hips.

"More," she said, looking him steadily in the eye. She was actually taller than he was now and he looked strangely frail next to her. "I need more. Find me more."

"An entire world awaits you," he replied. "Only be patient."

"I hate when you say that," she replied. "For thousands of years, 'Be patient.' Bah!" She folded her arms over her chest and frowned at him.

"We must wait for the others."

She looked around her, just then noticing the others who were beginning to stir. "If we must," she said petulantly. "But I will not wait long."

The next to emerge was Heram. Heram had been a blacksmith when he laid down his hammer to follow Melekath. A large, powerful man, Heram had been inordinately proud of his muscular stature. He had an anvil set out front of his blacksmith shop and he worked there whenever he could, stripped to the waist, swinging his hammer with limitless power. The men in Heram's town knew to stay out of his way, for he had a temper to match his strength and he did not bother to restrain it. His fists were their own hammers and they had pounded and flattened men for every offense offered to Heram, both real and imagined.

The stolen Song had changed Heram a great deal. His twisted leg had straightened. The cut running down the side of his neck had closed. The muscle he had been so proud of was returning as well. His arms and legs, thin and emaciated when he emerged from the prison, showed signs of returning muscle, though the muscles weren't quite proportioned right and bulged oddly in places. When he stood up, his first act was to hold up his arms, one after the other, clench his fists and flex his muscles. He nodded and swung his arms around experimentally. He looked at Melekath and something that might have been a smile touched his parody of a face. Almost none of the stolen Song had gone into rebuilding his face. His lips were little more than ragged strips of flesh and no new teeth protruded from his gray gums. His cheeks were withered and shrunken like a dried corpse's.

"Better," he croaked. "More. I need more."

"We will leave after everyone has revived," Melekath answered. "When all are ready to walk once more."

"Then I will rouse them," he replied, and turned away.

"Tell them to go to the plaza and gather there," Melekath called after him.

The first one Heram found was hiding under the wooden porch of a house. He grabbed the edge of the porch and pulled. The muscles in his arms bulged and he gritted his teeth. At first nothing happened, then with a squeal of protesting nails, the wood tore away. He leaned over and clamped one hand on the back of the man's neck.

"Get up," he growled. "It is time to go." He tossed the man into the street and went looking for the next one.

Melekath walked to the plaza. In the center of the plaza stood a large oak tree with a bench underneath it. Josef was kneeling by the oak, his hands clasped before him. Fresh, pink skin was beginning to show through the dead gray of his face. His nose, which had been mashed flat and hard to one side, was straighter and a torn flap of skin along the side of his scalp was knitting itself back to his head. But other than that he did not seem to have healed as much as the others Melekath had seen. Curious, Melekath walked quietly up behind him.

Josef had been a gardener in Karthije before he took the Gift. His talent with plants had been famous throughout the city, his services in much demand by the wealthy there. Josef could grow anything: trees, shrubs, flowers and grasses all thrived under his care. Even plants that would not normally grow in Karthije did well under his hands. Trees from the far south that should have died in Karthije's cold instead prospered.

Something was wrong with the oak tree. A black stain ran up its side and several limbs were dead. Josef was saying something, too softly for Melekath to hear. He seemed to be talking to the tree. Then, gently, Josef touched the tree trunk. Song flowed from his hands into the tree.

Melekath raised one eyebrow. This was something he hadn't expected. He edged closer, cautiously optimistic. Could this be a sign of his Children turning the corner? Did this mean they were starting to heal, that they would begin to think beyond themselves and their hunger?

A minute later the trickle of Song dried up. Josef rocked back on his heels and looked up at the tree, mute hope on his face.

The black stain on the trunk changed. It grew wider and longer, rising up the trunk. The limbs shuddered. Then, with a loud crack, the trunk itself split in half.

Josef sat unmoving, staring at the dead tree. Melekath heard an unusual sound coming from him. It took a moment to identify it.

Josef was crying, though there were no tears.

It took a couple of hours, but finally all of the Children were gathered in Ferien's plaza. They talked loudly and excitedly, showing off their newly-healed bodies to each other, boasting of what they would do now. Karrl and Linde danced an awkward jig. Linde's lost arm had grown partway back and she waved it in time to a tune only she could hear. Other Children gathered around them in a rough circle, laughing and shouting insults.

Reyna and Heram held themselves apart from the rest. Heram leaned against the wall of a building, his burly arms crossed over his chest. Near him, in a protective half ring before him, stood three of his followers. Almost on the opposite side of the plaza, as if in counterpoint to Heram, Reyna sat very straight and proud on a chair on the porch of a house, like a queen looking down on her subjects. Several of her most ardent followers sat on the porch near her feet, further completing the look.

How long would it be before one of them made a move against the other? Melekath wondered. They had plotted against each other for hundreds of years in the prison, constantly vying for the upper hand. There had been others who challenged them for supremacy – most notably Melfen – but one by one they had fallen away, until only these two remained.

Melfen was a tall, wiry man, highly intelligent, with a knack for getting others to follow him. Those who could be counted on to side with him nearly outnumbered the followers of Reyna and Heram put together. Melekath, who had given up trying to mediate the endless conflicts sometime in the first millennia of imprisonment, had been fairly certain Melfen would win out. He had actually hoped for it. Melfen did not have the vicious craziness of Heram, or the cruel capriciousness of Reyna. He actually seemed to care for his followers, albeit in his own somewhat twisted way.

However, there came a time when Melfen did not show for a feeding. When the feeding was finally over, and Melekath had pushed away the last whining member of his brood, he went looking for Melfen. He found Melfen's broken body lying under a pile of huge stone blocks. It appeared that Melfen had gone into one of the more unstable buildings and it collapsed on him. Melekath pulled the stones off of him, but there was nothing he could really do. Melfen was too far gone for Melekath to heal. The lower half of his head had been completely crushed, so he could not speak, but Melekath had been able to look into his eyes and what he saw there told him all he needed to know. Too strong for them to handle on their own, Reyna and Heram had joined forces to take out their strongest foe.

Another who did not join in with the excitement was Josef. Through it all he remained kneeling at the foot of the dead oak tree, his head down, unmoving. Melekath had tried to talk to him, but Josef did not respond and finally he left him alone. What thoughts went through Josef's mind? Even when one of the other Children knocked him over in her excitement, Josef did not look up or speak. He simply got back on his knees. Somehow, Josef tore at Melekath's heart more than any of the rest.

"Where now, Father?"

Melekath broke out of his thoughts. Orenthe was standing before him. She was a small woman, quite old when she accepted the Gift. She had not been one he expected to survive this long. There was no way to tell, really. Some who appeared most likely to navigate the treacherous path between holding their minds together and avoiding the worst of the violence that plagued the prison succumbed within a few hundred years. Others, like Orenthe, small and meek, perpetually unsure of herself, survived and emerged into daylight.

"Thrikyl, I think," he replied. "It is the closest."

She smiled. It wasn't a pretty sight. Her face was blotchy gray and pink. Her eyes were sunken and her mouth toothless. She held up one hand and rubbed her thumb and forefinger together. "It's coming back. Feeling. Isn't it wonderful?"

He nodded. "It is." And it was. It was one more step on the road back. His Children would return to him and all would be as it was.

The Children streamed down the main street that led to the front gates of Ferien in a giddy swarm. Reyna and Heram moved to the front of the pack immediately. Reyna was taller than Heram now, topping him by almost half a head, while Heram was thick with new muscle growth. They gave each other dark looks but neither pressed the issue and as they walked down the road that led out of town they walked side by side. They had not gone far when Karrl and Linde in their eagerness tried to push past them. Heram roared and hammered Karrl between the shoulders, hard enough that Melekath could hear bone crack. Karrl went down with a cry. Reyna grabbed Linde around the neck, threw the smaller woman on the ground and kicked her in the ribs.

Other Children who had been edging forward suddenly got the message and fell back. Melekath shook his head. When he created the Gift, Melekath had believed that immortality would end human conflict. With no death to fear and endless time on their hands, surely his Children would learn to live in harmony. Instead they had done nothing but fight and scheme against each other, all the things he'd so hated.

It was the effect of the prison, he told himself. That was what had caused this. They had been trapped there too long, cut off too long. But now they were free and they would recover. When they had finally fed enough to restore themselves, they would begin to settle down and they would see there was no reason to fight amongst themselves. There was enough for all.

In light of that, perhaps it was best they were going to Thrikyl first. There they would find enough Song to satisfy their hunger and when they finally turned north to Qarath, it would be as a unified people.

Orenthe walked near the back of the group as the Children left Ferien, still enraptured by the faint feeling that was returning to her hands. After feeding on the Crodin some of the Children had spoken of being able to feel once again, and she'd seen them complain when they fell in cactus, but she'd felt nothing and had resigned herself to never feeling anything again.

Lost as she was in her reverie, she didn't see the corpse until she tripped over it. She fell to her knees, her hands landing on its torso. Just like that she found herself face to face with what had been a young woman – though it was hard to tell. She was withered like an apple left in the sun, her hair bleached of color and brittle as old straw. The skin around her eyes had retracted so that the eyeballs looked unnaturally large.

With a cry, Orenthe pushed herself off the corpse and got to her feet. She hurried away, her face turned away from the horrid thing, her hands shaking. Unbidden, the memories of the previous evening's slaughter returned to her. She remembered screaming, the terror on their faces. Her first victim had been a child, a boy of probably ten that she found huddled in a hay crib, crying. Some tiny, inner part of her, a part that remembered who and what she had once been, had recoiled as she grabbed him, but the savage hunger overwhelmed all thoughts, all reason. She'd pulled him to her breast in an embrace as intimate as a mother's. The Song she drained from him was the sweetest nectar, a cooling balm for the fierce fever that had burned inside her for thousands of years.

There'd been another victim after that, a teenaged girl she thought, though she couldn't be sure. The night was a confused welter of images. Hunger and intoxication overwhelmed her, a flood that swept her away, leaving her high and dry this morning. She hesitated, half turning back. Guilt shook her and there was within her the feeling that she should find that boy, that young girl, and bury them, somehow atone for what she had done, however inadequate it would be.

Stronger than the guilt though, far stronger, was the hunger. It did not hurt as much as before, but it was not soothed and it would return in force.

She turned her back on the victims and hurried after the others, wishing there were still tears within her to cry.

THIRTY-FOUR

"King Perthen sends me to congratulate you on your victory and bids me ask you to join him at his table for a feast."

The Qarathian army had arrived at Karthije and a messenger had come out to meet them. The messenger was a young man with a wispy beard and nervous eyes. He sat on his horse as if he might jump off and run away. Rome and Tairus exchanged looks. "Give us a minute," Rome told the man, who moved off.

"What do you think?" Rome asked Tairus.

"I think you decline politely and we go as far as we can before stopping for the night. I don't trust Perthen."

"Neither do I," Rome mused, scratching his chin as he looked at the walls of Karthije.

"But you're going to go anyway, aren't you?"

"We need all the allies we can get. Now that the prison has broken, maybe Perthen has had a change of heart."

"And maybe pigs will fly out his butt," Tairus grunted sourly.

"You're not a very trusting soul, are you?"

"I trust my axe. I trust my men. Not much else."

"Not your macht?"

Tairus gave him a gimlet eye. "Not when he's like this."

"Like what?"

"You get in these moods, start thinking you're invincible and you can do anything, no matter how foolish. But a knife will go in you just the same as anyone."

"I know it's a slim chance that he's changed, but I have to take it anyway. He can help us."

"And if he takes you prisoner instead?"

"Then take the army and hightail it for Qarath."

"And leave you here? Just like that?"

"Just like that. This is bigger than me, Tairus. You know that. What happens to me doesn't matter."

"I don't know that the men will follow that order," Tairus said.

"They'll do what you tell them. We trained them, remember?"

Tairus sighed. "I knew I should have quit the army when I had a chance. I knew I should have gone back to farming."

"You'd hate it and you know it," Rome said, smiling. "You're not cut out to be anything else but a soldier."

"Just don't get yourself captured, okay?"

"I promise." Rome started unbuckling the straps that held the sheathed black axe on his back. "But just in case, I want you to hold this for me." He got it free and held it out to Tairus, who recoiled as if it were a snake.

"I don't want that thing."

"I can't take it with me. You know that. If Perthen does betray me, it's vital the axe not fall into his hands. If something happens, you have to take it to Quyloc. You'll need it to fight Melekath."

Grumbling, Tairus took the weapon, holding it at arm's length.

"Gods, man, it won't bite you," Rome said with a chuckle.

"Not if I don't give it a chance to."

A minute later Rome was following the messenger toward the city walls. Only Nicandro accompanied him. If it was a trap, more men wouldn't help, they'd just get themselves killed, and Rome didn't want that on his shoulders. His risk was his alone to take. As for Nicandro, well, he knew that if he tried to leave his aide behind it would have to be in chains and he'd prefer not to have to do that.

Behind the three men came the soldiers of Karthije, marching in orderly columns, thousands of grim men with armor and steel. They'd returned home, but there was none of the laughter or cheerfulness that would normally have accompanied a victorious army reentering its city.

"Nervous?" he asked Nicandro, as they entered the tunnel under the massive wall.

"I'm with the Black Wolf, ain't I?" Nicandro rejoined. "What's there to be nervous about?" But the whites of his eyes were showing a little bit too much and Rome saw him look up to the ceiling of the tunnel, noting the murder holes there.

"Just think about all the good food there'll be at the feast," Rome said. "Karthije is a rich land, after all. They must know how to put a proper feast on the table."

"I wouldn't mind that," Nicandro admitted. "I've been eating dried meat and wormy bread for so long an old boot would taste good."

Despite his outward confidence, Rome was worried too. Everything he knew about Perthen said the man would hold a grudge even if Gorim himself had his teeth in his foot. The man had been humiliated the last time they met and there was every chance he was looking for revenge, even if it cost him.

Rome knew all that, but he also knew the man had a powerful army and despite his fear that there'd be no place for normal steel in the fight to come, he'd still rather have all the soldiers he could get when Melekath showed up. That's why he had to take this chance.

The soldiers that formed up around them as they passed through the open portcullis stared at Rome bitterly, but none reached for weapons and for that he was grateful. It wasn't an easy thing, being nearly alone inside the stronghold of an old enemy. He couldn't remember when he'd last felt so vulnerable.

All in all the city seemed remarkably calm, though surely her citizens had felt the prison break just as the army had. But there was still an ugly undercurrent in the air that had Nicandro swiveling his head side to side, trying to watch in every direction at once. The people here at least partially blamed Rome for what had happened. Rome wondered if the soldiers marching around them were there to make sure they didn't escape, or to keep them safe from the populace.

Then they were at the palace. Only two soldiers escorted them inside, which eased Rome's concerns somewhat, though he knew it might not mean anything.

They were led to the main audience hall, a huge room whose high ceiling was supported by thick marble columns. The room was mostly shadows, lit only by two iron braziers flickering at the foot of the dais the throne sat on. Dimly visible on the throne was a hunched figure. Several guards stood at attention along the side walls and a figure stood to the left of the throne, but other than that the room was empty.

But Rome paid little attention to these things. What struck him most from the moment he stepped into the room was the stench. Incense burned in censers that flanked the throne, thick ropes of smoke coiling up to the ceiling, but they weren't enough to cloak the smell of rot. It was all Rome could do not to gag, and he thought of himself as a man with a strong stomach.

Where did the smell come from? he wondered. Was this all part of some elaborate ploy, something Perthen had dreamed up to get revenge? For the first time he began to seriously doubt the wisdom of coming here. For all he knew, Perthen was mad, and the mad were likely to do anything.

Rome stopped at the foot of the dais and fought the urge to put his hand over his nose.

"Welcome, Macht Rome," Perthen said. "I congratulate you on your victory."

Rome peered through the gloom, trying to see the man better. Perthen was no more than a dark shape slumped on the throne. From the corner of his eye, he noted that Nicandro's hand had dropped to the hilt of his sword.

"Thank you, King Perthen. It was only through your generosity and the bravery of your soldiers that we were able to win." The bravery part at least was true. Karthije's soldiers had fought as well as, or better than, Qarath's.

"So now we are done with the pleasantries," Perthen continued. "I've always hated them, polite, empty words that you exchange with those you'd most rather stick a blade in their guts."

Nicandro went into a crouch and drew his sword partway, but Rome put his hand on his shoulder to forestall him, though he wanted to do the same.

"There's no reason for that, King Perthen," he said calmly, though a part of his mind was noting the position of all the guards in the room and he was already planning which he would attack first and how they would flee from the palace. It would be futile, but he would not go down without taking a lot of them with him. "I brought your soldiers back like I said I would. We are heading back to Qarath and will cause you no further trouble, I assure you."

"Oh, you *assure* me, do you?" Perthen hissed. "The great and noble Wulf Rome assures me and now I feel all better. What a wondrous day it is!"

"I do not understand what you are angry about. I have done what I said I would. We defeated Kasai and I brought your army back."

"Did you notice that it smells in here? Surely you noticed it. Wouldn't you like to know where it comes from?"

Rome stared at the slumped figure, wondering what was coming next.

"I said, wouldn't you like to know where it comes from!" Perthen yelled.

"Yes." Though he knew for sure that he didn't. Rome had given up any hope of convincing Perthen to join forces. The man was clearly unhinged. Now he just wanted to get out of here in one piece.

"Come a little closer and I'll show you."

Rome took a deep breath and looked around the room. None of the guards had moved. What was Perthen's game? Was it a trap?

He took a step up onto the dais, then another. He could hear the rasp of Perthen's breathing now and the stench was, incredibly, worse. A dead horse wouldn't smell this bad.

"Just a little further," Perthen urged. "I want to make sure you really understand."

Rome took two more steps. He was breathing through his mouth. The room was too hot and sweat was trickling down his face. He was almost close enough to reach out and touch Perthen, but try as he might, he still could barely see the man, the room was so dark. "I can't see whatever it is you want me to see."

"Light is it? That's what you want? Of course."

The figure standing beside Perthen moved then, putting a handful of dried grasses onto one of the braziers so that the flames leapt up, illuminating Perthen.

With an oath, Rome stepped back, putting his forearm up to his mouth. Behind him he heard Nicandro gagging.

Perthen's skin had turned yellow. There were running sores covering most of his face and the one hand Rome could see. One eye was covered in a milky film and all his hair had fallen out. Perthen leaned forward, turning his head side to side to give Rome a good look.

"Now you see, don't you? What do you think?"

"What happened to you?"

"*You* happened to me. You did this!"

"What…how?"

"That's what I'd like to know, so that then I could return the favor. But I don't know. All I know is that it started that day when you came crawling up to my door."

All at once Rome realized what must have happened. Quyloc severed the flow of Song sustaining the man with his *rendspear*. Somehow that must have caused this.

"Ah, now you see," Perthen said, slumping back on the throne. "I can see it in your eyes. The good and noble Wulf Rome caused this." He coughed weakly, dark mucus flying from his mouth.

"I…had no idea."

"But you'd do it again, wouldn't you?"

Rome hesitated.

"Of course you would. Don't lie to me. Don't lie to yourself. What is the suffering of one man, what is the suffering of thousands, when it is necessary to achieve your goal?"

Rome stared at him, knowing he was right.

"When we parlayed that day you were so smug, so sure of your righteousness," Perthen croaked. "You can't imagine how much I hate you for that. You looked down on me because I was willing to sacrifice so many others to impose my will on you, yet now when you look on me you know the truth, that you are just as willing as I. That's why I brought you here. I wanted you to see. I wanted you to know. You do understand what it means to rule."

"If I had known—"

"Spare me your false guilt!" Perthen barked. "I see the truth of it. I see the truth of who you are. And now you do too." The grasses had burned down and the light was dwindling fast. Perthen was once again receding into shadow.

When Perthen spoke again his voice was so weak it was barely audible, as if the last outburst had taken the last of his strength. "Get out of here before I have you killed. Carry the truth within you. May it haunt you the rest of your days."

THIRTY-FIVE

That night, Rome dreamed.

He was in darkness and he couldn't move. He sensed that he was deep underground, encased in stone, the vast weight of it pressing on him on all sides. He'd been trapped there for thousands of years. Something had gone wrong and he couldn't escape. Some kind of poison had leached into him, immobilizing him. He couldn't cry out for help, couldn't do anything but wait.

Then, a change. A hand reached into the darkness and pulled him from the stone. He was out in the open once again, but still he could not move, could not even open his eyes. He cried out for freedom, but he had no voice.

Rome opened his eyes. The stars were bright overhead. The trapped, desolate feeling of the dream still filled him, an iron weight around his heart, mixed with the horror and guilt of what he'd seen in Karthije.

There was a hint of light in the east and Rome clambered to his feet, feeling the stiffness and the cold settled into his bones. He tried to shake it off as only a dream, but it stuck with him as he went through the motions of getting ready for the day's march. All around him soldiers dragged themselves up from sleep, rubbing their eyes, cursing softly, groaning. Rome saddled his horse and tied his armor and gear to it.

The last thing he picked up was the black axe and when he did he noticed something. The haft felt different. It wasn't as smooth. He squinted at it in the weak light. The entire haft had always had a design carved into it – feathers or very fine scales, he'd never decided which – but the carving was rougher now. Frowning, he removed the leather sheath he kept strapped over the head of the axe.

The eye was open.

The eye on the side of the axe head – always closed before – was open now. It was still all black, but now it looked somewhat shiny, as if it was wet. Cautiously, he touched it with his fingertip. It didn't feel wet. He flipped it over. The eye on the other side was open too.

Then he noticed something else different. The cutting edge of the axe, designed to look like a beak, had a notch in it at the bottom corner. As if the beak was open slightly.

Rome thought back to the day Lowellin unlocked his memories, when he learned that the axe had come from the wall of the prison. He'd also said something else, that the axe might be alive.

Was it alive? Was it waking up?

They were not pleasant thoughts. If it was alive, what manner of creature was it? How would it respond to being used by Rome? What if it was hostile? The last thing they needed was more enemies.

Tairus came walking up then. "What's going on?"

Rome held out the axe to him. "Look."

Puzzled, Tairus looked at the axe for a moment before his eyes widened and he stepped back. "Didn't the eye used to be closed?"

"It did."

"What's happening?"

Rome stared at the axe for a moment before answering. "I wish I knew. I think it might be waking up."

"What do you mean, it's waking up? It's stone. It can't wake up."

Rome raised an eyebrow. "Are you sure about that?"

Tairus glowered at him before answering. "No. I'm not sure about anything. Not anymore." His shoulders slumped. "What are you going to do about it?"

"I don't think there's anything I *can* do about it. I could ask Lowellin – if I had any idea where he is."

"That's one blessing we can count." Tairus started to walk away, but Rome stopped him.

"That's not all." He told Tairus about the dream he'd had. When he was done, Tairus was visibly upset. He threw his helmet on the ground and kicked it.

"Really, Rome? So now you're telling me you're dreaming that thing's thoughts? Do you realize how crazy that is?"

Rome nodded. "I wasn't going to say anything."

"Bereth's tail! I don't believe this! What next?" Tairus stomped off, angrily shouting at the soldiers to get themselves up and get moving.

Rome looked at the axe a final time, then slid the leather sheath over the head, slipping the loop that held it on into place, careful not to touch the axe head as he did so.

He mounted his horse and looked around. From horseback he could see the army camp spread out around him. The camp could barely be called that. There was no real order to it, no neat lines of horse pickets, trenches for latrines, or rows of tents. They were too exhausted for that. When Rome gave the order to stop for the day most of the soldiers basically dropped on the spot. Soldiers disappeared every night now and Rome made no attempt to chase them. His men were too tired to chase down deserters and, though it rankled his military nature to let them go, he understood their motivation well enough. They saw the end coming and nothing to look forward to but more battles against enemies who could not be killed by steel and muscle. Why not run to the family and spend what time a man could with them?

They'd lost a sizable portion of the army to Karthije. The army he had built with such pride and hope for the future was crumbling before his eyes. It tore at him, but Rome knew he had nothing to offer them. Now the axe, on which so much was built, was slipping from his grasp as well. He'd never felt so helpless in his life.

THIRTY-SIX

"Well, the city is still standing. That's something," Rome said to Tairus. They were about a mile from Qarath. It was mid-afternoon and the army, what was left of it, was strung out behind the two of them like a dying snake. The weariness Rome felt went clear to the bone. As bad as it was for him, at least he had a horse. He pitied the poor foot soldiers. The shoes of most of them had deteriorated to little more than scraps of leather held together with bits of string and faith.

The contingent of nobles led by Dargent didn't look very good either. Gone were the fancy shields and brightly waving banners. Some of that stuff was still being lugged along by their retainers, but Rome had a feeling that most of it had been quietly dumped alongside the road. Or maybe not so quietly. Word from the nobles' contingent was that the peasants serving them were being a lot more vocal about their loathing for their masters. Nothing like the end of the world to clear a man's head and make him question his lot in life. So far none of the nobles had been murdered outright, which Rome supposed was good. Not because he'd shed a single tear over the lot of them, but because he didn't relish hanging a man for doing what he believed in his gut needed to be done.

"Once I get off this horse, I'm never getting on one again," Tairus said. "I've a mind to knock this one on the head with my axe, rid the world of him once and for all." The horse Tairus was riding laid its ears back as if it understood his words. Maybe it did. Certainly the two of them didn't get along at all. Just that morning, while Tairus was saddling his horse, the beast had taken the opportunity to put its foot down on one of his. Then it shifted its weight to that foot and stood there with what Rome would have sworn was an innocent expression while Tairus swore violently and beat on it with his fists, mostly ineffectually.

As they drew closer a single rider exited the gates and came towards them. It was Quyloc. Rome saw nothing good in his expression. He motioned to Tairus to fall back a few paces, wanting to talk to Quyloc in private for a few minutes.

"How's the city?" he asked, as Quyloc reined in beside him.

"Pretty quiet, actually, though I'm told it was close," Quyloc replied. "Naills said a couple days before I got here a mob assaulted the palace."

"A mob?" Rome felt sick. "How many died?"

"No one. It seems Ricarn, the Insect Tender, convinced them to go home. Something about a swarm of stinging bugs."

"How did she…?" Rome waved off his own question. "Never mind. I don't need to know right now." His eyes felt full of sand. Rust coated his bones. What he really wanted was a bottle of rum and about two days of uninterrupted sleep. He wanted to be with Bonnie. But all that would have to wait. Too much was happening and there wasn't enough time.

"While we have a chance," Rome said. "You need to see something." He drew the black axe and held it out to Quyloc.

Quyloc looked at it, but made no effort to touch it. "The eye on the other side is open as well?" he asked.

Rome flipped the axe over to show him. "What do you think?"

"Didn't Lowellin say it might be alive?" Rome nodded. "Then it's waking up."

"That's what I was thinking," Rome said glumly. "Tairus thinks it's going to wake up angry."

"Probably."

"That's not all," Rome said, putting the axe back in its sheath. "I've been having these dreams every night where I'm trapped in stone and I can't move. It feels like I've been there for a very long time."

Quyloc looked thoughtful. The city walls drew nearer. "So you think the dreams are coming from the axe?"

"It makes sense."

Quyloc made a sound that might have been a bitter laugh. "What's the world come to when sharing a dream with an axe makes sense?"

"Isn't that the truth?" Rome sighed. "I think it's talking to me also."

Quyloc shot him a surprised look.

"Not aloud or anything like that," Rome added. "More like it's in my mind. All it says is 'Free me.'"

Quyloc was silent for a minute, digesting this. "My guess is something trapped it into this form – maybe one of the Guardians – and then placed it into the wall of the prison. Someone was meant to find it and pull it out, thus paving the way for the prison to be broken."

"What makes you think someone trapped it?"

"It probably wouldn't be asking you to free it if it was something it chose for itself."

Rome nodded. "True."

"It doesn't say anything about how you're supposed to free it?"

"No."

"And you've seen nothing else in your dreams that could be a clue?"

Rome shook his head.

"I had an argument with a god a couple days ago," Quyloc said.

"A god? No kidding?"

"Well, not a god. A Shaper. Same thing."

"Which one?"

"Khanewal."

Rome scratched his beard. It itched. His whole body itched. "I don't know that one."

"I don't think anyone's ever worshipped her. She's something of a bitch."

"What did she want?"

"She wanted me to ride out and attack Melekath."

"I'm guessing you said no."

"She wasn't happy. She doesn't like people very much. She threatened me a few times."

"Is she going to be a problem?"

"Maybe. She's scared."

"Who isn't?"

"Have you seen Lowellin?" Quyloc asked. Rome shook his head. "I don't think things are going much like he planned."

"Do you have any good news?" Rome asked.

"The city didn't burn down."

"That's something"

"Khanewal showed me what the Children can do. It was pretty bad."

"How bad?"

"They suck out all your Song and you die. They get stronger."

Rome swore. "Why'd they have to be immortal?"

"Based on how they look, I'd say they've had a pretty bad time of it. We're not going to be negotiating with them."

"Any chance Khanewal is going to help us?"

"I doubt it. We're basically talking bugs to her."

"We're probably better off without her," Rome said. "Perthen took his soldiers back." He told Quyloc about meeting with Perthen and what had happened to him.

Quyloc got kind of a sick look on his face. "T'sim told me there might be unpleasant side effects. I didn't think they would be that bad."

"What happened to him?"

"I don't know. My best guess is that some of the chaos power got into him when I cut his flow."

"Chaos power?"

"It's the power from the abyss."

"Which is…?"

"Some place deep underground. The Shapers used chaos power from that place to create the prison. Chaos power is poisonous to everything."

"You better make sure you don't cut yourself with it."

"I'll do my best."

"Did you have any trouble on your way back here?"

"You could say that."

"What happened?"

"The *sulbits* tried to eat us all."

"What? Why?"

Quyloc shrugged. "They were hungry."

"What happened?"

"It's not important. I'll tell you about it later. You're not going to like this, but we may have to evacuate the city."

"You want us to just run away?"

"You don't really understand yet what we're up against. If we can't come up with something, we've got nothing left but to run."

"What's the point of that? Where would we run to?"

"I don't know," Quyloc snapped. "You think I like this any better than you do? I don't want to run either. But what else are we going to do? Just sit here and let them slaughter us?"

"But you have the spear and I have the axe and there's the Tenders. Surely there's something they can do."

"I hope so. On the good days, anyway. Most days it just looks hopeless to me."

"Gods, Quyloc," Rome said. "We are truly fucked aren't we?"

They rode through the gates of the city. Niko was tired and a lot thinner than the last time he'd passed through these same gates, but the horse knew he was home and he lifted his head and perked up his ears. Rome patted the stallion on the neck, raising a cloud of dust. "I feel the same way, boy."

Rome saw scorch marks on stone and the blackened ruins of several buildings nearby. "They felt it here too, didn't they?" he said. "The prison breaking."

Quyloc nodded. "Apparently it got pretty bad. Way beyond what the city watch was equipped to handle."

"We didn't leave Naills very many men. It's a good thing he had Ricarn to settle them down."

"Ricarn broke up the mob, but it was the morning services that settled them down."

Rome gave him a questioning look.

"It wasn't Velma, the Tender Nalene left in charge. Some young girl named Cara. She's still doing them." Quyloc gave a half smile. "I went to listen. She's good. Not fire and death like the FirstMother, more softness and butterflies. But it works. They're still afraid," he said, gesturing at the city, "but they're not panicking anymore."

"The FirstMother isn't leading the morning services anymore?"

Quyloc shook his head.

"So long as she keeps them calm."

THIRTY-SEVEN

Once at the palace, Rome headed off toward his rooms, telling Quyloc that he wanted him to gather the others for a meeting in the tower in a few minutes. Quyloc sent out some messengers and then went to his office. As he was leaving his office, he heard his name called and turned to see Perganon hurrying toward him from the other direction.

"Can it wait? I'm in a hurry," Quyloc said.

"I know. I won't keep you for long. But what I have to say may have some bearing."

"What is it then?"

"If you will recall, a number of old books were found inside the wall that was torn out of the library." Quyloc nodded. "I have been going through those books and I found one that was written shortly after the fall of the Empire. As you know, records from that time are spotty at best. When the city finally fell, very few of its citizens escaped." It was true. Very little information about the Empire's final days had survived. What there was available was wildly contradictory and based almost completely on rumors, of which there were many.

"This book though, was apparently written by one of the Emperor's ministers, who was dispatched to Qarath on official business only days before Kaetria fell. The author said that in the final days the capital city of Kaetria was besieged by the encroaching sands of the Gur al Krin desert and by three monstrous creatures that roamed those sands. The creatures were the Guardians."

"Get to the point," Quyloc said tersely.

Perganon nodded. "My apologies. The relevant fact here is that apparently the Tenders were able to keep the Guardians at bay for some time by erecting a shield around the entire city, a shield made of LifeSong."

"Really?" Quyloc said. "I've never heard of that."

"Is it possible that something similar could be done here? I realize it would not solve our problem, but it might buy us some time."

"It just might. I will talk to the FirstMother about it. Keep researching. Let me know anything you find."

Perganon lowered his head. "Of course, Advisor. I will do all I can."

When Rome walked into the meeting room high up in the tower, the others were already there. Rome went to the window and looked down over the city while he caught his breath from the climb. From up here it looked perfectly normal, people moving about their ordinary days. The few burned spots were hard to see.

Rome turned away from the window and went and took a seat at the table next to Naills, who was sitting, his elbows on the table, his head in his hands. He did not look up as Rome sat down.

Nalene was sitting opposite Rome. Her thick hands were splayed before her on the table and she was staring at them. The ragged stubble of hair sprouting from her scalp – she still hadn't gotten it shaved again – looked white. She seemed smaller than he remembered her, as if some of the air had gone out of her. Her *sulbit* was crouched on her shoulder. It was the size of a cat now, still with the sinewy grace of a reptile, but with smooth, ivory skin and short, thick legs. The rear legs were longer, stouter than the front, and it raised itself partway on them, its front legs hanging like odd little arms, its blunt head turning this way and that while it peered at the others with its shiny, beady eyes.

Tairus was to Rome's left. Sweat stained his clothes and plastered his graying hair to his head. He was tearing at the plate of meat and cheese in front of him, all his attention focused on the food.

Standing a step back from the table to Rome's right was Ricarn. She might have been marble, so alien and bloodless did she look. Her crimson robe hid her feet. Her hair was a black mass of shadows in which hints of movement showed now and then. She regarded Rome without blinking, no hint of impatience, fear, concern or anything on her face.

They were all here, Rome thought, except Lowellin. Would they see him again? What was he doing?

There was a small cough at his shoulder and Rome started. T'sim stood there, as prim as ever in his long, brown coat with the polished silver buttons, his hands clasped behind his back. Rome hadn't seen him in three days.

Rome took a drink of water and dove right in. "How long until Melekath reaches Thrikyl?"

"Less than a day," Ricarn responded. "Maybe tonight."

Naills looked up then, his face haggard. "They still aren't leaving, are they?" he asked Ricarn.

The Insect Tender turned slightly to look at him. Her expression never changed. "Only a few."

Naills swore, which was unusual for him, who was always so proper and controlled. "The fools."

"It is their home. They are afraid. They convince themselves the danger is less than it is and so they believe what they wish to be true. It is no more or less than humans have done since the beginning." Her words were hard, but her voice had no inflection.

"Any chance they can hold out?" Rome asked. "It's a big wall."

"Melekath is a Stone Shaper," Ricarn said. "A stone wall is not a real obstacle to him."

"So what will happen when they get in?"

"They will all die," Ricarn replied. The words seemed to echo around the room. "And the Children will grow immeasurably stronger."

"Quyloc told me what happened to Ferien," Rome said. He remembered Ferien. He and Quyloc had passed through there after they emerged from the Gur al Krin, on their way to the army besieging Thrikyl. How long ago that seemed. "But I still don't understand. Melekath's Children are immortal, but they're still human. Why are they sucking out people's Song? What's in it for them?"

"There is a vast emptiness in them," Ricarn said. "The Gift severed them from LifeSong and three thousand years in darkness drove them insane. Consuming Song pushes the darkness back, at least for a while."

"Poor, miserable bastards," Rome said. "Why would Mclckath do that to them?"

"He thought he was helping."

"And eating Song makes them stronger?"

"It does. By the time they are finished with Thrikyl, they will likely be more powerful than the Shapers."

"How do we fight them? There must be something we can do."

"Not really," Ricarn replied. "We could run, but it will only delay the inevitable. There is no way to hide from them. They can smell Song no matter how it is hidden from them. Their hunger has no limits. They will feed until nothing lives, and then they will devour the River itself. After that, I do not know. Possibly they will consume the energy of the Spheres of Stone, Sea, and Sky as well. There is no way to know. Nothing like them has ever existed."

Tairus swore. Nalene jerked as if she'd been slapped and her *sulbit* hissed softly. Rome felt a sickness in his gut.

"If there is any hope, it is that they cannot yet feed on LifeSong directly, but only on Selfsong that they take from living things."

"I wouldn't call that hope," Tairus said, wiping his mouth with the back of his wrist.

"I refuse to believe there is nothing we can do," Rome said, looking around the table.

"Perganon told me that in the Empire's final days the Tenders erected a barrier of LifeSong around the capital city that was strong enough to keep out the Guardians," Quyloc said. "FirstMother, you put up some kind of shield to protect the Tenders from the wall of flames that the blinded ones sent against us at Guardians Watch. Can you do the same thing here on a bigger scale?"

"Are you serious?" the FirstMother replied, raising her head to stare at him.

"So that's a no?"

"We *might* be able to do it. But I'd need another hundred or so Tenders with *sulbits* and about a year to prepare them. You have no idea how difficult what you're asking would be. The Tenders of the Empire were vastly more powerful than we are, and there were a whole lot more of them. At best the most we could manage would be to block off the main gates."

T'sim stepped forward. "Lowellin is coming," he told Rome.

A moment later a shadow coalesced out of thin air. It grew wider and taller and then Lowellin stepped out of it. When he exited the shadow it collapsed and was sucked into his staff.

Lowellin sneered down at them. "It appears that finally you grasp the true gravity of your situation."

"Do you have anything useful to offer, or are you just here to say I told you so?" Rome asked.

Lowellin glared at him. "If we fail to stop Melekath and his spawn, my only consolation will be the joy I get from watching them devour you and your precious city, Wulf Rome."

"You came all this way to say that?" Tairus said.

Lowellin didn't even spare him a glance. "A short while ago, Melekath and his Children reached the city of Thrikyl. Any hope of convincing those fools to leave their precious city is now gone. Once the Children enter the city they will finally be able to feed freely. They will grow huge and vastly powerful, more powerful than you can imagine. More powerful than even I can imagine. Nothing we have planned so far will make the slightest difference then."

"So what are you suggesting?" Tairus asked. "You want us all to just kill ourselves?"

"If I thought it would help, but no. What I want you to do is twofold: first, you need to begin feeding the *sulbits* on human Selfsong. It is far more potent than the Song contained in animals and it will accelerate their growth." He was looking at Rome as he said this and did not miss the look on Rome's face. "Before you object, I remind you that you have no real choice. Some will, of course, die, but that is better than everyone dying."

Rome gritted his teeth. With an effort he said, "What's the second thing?"

"Hitting the Children with bolts of Song, the way you did at Guardians Watch," he said to the FirstMother, "won't work here. It will only make them stronger."

"I feared as much," she said softly.

"In order for the *sulbits* to be effective, they must be infected with chaos power."

The FirstMother's face drained of color. "That will kill them."

"It may not," Lowellin said. "These are not ordinary creatures. We don't know what they're capable of."

"And if it just kills them or drives them crazy? Then what? We'll be defenseless," Rome said.

"Which is why I will test it on just one at first."

"How will you obtain the chaos power to infect the *sulbits*?" T'sim wanted to know. "It did not go well when Bereth and Larkind first delved there." They were the first Shapers to discover the abyss, eons ago. When they tried to Shape chaos power Larkind was destroyed and Bereth was badly wounded.

218

"I'm not the idiot that they are," Lowellin growled. "I've been studying the problem and I know how to handle chaos power safely."

"There is no proof chaos power *can* be handled safely."

"Yes, there is. Since their escape, two of the Guardians have done it."

"So *that* is where the traces of chaos power have been coming from," T'sim said softly.

"The Guardians have been using chaos power?" Quyloc asked, shocked.

"Gulagh has been bleeding chaos power into the River for months now," Lowellin replied. "That is the source of the poison that keeps cropping up in the flows. And Kasai went there to get the *ingerlings*, the creatures that devoured Tu Sinar."

"The effects of those decisions will be felt for a long time," Ricarn put in. "It is possible that we will survive the Children simply to succumb to chaos power. And you wish to add even more to our world."

"Without it, we have no chance," Lowellin retorted. "You worry about what might happen, still not believing me when I tell you what *will* happen. By the time the Children are finished devouring the people of Thrikyl they will be so powerful they will be gods. They will be strong enough to reach into and drink from the River itself. You will be no more of a threat to them than a fly is to you. They won't even brush you aside. With each drink from the River they will grow ever more powerful and eventually they will consume it completely. There will be nothing left. This world will be a lifeless wasteland. Are you really so stupid that you won't take any chance, however great, to defeat them?"

They all looked at each other and Rome saw in everyone's face the sick realization that Lowellin was telling the truth. They really had no other options.

Rome spoke. "It's late and I'm beat. Let's see what happens in Thrikyl tonight. Maybe the Children won't get into the city right away. Maybe something else will come up. We will meet in the morning and I will give you my answer then."

"I will grant you this time," Lowellin said, pointing the staff at him, "only because I will need some time to obtain the chaos power. But I assure you of one thing: I will not let your idiocy doom our only hope. I will be at the Tender estate by dawn tomorrow and I will infect a *sulbit* then, with or without your permission."

He turned and stalked away. As he went, he threw the staff. It spun in the air and darkness flowed from it like ink. He stepped into the darkness and disappeared. Moments later the darkness was gone as well.

"So that's how he pops up wherever he wants to," Tairus said, a chicken leg in one hand. He hadn't stopped eating the whole time Lowellin was there. "Neat trick. I wonder what that staff really is.'

Rome looked around the room at all of them. "What do you think? Do we have any other options?"

"I don't think we do," Quyloc replied.

"Do you think it will work?"

Quyloc nodded. "It could. If the *sulbit* doesn't die or go crazy. LifeSong cannot withstand contact with chaos power. It's why the spear is able to cut flows of Song. In theory at least, if the *sulbits* were infected with chaos power, any attacks they make against the Children would contain chaos power. Perhaps the Children would be able to survive it, but it's possible that it would destroy them completely."

"What do you think?" Rome asked the FirstMother.

She nodded, her expression bleak. One hand was resting protectively on her *sulbit*, which was crouched in her lap. "What he says makes sense. I can think of no other weapon we could use against them."

"And you?" Rome asked Ricarn.

"It seems you are willing to destroy yourselves in order to survive," she replied. "I do not believe this is the answer. I believe there is another way, one we have not found yet. But I admit I am curious to see what happens."

Rome gave her a confused look.

"Why don't we just do it and get it over with?" Tairus said, throwing down the gnawed bone on his plate.

Rome said, "Tomorrow morning we will meet at the Tender estate at dawn. I want to be there when Lowellin does this, in case something goes wrong."

THIRTY-EIGHT

Orenthe had been a Tender once, millennia ago. She still carried faint memories of the day when Melekath first returned with his Gift. It had been raining all morning, not that it made any difference to her since she spent most of her days in her room, going ever deeper *beyond*, embracing the wonder of LifeSong.

Orenthe was one of the strongest Tenders of her day. She had journeyed down to the River many times. She had learned to manipulate the lesser flows of LifeSong to the point that she could pull one away from a living creature and attach it to another one. She could draw Song directly from the minor flows. Strong as she was, she had never touched one of the trunk lines. Though Xochitl had said more than once that any Tender was capable of doing so, it was generally thought to be impossible by the Tenders themselves. Two of their strongest had tried it in the past and each had been torn apart, the energy contained therein too much for them to control.

On that fateful day, one of the other Tenders – she could no longer remember who it was or anything about her – had shaken her out of her meditative state and urged her to come. When she asked what the fuss was, the woman excitedly told Orenthe that, after so long, the deceiver had returned and was entering the city. It was a momentous event and one she should not miss.

Still a little dazed from her time *beyond*, Orenthe had followed her, down the long, silent halls, across the elevated walkways, and up onto a balcony overlooking the main thoroughfare which led into Qarath.

"That's *him*?" Orenthe asked her now-forgotten guide.

"It is. Melekath himself." The woman scowled. "See how he carries himself, as if the city were his and we still his subjects. Can he really still believe that we are not wise to him?"

Melekath had been gone for hundreds of years. The stories said that Xochitl's anger was so great on the day that he left that she had

221

struck the floor in the main hall of the temple, splitting it asunder. Orenthe didn't know if the story was true: she had never been into the main hall of the temple. None of the Tenders she knew had. They were not allowed in there. None but Lowellin, he who was the Protector, had been in there for over two hundred years. On reflex Orenthe looked up the slope of Qarath to the massive, red quartz building standing at the apex of the city, its main tower impossibly tall and thin, reaching up as if to pierce the very heavens.

"I thought he would be bigger," Orenthe said.

Her memory said the other Tender did not respond, or it had simply been too long, but she clearly remembered Melekath. No more than average height, with a slight build and brown hair, he looked like an ordinary citizen walking down the street. Except that, like all the gods, there was something about him that made it impossible to confuse him with an ordinary person. It was a feeling that the body he wore was nothing more than a thin disguise, something worn to hide his full nature, and only mildly successful at it. He was a being of great power, perhaps even more powerful than Xochitl herself.

But on that day in the long-ago past Melekath had been leaning on a staff as he walked, as though every movement was a great trial. There was triumph on his face, but it was clouded with exhaustion. He appeared as a man who had accomplished an impossible task at great personal expense.

Orenthe watched him until he passed down the street and out of sight, caught by something about him she could not explain.

"He's not like Lowellin described him," she said to the other Tender.

"Yet were we not told that he would cloak himself in deceit, that he would make us doubt?" she replied. "Lowellin warned us that nothing would be as it seemed."

Orenthe agreed with her. What else could she do? She spoke with the words of Lowellin, after all. Who better to know the truth than he? Lowellin met every day with Xochitl, receiving her wisdom and sharing it with the Tenders. It was Lowellin who had brought them word to form the Tenders, said that it was Xochitl's will that those who were true of heart and courageous should swear themselves to her, become her priestesses, share in her beneficence. Lowellin had also told them that because a man, Radagon, had gone with Melekath when he left, Xochitl was angry with men and would allow none of them to join the Tenders.

It was Lowellin who had told them the truth in the first decade after Melekath's departure: Xochitl was the Creator, the one who created Life and the first humans, not Melekath as they had been led to believe. It was Lowellin who told them that Melekath hid because he plotted their downfall, because he was jealous of their Mother's love for them. Lowellin had said Melekath would return someday and that they should be ready for he was a creature of lies and they could trust nothing he said.

"I would like to see him closer," Orenthe said when he was out of sight.

The next day word spread throughout Qarath that Melekath would be speaking in the great amphitheater and all were invited to come listen. Since his return the city had been buzzing with rumors and anticipation. After his arrival, Melekath had gone directly to the great temple at the top of the city and disappeared inside. All knew of Xochitl's displeasure with the deceiver and they hunkered down for the eruption that was sure to follow. Would the temple be destroyed in the conflict when the two gods fought? Would the whole city be destroyed? Some citizens fled the city, but in the end it was anticlimactic. There were no explosions. The ground did not shake. The sky did not darken.

By late morning the great amphitheater was packed and more were streaming in from every corner of the city. By noon every street around the amphitheater was jammed. People had climbed onto rooftops. Several people had fallen to their deaths.

Shortly after noon Melekath walked out onto the field, still leaning on his staff, and Orenthe, sitting in the private box reserved for the Tenders, got her first chance to see him up close. Her first impression was that he had a sad face. There were lines around his eyes and mouth that spoke to her of heavy burdens carried. He looked up, and for a moment made eye contact with her, and something went through her. She couldn't have explained what it was, but at that moment she knew that the things she had been told about him, about his arrogance and his cruelty, were lies. He was neither of those. And she knew that the lines on his face were worry. Worry for her, for all people. She saw more in that instant as well. She saw the triumph that had carried him into the city the day before.

And she saw his anger.

A few seconds later Xochitl emerged from the tunnel and walked out onto the field. Most of the crowd gasped when she emerged and Orenthe did as well. Xochitl was a complete contrast to Melekath, tall, elegant, radiant. Her hair was golden and flowed down her back almost to the ground. Her gown trailed out behind her. Orenthe tried to see her face but it was hard to look directly at her. An aura of light surrounded her, as if the sun shone from directly behind her. Orenthe had an impression of vast beauty, and then she had to look away, blinking at the afterimages burned into her retinas.

Behind Xochitl came Lowellin. His face was dark and thunderous and he hurried to catch up to Xochitl. When he did he leaned close and Orenthe caught several angry words over the murmurs of the crowd. Xochitl turned her face away and Lowellin's features darkened further.

Melekath stopped in the middle of the arena and slowly surveyed the crowd. The murmurs stopped and the place went dead silent. Though she knew it was not possible, that there were tens of thousands in the amphitheater, Orenthe nevertheless felt as if Melekath looked directly at her when he scanned the crowd. She wondered briefly if others felt the same.

"My Children. It has been too long. I have missed you."

Melekath paused. If he was waiting for reciprocation from the crowd, he was soon disappointed, for the only responses he received were catcalls and hurled insults. It was only a small percentage of the crowd – most were silent – but it was enough that he frowned. He gave a sideways look at Xochitl, but she was turned away and he found only Lowellin's glare.

"But my long absence has not been in vain. For I have at last succeeded in my quest. I have found the answers I sought and now I come to share them with you."

Again he paused and again he was greeted with insults and derision. What else could they do? Every person in the amphitheater had been told since they were born that Melekath was the great deceiver, the god who would usurp Xochitl's place as their creator if he could. They had been warned that his every word would be a lie and to be prepared to resist him. Melekath's expression darkened further but he continued.

"I have brought you my Gift and it is the end of fear. No longer need you fear death, for I bring you immortality."

Now there was silence, as the audience grappled with his words. This was not something they had expected. Into the silence stepped Lowellin.

"It is a lie!" he cried. "He seeks only to mislead you, as I warned you he would. Reject him!"

The derision returned. Insults were hurled at Melekath. After a few seconds he lowered his head, both hands gripped around the head of his walking staff, his eyes fixed on the ground.

"What fools does he take us for?" a nearby Tender spat.

"Perhaps we are fools," Orenthe murmured, too quietly for the Tender, or any of the others, to hear. "Maybe we've already been misled."

"So you have made your choice," Melekath said, raising his head. The insults stopped, while they listened for what he would say next. Lies or no, there was something compelling about his voice, something that rang deep and resonated within the soul. His voice changed then, as a spark blazed to life in his eyes. "Never was it my intent to force any of my Children in any way. It is not how I created you." There were new catcalls at the last words. "You have chosen lies and death. So be it. I leave you to them."

With that he turned away, crossed the arena and disappeared into the tunnel he had emerged from.

The crowd cheered. Around her the other Tenders were hugging. Some were crying. They cried Xochitl's name. A few called out to Lowellin.

But Orenthe did not join them. She was already moving, pushing her way through the crush with muttered apologies. She wanted to see Melekath up close. She wanted to see for herself.

Outside the amphitheater the crowd suddenly recoiled as Melekath emerged. Even packed as tightly as they were they still managed to pull back and create an opening around Melekath. Somehow Orenthe managed to catch up and slip into that opening, gasping at the sudden freedom that came with release from the crowd. She was nearly close enough to touch him, breathing hard, suddenly unsure of what she was doing or why.

He regarded the crowd for a long moment, almost as if waiting for something. They did not insult him as those inside the amphitheater had. He was too close, too dangerous, for that. But they turned their faces away and it was all he needed to know.

Melekath started forward. The crowd parted for him. And Orenthe followed.

They had passed through the crowd and into the nearly-empty city streets when Orenthe realized she was not the only person following Melekath. A dozen or so had joined her, all hanging back, unsure but compelled all the same.

They were outside the city, the last homes and buildings behind them, when Melekath stopped and turned around. There were perhaps a hundred following him by then, a mixed bag of people of all ages, all confused with wonder and hope and fear. Melekath regarded them without speaking for a time.

Up close, Orenthe could finally see his eyes and what she saw there warmed her. Her whole life she had worshipped a god from afar, a god who never showed herself and then dazzled her to blindness so that she had to look away. But here was one who stood before her, almost ordinary in his humanness, his vulnerability and pain on open display. She was transfixed by him.

"I did not mean to be gone so long," he said. "I never believed you would forget me so easily."

His pain struck her deeply and she felt tears in her eyes. He had been wounded deeply and she had been the one to wound him.

"I wanted only to save you, my Children. I cannot bear to see you die. I cannot bear to have you taken from me."

His words pierced her and she felt the tears begin to flow.

"I did not dream that he would turn you against me, or that she would let him. Forgive me, my Children. I did not intend that it should be like this."

Without meaning to, Orenthe stepped forward. "I would like the Gift," she said quietly.

As if she had broken something, many of the others stepped forward as well, echoing her. Melekath seemed genuinely surprised. He gripped his walking staff so tightly that his knuckles turned white. Unshed tears filled his eyes.

"I made you in my image," he said, his words thick with emotion. "And yet it is I who am remade in your image. You have ever surprised me, my Children. You have ever humbled me."

A rider clattered down the paved road toward them then, a tall, red-haired woman on a magnificent horse. Two servants trailed her on lesser horses. Heedlessly she rode through their ranks and people scattered before her. Orenthe knew her, or rather knew of her. Reyna, powerful, beautiful, ruthless.

She rode between Orenthe and Melekath and slid down from her horse. She stood before Melekath, slightly taller than he, and looked him steadily in the eye. "Give me the Gift," she said.

And so it was that Reyna was the first to receive the Gift. She alone that day did not kneel to receive the Gift. She stood proudly while he placed his hands on her head. Orenthe watched as Melekath closed his eyes. She saw the sudden, intense glow as power flowed from his hands into Reyna. And she saw as well what it cost him, how he staggered slightly when he let her go.

Reyna saw none of those things, or if she did she did not care. Some new power flowed through her when she turned on the rest of them, a bright, cold smile on her face.

One by one Melekath conferred his Gift on the rest of them. Others crowded in before Orenthe, though she was closer. She did not resist as they replaced her. She watched quietly as he gave to each one and saw how each time it weakened him slightly. She felt almost guilty when it was her turn, but he motioned her forward with a small smile on his face and she could not have resisted him by then.

The Gift was a sudden, blinding flash that suffused her, washing over her, changing her irrevocably. She cried out softly in her joy.

Something else came with it, a distant feeling of loss, but she paid no attention to it. Something was always left behind when great changes came. It was only to be expected.

When he was done, Melekath faced them. "Thank you," he said simply. "Your faith has restored me." He looked over them at the city, shining behind them, and concern crossed his face. "I fear we cannot stay here. I know Lowellin and he will not tolerate this and Xochitl will not rein him in. Violence will come if we stay.

"Even though my other Children have turned their backs on me, I would not see bloodshed. We will have to go away, make our own home far from here where we can live in peace." He thought for a moment. "I have in mind a place of fertile lands and soft rivers, where the trees are thick and tall. We will build our home there and paradise will be ours." The people murmured at his words, and smiled to each other.

"Go now," he said. "Gather those of your possessions that you most value, but gather lightly. For all that you leave behind I will replace tenfold, a hundredfold. I will provide for you so that you never want again, never go in fear or hunger or pain. Gather loved ones if you can. Gather any you can who long for what I offer. There must be others, people who do not have your courage. Call them to join you, to join us out here as we begin our journey into a bright new future."

He stood there staring after them as they made their way back into Qarath for a final time. Orenthe looked back once and saw him still standing there, watching them, a smile on his face.

THIRTY-NINE

Melekath was true to his word. The city he created was a thing of wonder. Orenthe watched spellbound as he raised it from the very bones of the earth and shaped it with his will. She knew then why Lowellin hated and feared Melekath so. It was not just Melekath's power that Lowellin hated; it was his heart.

Each building was a work of art, formed from a single stone and shaped in beautiful, flowing lines crafted with an artist's eye. They were almost living things, an unknown life form that rose up from the ground, each blending seamlessly into the one next to it. Some looked like they were about to take flight, gently perched on the ground. Others appeared to have grown from the ground like a plant of a type never seen before. He crafted them from stone in every color of the rainbow. There were reds, pinks and oranges to put the sunsets to shame. Blues and greens that challenged the skies and the seas for depth and beauty. Near one edge of the city was a cluster of buildings made of quartz, interspersed here and there with buildings made of pure, translucent obsidian. One building was formed of a green-tinted granite and looked like a cliff face. The doors and shutters were so perfectly fitted that when they were closed they were invisible. The city contained great parks as well, trees and bushes growing thickly around a profusion of fantastic stone sculptures, realistic and fantastic depictions of creatures.

Last, Melekath shaped the great spire in the center of the city. It was formed of a single piece of deep blue crystalline stone, as if the whole thing was made from a giant sapphire. It rose a thousand feet into the sky, tapering to a fine point at the top. Around its circumference at regular intervals were balconies where people could stand to look out over their great city. The inside was open from the bottom floor to the very top, ringed at every floor with walkways and balconies. Opening onto the balconies were a thousand rooms, rooms designed to foster wonder and creativity. Creating, painting, sculpting, writing, dreaming. The spire was built to house it all, to provide a place for every one of Melekath's Children to gather, to follow any dream.

At the base of the spire and taking up the bottom twenty stories, was a huge auditorium. Rows of seats encircled the floor and in the center of the floor was a large, stone dais. There, plays could be staged, or the citizens could gather for a talk or to debate their future.

The city took Orenthe's breath away every single day. The colors changed as the light of the day changed. It seemed there was always something new to discover, some new wonder down a street she had never noticed before. Sometimes a street she was familiar with would appear differently the next day. She loved the place and yet...

There was something wrong. An emptiness inside that was only faint at first, but gradually grew stronger and stronger. At first, in the excitement of all the changes and the creation of the city, Orenthe didn't really notice it or when she did she put it down to fear, as what she had been used to was replaced by something completely new. After all, it wasn't every day that one became immortal. Endless time was now hers. There was no need to hurry. No need to worry about running out of time.

However she tried, she could not convince herself that nothing was wrong. The music of Song, that ceaseless background accompaniment to her life, had grown fuzzy and distant. Then came the day when she could not hear it at all. She was walking down the street when she noticed its absence. She stopped, feeling a stirring of panic within her. She looked around at the others going about their day, but none of them seemed to notice. But then, none of them were Tenders. They had not spent their lives attuned to Song.

There was a bench nearby and Orenthe sat down on it, trying to collect herself. She closed her eyes and went *beyond*. There, she received an even greater shock.

None of the people around her were connected to a flow of Song.

But...that couldn't be. She pushed her way deeper into the mists and her fear grew. Not only was no one connected to a flow, but there were almost no flows to be *seen*. There were a few, attached to plants, but even they looked somewhat thin and tenuous.

With her will, she reached out to take hold of one, a routine action that she had done thousands of times.

The flow moved away from her.

Fully alarmed now, she strengthened her will and snatched the flow before it could move away.

Before her eyes, the flow faded and flickered out. The plant it was attached to, a small, broad-leafed shrub, turned brown and died.

Horrified, Orenthe left *beyond* and began hurrying toward the center of the city. She could feel Melekath's presence – they all could; he was a lodestone they felt at all times – somewhere near the Spire.

She found him outside, shaping a piece of pink granite. He had made something that looked much like a great cat, crouched to spring, but he must have been unhappy with it because as she approached he frowned and set his hand on it. A second later the sculpture slumped, lost its shape and became a formless mass on the ground. She reached him just as he started to draw it up and form it anew.

"Father, can I speak with you please?" They all called him Father. He was, after all, their creator. Not Xochitl.

He turned to her at once. Seeing her distress, he released the stone so that it slumped back to the ground. He made the smallest gesture with his hand and it formed instantly into a bench.

"Sit," he said, motioning.

She sat and he did as well, taking her hands in his and looking into her eyes. His eyes changed as the weather changed, and today they were a depthless blue. For a moment she couldn't speak. When Melekath spoke with one of his Children, he gave that person complete attention. The feeling Orenthe always had – as she did now – was that he had nothing else in the world to do that could compare to being with her, that his whole day he had merely been waiting for her to arrive so he could sit with her.

"Talk to me," he said.

"It's the flows…we aren't connected." She told him what she had seen.

"It is nothing to worry about. With my Gift I have set you beyond the need for Song to sustain you. You are, each of you, your own perfect circle. You do not need to be sustained by anything outside you. It is the essence of the Gift."

"But I…I touched one and it…" She had to gather herself. "It *broke*. It disappeared."

Now concern did touch his features. He stroked the back of her hand. "I was not aware of that. I will look into it. I knew there was a chance of unexpected consequences, but I am certain there is nothing to be concerned about. I will take care of it."

Orenthe nodded. She trusted him. If he said it would be okay, she believed him. She stood up. "I will not keep you longer," she said.

He rose too. "You are keeping me from nothing. You are one of my beloved Children and I am always here for you."

Orenthe started to turn away, then paused. "There is one other thing. It might be nothing."

"Go on."

"There is a growing emptiness inside me. There are times when I suddenly don't know where I am or where I am going. I look around and nothing seems familiar. I can hardly hear the music of the Song anymore." The words rushed out of her and she was surprised at how badly she'd needed to say them.

Melekath laid his hand on her shoulder. "Do not worry. It is only temporary. You have made a great change in your life. It is only natural that you have misgivings. It will pass."

She nodded and left him then, but she did not feel reassured by his words and in the coming days the sense of emptiness grew ever stronger.

⚒ ⚒ ⚒

Then there was no more time to worry about it. Melekath gathered them one day in the great auditorium at the base of the Spire and they could see right away that something was terribly wrong. He paced the raised dais with his hands behind his back as they gathered, his face turned down, and for Orenthe it was as if a dark cloud rolled across the face of the sun. She felt his anger and fear as her own and it was difficult to remain seated as the rest of the Children made their way in, so slowly, too slowly. She wanted to shout at them to hurry. They numbered nearly ten thousand now, as more entered the city every day in search of the Gift.

On the dais with him were the three Guardians: Kasai, tall, narrow and white-skinned; Tharn, stone made life, thick and blocky; and Gulagh, most mysterious of them all, wreathed in shadows where none should be.

"They are coming," he said, when they were all seated. His eyes were very dark and his hair was tangled as if he had been dragging his fingers through it. "Xochitl and seven of my most powerful brethren. With them comes an army. The Guardians have brought word."

"But why?" cried a woman. "What have we done to them?"

Melekath's shoulders slumped. "I don't know," he said at last. "Somehow Lowellin has convinced Xochitl that we are a danger to them and she in turn has convinced the others. It was something I would not have considered possible. My brethren do not work well together. We never have."

"What will become of us?" the same woman asked. She was a matronly woman, holding the hands of two small girls, twins by the look of them. "What should we do?"

"Stay calm," he replied. "When they get here I will speak with them. It is still possible that I can sway them from this madness."

"And if they won't listen?" Orenthe murmured softly.

Melekath looked up and met her eyes. Somehow he had heard. "We are not helpless. I know something they are unaware of. I know how to tap into the power of the Heart of the Stone directly. I can raise a shield of this power around the city. Nothing they can do, even with their combined might, can breach this shield."

There were sighs of relief at this and the crowd relaxed visibly. Then one man with the thick arms and shoulders of a blacksmith stood up. Orenthe thought his name was Heram.

"I say we arm ourselves and take the fight to them!" he shouted, shaking his fist. "Let us make an example of them to everyone who threatens us." He looked out over the crowd. "How can we lose? With the Gift we are immortal!"

A number cheered at his words, though they were in the minority. Orenthe personally recoiled at the thought of shedding the blood of her people. Fortunately, Melekath felt the same way.

"No. We will not shed the blood of our brothers unless we have no other choice. We will not give in to hate or fear. We must remember that they are our blood, that they are not evil, only confused and afraid."

Grumbling, Heram sat down. Then the red-haired woman, Reyna, spoke.

"Well enough for the human army, but what about the ones who lead them?" Her voice was very clear and cold.

Melekath's face darkened. "For them I have no mercy," he grated. "They are not blinded by the fears of those who are mortal. If they do not desist, they will answer to me for this. But that is for me to do, not you. Even the Gift cannot enable you to fight them."

The human army was vast, covering the green, rolling hills around Durag'otal in every direction. They came from many cities across the land, cities where gods other than Xochitl were worshipped, and their colorful, varied banners filled the air. They marched to the sounds of drums and horns and the light flashed off weapons and armor of every type.

At their head strode the Eight: Xochitl, remote and awesome in her beauty; Tu Sinar, thin and blade-like, a perpetual scowl on his face; Sententu, huge and grim, like a slab of living white stone; Gorim, shorter and broader than Sententu, with fierce, craggy features; Khanewal, lithe, dark-skinned, with a sharp, feral face; Bereth, moving on all fours, his tail whipping ceaselessly behind him; Protaxes, tall, regal and gold-skinned; and Golgath of the Sea, the only *shlikti* among them, face and body as changing as the surface of the ocean. Trailing slightly behind Xochitl was Lowellin.

Aranti raced shrieking through the skies overhead, building mighty thunderheads out of thin air only to dissipate them the next moment. They were not there to take sides. They were drawn, as they always were, by the excitement. They would come and go many times, whirling in and out as interest and boredom waxed and waned.

Hundreds of lesser Stone Shapers accompanied the army as well. Some moved on the surface, animated creatures of every type of stone imaginable. Most bore no resemblance to anything living, no mouths or eyes or ears. Others moved below the surface, passing through solid rock as easily as a fish swims through water. Sometimes ripples marked their passage.

Melekath walked out alone to face them. There were those who tried to join him, but he refused them and sent them back. There was no wall to pass through, no mighty gate to open. Unlike the other cities of the land, Durag'otal had no walls, no defensive fortifications at all. Every other city owed allegiance to a god and when the gods warred against each other – as they often did – their human followers warred as well. When Melekath built Durag'otal, he told his followers that they were witness to the dawn of a new age. Never again would he be drawn into the endless conflicts of his brethren.

The Eight stopped before Melekath and the two sides regarded each other for a minute. Melekath seemed small and frail before them, no taller than the average human. Sententu, the largest among them, was five times his height, like a small hill. Even Khanewal, the smallest of the Eight, was twice the height of a human.

"There is no need to do this," Melekath said, speaking to Xochitl. "We have no quarrel with any of you."

Lowellin stepped up beside Xochitl. Gorim darkened as Lowellin pushed against him and raised one block-like fist, but Lowellin ignored him. "It is too late for that," he spat. There was triumph in his eyes and a cold smile on his face. "You have broken the pact which you set at the dawn of Life and now you and your creatures will be destroyed." He would have said more, but Xochitl laid her hand on his arm and restrained him.

"So now one of the Second Ring speaks for you?" Melekath said, ignoring Lowellin and addressing the Eight.

Lowellin hissed with rage but before he could speak Sententu grabbed his shoulder with a hand the size of a boulder and yanked him backward. "Do not speak again or I will break you," he growled.

"It is not too late to undo what you have done," Xochitl said.

"And what have I done?" Melekath blazed, suddenly angry. "What is my crime? The only crime I am guilty of is loving my Children too much. I cannot bear to see them die."

"The pact comes from your own mouth," Sententu rumbled.

"It was long ago," Melekath replied.

"The *shlikti* agreed to the existence of the new Circle, Life, only because it dies and returns what it has stolen," Golgath interjected. "It is an agreement we have regretted many times since, but we have honored it. Now you yourself break it."

"I would that it not come to this," Melekath answered. "But if you persist, you must know that you will not defeat me."

"Brave words," Khanewal said in her mocking manner. "And perhaps once true. But we know the truth: the Gift has weakened you."

"In my search for it I learned the secret of tapping the Heart of the Stone."

That gave them pause. It was Protaxes who spoke first. "Impossible," he said. The golden radiance around him seemed to have dimmed somewhat. "Not even you can do that."

"But I have. As you will see if you continue with this threat to my Children."

"Please don't do this," Xochitl said, her voice earnest and soft. "If you care for your children as you say, you will stop. If it comes to war, many of your children will suffer," she said, motioning to the army the Eight had brought with them.

"They have refused me," Melekath replied. "What happens to them is beyond me now." His voice took on a harder edge. "They no longer recognize me as their Father. I expected no less from the followers of the others gathered here, but you, at least, I did not expect to lie to them and turn them against me."

His words struck Xochitl like a physical blow. Her eyes clouded. She made as if to turn and look at Lowellin. "You do not understand."

"There is nothing to understand. While I was gone, you turned them against me."

"It is not so simple as that," she protested.

"We are done here," Melekath stated flatly. "Do your worst. You will never defeat us." With that he turned and walked back to the city and the siege of Durag'otal began.

$$ \text{X} \quad \text{X} \quad \text{X} $$

The shield Melekath erected held strong, and for three years it seemed all they must do was be patient and eventually the besieging army would give up and go away, leaving them in peace once again. During that time the sense of emptiness grew strong enough that no one could deny its existence. With the emptiness came fear and hard behind that anger. The once-placid streets became filled with conflict and Melekath was forced to spend much of his time mediating.

Then came the day when their world changed forever. Orenthe saw people hurrying to the edges of the city, heard them talking about something different the besiegers were doing. She arrived in time to see the ground split open around the city and a second later a sick horror filled her and she knew that whatever the Eight were drawing up from below was dark and wrong.

All at once a wave of seething purple-tinged blackness rose up out of the ground. Every instinct she had screamed at her to run, to get away, but it was too late. The blackness flowed over the city and the sunlight disappeared forever.

When the prison closed the emptiness inside was suddenly a bottomless abyss. Orenthe knew instantly that it was because they were completely cut off from LifeSong. She staggered and fell to the ground, clawing at her throat. She couldn't breathe. She was suffocating.

And then the worst horror of all: she did not die.

She did not die!

How many times in the following years had she prayed for death? How many times had she gone to Melekath and begged him to take the Gift back, to give her the new gift of oblivion? She tried going *beyond* of course, but there was nothing there. Nothing at all. Just a blankness that frightened her so badly she never attempted it again.

After that came a long period of madness populated with random, disjointed images and memories. Riots in the darkened streets. Anarchy and chaos beyond Melekath's ability to quell. The constantly shifting factions of bullies and thugs. Violence that claimed so many.

Then, long after all hope was gone, the prison opened. With the rest she crawled out into the sunlight and turned her face to the sky. She was cold, terribly cold, but the sunlight could no longer warm her. When they came upon the Crodin nomads she tried to resist when the others charged at them and began feeding, but her resistance crumbled after only a few seconds and she rushed into the melee after them. She didn't get much, only scraps from a dying woman, but it was heaven, the first light in the darkness for far too long.

Now she had fed again. People were dead at her hands.

What had she become? Was there no end?

FORTY

Thrikyl sat on a wide hill with its back to the ocean. It was a smaller city than Qarath. Thrikyl's most distinguishing characteristic was its massive outer wall. A hundred feet high and nearly half that wide at the base, that wall had never fallen to an invader until Wulf Rome broke it with his axe. Local lore held that it had originally been raised by Bereth thousands of years ago from the very bones of the earth, and it certainly looked it. If the wall had been built by hand, the stones had been so cunningly and precisely placed that no seams or joints were visible anywhere in the wall, except where Rome had broken them, of course. That section of wall had been rebuilt since then and it could not match the original stonework.

So it was that the citizens of Thrikyl mostly ignored the warnings that came from Qarath. They believed in the strength of their wall.

"Has the messenger from Qarath left yet?"

"Yes, Noblewoman. This morning. The Qarathian troops and their governor will be leaving tomorrow morning." Wels kept his eyes down as he spoke. Noblewoman Ophira was notoriously touchy and prone to rash violence if she felt slighted in any way. Under the new laws imposed by Qarath, no citizen could be executed without a trial, regardless of how powerful or angry a nobleman was, but it was not a stretch to say that the old ways were a long way from dead. At the very least Noblewoman Ophira could cost Wels his position in the government, leaving him ruined financially and living with his family in the streets. Wels was powerfully fond of his home and his lifestyle.

"Something good has come out of this, then," Ophira mused. "Anything that rids us of Qarathian interference is a good thing."

Wels shifted uncomfortably. The coat that was the symbol of his office was hot and constricting. He longed to be back in his offices, the coat off and hung up, a cool cup of wine at hand.

He did not share her belief, unfortunately. He had been the first to question the survivor of Ferien who stumbled into town a few days ago and what he had heard had caused him sleepless nights ever since. *The stone wall burned? Broken, misshapen people that sucked people dry and couldn't be hurt by any weapon?* It sounded impossible, but Wels no longer believed he knew the meaning of that word. Too many bizarre happenings in the last year, too many unexplainable creatures. And ever since that afternoon not so many days ago – when it felt like the world itself ripped in half – he was less sure than ever that the word impossible meant anything at all. Something bad was coming, and no confident words from the nobility could change that. His best hope was that whatever came would kill the nobility first.

Not for the first time he considered leaving in the morning with the Qarathian soldiers. But Thrikyl was his home and he had worked hard to climb to his position in life. The thought of starting over was nearly unbearable.

"Is that refugee from Ferien still locked up?" Ophira asked.

Wels ducked his head. "He is. Awaiting your command."

"Once the Qarathians are gone, have him quietly executed. I can't have him upsetting people."

"As you command," Wels replied. After the refugee had been questioned, he had been released. However, right after his release, he had gone to Victory Square, the largest market in the city, and started loudly telling everyone who would listen about what would happen to the people of Thrikyl if Melekath and his Children came that way. Wels had been forced to have the man arrested before he caused a panic. It wouldn't have taken much. There were riots every few days now. So far they had suppressed every one before it could get out of hand, but that didn't mean they could handle another one.

"Have any of our scouts returned?" Ophira asked, ceasing her pacing long enough to stare out the big window with its commanding view of the city. She was a tall woman, well into her middle years, still beautiful but in a hard-edged way that said her beauty was merely one of the many weapons at her disposal.

"None, Noblewoman." Wels frowned.

"How can that be?" Ophira demanded. "Didn't you order them to send reports back every day, regardless of what they did or didn't find?" She turned on him, fixing him with an icy glare.

"I did, Noblewoman."

"Have you sent out more?"

"Every day, Noblewoman."

"So we have no more information. Have you alerted the guards at the front gate to question any who come from the villages between here and Ferien?"

"Yes, Noblewoman."

"And…?"

"They had nothing to tell us. They fled their homes long before Melekath arrived."

Ophira hissed to herself. She seemed to take the lack of information as a personal affront. Wels tried to make himself smaller.

"Get me some information," she grated. "Or I will have a new seneschal."

Wels bowed, wondering: *If I decide to leave in the morning with the Qarathians, will you let me go?*

Wels entered Noblewoman Ophira's office in a rush, collected himself and managed to close the door gently behind him. Then he stood at attention, waiting for her to notice him. The office was one of the biggest in the palace, with tiled marble floors covered in thick rugs, highly polished columns rising to a ceiling two stories high, and huge windows that looked down over the city. Ophira's desk was massive as well, so large it had been put together in this very room since it would not have fit through the doors. Ophira, dressed in a floor-length, blue dress that glittered with semiprecious stones, sat at the desk, writing on a parchment. Her graying hair was tied up in a perfect bun from which no stray hairs escaped. Her makeup was flawless, her fingernails long and carefully painted.

Time passed and Wels fidgeted. Sweat ran down the back of his neck and gathered under his arms. The Noblewoman seemed completely oblivious to his presence. He resisted the urge to cross the room, grab up the parchments on her desk and throw them on the floor. What he had to say could not wait.

Finally, after what seemed like an hour, the Noblewoman looked up. She frowned slightly when she looked at him, as if irked by his very presence. "I am busy," she said.

"This is important," he replied, trying to keep his voice calm and even. *I should have left with the Qarathians.* She gestured for him to continue. "They…they are here."

"They?" she asked.

His frustration nearly boiled over then. He wanted to slap her so badly that his muscles ached from holding back. "The…Melekath and his followers. They have arrived."

"Indeed." She remained sitting for a few more moments, not looking at him, seemingly lost in thought. Then she stood and walked to the windows, her steps echoing loudly on the marble floor.

Wels broke protocol then, following her to the window without first receiving permission. She frowned at him, but said nothing. Melekath and his Children were just visible out beyond the wall, a small mass of bodies. No details were distinguishable at this distance.

"That is them?" she asked. "They don't look so frightening. Why, there are hardly any of them at all." She nodded, turned to the seneschal and gave him a smile. "You can leave off sweating now, Seneschal, before you stain my floor. It appears we have been misinformed as to the gravity of our situation. I hardly think we need worry about this."

"With the greatest respect, Noblewoman, but I think you are mistaken."

One carefully painted eyebrow rose at his words and her smile became noticeably colder. "I do not believe I approve of the way you are speaking to me."

Wels ducked his head, more to keep her from seeing the sudden rage he felt than as a sign of deference. When he felt enough in control he said quietly, "What do you want me to do about them?"

Ophira looked out the window again, then dismissed them with a negligent wave of her hand and started back to her desk. "I think we will just wait. They don't seem to be doing anything. We will wait and hear their demands. We don't want to appear frightened."

"That's it?" Wels asked, his voice strangled. "We're just going to *wait*?"

The look she gave him was very cold. "Just this once, in light of your excitable nature, I am going to let this pass. Never let it happen again. Am I clear?"

Wels had to clamp his hands together in order to control them. "Yes, Noblewoman."

"I didn't hear you."

"Yes, Noblewoman. My apologies, Noblewoman."

She tapped her fingernails on her desk while she considered him and his apology. Then she gave a short nod. "Very well. Now go. You have taken up quite enough of my day already."

A moment later Wels found himself outside her door. Neither of the two stone-faced guards stationed there betrayed a sign of his presence. He might have been invisible. For a moment he did not know what he would do next. He felt like he was lost in someone else's body. Had any of that just happened? Was the de facto ruler of his city just going to pretend that the greatest threat they had ever faced was nothing more than an unruly mob of bandits?

I should have left with the Qarathians.

Wels had just left the palace when his aide, a short man with wispy yellow hair, came running up to him.

"Seneschal!" he cried. "Seneschal, you must come at once!"

"What is it?" Wels asked, trying to appear calmer than he felt.

"It's High Priest Tenschall," the aide gasped, trying to catch his breath. "He has sent novitiates throughout the city, telling people to come to the Great Temple to hear Bereth's word on Melekath and his Children." He leaned closer, making sure no one was around to hear him. "It's not going to be good. I think you should come."

"Have you spoken to the captain of the city guard?" Wels asked.

"He was the one told me to find you. He's sending every man he can down there right now."

A servant came forward with two horses and the men mounted and clattered through the gates and down into the city. By this time everyone in Thrikyl knew of those who had gathered outside the gates – they could *feel* their presence – and the fear in the air was palpable. People looked up imploringly at Wels as he rode by, but he had nothing to offer them. He felt like he was standing on the edge of a pit, just on the edge of falling in, and in the bottom waited a sleepless beast eager to tear and rend.

A massive crowd had already gathered in the huge square before the Great Temple and Wels had to kick his horse savagely to force his way through the crowd. He saw the captain of the city guard, surrounded by armed and armored men, and made his way over to him.

"I'm powerful glad to see you, Seneschal," the captain said. He was wearing full armor and his sword was in his hand. His horse sidestepped skittishly and he worked to control it. All the horses were skittish. Part of it was the mob, but mostly Wels thought it was because they, too, sensed the hunger waiting outside the walls. The animals would have been smart enough to leave if they'd had the chance, he thought.

Several stories up the front of the temple was a small balcony, big enough for maybe four people. As Wels looked up, the door at the back of the balcony opened and Tenschall emerged. He was a tall, broad-shouldered man, his hair silver, his robe of the finest cloth-of-gold. Normally he was the very picture of composed confidence, but on this day his face was pale and his hand shook as he wiped at the sweat that gathered on his brow. He looked side to side at the aides who flanked him, saw nothing there, and turned his gaze back to the crowd.

"Bereth has spoken to me," High Priest Tenschall said. The crowd went completely still.

Tenschall seemed to waver. He gripped the railing that lined the balcony and Wels had a sudden, irrational feeling that he was about to fling himself over it. His next words came out in a croak.

"There is no hope."

The crowd gave off a collective moan of despair. There were cries and a number fell to their knees.

Wels started to turn to the captain. Ophira's orders had been very clear. No one, not even Bereth's High Priest, was to rouse the citizens to riot. But what did her orders really mean now? What point was there in following anything?

I should have left with the Qarathians. Forgive me, my wife, my children.

Wels met the captain's eye, then shook his head. "We will hear what he has to say."

"But the Noblewoman – "

"The blame is fully mine." *Not that there will be any to cast that blame after today. Today, Thrikyl dies.*

"The walls will not stop Melekath and his spawn," Tenschall said. "Our weapons will not stop them. They will enter Thrikyl. And we will all die."

There were screams from the crowd. A scuffle broke out nearby, quickly growing until at least a score of people thrashed on the ground, tearing at each other's throats.

One of the High Priest's aides leaned in and spoke in his ear. Tenschall shook his head and waved the man away. "They deserve to know," he said loudly. He looked back at the crowd.

"We cannot fight them. We cannot hide from them. It is too late to run. When they come in they will drain every person in this city of life and each one they do will only make them stronger."

"But what can we *do*?" wailed a woman.

"There is nothing you can do but choose how you wish to die," Tenschall replied, tears in his eyes. "At their hands or your own." As he said this he drew a long dagger from the depths of his robes. His aides reached for him but they were too late. The blade flashed and then he buried it in his own chest.

The crowd streamed from the square and the panic began.

"Well, I think we've kept them waiting long enough," Ophira said, drawing on her elbow-length riding gloves. Despite her wealth and status, she still preferred to ride her horse when she got a chance, and only took a carriage in foul weather or to formal meetings. "We'll go down there and find out what they want. Now that they've had time to see we're not the type to panic easily we will better be able to negotiate." She and Wels were standing outside the palace. The sun was near the horizon. Ophira sounded utterly calm, as if she were talking about meeting with a trade delegation. Wels wondered if she had gone insane. He wondered if he had as well. Why was he here, still waiting on the beck and call of this madwoman when he should be with his wife and children?

"There's nothing to negotiate, Noblewoman," Wels said.

"Ridiculous," Ophira said, grabbing onto the saddle horn and swinging herself up onto her horse. "Every conqueror will negotiate. It is only a matter of finding what he wants and giving it to him." She adjusted her fur-lined riding cloak and touched her hair to make sure the combs which bound it up were still in place. "And I grow weary of your constant whining. If you value your position, you will rethink your tone."

Wels felt the sense of unreality wash over him again. His horse was brought up and somehow he got up into the saddle, though he seemed to have lost all life in his hands. He turned to the side. Noblemen Patric and Letrolec were standing on the steps of the palace. They had been in Ophira's office when Wels brought the news of the High Priest's suicide and they had followed Wels and Ophira down here without speaking. Patric had a carafe of rum in one hand and was drinking directly from it. Letrolec was fingering his belt knife. Neither one of them met Wels' eye.

"There. I am ready," Ophira announced. "Let us go speak to this Melekath character now."

She looked at Wels as she spoke and all at once the calm mask slipped and he saw the terrible desperation in her eyes. She was barely holding together. She badly needed one person to believe her, to bolster the dam that was collapsing fast.

Wels started to tell her just how crazy she was, how crazy they both were, but then he nodded. "As you command, Noblewoman Ophira."

Let us be the first to die.

Normally only soldiers were allowed on the walls, but nothing was normal anymore and no one moved to stop those citizens who climbed the stone steps to the top to witness as Noblewoman Ophira and Seneschal Wels headed out to meet the invaders. When the gates opened, the horses nearly bolted and it took all of their riders' skill to keep from being thrown off. In the end they simply dismounted, handed the horses over to waiting soldiers, and proceeded on foot to their deaths.

The sun was nearly gone and the wind off the ocean was bitingly cold, lifting Ophira's riding cloak and swirling it around her. To their credit, the two emissaries from Thrikyl did not hesitate, but walked steadily across the open field.

Waiting for them was an old, ordinary-looking man in a tattered cloak. Behind him waited five score twisted, misshapen parodies of humankind. They seethed and twice began to surge forward, only barely restrained by the old man, who had to knock several of them down before they would stop.

Ophira and Wels stopped before the old man. Ophira raised one hand and began to speak.

The old man was replying when all at once it was like a dam breaking.

The misshapen ones surged forward and broke over Ophira and Wels. They screamed, but not for long.

Those who watched from the walls fell back in horror as they saw their future and word of what they had seen spread through the city.

FORTY-ONE

Melekath watched with a sick feeling in his heart as his Children fought over the scraps of the two people. Was this all there was? Would they never get better?

"Why, Xochitl?" he said softly. "Why could you not have let us be?"

His expression hardened then. It was not his Children's fault. It was Xochitl and the rest of the Eight.

It was Lowellin.

He looked to the north. He could feel Lowellin's presence in that direction, probably in Qarath. "This time I will not let you escape," he said. "This time you will answer for what you have done. I turned my back on you once before, but never again."

He began wading into the mass of his Children, yanking them back and tossing them aside. "Stop it!" he shouted. "Stop! There's nothing left!"

Gradually they fell back and stood panting, watching him. Those who had been closest had blood smeared on their faces and hands. The two bodies were little more than ragged flesh and bone. Melekath looked down on them and shook his head. Then he turned on his Children.

"I told you to wait," he snapped. "I wanted to speak to them."

"Why?" Reyna asked sullenly. After Ferien most of the skin on her face had been new and pink, with only a few patches of gray. But now the gray was creeping back. Her red hair, which had mostly grown in, had started to fall out again. There had been precious little Song for them to steal since Ferien – the few miserable, pathetic villages they came across were empty and the scouts Melekath caught were few and far between – and they were all showing signs of regressing. "Why are you always telling us to wait? We are sick of it."

There were angry mutters from the rest and Heram scowled. The thick, brute strength which had filled his chest and shoulders after

Ferien had diminished rapidly in the last few days and his mood had soured badly. "We are here," he growled, gesturing at the city. "Finally there is enough. Right there. Still you hold us back."

"Have you learned nothing? Are the lessons of three thousand years lost on you?" Melekath retorted. "I made you wait because I knew they would send emissaries out eventually. I wanted to take them and learn what they know. I wanted to know more about the threats we face."

"What threats?" Heram asked. He kicked at one of the bodies on the ground. "They are pathetically weak. There's nothing they can do to stop us."

"And the one who broke the prison for us? The Tender? Was she weak as well? We do not know what they are capable of," Melekath continued. "The Gift has made you immortal, it is true. But you are not invulnerable. You can be wounded beyond your power to heal yourselves, like so many who are still in the prison." He waited while that sank in. They had seen so many torn beyond life, yet unable to die. "What if they have learned to control chaos power?" he asked, and at those words they went deathly still. It was chaos power that formed the walls of the prison.

Heram frowned uncertainly and looked to Reyna for reassurance. "I agree with Heram," she said. "No one has shown themselves during the time we've been free. That Tender broke the wall, it is true, but she fled before us. And since then she has done nothing to stop us."

"Let me ask you something then, since you've figured it all out," Melekath replied. "If nothing in this world can threaten us, then where are the Guardians? Where is the army they were raising for us?"

Reyna recoiled and now it was her turn to look uncertain.

"If we have nothing to fear, *then where are the Guardians*?" Melekath asked relentlessly.

The Children went quiet, processing this new information. Worried looks were cast over shoulders, as if fearing an army would appear over the horizon at that moment and charge at them.

"I know you don't like it," Melekath continued. "I know it has not gone well for us. But you must trust me. When I say to wait, to be patient, it is only because I would not have us make the same mistakes again."

"*We* didn't make the mistakes," Reyna retorted. "*You* did."

That struck deep. Melekath could not deny the truth of what she said. His voice was softer when he continued. "What was done, is

247

done." How many times over the millennia had he questioned his decisions? He had trusted the strength of the shield he had erected. He had trusted that Xochitl would never harm his Children. She loved the stubborn, unpredictable, volatile creatures as much as he did. He had believed that ultimately she would leave him and his followers alone. But he'd been wrong and his Children had paid a terrible price. "From here we proceed cautiously. I don't want us to run headlong into a trap. I have to learn as much as I can. Which means that tomorrow when we enter Thrikyl you will do what I say."

When he said tomorrow a collective groan arose from the Children. "Why must we wait?" Heram growled. "Let us take the city now." The rest voiced their agreement with him.

"You will wait because I said so," Melekath replied. Part of him agreed with Heram. There was no real reason to wait. But another part said he was losing them, that he must exert control over them while he still could. Once he was sure this world was safe for them he would let them go, allow them to do as they wished. But until then he must protect them and he could not protect them if he could not control them. "And when we enter the city you will each take only one until I have had a chance to question the leaders. Once I am satisfied that I know what they know, then you will be allowed to feed freely."

More whining and complaining greeted his words. Melekath gave them a minute to vent, then added, "Agree to my terms or I will not open the city for you."

"What are you saying?" Reyna asked.

"We will do this as I say, and how I say, or I will not break that wall for you. Look at it. How will you get in without my help? Do you think you can climb that wall? Or will you burrow under it?"

That gave them pause. They looked at the wall with new eyes. Finally they looked back at him. Melekath waited until he saw resignation and acceptance in every face before he nodded. "In the morning then. We will speak no more about it."

FORTY-TWO

At the first streaks of light in the east, Melekath stood up and announced that it was time. Only a couple dozen Children gathered around him. The rest had slipped away during the night, sneaking off to the wall, looking in vain for a way in. Melekath had seen them leaving but chose to do nothing. He would not spend the entire night chasing after them and dragging them back. It would have been a futile task. Instead, he announced to those who remained that he would not open the wall until every last one of them had gathered around him.

Those who were left cried out and complained bitterly, saying they should not be punished for the misdeeds of the others, but Melekath was unmoved. Still complaining loudly, the obedient ones went to gather the rest.

It took an hour, but finally all the Children were gathered around Melekath. Reyna and Heram had been the last two to show up. As they walked up, he saw that they were talking but they stopped before they got close enough for him to hear what they were saying, fixing him with angry looks.

"Something's wrong," Heram said, sniffing the air. "There's not enough Song in there. Not for that size city."

Melekath shrugged. "They knew of our approach. Many no doubt fled before we got here. There is still enough for everyone."

"There better be," Heram said darkly.

"Remember what I said," Melekath said. "You will control yourselves once we are in. Take one for each of you, but no more until I have questioned the leaders and learned what they know."

The Children did not respond.

"Then you will wait here and I will go in alone," he added.

"Okay," Reyna said. "It will be as you say."

Melekath started walking to the city and the Children fell in behind him, Reyna and Heram at their head. Halfway there, one of the men who had lost an arm during his time in the prison – a vestigial stump had begun to regrow since Ferien, boneless and useless – lost his self-control and tried to run past the rest. Heram clubbed him on the side of the head and he went down. While he was down, one of the other men jumped on him and tried to steal Song from him, but Heram kicked him off with an oath. After that there were no more problems.

Melekath had spent the night reaching deep into the Stone, trying to learn more. But he was still very weak and his control had rusted over the millennia he had been cut off from his native Sphere and he learned almost nothing. He was able to vaguely sense the three Guardians, enough to know that two of them – Kasai and Tharn – were wounded. But they were not together and they were not anywhere nearby, which was alarming. Had they been that badly defeated by Lowellin? Even more alarming was the fact that he picked up traces of chaos power. Had Lowellin used chaos power to defeat the Guardians? Surely even he would not do anything so insane. The Eight combined had barely been able to control chaos power long enough to construct the prison. Melekath couldn't even imagine the destruction that would happen if chaos power was allowed to leak uncontrolled into this world. Even the Nipashanti would not survive that. Did Lowellin hate and fear him enough to attempt something so inherently foolish?

There was still so much that did not make sense. During the night Melekath had felt the hole where Tu Sinar had once existed. While he was happy to learn that one of his old enemies had been destroyed, what bothered him was the fact that he felt traces of chaos power around the hole where he had been. Was it Lowellin's doing? But why would Lowellin attack Tu Sinar? If anything Tu Sinar would be a likely ally. It made no sense to destroy him, unless Tu Sinar had protested his use of chaos power and Lowellin had then turned it on him.

If Lowellin had grown that powerful, then Melekath and his Children had much to fear. Either Lowellin had found a way to control that which was, by nature, essentially uncontrollable – in which case Melekath would not be able to defeat him – or he had found a way to use chaos power but could not control it. If the latter were true, then even if he managed to defeat Lowellin, there would be no world for his Children to inherit.

Consumed by these worries as he had been all night, Melekath had given no thought to the city they waited outside. Now, however, as they approached the city, Melekath quested outward with his senses, taking the pulse of the city. He expected fear and despair. Perhaps desperate, hopeless courage.

But what he found made him break into a run.

Suddenly Father began running. Reyna hesitated for only a second, then took off after him. One leg was still quite weak and she cursed as he drew further ahead. Heram drew up beside her.

"What is it? What's wrong?" he demanded.

"I don't know," she hissed. *Idiot*, she thought. Heram had been a useful enemy-slash-ally during their years in the prison. He was strong enough, and controlled enough followers, that together they had been able to take down all the others who contended for rule of the Children, but at the same time he was stupid enough that controlling him was not that difficult. As it was, he was still useful to her. Eventually his usefulness would end, and she would destroy him as she had destroyed so many others both before and during her years in the prison. But for now she still had to tolerate him and it was all she could do to put up with him sometimes. Why should she know what was wrong? Was he really that stupid? Surely it could not be an act. She would have figured it out after all this time.

Melekath reached the wall before them and stopped, looking up at it. He had gone for the nearest section of wall, a stone's throw or so to the left of the city gates. Reyna and Heram caught up to him just as he put his hands on the wall. He closed his eyes.

"What is it?" Heram asked again.

Reyna started to curse him and then suddenly she *knew*.

There was not enough Song.

She barely kept herself from screaming. More of the Children came running up then, but they sensed the foulness of her mood and stayed back from her. "Hurry up," she said to Melekath through gritted teeth. "*Hurry up!*"

Gradually Reyna felt a tremor deep in the earth underfoot. The tremor grew stronger and several of the more idiotic Children cried out in alarm. Then the wall began to shake. The shaking grew stronger and an almost-human cry came from the stone as it split with a loud crack, opening a ragged gap several feet wide and reaching to the top of the wall. Chunks broke off and rained down around them, a fist-sized one hitting Reyna on the shoulder hard enough to hurt.

But she cared nothing for any of it. As soon as the gap opened she thrust her way past Melekath and into the city. Melekath did not try to stop her. He didn't try to stop any of them as they fought to get through the opening as fast as they could. He was shoved to the side like an old man and they streamed into the defenseless city.

They were all dead!

Bodies littered the street. Some were broken, having clearly jumped to their deaths from the heights. Others lay in pools of blood, knives lying near hands frozen in death. One bore no visible wounds, but his face was blackened and an empty vial lay on the ground by him.

Reyna stopped and stared, aghast. The others spilled in around her, slowing and stopping as the reality hit them. She heard Heram's furious bellow.

It couldn't be.

She hurried to the nearest door. Though weakened by the days since Ferien she was still far stronger than a normal human and she only had to strike the heavy wooden door twice before it cracked open.

She forced her way through the remains of the door. As her eyes adjusted to the gloom she began to scream with rage.

Two children lay on the floor before the fireplace, congealed blood pooled around them from their slashed throats. Lying across them was their mother, adding her blood to their own. Slumped against the wall was the father, dead, the knife lying where it had fallen from his hand.

Reyna ran back outside. The other Children were scattering, kicking down doors, tearing into corpses. She saw Melekath standing near the breach he had made in the wall. He was staring at one of the dead bodies and there was shock on his face. "You did this!" she screamed. She ran at him and began pummeling him, venting thousands of years of fear and desperation on him. He fell back before her onslaught. She clawed at his eyes, missed and tore a gouge down one cheek, her fingernail ripping away in the process. There was no blood. Though the Nipashanti could appear as human, they were far from being human.

Melekath made no move to protect himself. He turned his face away and allowed her attack to run its course.

"This is your fault!" she screamed over and over as she struck him. The fact that she could do no real damage to him maddened her further.

Finally, he grabbed her and held her still, forcing her to stare into his eyes.

"They are not all dead," he said.

At first the words did not sink in and she continued to fight him but he shook her and repeated himself and all at once it made sense.

"There are still hundreds of them," he said. "They are hiding, but you can find them. You can follow their Songs right to them."

She let go of him and turned around. Most of the others had already figured out the truth of what he said and had scattered into the city. She turned back, slapped him one more time, then took off running.

Melekath watched her go. Then he set off into the city himself, heading for the towers of the palace. He didn't have much time to waste. If he wanted any answers, he had to ask whatever leaders this city still contained before his Children found them. The moment he'd realized his error, he'd known his chances of controlling them had disappeared. He wondered if they would listen to him at all after this. Why would they? Everything he had promised them had turned to ashes. He had failed them at every turn. He remembered long ago days, as he Shaped Durag'otal, his joy at seeing the light in their eyes as he shared their new city with them. The future had held so much promise then. How had it all gone so wrong?

There was nothing he could do about his Children's feelings toward him. He accepted their hatred as his just due. The only thing left to him was to do everything in his power to see that they were not destroyed by their enemies. Whatever Lowellin and his allies had managed to do to defeat the Guardians, Melekath would make sure they could not do to his Children. They could hate him all they wanted; he would still spend every effort to see them safe.

At the palace he saw a soldier on top of the wall surrounding the grounds. The man looked down at Melekath with wide eyes, the point of his spear wavering in his shaking hand. Melekath ignored him. He needed leaders. People who knew something.

He placed his hands on the wall and summoned Stone power up from below. The power came, though slower this time. He was still weakened by his efforts during the night and breaking through the outer wall. But at last it did come. The wall shook and then cracked. Melekath leaned against the wall for a moment afterwards, collecting his strength.

He found others in the palace as well. Two were hiding in a small storage room. They had barred the door, but it was not difficult for him to break it down. It was a man and a woman, servants by the look of them. The woman cried out when he stuck his head in the room and the man pushed her behind him. They both looked at him with the eyes of people who are already dead. Melekath looked down at them and felt a great sadness spread through him. But for the interference of Xochitl and the rest, these two might have chosen to follow him as well. Instead of huddling in here waiting to die, they could be free of the fear of death forever.

He left quickly, uncomfortable with the feelings churning inside him. There were too many doubts, too many questions. He was no longer sure about anything he had done. He was no longer sure about anything he would do.

There were other servants here and there and Melekath began to fear he would not find what he sought, but at last he came to a large, brightly painted room with a high ceiling, several ponderous chandeliers and a dais at one end with a high-backed, ornate chair sitting on it. Sitting on the chair was a man, probably in his middle years, though it was hard to tell. None of the chandeliers had been lit and the room was dim. The man's face was so haggard with fear and exhaustion that he might have been twenty years younger than he appeared to be. He was not dressed in the simple clothing of the servants Melekath had found, but in a richly brocaded shirt and black leather pants with silver stitching down the side and knee-high, polished boots. A thick gold chain was around his neck. A crown, heavy with jewels and gold, lay on the floor by his feet.

As Melekath approached the man raised his head. His head wobbled on his neck as he tried to focus bleary eyes on the figure approaching him. Then he shook his head and gave up. He took a long drink from the bottle he held in his hand, belched and looked at the crown near his feet.

"I always wanted to know how it felt to wear that thing, to sit here," he said, his words slurring. "And you know what I found?" He made another attempt to focus on Melekath. "It's damned uncomfortable, that's what it is. The hat. The chair. All of it. I think I would have been a shit king." He took another drink off the bottle and squinted at Melekath. "Are you here to kill me?"

Melekath took the bottle from his hand and set it on the floor.

"Will it hurt much?" the man asked. "I can't stand pain. I'm a coward that way. A coward all ways, I guess. That's why I didn't kill myself like all the smart people." He held out one arm. There was a shallow cut across the wrist. "I couldn't do it at all," he confessed. "That's Patric, he's nothing but a coward."

"Tell me what you know about Lowellin's plans," Melekath said.

Patric looked at him, confusion on his face. "Who's Lowellin?"

"He is the one who is leading you. With his help you defeated the Guardians. I need to know how you did it."

"I've never heard of anyone named Lowellin," he slurred. "Maybe you're thinking of Wulf Rome. He's our leader now, at least since he took down our walls with that damnable axe of his." The man proceeded to softly curse Wulf Rome.

"So Wulf Rome is the one who pulled the axe free. Does he still have it? Has it awakened yet?"

Patric shook his head. "No. I'm not going to answer your questions. You're just going to kill me anyway. Why should I help you? And don't think torturing me will help." He pointed at the bottle Melekath had taken away. "I drank three of those already. I can't feel a thing." Tears started to run down his cheeks. "I was hoping the rum would kill me. I've heard it can happen. It's the only kind of courage I've ever had."

"I'm not going to torture you," Melekath replied. "But I do have something to offer you."

Patric's eyes seemed to take a long time to settle on Melekath's face. "What?"

"My Children are coming. I don't know how long it will take them to get here, but eventually they will come and they will find you. Then they will drain your life from you. I can't tell you how that feels, but I have seen it happen. It is not pleasant. I could spare you from that, take you from the city and let you go."

"Go?" Patric laughed amidst his tears. "Where would I go? My home is gone. You'll have to offer better than that."

"A painless death then. A sleep you do not awaken from."

Patric nodded. "That's better," he mumbled. His eyes went to the bottle on the floor and after a moment Melekath picked it up and gave it back to him. He took a drink.

255

"Now tell me how you defeated the Guardians."

Patric shook his head. "I have no idea what a Guardian is. There are lots of stories about strange creatures about these days, and we heard that one took over the city of Nelton, but I never heard of a Guardian."

"Tell me about this creature that took over Nelton."

Patric shrugged. "I don't know much. Tall and thin, looks like a starving man. It did something to the people there, turned them all into slaves devoted to it."

Melekath pondered this. It wasn't much to go on, but that could be Gulagh. The Guardian could have changed much in the three thousand years Melekath had been trapped in prison. The Guardians had all managed to flee Durag'otal before the prison was completed, but somehow they had been bound to the area, unable to go beyond the boundaries of the Gur al Krin. Melekath had had limited contact with the Guardians as the years went by and the door of the prison weakened, but he had not been able to see them.

But why would Gulagh be turning people into slaves? Gulagh's orders had been to prepare for the Children's return, to find those who were faithful, who would choose the Gift, and from them raise an army to defend the Children until they could defend themselves. Melekath had never intended that it raise an army of slaves.

"What about the other Guardians? Have you heard anything about any others?"

Patric took a long drink and stared into the depths of the bottle before answering. "When the last messenger from Qarath came, telling us to evacuate the city, he said that Qarath's army had defeated an army led by a white-skinned creature, up near the Plateau."

"How?"

"He didn't know much. But he said Quyloc – that's Rome's chief adviser – used some kind of spear. He said he used it on some other monster as well, a thing like red stone brought to life."

A spear? No spear made by man could harm one of the Guardians. This, then, must be the weapon that Lowellin had discovered to defeat him. He'd had thousands of years to prepare, after all. He surely knew that once Melekath got free that he would come for Lowellin. But what kind of spear could do such a thing?

Chaos power.

There was no other possibility. Somehow this weapon was formed of chaos power. Melekath couldn't imagine how Lowellin had done

256

such a thing. There was no way he had the power to control chaos power enough to make a weapon from it. But then, there was no other weapon which could have injured one of the Guardians.

Melekath questioned him some more, but it soon became apparent that Patric had nothing more to tell him. He put his hand on the man's head. Patric looked up at him one last time.

"It's going to get a lot worse, isn't it?"

Melekath thought about his Children, what they had become. He thought about chaos power loose in the world. He nodded.

"Then I'm glad I won't be alive to see it."

Patric closed his eyes. Melekath looked deeper, *saw* the glow of Song around his physical body. It was a simple matter to slit the glow and let the Song flow out of the man. In moments he slumped over dead and Melekath was left alone in the throne room.

FORTY-THREE

The next morning Rome and Quyloc rode down to the estate before the sun rose. Quyloc thought that the city had never looked as beautiful to him as it did that morning. What would the future bring? Would all this be destroyed in just a short time? He looked to the south, wondering what it was like in Thrikyl right now.

When they rode onto the estate, the FirstMother and Ricarn were standing on the carriage way in front of the estate house, a handful of other Tenders gathered around them. Quyloc saw that the FirstMother and the other Tenders looked pale and shocked. He didn't have to wait long to find out why.

"The people of Thrikyl did something I did not expect," Ricarn said. "They killed themselves."

"What?" Rome exclaimed, dismounting and handing his horse over to a servant waiting nearby. "When? All of them?"

"During the night. Not all, but the great majority. I believe that, at the end, they stopped deluding themselves and accepted what was going to happen. I did not think they were capable of this." Ricarn honestly looked surprised, an expression that Quyloc had never seen on her face before. "For some reason Melekath and his Children did not enter the city yesterday, but waited until this morning. By then most of the citizens had killed themselves. It is most surprising."

"Goddamn," Rome breathed. "They bought us some time." He looked stunned, unable to quite grasp the enormity of it all. Quyloc knew how he felt.

"And we will not waste it," Lowellin said, surprising them all by walking up right then. "This morning, after the service, you will begin feeding your *sulbits* on people," he told the FirstMother.

"You will ask for volunteers," Rome said sternly, pointing a thick finger at the FirstMother. "No one will be fed on without it being their choice. Do you understand me?"

The FirstMother nodded.

"And now," Lowellin said, holding up Ilsith, "it is time to infect one of the *sulbits* with chaos power."

"But we don't—" the FirstMother objected.

"Shut up!" he barked, causing her to flinch. "Enough talk! Those idiots in Thrikyl have given us a chance and I'm going to take it."

"I volunteer," a tall, young, dark-haired Tender said, stepping forward.

"You're Bronwyn, aren't you?" Lowellin said. "I saw you at Guardians Watch. I know how powerful you are becoming." He shook his head. "I won't risk you. One of the useless ones will go first, one whose loss will not matter."

"Then I guess that should be me," a small voice said from the midst of the small group of Tenders. They parted to reveal a nervous-looking woman with a long face and downcast eyes.

"You are my aide, Velma," the FirstMother said. "I don't want to risk you."

"Please let me do this before I lose my nerve," she said. "You know as well as I do that I'm not good for much of anything anyway. Maybe this is the way the Mother has planned for me to serve."

"I still don't..." the FirstMother began, but Lowellin pushed past her, took hold of Velma's arm and pulled her forward.

"Put your *sulbit* there on the ground," he said, pointing.

Velma looked around at the other Tenders, then at the FirstMother. "It will be okay," she told the FirstMother. "He's the Protector. He knows what he's doing." The FirstMother looked like she would respond, but a dark look from Lowellin silenced her.

Velma knelt on the ground. Her *sulbit*, as if sensing something about to happen, was hiding in her sleeve and it took her a minute to get it out, while Lowellin stood over her, muttering and fuming. When she finally got the creature out, she held it to her cheek for a moment, murmuring to it. When Lowellin angrily told her to hurry up, the FirstMother stepped forward.

"One minute won't make any difference," she snapped at him.

He turned on her, his eyes flashing, but Velma spoke up before he could. "It's okay, FirstMother." To Lowellin she said, "I'm ready now." She set her *sulbit* on the ground and stepped back. The creature, not much bigger than a mouse, crouched there, its small head swiveling side to side in confusion. When it started to scurry toward Velma, Lowellin stopped it by putting the end of his staff down in front of it. The *sulbit* froze when he did that, and chittered at Ilsith, then backed up.

Lowellin threw Ilsith into the air above the *sulbit*. The staff hung there and dark smoke began to pour out of it. The cloud of smoke obscured Ilsith, then drifted down and covered the *sulbit*, which started to whine. Everyone took a step back.

From the depths of the smoke a tiny purple spark appeared. The spark dipped down and settled onto the *sulbit*, which was only dimly visible.

As soon as the spark touched it, the *sulbit* started wailing, a high-pitched sound not unlike a crying baby. Velma blanched and took a step forward, but was stayed by the FirstMother.

Gradually the black cloud lifted and reformed into the staff, which Lowellin plucked out of the air. "Now we will see," Lowellin said, staring at the *sulbit* intently.

There was a dark purple stain marring the *sulbit*'s ivory skin, on its back right behind its head, but other than that the creature seemed unaffected. Quyloc relaxed fractionally. Maybe this would work.

But then the *sulbit* began to shiver. It turned its head as far as it could, biting at something on its back that no one could see.

Suddenly it flopped over on its side and began to spasm. Velma cried out and put her hand over her mouth. After a minute the creature went still and lay with its tiny mouth open.

"So much for that idea," Rome said.

"It's not dead," the FirstMother said.

Purple-black streaks began to flow outward from the stain on its skin, soon covering most of its body. The *sulbit*'s eyes opened and it stood unsteadily.

Since he had the *rendspear* bare in his hand, Quyloc *saw* what happened next.

With a sob, Velma started to go to the *sulbit*, but as she bent over it, the FirstMother lunged forward, grabbed her arm, and jerked her back.

At the same instant the *sulbit* snarled, tiny flecks of foam appearing at the sides of its mouth, and leapt. But it didn't leap at Velma. It leapt at the flow of LifeSong sustaining her. Only the FirstMother's intervention saved the woman, pulling her aside just a heartbeat before the *sulbit* acted. Thus, the *sulbit* missed Velma's flow and instead bit down on the next flow beyond it.

With a cry, one of the other Tenders standing there collapsed on the ground, sores appearing instantly all over her body. As she fell, her *sulbit* lost its hold on her shoulder and hit the ground. Tiny sores appeared on its body as well and it staggered about drunkenly.

The flow of Song was severed instantly. Golden LifeSong poured into the diseased *sulbit*, but only for a second and then the flow shriveled up and turned black and dead.

The effect on the *sulbit* was nearly instantaneous. In the blink of an eye it increased in size, so that it was now the size of a small cat. Lowellin was shouting to leave the creature alone, but Quyloc ignored him, stepping forward and stabbing with the spear.

But, as quickly as he reacted, he was too slow. The *sulbit* dodged his attack with lightning speed.

The FirstMother's attack came right after Quyloc's. She threw her arms out, drawing Song off the flows around her, then threw a bolt at the infected *sulbit*.

The bolt struck the creature, but instead of harming it, it absorbed the energy, instantly growing larger. Its mouth stretched open and it belched out a glowing, crackling ball of purple and black energy. Quyloc cringed inwardly, expecting to see the FirstMother killed by the attack.

But at the last moment the FirstMother brought her hands together, gathering Song, crying out as she did so. A glowing shield of golden light appeared before her. The crackling ball of energy struck the shield and devoured it. The shield evaporated and the FirstMother was knocked backwards and fell down.

The *sulbit* bolted toward the front wall of the estate. Near the wall was a group of workmen who didn't see the *sulbit* approaching. As it ran by them, it slashed at the flows of two of them.

The two men immediately dropped to the ground and the Song sustaining them was consumed by the *sulbit*, which caused it to double in size.

It leapt to the top of the wall, balanced there for a moment, then jumped off the other side and disappeared.

Rome turned to Lowellin, only to find him gone. He swore and turned to Quyloc. "How are we going to stop that thing?"

Quyloc was already heading for the horses. They were rearing and whinnying, their eyes rolling, and the man was having a hard time holding them. "I don't know. But whatever it is, we have to do it fast." He took the reins of his horse from the man and managed to calm the animal enough to climb on. As Quyloc rode away he heard the FirstMother shouting something behind him, but he didn't turn back to figure out what it was.

It wasn't that hard to tell which direction the *sulbit* had gone. One body lay about fifty yards away, in the middle of the street, and another lay just down a side street.

The two men galloped down the side street. It led between two estates. A couple blocks further on they came upon another body, a young woman, clearly a servant, with a spilled basket of bread near her. Her skin was covered in sores like the others.

"There it is!" Quyloc yelled, pointing. The *sulbit* was just visible rounding a corner. It was now the size of a large dog. Quyloc's horse reared when it saw the creature, and it was only with difficulty that he managed to calm it and get it back under control.

The creature turned onto a street that led downhill. It was moving fast and without the horses they wouldn't have been able to keep up. As it fled, the creature killed two more people, growing each time, and Quyloc realized how lucky they were that this was happening so early, when few people were up and about. In an hour this same street would have hundreds of people in it. With so many to feed on, the *sulbit* would grow huge and so powerful they'd have no chance against it.

In a couple of minutes, the street flattened out. The homes of the wealthy gave way to large, well-maintained warehouses. The warehouses were built up against each other so there were no alleys or side streets. None of the warehouses had windows on the bottom floors; those windows on the upper floors were all barred. Stout doors provided the only entrances from the street and they were all closed. They might be able to bring the creature to bay here.

"The street dead ends just ahead!" he yelled to Rome.

At the end of the street was one of the biggest warehouses, four stories tall. The *sulbit* reached the building and turned around, its head turning as it sought an escape route. Rome and Quyloc slowed down and spread out, readying their weapons.

"We're only going to get one chance at it," Rome said grimly, the black axe in one hand. "Let's make it count."

Just then the door of the warehouse opened and several men emerged, arguing with each other.

"Get back inside and shut the door!" Rome yelled.

The men looked up, surprised and confused. Their confusion lasted only a moment. Their eyes fell on the nightmarish creature that was even then turning on them, and they began fighting to get back into the warehouse.

But it was already too late.

The *sulbit* ran into their midst, claws flashing. Two of them dropped instantly and the air rippled around the *sulbit* as it absorbed their Songs and grew larger. It paused in the doorway for an instant to look back over its shoulder at Rome and Quyloc and snarl at them, then it ran inside and disappeared.

Rome and Quyloc clattered up to the door of the warehouse and jumped off their horses. As soon as they dropped the reins, the horses bolted back up the street.

"Stay behind me, Rome," Quyloc said as Rome headed for the door.

"And miss all the fun?"

"I'm serious, Rome. "That thing is killing people by cutting their flows, which you can't *see*. If it gets near yours, you're dead."

"Then you'll just have to be my eyes," Rome said grimly, entering the building.

Quyloc swore and followed him. Another body lay sprawled just inside the door. Rome stepped over it, scanning for the creature.

To the right was a stairway leading to the upper floors, which probably contained offices. A hallway stretched straight ahead, doors on either side of it. Dim light filtered in from the far end of the hall, enough to see that that it was empty.

"What do you think?" Rome asked softly. "Forward or up?"

Quyloc paused, closing his eyes and feeling for the creature. He opened his eyes. "Down the hall."

The two men made their way cautiously down the hall. At the end of the hall was a door that was open halfway. A body lay in it, the man's eyes wide and staring, sores covering his face. With his axe, Rome pushed the door open the rest of the way.

Beyond was a large storeroom, easily a couple hundred feet across and two stories high. The light came from two small windows in the far wall, set high up, with heavy bars across them. Stacks of crates and barrels filled the room. At the base of one lay another body. A dozen or so thick stone columns rose up and disappeared into the gloom, supporting the upper floors. On the far side of the room was a large, sliding door, used to give wagons access for moving goods in and out. It was closed.

"Perfect," Rome said. "It's trapped in here."

Quyloc doubted that, but chose not to say anything.

"You go right," Rome said, "and I'll—"

He didn't get to finish his sentence. Quyloc saw movement on top of one of the stacks of crates. It was the *sulbit*, now the size of a bear, but slender like a cat, with a long tail. Its smooth skin was patterned with streaks of purple and black. Its head was huge, its snout blunt, its mouth wide and lined with fine, needle-like teeth. It opened its mouth and Quyloc reacted without thinking, shoving Rome to one side and diving the other way.

A ball of crackling, purple and black energy spat from its mouth, striking the wall right behind where the two men had been standing. There was an explosion and a whole section of the wall turned into splinters. A moment later a section of the ceiling crashed down onto the floor. The *sulbit* jumped down off the other side of the stack and disappeared.

Rome got to his feet. "That was a lot bigger than the one it threw at the FirstMother."

"It's just getting stronger and stronger."

"You circle around to the right and I'll go this way," Rome said. "Find a way to distract it and I'll come up behind it and kill it with the axe."

"What makes you think the axe will work on it?"

"You have a better idea?"

"This." Quyloc held up the spear. "We know it works on creatures from the *Pente Akka*. It should work on this thing."

"It might," Rome conceded. "We don't have time to stand here arguing about it. Move out, try to flank it. Whoever gets a shot at that thing takes it." He ran off into the gloom.

Quyloc watched him go and swore under his breath. Sooner or later that man was going to charge at something he couldn't handle.

Cautiously, he began to circle along the edge of the storeroom, eyes straining for any sign of movement. He made it to one of the stone support columns and ducked behind it, then peered around it.

Almost too late he saw the infected *sulbit* between two of the stacks and he threw himself backward just a heartbeat before it coughed out another one of the crackling balls of energy. The ball of energy struck the stone column, obliterating it. He felt a strange, prickly heat pass over him in a wave and a number of blisters appeared on his skin.

Some debris drifted down from the roof overhead, where the column had been, and Quyloc got an idea.

"Stay near the edge of the room!" he yelled to Rome. "I'm going to bring the roof down on it!"

"I can help with that!" Rome yelled back.

A moment later Quyloc heard an odd hissing noise, followed by a cracking sound and one of the stone columns on the other side of the storeroom collapsed. He looked around. Two down; it looked like there were about ten remaining. How many would it take before the building came down? Were there people in the offices overhead? Would he and Rome survive the collapse or would the whole building fall?

He ran to the next column and peered around it. Nothing. "Hey! Over here!" he called, rapping the butt of his spear on the floor. On the other side of the room another column collapsed.

He heard the faint scratch of claws on stone as the *sulbit* came around the edge of a stack of barrels and coughed out another crackling ball of energy. He turned and dove for the floor. The column exploded in a spray of stone fragments and another wave of the prickly heat washed over his head. When he rolled and came to his feet he saw that his clothes were smoking. Pain in his back told him some of the stone chips had hit him. That one was way too close.

This time the *sulbit* didn't retreat. Instead it growled and charged at him. Quyloc ran for the cover of a tall stack of crates, with each step sure he was about to be blown into pieces.

For some reason the attack didn't come, making him wonder if the *sulbit* needed time to recharge. Maybe it had used up the Song and couldn't attack until it killed again. He reached the cover and ducked behind it, his heart pounding.

From the other side of the barrels he heard the sound of claws on stone, stealthily moving closer. The thing was stalking him. The thought made his blood run cold. How dangerous would this thing become if they didn't kill it here?

On the other side of the room he heard another column collapse and he looked up, eyes straining to see through the gloom. Was it his imagination, or was the ceiling beginning to sag?

The clawed footsteps came closer. He scanned the room for the nearest column, then took off running for it. Before he'd taken three steps he heard a growl behind him and knew his death was only moments away.

He made it to the column, skidded around it and dove to the floor, just as the column exploded. The concussion dazed him and he felt a number of sharp pains as more stone shrapnel embedded itself in his side. He rolled over and tried to stand up, trying to shake the cobwebs from his brain, knowing he was out of time. At this point it was only a matter of whether the thing would blow him up or sever his Life-line and kill him that way.

"Over here, you ugly, over-sized rat!" Rome yelled from beyond the *sulbit*. "Come and get me!"

Quyloc lifted his head and saw Rome on the far side of the creature, waving his arms in the air.

The *sulbit* hissed and turned part way toward Rome, clearly unsure which threat to deal with first. Quyloc took his chance and started to crawl away. He just needed a minute to get himself together.

"That's right," Rome said. "You don't want him. You want me. I'm the tasty one." He was backing away as he spoke and now the *sulbit* was facing him completely. It growled and took two steps his way.

Rome kept backing away, but at an angle. As Quyloc glanced back at him he saw that Rome was making his way toward one of the few remaining columns, this one near the center of the room, and he knew exactly what he was doing.

The time for crawling was over.

Quyloc lurched to his feet and took off running for the edge of the storeroom. At almost the same moment, Rome did the same, though his path took him behind the column. Quyloc reached the dubious safety of the wall and turned to look just as the *sulbit* coughed out another crackling ball of energy.

The ball of energy missed the column.

Instead it struck a stack of crates just as Rome dove behind them. Most of the stack exploded into fragments.

The *sulbit* continued moving toward its prey, but slower now, as if the creature was sure of its kill.

"Rome! Rome!" Quyloc yelled, but there was no answer. He could see no movement.

"Over here!" he yelled at the *sulbit*. "I'm the one you want!"

The *sulbit* looked over its shoulder at him but continued on, clearly seeing him as no threat.

Quyloc tensed to chase the creature down, even though he knew it was hopeless. He could barely stand. It felt like he had sprained his ankle. His vision was still blurry and he was dizzy. The thing would most likely kill him easily. But he had to try. He had to at least do that.

As he pushed himself away from the wall and took his first shaky step toward the *sulbit*, which was just passing by the stone column, he thought he saw something black fly through the air, but he couldn't be sure.

It was the black axe, thrown from behind the remains of the stack of crates. It wasn't a good throw. The axe only struck the stone column a glancing blow...

But it was enough.

The column fell. The *sulbit* looked up just as the ceiling trembled and collapsed with a roar. Quyloc threw himself against the wall, putting his arms over his head. He felt debris strike him and for a moment thought they'd badly miscalculated. He and Rome were both going to be killed here.

Then it was over, only a few pieces still falling from above. Quyloc shook off the pile of wood and plaster that had fallen on him and stood up. Sunlight poured in from the huge hole in the roof above. Not just the ceiling had fallen in, but all of the offices above the storeroom as well. The front of the warehouse was still largely intact, as were two of the walls enclosing the storeroom, though they were swaying, dangerously close to falling as well. A huge timber lay just a foot away. It had barely missed crushing him.

"Rome!" he called. The pile of debris was huge. It seemed impossible that Rome was still alive in there. He began climbing up onto the pile, still calling Rome's name.

He hadn't gone far when he heard a familiar voice on the far side of the pile call his name. "Quyloc! Are you all right?"

Quyloc looked down at himself. He was bleeding from a dozen places. His ankle hurt terribly. There were strange burns on his skin and the side of his face.

"Yeah!" he called back. "I'm all right."

Rome clambered across the debris and approached Quyloc. "You look terrible," he said.

"I feel terrible."

"That's what you get for playing tag with a monster. I thought you were dead."

"So did I."

Rome reached him, then turned and looked back at the mound of broken stone, shattered timbers and random debris. "You think it's still alive?"

"It might be."

"I'll get some men down here to move that pile and find my axe. I'm thinking it would be a good idea to be ready with your spear when they do."

Quyloc nodded.

"Nice of Lowellin to stick around and help clean up his mess."

"I don't think we're going to see much more of Lowellin."

"I can't say that upsets me." There were shouts from the front of the building, then the sound of voices getting closer. "I guess we need a new plan, don't we?"

"Maybe one we come up with. No gods involved."

"I think Lowellin was right about one thing."

"What's that?"

"I hate to say it, especially after what just happened here, but I think we need the *sulbits* to be more powerful."

"You're going to let them feed on the people?"

"Only those who volunteer. I'm going to tell them the truth, and then if they want to, they can. If not…"

"You're going to tell them the truth about the Children?" Quyloc asked. Rome nodded. "There may not be anyone left after that. We might end up defending a deserted city."

FORTY-FOUR

Quyloc stayed behind to make sure the creature was dead and oversee the men who were digging out the black axe. Rome got to Seafast Square about the time Cara was wrapping up the morning services. He stood at the back of the crowd and listened to the last few minutes. He had to admit that she was good at what she did. Listening to her made him feel a lot more positive about their chances.

When he sensed that she was almost finished, he made his way through the crowd to the front. He'd sent word to the FirstMother, telling her to meet him there, and she showed up about that time, hurrying to catch up to him. The crowd, seeing their macht and the FirstMother converging on the speaking platform, didn't disperse but stayed around to see what was coming next.

The FirstMother took hold of his elbow. "It's dead?" she whispered.

"I think so. We dropped a building on it."

"Thank the Mother," she breathed. "I didn't think…"

"I know how you feel. It was close."

"I haven't seen Lowellin since."

Rome shrugged. "We don't need him."

"What are you planning to do?"

"The *sulbits* need to be stronger. I'm going to give them a chance to help." He gestured toward the crowd.

"What are you going to tell them?"

"The truth. They deserve it."

"I'll oversee every feeding. I won't let anyone die."

"I hope not." Rome turned and went to the front edge of the platform.

"Citizens of Qarath!" he called out. Every voice went silent and every eye turned to him. "I'm here to tell you what is going on, and I'm here to ask your help."

269

Then, as he'd done with the soldiers after the battle of Guardians Watch, he told them, in plain, straightforward language, what was coming for them. He told them what the Children were capable of. He told them what he knew about what had happened at Thrikyl.

"They're coming here next. I don't know if we can beat them, but I know I'm going to fight with everything I've got. You don't have to stay and join the fight. If you decide to leave, none here will judge you or hinder you. Melekath and his Children won't be here for a few days at least, and that should give you time to get a pretty good head start on them. But if you decide to stay, we need your help. You know about the *sulbits*. You have some idea what they can do. We wouldn't have defeated Kasai's army without them. But they have to be stronger, and that's where you come in."

He told them about the plan to make the creatures stronger by letting them feed on people. He didn't sugarcoat it. He told them that some of them might die, though they'd do everything they could to keep that from happening. He told them it wouldn't be pleasant.

When he was done he stood there silently and watched them. He wasn't sure what would happen. Would they simply flee the city en masse? Would they panic? He saw some talking excitedly amongst themselves and a few left the square as if they intended to run straight out of the city, but most just stood there, as if unsure what would come next.

Then a middle-aged woman came forward. A plain white cloth was tied over her graying hair. Her dress was faded and frayed, but clean, her hands thickened by years of hard work. She stopped at the bottom of the steps and looked up.

"It seems to me we either fight and die here or we run and die elsewhere. This is my home. I'd rather die here than in some strange place." She held her head up high. "What I'm saying is, I'm staying and you can take what you want from me."

Rome and the FirstMother exchanged looks and she nodded. Then she walked down the steps, held out her hand to the woman, and escorted her up onto the platform.

"You're sure about this?" she asked her. Her *sulbit* was crouched eagerly on her shoulder, beady eyes fixed on the woman.

"I said I would, didn't I?" the woman said irritably. Though she hid her fear well, Rome saw the smallest tremor in her hands as she stared into the FirstMother's eyes. "Let's get this over with already. I have things to do and I reckon you do too."

The FirstMother took the woman's arm. Her *sulbit* had grown very still, though its whole body was taut. Its smooth, ivory skin seemed to glow in the morning light. "What's your name?" the FirstMother asked softly.

"Enerva."

"Thank you, Enerva."

The *sulbit* looked at the FirstMother, its head tilted to one side. Without looking at it, she nodded. With a small squealing sound it scurried down her arm. Its mouth opened and it clamped down on Enerva's wrist.

Enerva went rigid and her eyes widened. A spasm passed over her and her eyes rolled back in her head. Her skin grew very pale. A trickle of blood leaked from the corner of her mouth and she sagged to one side. Rome stepped forward and caught her. When he touched her a shock went through him. The day went very dark and he had the sensation of falling into bottomless darkness.

Then the feeling passed and he was blinking in the sunlight. Enerva was limp in his arms. He looked up as the FirstMother stepped back. Her *sulbit* was standing on her forearm. He saw a thin, gray tongue emerge from its mouth and swipe across its upper lip. It almost seemed to be glowing slightly. He looked back at Enerva. "Is she going to be all right?" he asked. His tongue felt very thick and it was hard to form the words.

The FirstMother looked at Enerva, her eyes distant and unfocused. After a moment she nodded.

She stepped up to the front edge of the platform and looked out over the crowd. "Spread the word," she told them. "All who want to volunteer should come to the Tender estate."

Rome meant to ride up to the palace when he left Seafast Square – no doubt a thousand details demanded his attention – but for some reason when he got back on his horse he rode to the Grinning Pig. It was dim inside, almost dark after the brightness of the morning, and Rome stood just inside the entrance letting his eyes adjust. Gelbert looked up from behind the bar where he was wiping a glass with a rag.

"Rome," he said, and nodded. Gelbert had known Rome long before he was macht, before he even rose to the rank of sergeant, and he never bothered with his title. Rome didn't care either way. It was part of what he liked about coming here. It felt like, at the Grinning Pig, he could be himself again, not Macht Rome, just Wulf Rome.

"Heard you had some trouble here with a mob," Rome said. He'd seen the scars on the stone outside, noticed that the door was new. Also, one of Quyloc's men kept an eye on the place for him, on Bonnie really, and the man had reported everything to him last night, especially the part about how Bonnie was safe.

"Nothing we couldn't handle," Gelbert replied.

From his stool just inside the door Arls grunted. "With a little help from that Musician."

Gelbert waved his words away like they were flies. "She's upstairs, in her room. Unless you're here to make pretty talk with me."

"I'd sooner talk to my horse," Rome said, and headed for the stairs. Gelbert muttered something behind him, but Rome ignored him. This close it was all he could do to stop himself from running up the stairs two at a time like a kid. He didn't have time for this. He had so much else he needed to do, that his city needed of him, but right then none of it seemed more than a pile of sticks. He needed to see Bonnie and he needed to see her now.

He knocked on her door but didn't speak, waited as he heard her steps cross the floor, the sound of the bar being pulled back. She opened the door with some harsh words at being disturbed, but when she saw who it was the words died. A light came into her eyes and a sound that might have been a cry and might have been a gasp escaped from her lips. She nearly knocked him down throwing herself at him, crushing him in a hug so hard he heard a bone in his back pop.

They held each other for some time in the doorway, wordlessly, and when at last Bonnie pulled back to look up at him Rome felt tears in his beard and knew that not all of them were hers.

"I can't tell you how good it is to see you," he managed finally.

"Oh, Rome," she said, and crushed him to her again.

This time when they parted she pulled him by the hand to the room's lone table and pushed him down into a chair. Then she bustled about, getting him some tea from the kettle that hung over the tiny grate, getting him a thick slice of bread with jam. She didn't look at him again as she did so, didn't answer any of his questions or respond to his protestations that he wasn't hungry. It gave him a chance to look at her and what he saw concerned him. Though it was nearly midday, she was wearing her sleeping shift, and her red hair hadn't been brushed.

"Are you sick?" he asked her.

"Not anymore," she said. "Not since you walked through that door."

Rome felt the tears in his eyes again and brushed at them with the back of his hand. "It's been too long. I just…it was too long."

"Praise the gods you're safe."

"And you too. I heard about the mob and the thing that smashed through the door."

"It wasn't all that," she replied with a dismissive gesture.

"Listen," he said. "I want you to move up to the palace. This time I won't take no."

"Because of the mob? But it's settled now and I'm safe here. You needn't worry about me."

She reached for his cup to refill it – though he hadn't had any of it – but he caught hold of her hand and held on tight. After a moment she quit resisting and looked into his eyes. "It's not about your safety," he said. The next words were hard, but once he started them he couldn't stop them. "It's for me. It's…I don't think we're going to survive what's coming. I don't know what to do. It's too much. The whole city looks to me. I see them thinking, 'the Black Rome will save us,' and I wonder what they would think if they know how lost I really am. There's nothing I can do. This might be the end and I want you with me. I want to see you as much as I can before it's too late."

He let go of her hands, shocked at himself, at the words he'd just uttered. He hadn't meant to let that out. Bonnie looked shocked too, her eyes wide. Then she burst into tears, both hands coming up to hide her mouth as she bent over.

"Hey," Rome said awkwardly. "I didn't mean to…forget I said anything, will you? I'm just tired and – "

Bonnie cut off his next words with a kiss, sitting in his lap and wrapping her arms around him. Now Rome was really confused.

She pulled back to look at him. "Of course I'll come."

"Just like that?" Rome hadn't expected her to agree at all, and for sure not without a fight. "Why?"

"You really don't know, do you?" Bonnie laughed at his puzzled expression. "This is the first time you asked me to move to the palace just because you need me."

"What?" Rome was still lost.

"Before you just wanted to own me."

Rome frowned. "I never wanted to own you."

She shook her head. "Of course you did. I've been a prostitute too many years. You can't pull that over on me."

"But now I don't?"

"No."

"Okay," Rome said. He'd have to think about this later, try to puzzle out what had just happened. For now he was just happy she'd said yes. "When can you leave?"

"Now," she said, "if you don't mind carrying a small chest for me. I have to have some clothes."

"Of course." Rome's head was swimming. Was he awake? Was this a dream?

"I want to keep these rooms, though," she said. "Can you promise me that?"

"Sure. I'll talk to Gelbert. He'll charge me too much and I'll have to threaten to gut him, but we'll work it out."

Bonnie's face suddenly became serious. "I have to tell you something first, though."

"What is it? Are you sick? I see you're wearing your night clothes. I'll get the best healer in the city – "

"Hush." Bonnie put a finger over his lips. "It's not that. I mean, I am a little sick, but it's all normal. You see, I'm pregnant."

Rome's heart stopped. His mouth was dry and he couldn't get a single word out.

"What's wrong?" she demanded. "If you don't want a child…I'm not getting rid of it. It's my baby. I understand if it's not what you want. You're under no obligation here, mister."

Now it was Rome's turn to cut her off. "You are completely wrong, Bonnie. I'm just surprised is all. And I feel like the world's hairiest dunce for not noticing it before. But I can't think of anything better in the whole world than to have a child with you. This is the best news I've ever heard." He meant it too. Just like that the doom that had gripped him since Guardians Watch cracked and a ray of light shone in. He and Bonnie were to have a child. Nothing felt nearly as fine as rolling that thought around in his head.

Bonnie was crying again and apologizing for it, saying something about how it was the pregnancy riling up her emotions and not to mind her but Rome stopped her with a kiss.

FORTY-FIVE

Reyna rolled over and opened her eyes. At first she did not remember where she was. Then her gaze took in the thick blankets, the silken pillows, the heavy drapes over the window, and she remembered. The mattress was goose down, as soft as a cloud. She stretched lazily, luxuriating in the feel of luxury and comfort, sensations gone for so long she had nearly forgotten them. She sat up. Sunlight flooded in through the window. Heavy furniture lined the walls. Thick rugs lay on the floor.

She got out of bed, careful to avoid stepping on the body sprawled on the floor. She remembered more. There had been more survivors in the city than she'd thought, several times as many people as Ferien had yielded. She'd been drunk on stolen Song when she came upon this estate. The ornate, iron gates were locked, but by that point she was so filled with power that it had taken almost no effort to rip them down and toss them aside. Through a haze, she remembered staggering across the vast grounds, soaking in the wealth, the neatly-trimmed hedges, the sparkling fountains and opulent carriages, all parts of a world she had enjoyed so long ago.

She kicked in the front door and stumbled into the massive foyer, the floor tiled in marble, fluted columns supporting graceful stairs that led to the upper floors. It reminded her somewhat of her own estate, the one she walked away from so many years ago. She climbed the stairs, her fingertips sliding over the glossy wood of the banister, her bare feet slapping on the marble tiles. Why had she ever left this? She should have taken Melekath's Gift, then gone back to her own life. Instead she'd been seduced by him, by the picture he drew of the utopia he would create.

Durag'otal hadn't been utopia at all. What it had been was boring and frustrating. It was frustrating because Melekath gave wealth to his followers indiscriminately. What was the point of wealth if it did not confer power over others? In Durag'otal everyone shared equally in

Melekath's largesse. There were no servants, no commoners at all. By giving it to everyone, Melekath succeeded in making wealth meaningless. It was boring because there was no political intrigue. Politics was a game she loved: the manipulating, the scheming, the seducing, all to climb ever higher.

By the time the Eight and their army showed up, she was ready to leave Durag'otal. She decided right away to sneak out of the city as soon as it got dark and join up with the besiegers. Maybe she knew something that would help them, that she could use as leverage to set herself up in a position worthy of her. But Melekath ruined that plan with his shield. It kept the Eight out all right, but it kept her in as well, which she discovered when she tried to pass through it.

So she'd been stuck there while the siege dragged on. Sieges were dreary affairs and that one was no different. Day after day with nothing to do but wait and hope the besiegers would give up and go away. She was sure she would go mad from the idleness.

Then the walls of the prison rose and the dark years came. It was bad in there, very bad. The feeling of being cut off from something indefinable, a hole inside her that felt as if it would swallow her whole. The cold weakness that gradually stole over her body, only partially alleviated by feeding from Melekath. The only good thing about that time was that at least the foolish notions of utopia disappeared. What good was utopia anyway? Life was about struggle, about clawing and scratching, beating your enemy and then standing on his body to reach higher. And there'd been plenty of struggle in the prison. Treachery, intrigue, shifting alliances. It was a harder, darker version of the game she loved, but it was something and playing it was what had kept her alive and moving when so many gave up and crawled away to hide in the darkness.

Now she was free and her power was returning. When she was done with him, she would destroy that fool Heram. Then she would lead the Children herself and the world would be hers to do with as she pleased. The Song she had taken burned like a forge inside her, making her stronger than ever before. She squeezed the bannister and felt how the wood gave under her hand like parchment. She tore a section away and flung it over the edge. It appeared that there was more to the Gift than simple immortality. Clearly there was power here as well. She felt huge and strong. She felt limitless. When she could feed on the ordinary humans in the thousands, in the tens of thousands, there would be nothing she could not do.

Melekath. She frowned at the thought of him. He would resist and complain. He still felt attachment to these weak creatures for some reason. He would no doubt try to stop her. But she had been watching him. She had seen how difficult it was for him to open a breach in the wall of this city. Once she could feed freely, she felt certain she could overpower him as well.

As Reyna reached the top of the stairs she realized that the estate house was not empty. The fool who owned the estate had not fled or killed himself and she found him huddled in the master bedroom, a middle-aged man with a heavy paunch and a carafe of brandy in one thick hand. He'd shrieked when she came into the room, and threw the brandy at her. It broke and the shards cut her bare feet, but after so many centuries of numbness, even pain felt like ecstasy.

The man tried to run then and she caught him at the doors leading out to the balcony and dragged him back to the bed, where she wrapped herself around him, ignoring his feeble struggles, and drained his Song slowly, then pushed his lifeless body to the floor and collapsed into sleep.

Reyna smiled down at the man's lifeless body. "No lovers I had when I was human ever matched you," she told him. And it was true. Sex was only a pale shadow of the ecstasy that came with feeding on Song. By the end of her time as a human she had not enjoyed sex for many years anyway, being to her nothing more than a weapon to be wielded against men and occasionally women. It was how she thought of the past now, *when she was human.* For she no longer considered herself as such. She and her brethren were a new breed completely, superior to humans in every way.

"Your time is over now, you know," she told his corpse. "We are your betters in every way. You will live only as food for us." He did not seem to care.

A huge mirror hung on one wall. Reyna walked to it and looked at herself. Only a few scraps of the gray skin remained, most replaced by fresh, pink skin. She scratched at a gray patch on her forearm and succeeded in peeling it away. Her lips were lush and full, exactly as she remembered them. Her red hair was long and spilled over her shoulders. She frowned and leaned closer to the mirror. There were still flaws. Her nose did not look quite right. It was bent to the side slightly.

Concentrating, she drew on the stolen Song, focusing it with her will. After a moment her nose began to change, like wax left in the sun. Her brows drew together as she concentrated and slowly her nose assumed a new shape. She relaxed and touched it with one finger. Better. Not perfect. Not yet. But better.

She looked down at the rags she was wearing. This would not do. She tore them away and threw them down, then studied her body in the mirror. Her arms and legs were straight and smooth, her breasts full and round. There was no sign of the sag, the wrinkles that had so horrified her in her old life. She could still do better, but it was a start.

"Goodbye, lover," she said to the corpse, blowing him a kiss. She left the room and walked down the hall, searching for one that had belonged to his wife or a daughter.

Three doors down she entered a room with a wardrobe filled with dresses. She found one she liked, red satin with pearl buttons. But when she started to put it on the dirt on her skin caused her nose to wrinkle. It would not do to ruin such a beautiful dress with filth.

In a side room was a tub that had been filled for a bath. Floating in the tub, face down, was a young woman, her hair spread out in a fan around her.

"A better choice than your father made," she said, lifting the body by its hair and tossing it aside. It was so easy to do. Being strong was quite a wonderful thing. One of the things she had hated most in her old life was that men were physically stronger than she was. It made her more dangerous than they, since she had to win with her wits and could not resort to blunt force, but still she hated it. Now that would never be a problem again.

Then she climbed into the tub and treated herself to her first bath in three thousand years. There were no maids to wait on her, and the water was cold, but it felt wonderful all the same and she was a new woman when she emerged. She sat in front of the vanity and brushed her hair, then tied it up in ribbons. She drew on the dress, added some shoes and did a slow twirl in front of the mirror.

"Much better," she said to her reflection. It would be nice to find some jewelry she liked, but she was, at the very least, presentable once again.

She frowned. The stolen Song filled her veins, finer than any wine, filling her with light and energy and power, almost enough to push back the shadows of the prison. But it would not last. Though it was still very slight, already she could feel the wild energy abating. She would need more.

It was time to go to Qarath. No doubt Father would seek to delay them. He would fuss and worry and come up with reason after reason why they should be patient. Furious suddenly, she struck the heavy vanity table with one fist so hard it cracked in half. She was done with patience. She was strong. She was invincible. It was time to act.

She was walking out the front door of the estate house when a faint trickle of Song wafted over her, sweet and gentle as a spring rain. She froze, her head turning as she sought to find its source. She reentered the house and walked down a hallway, finally passing through a small door into the servants' quarters. In the kitchen she found another door that opened onto a narrow set of stairs leading down to the cellars. A smile lit her face. The Song came from down there. Even better: there were two sources.

The cellar was dark, but she needed no light. Three millennia in a lightless prison had taught her well how to navigate in the dark. At the bottom of the stairs she stopped and listened. The air was redolent with the odors of onions, potatoes, apples, drying hams and sausages. She smelled spices and wine and wondered how wine would taste to her, after all these years.

And, very faintly, she could hear the rapid beating of two hearts.

She lit a lantern that stood on a shelf and held it up before her. It was not for her. It was for them. For an idea had come to her as she searched for these two. A way to stave off the growing hunger. She smiled at her own cleverness.

She found them huddled in the far corner, behind two enormous sacks of grain. They were young women, probably just finishing their second decade, twins. They stared up at her with huge eyes, too frightened to move.

She gestured to them to come out. "Don't be frightened," she said.

When they didn't move she grew irritated suddenly. "Are you deaf? Come here!" They cried out and buried their faces against each other and suddenly she had had enough.

Making an aggravated sound, she picked up the grain sacks and tossed them aside. Then she grabbed the two women, yanked them out of their hiding place and dragged them upstairs. In the light of the kitchen, she looked them over. Dark-haired, wearing matching red and white dresses with what was probably the emblem of their master sewn to the breast. Their faces were round and plump. Favored, pampered servants then. They clung to each other, crying.

"Come with me," she said, and started back toward the front door of the estate house. They ran the other way.

Now she was getting angry. She caught up to them at the door leading to outside, where they were struggling with the heavy bar. She grabbed them by the scruffs of their necks and banged their heads together a couple of times. They screamed but stopped struggling and hung limply in her grasp, giving themselves over to their fate. This time when she told them to follow her they did meekly.

In the stables Reyna found that most of the stalls were open, the horses gone, but two of the stalls were still occupied. A new idea occurred to her and she started toward them. The animals went mad as she drew closer, rearing and flinging themselves at the gates to their stalls. Reyna stopped. So much for that idea. She had thought to use the horses to draw a carriage so she could ride in style from this city. At the very least she could ride one and save herself all the walking. But clearly the beasts were not going to allow that.

She ignored the horses and looked until she found the tack room. Hanging on the wall were halters and lead ropes. She fastened one around the neck of each woman, knotting them tight. Now it would be easier to keep a hold of them.

Outside, she realized that her hunger was starting to once again make itself known. It was mild still, but she had to make a real effort not to drain Song from the women as she secured them. She would save them for later. When the others were crying with hunger, she would have food. If she fed and watered them, and didn't take too much from them, perhaps they would feed her for some days. She took them to the kitchens and told them to gather food for themselves, as much as they could carry.

Then it was time to find Heram. It appeared she needed her temporary ally a bit longer. They needed to be united against Melekath. She wasn't yet ready to go up against him alone, especially when conflict with him might weaken her to the point where she was vulnerable to Heram.

As she passed through the city she saw other Children beginning to stir from their torpor. They looked better after feeding, but most still looked pretty mangled. It was only as she had expected. They were weak. Their minds were shattered by the prison and so they had not been able to restore themselves as well as she had. Each one she encountered she told to meet her at the break in the wall where they entered the city. Tell any others they saw. It was time to leave. There was a whole world waiting for them.

All of them looked hungrily at the women she led, but for most it only took one look from Reyna to convince them that acting on that hunger would be foolish. One, a pathetic little man whose name she thought was Lerek, actually lunged at her captives. Reyna swatted him aside, releasing just enough power to give her blow real force, and he slammed into a nearby wall hard enough that one of his bones in his shoulder cracked loudly and he yelped in pain. She strode over to him, lifted him by his broken shoulder and shook him, eliciting a scream from him.

"Next time I will tear both your arms from your body. Remember that."

He stared at her for a long moment, his eyes rolling wildly in his head, then nodded.

She found Heram in a small square with an ornate stone fountain in the center. Heram had hold of two of the weaker Children and was slamming their heads into the side of the fountain over and over. He had fed well, and his arms and legs were grossly swollen with muscle. Each arm was as big around as a normal man's waist and his legs were stumps. His neck was bigger around than his head, which was basically a square block. Veins bulged everywhere. He was also at least a head taller than before, but Reyna had grown as well and she was still taller than he, a fact that she noted with satisfaction.

He looked up as she approached. His eyes were red. His nose was misshapen like a potato, his ears hard knots of cartilage and he had only scattered teeth in his mouth. Clearly he had put no effort into his appearance, focusing all his energy on strength. Reyna found him repulsive and thought longingly of the day when she could destroy him.

He ceased his banging and scowled at her, noting the dress she wore, his eyes lingering on her two prizes. Freed from his grip, the two weaker Children scrambled to their feet and ran from the square.

"Where did you get them?" he asked.

She cocked her head to the side, looking down at him, making no effort to hide her disdain. The man was little more than a brute, like a bull. But a bull that, pointed in the right direction, could do a great deal of damage. "They are for later. When my hunger returns. Did you not save any for yourself?"

He shook his thick, block like head and his scowl deepened. "They were gone too soon. There were not enough of them."

"And that is why it is time we speak of Father."

Heram looked around. There was so much muscle in his neck that he appeared to barely be able to turn his head. Satisfied the square was empty, he turned back to her and crossed his thick arms with an effort. "So talk."

"This is what I have always appreciated about you, Heram. You are not a man to waste time on subtleties," she said sarcastically. He did not rise to the bait, only stared at her with his red eyes. Probably he did not even know what sarcasm was. "You saw what happened here. He made us wait. We did, and because of that we were cheated of what was rightfully ours. There were tens of thousands of them here, enough to sate us for days and days. Instead we were left with only a handful. Even now the hunger begins to return. You feel it as well as I do."

Heram's glare remained suspicious, but he nodded. "It is true what you say." He shifted his stance, standing with his thick legs widespread, and looked once more at the women she led. She let him look, let him feel desire. With men it was always the same: once they felt desire, they quit thinking. That was when they were easiest to manipulate.

"This is why I have come to you. You of all of us understand the need for strength. You and I, we have always thought alike, have we not?"

"I am not interested in your flattery," he grunted. His lips were still badly misshapen and his words were difficult to make out. "I know what you are. Speak what you intend and be done with it."

"Forceful and direct. It is what I have always admired about you."

"Save it, Reyna. You have never admired anyone. You have eyes for only one person, and that is you."

Reyna nodded. "Fair enough. I simply wished to be sure that we understood each other."

"It was three thousand years," he said angrily. "We understand each other far better than I would ever wish. Speak or go away. You are beginning to anger me."

Reyna felt her anger rising and worked to push it back down. She needed Heram on her side. For now at least. She could not manage him and Melekath at the same time. She forced herself to smile. "We need to make sure that this never happens again."

"You would turn on our Father?"

"I am not saying that. Only that we must keep our options open."

"He is still more powerful than you realize. Even together we could not bring him down yet."

"I am aware of that. I am only saying – "

"And there is the matter of the Guardians. We would have to deal with them too."

Reyna paused. So there were thoughts inside that thick skull. What a surprise. "They are still far away."

"As far as we know." He stabbed at her chest with a thick finger and she fell back a step. "You are not the only one who thinks, Reyna. You are not the only one who plots."

She drew herself up. "So you refuse my offer of alliance?"

"I do not," Heram replied. "I agree with you. Father has been too cautious. He has cost us a great deal here." He waved a thick arm. "But there are still more cities out there, many more. This will be as nothing in time."

"And if it is not?"

"Then we will act. But I will not be your soldier. We will be equals in this, of that I want you to be very sure."

"Of course," she replied sweetly, smiling and showing him all her teeth. "How could you think it would be anything else between us?"

FORTY-SIX

Josef remembered the last day. He remembered the fear in the
streets of Durag'otal when the Shapers began their strange ritual, the
wild eyes, the crying, the fights that broke out. He hadn't been as
frightened as most were. His faith in Father was strong. He calmed
the weeping. He broke up fights. Over and over he told people
"Father will take care of it. Father will take care of us. Trust in
Father."

But as the unearthly, boiling, purplish-black walls climbed higher
into the sky, even he began to doubt. He ran until he found Father, in
Heaven's Plaza near the main entrance to the city. The floor of the
plaza was all of a translucent, reddish stone. In the center of the plaza
Father had shaped statues of a man and a woman side by side. The
statues had looks of transcendent calm on their faces and slight smiles
on their lips and faced outwards as if they were looking at the
besieging forces. Father stood near them, watching the blackness
cover the city, doing nothing. He looked small and insignificant next
to the statues, bent over and tired.

Josef ran to join the mass of people around Father. They were
crying out to him, pleading, begging, but he seemed not to hear any of
them. It looked like he was staring at Xochitl, as she fought with the
other Shapers to control the chaos power they were drawing from a
deep fissure in the earth. Even then, Josef did not doubt his Father.

It wasn't until the visible sky had narrowed to a tiny disc overhead
that he began to doubt. Then even that opening closed, and everything
changed.

He was suffocating. People around him clawed at their throats.
There was a roaring in his ears. A terrible emptiness loomed around
him and though people pressed against him on all sides, he knew that
he was utterly and forever alone.

Lights rose in the darkness as lanterns were lit. Frightened faces
loomed around Josef. They were speaking, but he could not hear them

over the roaring. He turned and Father was there, only an arm's length away, with his back to Josef, holding a lantern over his head. Josef reeled towards him, a refuge in the dark of the storm. Father would fix it. Father would make the desolation go away. He clutched Father's cloak. Father turned, and that was when the rest of the light went out of the day for Josef. That was when he truly abandoned hope.

Father was lost too. Josef could see it in his eyes.

Someone fell into Josef from the side and when that happened Josef felt something give way inside him. The desperation and fear came to a head then and he just snapped. He gave the man a hard shove in return. Josef was not a small man and he was stronger than most. The one he shoved went flying, slamming into several others. Father yelled something and tried to reach out. But the man Josef shoved had gotten his feet back under him and he came at Josef, howling mindlessly. He struck Josef twice and then Josef tackled him, knocking down two other people in the process.

And that was how the first riot started.

The panic which rose with the walls of the prison overwhelmed those people known as the Children. They turned on each other with a savagery so complete that it was hard to imagine they had been civilized folk only minutes before. Josef had not been in a fight since his youth. He was a peaceful man at heart, dedicated to the plants he loved so much. He was soft spoken, slow moving and generally kind. But all that disappeared in those first few crazy hours after the prison closed around them.

In the melee he quickly lost sight of the man he was originally fighting with. But that didn't matter. There was no lack of foes. He struck out at them all. He attacked men, women and children with equal ferocity and they attacked him in return. He punched, he bit, he kicked and scratched and clawed. At some point someone bit off part of his ear and he caved in the person's cheekbone with an elbow.

It was hours before the riot burned itself out. When Josef first came back to his senses he was sitting against a wall, throwing up blood. When the spasm passed he raised his head and looked on a scene from a nightmare. Here and there were knots of people still fighting, but most had stopped. Scores of people were down. Some were motionless. Others were dragging themselves with their arms. People were moaning and crying. A woman off to his right was screaming. A child lay nearby, his head twisted back and around in an unnatural way that said his neck was broken. As Josef looked at him, the child opened his eyes. He couldn't have been more than eight.

"Help me," he said. His eyes rolled wildly. "I can't move. What's wrong? I can't move!"

Josef turned his face away. The gulf yawned around him. There was no way to reach across it. He was utterly alone. After a while he rose, hurting everywhere, and stumbled out of the square. Father was standing in the middle of the square, saying something, but Josef ignored him. Nothing he said would make any difference. Nothing would ever again make any difference.

FORTY-SEVEN

Orenthe fled down a black street. She caught her foot in a hidden crack in the ground and pitched forward, falling amongst a litter of broken stone. She came to her knees. Out of the murk she saw the dim outline of a fallen stone statue lying before her, a beautiful woman of reddish stone, lying on her back, one arm broken off, the other reaching for the sky that wasn't there. She grabbed the statue's remaining arm and pulled herself to her feet. Behind her she heard the hue and cry of the mob, coming closer.

But when she tried to run again she found herself in deep sand. It was up to her knees and she was sinking deeper with each struggle for freedom. The cry of the mob grew closer, wild animals that had found the prey upon which they would temporarily sate their madness. The city had disappeared. Huge sand dunes surrounded her.

With a gasp she woke up. She was in a small room, almost completely dark except for the thinnest line of light from underneath a door to the side. It was only a nightmare, she told herself. Only a nightmare.

Then the memories of the past day flooded back and she knew for a fact that the nightmare had not ended, only shifted, as nightmares do.

She'd sworn to herself that she wouldn't give in again. During the long night that the Children waited outside Thrikyl Orenthe had spent the entire time praying. She couldn't have said who or what she prayed to, only that she did, and fervently. She prayed for strength against the hunger that was a living thing inside her, like a rat crawling through her bowels, endlessly chewing. She prayed for courage. Mostly she prayed for an end, a release from the hell that was her life.

When the morning came she thought she could handle it. The hunger was bad and getting worse, but she could keep from giving in to it. She could keep it from controlling her. If she stole no Song, she would get weaker and hungrier. She wouldn't die, but she would eventually get so weak that she would be unable to move. Then, at least, she would never kill again. It would not cleanse her of the deaths already on her hands, but it was something.

When Father announced that it was time to enter the city, she turned her face away and ignored his call. She sat down, facing back the way they had come. Looking at the devastation they had made on their way here – a wide swath where everything was gray and dead – strengthened her in her conviction. She would no longer be a part of this destruction.

She felt the inner tug as Father used his power to breach the wall, then the outraged cries that followed. She looked over her shoulder and saw her brethren streaming into the opening. It didn't take her long to guess what had happened, but somehow, knowing that most of the inhabitants of Thrikyl were already dead made the hunger worse rather than better. She turned her back on the city once again, gritting her teeth, her hands balled into fists.

She would not give in.

She sat there for some time, listening to the desperate cries of her brethren as they hunted, now and then the scream of an unfortunate soul that met its end. Suddenly she couldn't sit there any longer. She had to move.

As she started walking toward the breach in the wall, she told herself that she was only going peek in. She would not enter the city.

At the breach she stopped. The pull to enter the city was nearly overwhelming, so strong that her whole body shook as if with a fever. She made herself sit down on one of the fallen blocks of stone that littered the ground near the breach. She promised herself she would go no further, no matter what happened.

Sometime later she was sitting there, perched on the edge of the stone, staring intently into the city, when she saw movement. A boy emerged from an alleyway and ran toward her. Something rose within her, like a massive wave in the midst of a wild sea, and she gripped the stone so tightly she heard a bone in her finger snap.

The pain helped to calm her enough that as the boy drew nearer she was able to stand up and move back so as to allow him through the breach. When she did, he saw her and stopped in his tracks. He stared at her, his eyes big and round, his chest heaving. He was probably twelve, wearing torn pants and a badly stained shirt. His brown hair was ragged, his limbs painfully thin. He glanced over his shoulder, then back at her.

"It's okay," she said softly, trying to sound nonthreatening. It was hard to form the words because her lips and tongue had not regrown properly, but she thought she did well enough. "I won't hurt you."

He backed up a step, looked back over his shoulder again, then back at her. She saw faint scarring on the side of his face. In his eyes was a wisdom beyond his years, a wisdom that comes from surviving on the streets alone. He held a rough club in one hand and he raised it. "What are you?"

"I'm...Orenthe," she replied, holding her hands with palms up. She saw that her hands were shaking badly. This close to the boy's Song she could almost taste it. It was maddening. The boy saw the shaking too and his eyes narrowed. "I won't hurt you. I promise." She motioned him through. "But you need to hurry."

He hesitated, glanced over his shoulder again. "What are you?" he repeated, waving his club to encompass the city behind him and the crazed creatures that hunted within it.

Orenthe looked at the gray skin that covered much of her arms, the old, unhealed wounds, the merest rags which served as her clothing. "I don't know anymore," she said softly. "But we were once human. Like you." She looked back into his eyes. "It doesn't matter. You have to leave before it's too late."

He stared at her, trying to judge whether she could be trusted. There was a shriek behind him and a gurgling moan. Suddenly making up his mind, he ran forward, picking his way through the rubble of broken stone. Orenthe knotted her hands tightly together as he drew near. There was a pounding in her ears, drowning out all thought.

The breach was narrow. Orenthe realized he would have to pass very close to her and she stood, thinking to move back out of his way. Just at that moment, like a rabbit fleeing a fox, he darted by her. Orenthe leaned back.

His foot caught on a stone and he pitched forward, throwing his arms out to catch himself.

One hand struck her leg. His touch was white-hot fire.

The flood she'd been fighting to hold back burst free.

Orenthe snarled and jumped on him. He twisted as they went down together, managed to hit her with the club hard enough that her head snapped back. Pain burst in her head and any chance of controlling herself disappeared completely.

She wrapped both arms clumsily around his legs and then her mouth closed on his leg.

He screamed, a high, forlorn sound, but Orenthe couldn't hear it over the pounding in her ears.

When it was over she rolled off of him, sick at what she had done and maddened by how it made her feel. The coldness, the darkness, the emptiness – they had all been pushed back. Not very far, but enough. His Song roared through her, all golden light and endless possibility.

Then she took off into the city, desperate to find more, desperate to drive the blackness back once again.

How many she killed after that she didn't know. Two or three probably. The rest of the day was a jumbled, disjointed memory. At some point the Song she had taken in grew overwhelming and the pain started. It felt like her bones were moving under her skin. At any moment she expected her skin to split open. That was when she sought out a place to hide, to rest and let the Song work through her.

⚒ ⚒ ⚒

Orenthe made her way toward the light coming from under the door. She was in a cellar, dim outlines of crates stacked to the ceiling on one side, kegs and barrels on the other side, the smell of stale beer and sour wine. The stairs leading up were rough, but stout, and the door opened soundlessly when she pushed on it.

She stumbled through a tavern, trying to avoid looking at the four bodies sprawled around a table, empty wine cups near their dead hands. At least she had not killed them. Not directly, anyway.

Outside, for a moment she couldn't see; the light was too bright. She put her hand on the wall of the tavern and waited for her eyes to adjust. As her vision returned, she saw a woman lying nearby in the street. She had not had the good sense to face death on her own terms. The woman's belly was distended by pregnancy. Her arms were wrapped around her belly, trying to shelter her baby with her last strength. Her mouth was stretched wide in a scream and her flesh had the same wrinkled, sunken look that all the Children's victims had.

Orenthe had no memory of the woman; there was no way to tell if she was one of Orenthe's victims or someone else's. But it didn't matter. All at once the enormity of her guilt struck her like a physical blow and Orenthe collapsed to her knees. She wanted to cry. She wanted to release the pain in a flood of tears, but she was completely dry inside and so there was nothing, only the intense pain building and building with nowhere to go.

"What have I done?" she moaned. She pressed her fingers into her eyes, but the pain did not relent. "What have I become?"

Choking on her self-hatred, she came to her feet and stumbled down the street away from the dead woman's accusing corpse. She walked blindly, staggering into walls, tripping over refuse and the occasional body. At some point she stopped, turned her face to the sky and began to scream. She tore at her hair, pulling out great chunks. The pain was intense, but it barely penetrated the pain where her heart used to be. Her screams brought no answers.

When her passion subsided and she could again see she was surprised to discover that she was in a small plaza not far from the city wall. On one side of the plaza was a temple. Unlike most of the temples in Thrikyl, this one was not dedicated to Bereth, but to some god she did not recognize. There was something familiar about it, though, and she stumbled closer, trying to figure it out.

All at once she realized it had once been a temple to Xochitl. There were still faint traces of the many-pointed star in the stonework of the façade, though the stones had been scoured to remove them.

"Mother?" she whispered, taking a hesitant step toward it.

Then she stopped. She knew what Xochitl was, knew that she was no god, any more than Melekath was. It was Xochitl who had led the army that imprisoned all of them. Xochitl had already judged her. There would be nothing for her there.

Moaning incoherently, she stopped. There was no hope anywhere. No redemption. No promise. Even the doors of death were closed to her.

An idea came to her then. A way to kill herself perhaps. It was worth trying. She had nothing else to lose.

Drawing on dusty memories, she gathered her attention and turned it inward, falling down within herself, down to the place *beyond*. The mists billowed around her but she ignored them, diving deeper, pushing as far as she could. She *saw* flows of Song, faint and gossamer in this place of death. They were already fading. Soon the city would be completely dead. She did not have much time.

She dove deeper, following the flows down and down. Finally, she found what she sought.

A trunk line.

Thick and powerful it pulsed softly, massive quantities of Song flowing through it.

She lurched forward and embraced it. Power unimaginable coursed through her, blinding, tearing pain. She was thrown back and down.

She was lying on her face in the street. Her body was in agony everywhere. She knew without looking that the power of the trunk line had literally torn her open. Muscles and flesh were shredded like tissue paper.

The death she longed for still eluded her, but at least she would never hurt another innocent again.

FORTY-EIGHT

"What is this?"

Melekath had sensed his Children gathering at the main gates of the city and gone there to see why. Almost all of them were there, gathered around Reyna and Heram. As he spoke, Melekath gestured at two young women who had halters knotted around their necks; Reyna was holding the lead ropes in one hand. The two women were clinging tightly to each other, staring at the Children who crowded around them with wide, rolling eyes. Reyna looked at Melekath and smirked. Her dress was a vivid red and she stood out amongst the others, most of whom were still only dressed in rags.

"Shatren," she replied.

"I don't like it," he said. "It is enough that you slaughter them. You don't need to torment them as well."

"You don't have to like it," she retorted, an intense, almost predatory look on her face. Then she turned to Heram. "Are we ready to go?"

Before Heram could reply, Melekath said, "Not everyone is here. A few are still in the city. At least one is badly injured."

Reyna shrugged. "They can catch up with us. Or not. Either way."

"They are your brothers and sisters," Melekath protested.

She snorted. "They are no more my brothers and sisters than you are my father."

That shook him. He had thought of them as his children for so long. What did it mean, really, to be a father? He knew only that her words left a dull ache inside.

"We have changed," she said. "Look at us. We are no longer your children and you are no longer our father." She turned to look at the rest of them, gathering close to hear. The stolen Song had changed them greatly. Broken limbs had been mended, gray skin replaced by new, pink skin. Hair was sprouting, backs were straightening. Most had not the control Reyna did, and their forms had not come out as well as hers. Success or failure had a great deal to do with the relative sanity of the mind directing the healing and the minds of the Children were mostly shattered. As a result, missing limbs had regrown too long or too short, with joints in the wrong places. Facial features were recovering, but they did not look right. "You know the truth of my words. Look at the changes we have wrought on ourselves. *We* have done this." She turned back to Melekath. "We do not need you. We do not need any of the old gods. We are becoming our own gods." She pointed to the north. "That way lies Qarath. A city filled with Song. With *our* Song. It is *ours*. We need only reach out and take it. But only if we do not stand around and waste time. Only if we move, and now."

"It is not so simple as that," Melekath replied, still struggling to find his balance under the impact of her words. "We risk much if we run headlong. Remember, these people defeated your Guardians. You do not know what they are capable of."

That gave them pause. They exchanged uncertain looks.

But Reyna did not give up so easily. "Yes, *Father*," she said, putting mocking emphasis on the title, "let us follow your wisdom once again. It worked so well here." She gestured at two bodies lying sprawled nearby. They appeared to have jumped from the wall to their deaths. "You may stay and tremble once again behind a wall with him, if you want," she said, and he saw how she had cleverly tied his mistake here to his mistake during the siege of Durag'otal. "But I choose to go on the attack. Heram, open the gate, if you will."

Heram was already standing by the inner portcullis and Melekath saw that Reyna had planned this as well. This was why she had gathered them here, rather than by the breach he had made in the wall for them yesterday. She meant this as a display. She had known he would try to stop her and she was ready for him. He would not win this contest. His best hope was to back off and try to salvage what he could later on.

Heram's skin was oddly red, as if he had been badly sunburned. His body was layered with thick slabs of muscle. He laid thick hands on the portcullis, which was made of heavy, interwoven bands of iron. The muscles in his shoulders and chest swelled. He began to strain. At first, nothing happened. He pulled harder. There was the squeal of tortured metal and then the portcullis bent outward. He yanked at it and all at once it gave, tearing completely away from the wall.

Balancing it over his head, he turned, glared at Melekath, then threw it. The Children ducked to avoid it as it flew over their heads.

But he was not done yet. He walked into the tunnel that led through the mighty wall, under the silent murder holes, and up to the outer gates. Easily two feet thick, they were banded in iron and secured by crossbars the thickness of trees. Heram clenched his massive, block-like fists. With a roar, he struck the gates with a two-handed blow. Then again. On the third blow the gates tore away from their hinges and sagged outward. Heram tore them free the rest of the way and tossed them outside, one at a time.

Without speaking, the Children followed, passing around Melekath, flowing through the passageway and spilling out of the dead city. After a moment, Melekath followed. Reyna did not even deign to glance at him as she moved to a spot at their head, Heram at her side. Like a queen addressing her subjects, she drew herself up and gazed down at them from her proud height. "Follow me," she said. Heram made a grunting sound and she amended her words. "Follow *us*. We are the Reborn. We are the new gods of this world. Together we will take it and make it our own and none will hinder us." As she said the last she shot a challenging look at Melekath.

Melekath could do it. Reyna had misjudged him. As weakened as he was, he was still strong enough to slap both Reyna and Heram down and make an example of them.

But in the end he couldn't. They had suffered far too much at his hands already. It was his fault that they had spent thousands of years in a lightless, Song-less hell. It was his fault they had become as they were now. He could not visit more pain upon them. Not now, maybe not ever. Best would be to let them have their heads for a while, to follow and guide them as best he could. They still needed him. Of that much he was sure. There would be other chances. He let the power which had begun to build within him go.

Now Reyna's look was triumphant. Her lip curled slightly and she turned away, dismissing him, and began walking north along the coast, Heram matching her, the Children – the Reborn – falling in behind them.

FORTY-NINE

Netra opened her eyes and had no idea where she was. For a moment, just a moment, she was in her old room in the Haven. Cara was in the bed next to her. She must have overslept though, because the sun was already up, flooding through the window. Then Shorn put his hand on her shoulder and it all came crashing back on her.

The Gur al Krin. Melekath. Breaking the prison.

Netra sat up and what she saw made her gasp. They were halfway up the side of a small valley, at the foot of a low run of cliffs. The ground underfoot was covered with a plant the consistency of moss but a deep yellow color. Everywhere in the valley plants grew in riotous profusion, but they were unlike any plants Netra had ever seen before and they grew in colors she had never imagined: vivid reds, yellows, blues and oranges. Nearby was a row of plants that were taller than trees, with thin, willowy stalks and delicate, almost lacy red leaves. There was a patch of emerald blue plants that were waist high and leafless, with hundreds of intricately-branching limbs. There were plants that looked like tall ferns, the leaves orange and shading to a deep crimson along the edges. And the flowers. They grew everywhere in every color of the rainbow.

Moving through the strange plants were a number of creatures: tiny scarlet and black birds that seemed almost to float from plant to plant rather than fly, wide-bodied creatures with silver fur that moved slowly through the ferns. From the limb of a tree with rippling, silver leaves a furry creature with a long nose hung upside down. It opened its eyes, regarded them sleepily, and then closed its eyes once again.

"It's beautiful," Netra whispered. "There's so much life. And look," she said, taking a step toward something that reminded her of a rabbit but with long, white fur and long, drooping ears that was nosing around in the plants near their feet, "it's not afraid of us." She turned to Shorn but he wasn't looking at the rabbit-like thing. His head was turning side to side, alert for an enemy. "I have never heard

LifeSong as strong as it is here." She stopped, concentrating on what only she could hear. "There's something different about it though. It's mixed with something else." She went still again, concentrating, then realization dawned in her eyes. "It's mixed with Sea force."

She slipped *beyond* and reached past the mists. She *saw* myriad *akirmas* all around them, connected by an intricate web of LifeSong, but LifeSong tinged with an emerald green that was the Sea. Further out she *saw* something else and she came out of *beyond* and turned eagerly to Shorn.

"This isn't a...we're in a..." She hesitated, unsure how to put it into words. "This whole valley, everything you see here...it's *alive*. It's alive and it's aware of us."

She waited for his response and was annoyed when all he did was shrug. "That's it? All of this around you and all you do is shrug?"

"Where is the one who brought us here?" Shorn rumbled, his eyes once again moving over the landscape. "Why did it bring us here? These are what I wish to know."

"I may be able to help with that," said a soft voice.

Shorn spun, his fists coming up. Netra put her hand on his arm to forestall him.

"Wait," she said. "It's not the same one." Though the creature that faced them from the other side of the small clearing had the same slight, almost delicate build as their attacker, with bulbous eyes set very wide on its face, a wide, lipless mouth and the lines of gills on the sides of its neck, it was clearly different. It was smaller and slighter than their attacker, for one thing, and its color was different. Their attacker had been a deep, ancient yellow, but this one was a lighter, fresher yellow, and it had streaks of green tingeing the skin around the eyes and mouth and along the backs of its slender arms. "I don't think it is here to harm us," Netra finished.

"Indeed, I am not," the creature said. Its voice was soft and somewhat musical and, Netra thought, female, though she could not be sure. The creature wore a thin shift of some kind of shimmery material that went up and over one shoulder, was belted at the waist and ended at knees that bent backward. The creature crouched and lowered her head, showing the back of her neck. Her clothing moved as if part of her, catching the light and reflecting it in a variety of muted colors.

After a long moment she stood and faced them once again. "I am Jenett, a Seeker of the Lementh'kal. Welcome to ki'Loren."

"You speak our language," Netra said.

"Perhaps. Or I am helping you to understand ours. It does not matter." Her eyes were very large and luminous. She held her hands out with the palms up. She appeared completely nonthreatening.

Shorn was not convinced and he advanced on her, looming over her. She looked immensely frail before him. It seemed like if he simply fell on her she would be crushed. "Why have you brought us here?"

"It wasn't her, Shorn," Netra said, but he held up his hand to stop her and did not look at her.

"If you mean no harm, then why were we attacked?" he growled.

"That was Ya'Shi," Jenett said. She blinked slowly – her lids rose from the bottom of her eyes and they were translucent – and turned her head to the ground. Netra sensed regret in her Song. "He is...his ways are unorthodox. I cannot say why he did so. Though I have been his student for many years, I still often do not understand him." She raised her head, gazing first into Shorn's eyes, then Netra's. "I can say this with certainty: Ya'Shi has his reasons and they are not empty ones."

Netra approached her. The Lementh'kal did not move, only stared into her eyes. "I believe her," she told Shorn. To Jenett she said, "I am Netra. This is Shorn."

Jenett's mouth opened very wide in what Netra assumed was meant to be a smile. Instead of teeth she had rough bristles covering the inside of her mouth.

"Your eyes are open to the currents," she said. "You *saw* the truth of ki'Loren."

"Ki'Loren? You mean all this?" Netra asked, indicating the landscape.

Jenett nodded. "She is pleased that you have noticed and she welcomes you," she said.

"What is it...she?"

Jenett tilted her head to the side, considering this. "She is our home. She is our mother."

"Okay," Netra said, "but that still doesn't tell me what she is."

"Maybe this will help you understand." Jenett walked past Netra to the low cliff behind her. The cliff was of a type of stone that was a bleached blue color and very porous. Jenett placed her hands on the cliff face and began to sing, a strange, rhythmic sound that made Netra think of waves crashing against the beach. Under her hands the stone began to move. She stopped singing and stepped back. There was now an opening in the cliff big enough to stand in. Sunlight flooded in through the opening and only then did Netra realize that the light in this strange place did not come from the sun and in fact was a different shade of yellow all together. Jenett motioned her to come forward.

"Shorn, you have to see this," Netra said when she stood in the opening. He moved up beside her, still wary. "Look."

They were looking out over the ocean. The sun was setting, and in the distance, just visible, were the orange and red dunes of the Gur al Krin.

"Is this an island?" Netra asked. She could see that they were about halfway up the side of a long, steep slope. From what she could see, ki'Loren was huge.

"If it helps you to think of it as such," Jenett replied.

Shorn was still staring at the distant coast. "We are moving," he said.

"Yes," Jenett agreed.

"Where are you taking us?"

"I don't know. Ki'Loren takes us where she will."

"We need to go back," Netra said. "We have..." She trailed off, not sure what to say. "There is a great danger threatening our people. We have to help."

"I know of this," Jenett replied. "The currents are roiled. The sea feels the taint."

"Then you will help us? There is power within the water. I *saw* it." Netra felt hope rise within her. Maybe these people were the help she sought.

"I would be honored to do all I can to help. But I am only one. I am afraid I do not speak for my people. There are others who feel this is not our fight. They feel this is between Melekath and the land dwellers." She looked away and blinked. "It seems Golgath feels the same. He has ordered us to stay out of it."

"Golgath?" The name sounded familiar. Then Netra remembered. "He was one of the Eight who besieged Durag'otal."

"Yes."

"And you *talk* to him? To your god?"

"When there is occasion to, yes. Though we have not in some time now."

Netra was stunned. To be able to talk to your god. It was unthinkable. How different would their lives be if Xochitl was still there to hear them? She managed to overcome her surprise – and jealousy, it must be admitted – to say, "Then he knows what a threat Melekath is. Surely he will help. Maybe if I could talk to him."

Jenett was already shaking her head. "No, no. He will no longer see his own children. He will not respond to our cries for guidance. There is no chance he will see you." She hesitated. "In fact, he has ordered your death."

"What? But why?"

"You touched the currents. You touched Sea force. No land dweller may touch the source of Golgath's power." She lowered her head once again and Netra heard shame in her Song. "Thus were the people of Kaetria killed, for this crime."

Netra stared at her. "They were killed by *Golgath*? But I thought it was the Guardians. The sands were getting closer…"

"Golgath sent the *zhoulin*." She regarded Netra sadly. "Just as one was sent to kill you two. Only Ya'Shi's arrival saved you."

"Golgath killed the people of Kaetria," Netra said, still trying to process this new fact. She shot Shorn a look. "You knew. You tried to tell me."

Shorn looked back at her, unblinking. He offered no comment.

"But doesn't Golgath understand what is at stake? Melekath will–" Netra suddenly sensed something wrong, a deadly intent, and she spun. Jenett turned at the same time. On the slope below them was a thick patch of what looked like tall, thin trees, their trunks no bigger around than Netra's wrist, with showers of delicate red leaves that hung down on long stalks. Something – she couldn't see what – was coming through the thin trees. Only glimpses of yellowish skin were visible.

"I must leave now," Jenett said. "I will not be able to help you if I stay." She touched Netra's arm and Netra felt her sincerity like a physical sensation. "I will try and find Ya'Shi." Then she ran off to the left and disappeared into a patch of what looked like very tall ferns, yellow in the middle but shading toward red along the outside edges.

"We need to leave," Shorn said. But when Netra turned, she saw that the opening in the cliff was gone.

A moment later the bushes parted and three more of the Lementh'kal emerged. They were all taller than Jenett and their yellow skin was streaked with brown across the tops of their skulls. Spots of brown speckled down their arms and legs. Netra could not fully understand the expressions used by these beings, but to her they looked grim, serious. She could feel hard intent, hear it in their Songs.

Shorn moved in front of her. He raised his hands.

The three Lementh'kal stopped a short distance away, fanning out to face them.

They spread their arms and from them came a rough chittering, scraping noise.

Shorn instantly exploded at them.

Their eyes widened and one fell back a half step as they grappled with the reality of this huge, brute-like creature running amok in their midst.

Shorn grabbed the middle one around the chest with one huge hand and started to lift him into the air –

Glowing, scuttling things suddenly broke from the ground at Shorn's feet, a half dozen of them. They ran on six chitinous, segmented legs, and they had claws like those of a crab. Long eyestalks protruded from their ugly, flat bodies. In a flash they scurried up Shorn's legs.

Netra felt something on her foot and looked down: two were on her shoe. She shook her leg wildly. One went spinning, but the other made it to her ankle. She bent and slapped at it, but her disgust at touching it made her hold back and it dodged her blow.

Two ran up her other leg.

Netra attacked the crab-things with a frenzy. She hit the first one hard with her fist. There was a cracking sensation, felt more than heard, and it was knocked flying. She straightened, started to turn –

A sudden pain in the top of her skull. Another on her spine at the base of her neck.

Her muscles quit working. Icy venom burned through her veins. She fell to her knees.

She looked desperately to Shorn to save her.

Four of the crab-things were on him. Two were perched on his skull, and the others stood on his spine. He was frozen, half-turned towards her, only his eyes able to move. Suddenly the legs of the crab-things grew, wrapping around and around Shorn, binding him tightly. Somehow he remained on his feet, but she knew he wouldn't for long. She felt the same thing happening to her and came close to toppling over.

The three Lementh'kal came closer. The one in the middle spoke, its voice deeper than Jenett's. "Once before your people sought to steal our power and you paid with your lives. Is it that your kind cannot learn?"

"I...I didn't know," Netra gasped. "I thought the Guardians..." She'd never been so cold in her life. Her whole body was shaking uncontrollably. She was having trouble thinking.

"It does not matter," he replied. "Golgath has spoken your death." He held up one hand, and clenched his fist. Netra felt the legs wrapped around her tighten more, forcing a cry from her.

"We didn't...please..." Blackness crowded her vision. Shorn seemed to be saying something, but she couldn't tell what it was. She knew she was dying and all she could think of was that she wanted to apologize to Shorn, to tell him how sorry she was.

She slipped further into the icy darkness and suddenly it didn't seem so bad. Why should she fight so hard? What had it really gotten her? She had caused the deaths of those she loved and in her arrogance and pride she had released Melekath. The world would be better off without her.

Then her eyes met Shorn's. She saw his helplessness and his rage. And she saw that he had not quit fighting, even though it was useless. It touched something within her.

Something sparked.

She knew what to do.

She let the hunger take over. As the things' legs wrapped tighter about her, slowly suffocating her, she simply quit trying to hold back her craving.

Sweet Song like liquid honey bloomed all around her. She brought it to her lips, tasted it.

And found it good.

The legs of all three of their attackers suddenly buckled and they staggered. Netra drew in deep, drinking greedily, luxuriating in the stolen Song. Why did she resist this feeling? All her pains. All her fears and doubts. All just gone. This was how she should feel all the time. It was silly to fight something that felt so right.

These beings were far beyond the Crodin. Their Song was exhilarating in a way she had never experienced. The Crodin had been heavy and dull in their fear. These beings were light and air. Torrents of Song flowed and crashed within them. And it was all hers.

Soon they would be empty. It was a good thing she could smell others, not far away. She would take their Songs next. They had attacked her. What happened now was their fault. She would feed without remorse and she would be strong.

Shorn saw Netra slump to her knees. The yellow-skinned creatures walked up to her and the one in the middle squeezed his fist in the air. Netra cried out and he knew she was dying. There was nothing he could do. His helplessness infuriated him. Once again he could not save her. He fought, throwing everything he had in it, but he could not budge the things' grip. His muscles felt distant and disconnected from him.

Then Netra looked up and met his eyes. He saw the fear and uncertainty fade and a new look enter her eyes, a look that he had seen before.

Outside the Crodin village. A look of animal hunger.

There was a tug inside him, as if he was on the edge of an eddy, with a powerful current just starting to pull at him.

The three Lementh'kal sagged suddenly. Their eyes widened in disbelief and they looked at each other in horror. Before Shorn's eyes the yellow color began to leach from them, streaks of white moving in and taking its place. The one on the left dropped first, giving a sigh like a punctured bladder. The one on the right toppled over sideways and the middle one staggered and fell to his knees.

The things' hold on him weakened. Shorn gave one more mighty heave and with a sound like snapping twigs their legs shattered.

Freed, Shorn knelt by Netra. He grabbed the thing attached to the top of her head. It bit him when he took hold of it, but he ignored it and tore half its body away. Taking the head of the other one between two fingers he ripped it off. It took only a few moments to pull the lifeless legs from her.

"What you have done..." the middle Lementh'kal said, raising one hand. "I..." He fell onto his side, his eyes rolling back in his head, and did not move.

Shorn glanced at the other two, but they were limp in a way that said they were unconscious. He did not need to worry about them. Not for a while. He turned his attention back to Netra.

The tugging within him had grown stronger. It would not be long before he was sucked in, his LifeSong drawn into the vortex that was Netra. Already a numbness was spreading up his arms.

"Netra. Listen to me. You have to stop."

She did not respond. Her eyes were fixed on the middle Lementh'kal. There was a cold smile on her face.

Shorn shook her. "Fight it, Netra!" he growled. When she did not respond, he slapped her on the side of the head, hard enough to make her ears ring, then gripped her shoulders and shook her again.

Finally, she looked at him. But what he saw in her eyes chilled him to his core. He saw only animal hunger there. And rage. "They attacked me," she whispered. "They tried to kill me. They deserve to die."

"Not like this, Netra. If you want to kill them, I will help you. But not this way. You will never be yourself again."

Tears suddenly filled her eyes. "I'm so hungry, Shorn," she said. "I can't fight it."

"You can. You have to."

The middle Lementh'kal twitched and moaned. Shorn looked over at him. His skin was nearly white.

"Let them go, Netra."

Netra shuddered suddenly. The tugging sensation stopped. The feeling began to return to Shorn's arms.

Netra put her hand on his arm. "It's me again. You can let me go."

Shorn stood and went to the three Lementh'kal. Somehow, they were still alive. As he watched, color began to leach back into their skins. The one in the middle recovered first. When he tried to sit up Shorn gave him an open-handed slap and he went down like a stone. From the ground he gave Shorn a look of pure malice.

"You'll still die," he whispered. "This changes nothing."

"Maybe I should let her kill you," Shorn replied.

The Lementh'kal's eyes flicked to Netra, who was crouched with her arms wrapped around herself and he closed his mouth.

"I'm so cold, Shorn," Netra said. "How do I get warm?"

Shorn gave the three Lementh'kal another look. It didn't look like they would be any trouble for a while. He walked over to Netra.

"Maybe we should find this Ya'Shi," he said. He didn't like saying it. The memory of their last encounter was still fresh. Never had he seen anything or anyone move so fast.

"Ya'Shi won't help you," the Lementh'kal croaked. "The old one is crazy. Next time he might kill you instead of saving you."

Shorn ignored him. He looked around, hoping to see at least Jenett returning. Maybe she knew a way they could get off this floating island and back to land. Netra's sudden grip on his arm made him turn back to her.

Ya'Shi was walking up the hillside toward them. Though they had seen him only once, there was no mistaking him. All the Lementh'kal were graceful, but with Ya'Shi the gracefulness was unworldly. It seemed almost as if the world moved for him, instead of the other way around. He flowed over the ground seemingly effortlessly, like water flowing downhill. In seconds he had covered an astonishing amount of ground and was already up to them. His skin was the yellow of ancient ivory. There were lines around his mouth and eyes that spoke of great age, but none of that age showed in his movements.

The three Lementh'kal who had attacked them were getting to their feet when he walked up. He stopped by them.

"I see you have met our guests, Kelseth," he said with a careless wave toward Shorn and Netra. "Did it not go well?"

The one he called Kelseth scowled. It was the one who had stood in the middle. "We act with the authority of the Council," he said.

Ya'Shi shrugged. "So?"

"Golgath has ordered their deaths."

"I don't want them to die right now," Ya'Shi replied. In contrast to the other Lementh'kal they had seen, who were all completely hairless, a handful of long, wispy white hair sprouted from the top of his head. He was looking at the back of one of his hands as he spoke, seemingly completely disinterested in the conversation.

"Golgath is our god," Kelseth spluttered.

Ya'Shi nodded. "Very true." He gave Kelseth a sideways look, then quickly turned away from Kelseth's angry face.

"You cannot gainsay our god."

Ya'Shi nodded again, more vigorously this time. "This is also very true."

"Then you will let us finish what we came here to do."

Ya'Shi shook his head. "I must point out to you that Golgath is not here. However, I am."

Ya'Shi made no threatening moves. In fact, he looked down as he spoke and idly kicked at something on the ground. But Kelseth blanched and took a step back. "We will go to the Council," he said.

"I hope so," Ya'Shi replied. "You should be given your chance to speak. Now go, so that I may hear our guests speak."

After they were gone, Ya'Shi turned to them. "Welcome to ki'Loren," he said, bowing. "We are honored to have you."

"It is no honor," Shorn growled. "You brought us here against our will."

Ya'Shi shrugged. "It was simply the easier route. I could see that you would not quickly listen to reason and I did not wish to argue."

"Why have you brought us here?" Netra demanded. She was still pale and she still had her arms wrapped around herself, but she was looking better.

"To save you from the *zhoulin*?" Ya'Shi said, tilting his head to the side and opening his eyes very wide.

"This is not your reason," Shorn said.

"Well..." Ya'Shi cupped his chin and stared at the ground, for all the world looking like a man lost in thought. He looked up. "For company?"

Shorn growled again and took a step forward, but Netra restrained him. "Did it have something to do with Melekath? Is that why you brought us here?"

Ya'Shi thought about it, then shook his head. "Probably not. Probably I was just bored. It happens when you're as old as I am."

"You will get nothing from him, Netra," Shorn said.

"If you don't want us here, then we'll leave. Do that thing that Jenett did to the cliff wall and let us out."

"At once," Ya'Shi said, and hurried to the cliff. He laid his hands on the stone and began to sing. But the song that came from him was halting, lacking all melody, and full of pauses. He frowned, moved to another spot and tried again. This time the song sounded suspiciously close to a children's melody Netra remembered from her childhood. Again, it didn't work. Suddenly he seemed to lose patience and began banging on the stone with both hands.

"Open up, you stupid wall!" he shouted.

As quickly as it came, his anger subsided and he turned to them, shaking his head. "It won't work anymore," he said sadly.

"Do not waste any more time talking to him," Shorn said. "He toys with us for his own amusement."

"Is it amusement you're looking for?" Ya'Shi asked, frowning. "I thought you wanted to leave." He came over to them and lowered his voice. "It wouldn't help anyway, if I opened the door. You would only drown. It is a long way to land and these," he took hold of one of

Netra's hands and looked at it sadly, "are almost completely useless for swimming." She noticed then that his fingers were webbed.

"Look," Netra said, yanking her hand back. "Just take us back to land. I'll leave the Sea force alone. I promise."

"Oh, not yet," Ya'Shi said. "I brought you here for a reason. You are not finished here."

"What reason is that? Why did you bring us here? I don't have time for this. I have to get back. I have to find some way to stop Melekath."

Ya'Shi shook his head. "You worry far too much about Melekath."

"What? Of course I do. Why shouldn't I?"

With one long finger Ya'Shi beckoned her closer, as if to share a great secret. "It is not Melekath you should fear. It is his Children."

"His Children? I don't understand."

"You think you hunger, but yours is nothing compared to theirs. Three thousand years they have hungered and now they are free to feed that emptiness inside them. But the emptiness can never be filled. No matter what they take, they will always desire more. That is why you should fear them."

"I still don't understand. Melekath's Children? Are you talking about the ones who went with him to Durag'otal?"

"Yes." Ya'Shi rocked back on his heels, a curious look on his face. He seemed almost amused.

"But they are only people…and wouldn't they be dead after all this time?"

"Oh, not dead. Very much alive. Well, not alive. Not exactly. But not dead. Definitely not."

"How can that be?"

"You do not understand the nature of the Gift, do you?"

"No. The Book doesn't say much about it, except that it turned Melekath's followers into abominations."

"I suppose it did," Ya'Shi said thoughtfully.

"I still don't understand why we should be so afraid of them."

"Because they hunger. Because they cannot die."

"Can't die? That doesn't make any sense."

"The Gift was immortality," Ya'Shi said.

"But that… it's not possible."

"Perhaps I should show you what you face." Ya'Shi beckoned her to follow. He led her to a small pool of water. He leaned over the pool of water, so far that Netra was sure he would fall in. But he didn't. Instead he made circular motions over the pool of water, as if he was stirring it. Then he leaned back and pointed.

Curious, Netra approached the pool and looked in. Then she gasped.

Instead of water, she was looking at a village with a wall all around it. "What town is that?" she asked.

"It is Ferien. Melekath's Children recently left there. Look closer."

The image drew closer, and as Netra realized what she was looking at, she gave a soft cry and put her hand over her mouth.

Dead bodies lay in the streets, mouths open, eyes staring sightlessly at the sky. They looked shriveled, desiccated.

"What happened to them?" she asked.

"They met the Children's hunger."

All at once it was too much and Netra staggered back from the pool. She held onto Shorn, trying to hold herself upright. The world swayed around her. Guilt soared up from within her and wrapped her in its black velvet wings. *All those people dead. All because of me.*

Ya'Shi sighed loudly. "That's annoying, you know."

Netra was shaking hard, both hands gripping Shorn tightly. "I don't..." she said brokenly.

"Quit doing that," he barked at her, so loud she jumped.

"Doing what?" she asked shakily.

"That," he said, pointing an accusing finger at her. "The carrying on. The guilt that you love so much."

"What?" Netra asked, shock overcoming some of her guilt.

"With you it's all 'Poor me. I let Melekath out. Now everyone's going to die and it's all my fault.'" He glared at her. "I don't like it. It means the rest of us don't count."

"But I did," Netra said, fresh tears coming to her eyes. "It's all my fault."

Ya'Shi looked around. There were some Lementh'kal down in the valley. He looked at Shorn. He seemed to be counting on his fingers. Then he shook his head. "No. No matter how I count, I keep finding other people in this world. You're not the only one."

"But none of you let him out."

Ya'Shi shrugged. "So it was you. Big deal. If it hadn't been you, he would have found another pawn." He leaned in close and jabbed

308

his finger at her. "Your problem is you think you're special. You think the whole world revolves around you."

"I do not," Netra said, letting go of Shorn and straightening up.

"Oh, really? Let's think back." He began to tick points off on his long, spindly fingers. "As a girl, you always thought you were marked by Xochitl. You could hear Song better than the other Tenders in your tiny little world." He pointed at the *sonkrill* hanging around her neck. "The rock lion chose *you* when you Quested. Then Melekath started breaking his prison and you had more proof of how special you are.

"*You* survived Tharn's attack. *You* saved yourself and Siena from Gulagh in Nelton. The ancient tree in that village, it spoke to *you* before it died. The creature within the poisonwood on the Plateau attacked *you*." He finished ticking off the points and turned to her. "With all this, how could you be any less than the center of all that happens on this world?" He stared at her for a long minute, daring her to say something.

"Get over yourself," he said finally. "You are only one among many. There is plenty of blame to go around. What about the fool king from Qarath, the one who pulled the axe from the wall, causing the first crack? What about Xochitl, losing her hold when she was building the prison?" He was nearly shouting now. "What about the woman who birthed Rome? Or the farmer that grew the crops that fed him while he was a child? What about the mother who birthed you and then left you at the Haven?"

His voice returned to its normal volume. "The point is that we're all connected to this, every one of us. We're all facing the same threat. There's plenty of blame to go around. So yours was the hand that cracked the final piece. So you were in the wrong place at the wrong time and you happened to be the one Melekath tricked into doing what he wanted. So what? What's done is done. If you really want to do something about it you'll stop wallowing in self-pity, stand up and help us fight back."

"That's not fair!" Netra yelled. "You can't heap all that on me!"

"Now that's what I'm looking for. Some fire. Use that and let's take care of this." Suddenly he was completely calm. "Or don't. It doesn't really matter either way."

"What?"

He gestured at everything around them. "None of it's real, anyway. It's all a bad play, filled with bad actors who believe far too much in their pathetically tragic roles. Do what you want. I don't care."

He turned and walked away, circling around a low shrub just a few feet away.

"Hey wait!" Netra called, hurrying after him. "You can't just..."

Ya'Shi was gone. There was nowhere he could have gone, and yet he wasn't there.

Netra stared openmouthed at the spot where he disappeared, then turned to Shorn. "What...?" She swallowed, not sure what she meant to say. "What just happened?"

Shorn looked genuinely puzzled. "I don't know."

"What do I...what do we do now?"

Shorn shrugged and looked around. Down in the bottom of the valley small groups of Lementh'kal could be seen walking, all seemingly headed to the same place. "We could go see where they are going. Hiding up here isn't doing us any good." Several of the Lementh'kal were looking at them.

FIFTY

They were walking down the slope when Jenett caught up to them. "You are well. Good."

"You left us," Shorn said, stopping and standing so as to bar her way. "You do not know the price Netra had to pay to save us."

"I do know," Jenett said, looking down. She made no effort to go around him. "I did not want to."

"It did not look that way to me," Shorn replied, his thick arms crossed over his chest. "It looked to me like you ran away to save yourself."

"I accept that," she replied, still not meeting his eyes. To Netra, her color looked different, almost faded.

"Let her be, Shorn," Netra said, putting her hand on his arm. "We don't know what's really happening here. I don't think she had any choice."

Jenett gave her a look that Netra could not interpret, but said nothing. After a moment Shorn relaxed and let Netra pull him away. They started down again, Shorn leading. Netra waited for Jenett and then walked beside her.

"You said you were Ya'Shi's student. Is he always...like that?"

"Ya'Shi's path takes him beyond our understanding."

"I don't envy you."

"It is a great honor to be chosen by Ya'Shi as a student. Even among the Ancients he is unusual."

They made it down to the bottom of the valley. The numbers of Lementh'kal had increased, all going in the same direction, some walking alone, some in small groups. They all wore shifts similar to Jenett's, their clothing seeming to change color as they walked. They were a tall people, all of them quite slender. Shorn and Netra received some curious looks, but none spoke to them and for the most part ignored them completely.

"Where is everybody going?" Netra asked.

"The Council is meeting," Jenett said.

"Is it about us?"

"Yes," Jenett admitted.

"I want to go."

Shorn shook his head. "This is not wise."

"Ya'Shi has said that you are to be untouched," Jenett replied.

"That did not matter to those who attacked us," Shorn put in.

"Where else can we go, Shorn? There's nowhere we can run to. We need to go to this meeting. Maybe I can convince them to ally with us. Maybe I can get them to see that Melekath threatens them as much as he does us."

"I think this is what Ya'Shi believes," Jenett said. "Though he has not openly said so. There has been much talk since Melekath and his Children escaped. Most believe that the war will not touch us if we don't interfere."

"What do you believe?" Netra asked her.

Jenett turned to her. She blinked slowly, the eyelid sliding up, over her eye, then back down. "Golgath became involved with the problems of the land dwellers once before. As you can see, it did not go well."

"So you are against us as well," Netra said flatly.

"I did not say that. I only observed that when we become involved in your world it is of no benefit. But we may need to become involved once more, to clean up the problem we helped create."

Netra stared at her for a long moment. "I guess that will have to be enough," Netra said. She turned away and began following the others. Shorn and then Jenett fell in behind her.

As they walked, the small valley grew narrower. The hills were more thickly covered with brightly-colored plants of a bewildering variety. At length they came to a place where the small valley boxed up, ending in stone cliffs. Pouring over the edge of the cliffs was a waterfall, the water gathering in a pool of water at the base. Sitting on the sand at the edge of the pool, where the spray from the waterfall misted over them, were seven Lementh'kal.

"That is the Council," Jenett said.

Before the Council, sitting cross-legged on the ground, were several hundred Lementh'kal. Only one was standing, and he was right in front of the Council.

Jenett bowed to the Council, then sat down as well. Netra looked at Shorn. She looked at the Council. They, and the one who stood before them, were looking at her. She looked down at Jenett. No one spoke.

"What do I do?" she asked Jenett.

Jenett shrugged. The gesture did not look natural on her and Netra had the feeling Jenett had copied it for her, that she had never known of such a gesture before today. "Do whatever you think is right," she said softly.

Netra looked around. It seemed everyone was looking at her. She sensed no impatience, no hostility. They seemed simply to be waiting to see what she would do.

"I guess we talk to them," she said to Shorn.

He did not reply but simply waited as well.

Gathering her courage, Netra headed for the Council. Though the Lementh'kal were gathered thickly, they appeared to have left her a path. She heard Shorn's heavy, purposeful tread behind her and drew strength from it.

As she drew closer to the cliffs, she realized something suddenly. They were not made of stone. She wasn't sure how she knew this at first, only that the cliffs did not *feel* like stone to her. Something was missing. Then it occurred to her that she sensed no Stone power within them. She had not realized that she'd become sensitive to the power within stone; somehow it had happened during her time in the dead city of Kaetria.

The one who was standing before the Council was Kelseth, the leader of those who had attacked her. He watched her as she approached. Surprisingly, she saw no sign of resentment or hostility in his stance or his expression. Nor did she sense any in his Song. When she was in place before the Council, he turned back toward them and began speaking.

"Ya'Shi speaks and says we are to leave them alone. Golgath speaks and says they are to die for the crime of touching Sea force."

One of the Council spoke then. By the voice, she was female. Her skin had faded so that in spots it was nearly white. She gave the impression of great age, as did the rest of the Council. But she did not appear feeble in any way. "You and two others attempted to carry out Golgath's sentence." It was not a question.

"Yes, Zerin."

"But you did not."

"The female defeated us."

"Three of our strongest in the Way."

"She took our power from us. We almost died." There was no hostility, no regret, no shame in his voice. Kelseth simply stated facts.

The eyes of the Council turned to Netra. "There is a vast hunger in her," Zerin said. "Awakened, it could consume many of us before we could stop her."

"I didn't mean to," Netra blurted out suddenly. "I mean, I had no choice. They were killing us."

The Council stared at her unblinking. No one spoke. They seemed to be waiting to see if she would say more.

"We didn't do anything wrong," Netra added.

"You touched Sea power. This is forbidden to land dwellers," said one of the Council who had brown spots across his forehead and running down the center of his face. He spoke with his eyes closed.

"I didn't know that. I was just…I'm desperate. Melekath is free. I will do anything to stop him."

The brown-spotted Council member frowned. Though his eyes were closed, Netra could feel them boring into her. "You freed Melekath."

Netra went cold. "I didn't mean to."

"You said that before," Zerin said. "What is it you *mean* to do?"

Netra felt herself trembling. She seemed to be having trouble breathing. She fought to get a hold of herself. "I will do anything," she repeated.

"You ignored Sententu's warning and broke the prison."

Dimly Netra remembered the stone hands that came from the door in the prison, gripping her wrists, the voice that told her to stop. That had been Sententu, trying to stop her. But she had broken him with the Song stolen from the Crodin. She had thought she was saving Xochitl, but it had only been a lie.

"You are not a child, to throw your power about so recklessly," Zerin said. "Do you land dwellers care nothing for responsibility?"

"I'm trying," Netra said in a small voice. "But I don't know what to do."

"This is why I have come before you," Kelseth put in. "She is a danger to herself and others. Golgath has sentenced her to die."

Netra felt Shorn tense beside her. At the same time, she felt her hunger return and with it the mad desire to simply give in to it, to let it sweep her away.

"She does it again," said the Council member with his eyes closed. "She is dangerous."

"You will stop threatening her," Shorn growled. His weapons were gone, probably still lying by the underground pool, and he stood there unarmed, his fists clenched. Kelseth took a half step away.

Zerin spoke to Kelseth once again. "Why have you come to us?"

"To carry out the sentence."

"Ya'Shi brought them here," said the Council member with his eyes closed.

Kelseth nodded. "Yes, Jeng."

"And he told you what?"

Kelseth shifted uneasily. "He said to leave them alone."

"Ya'Shi told you this, Kelseth?" Zerin asked. "Directly?"

Kelseth nodded again.

"Yet you come before us?"

Kelseth hesitated, then nodded.

"Why?" The old female seemed genuinely puzzled by this.

"Golgath decreed that they must die. He is our god."

The Council members exchanged a look. Netra sensed that they were communicating, but there were no words. Zerin turned back to Kelseth. "Golgath is not here. Ya'Shi *is* here." Several of the Council members nodded.

"But Golgath is our god," Kelseth protested. "Ya'Shi has no place to defy him."

The Council members looked at each other again for a long moment, then Zerin looked back at Kelseth. "You are correct in what you say. Ya'Shi has no place in this. We are behind you. The outsiders must die, as Golgath has decreed."

Shorn moved to place himself between Netra and the Council.

"However," Zerin continued, "you must tell Ya'Shi yourself. You, directly. Then come to us and we will support you."

Kelseth stared at them, then lowered his head.

Softly, Jenett said, "He knows Ya'Shi will kill him if he does that." Netra was surprised. She had not realized that Jenett had followed them to the front. "Or he will change his mind and say okay. With Ya'Shi there is no way to tell."

The Council members rose. One by one they turned and headed for the pool of water behind them at the foot of the waterfall.

"Wait!" Netra cried. "What about Melekath? Will you help us?"

All of the Council members but Zerin ignored her. The first reached the pool, walked into it and disappeared. The others followed.

Zerin turned back. "Golgath will have no part in the problems of land dwellers."

"But this will affect you too. The Children devour Song. Eventually they will come for you as well."

Something like a smile touched Zerin's lipless mouth. "That is not Golgath's concern." She turned away and entered the pool. Within seconds she was gone as well.

To Jenett, Netra said, "What do we do now?"

Jenett shrugged. It looked somewhat more natural on her this time. "Only Ya'Shi knows that."

"Just let us leave. I promise I won't touch the Sea again."

"That is beyond my power," Jenett replied calmly. "But I will show you a place where you can rest while you wait, and something for you to eat."

Netra looked at Shorn, saw no answers there. When Jenett began walking away, she fell in behind her. What else could she do? How long had it been since she'd had choices, real choices? It seemed every day a new wind rose up and blew her in a different direction. How were they supposed to get back to land? What did Ya'Shi want with them? Where were the Children now? How many more had they killed?

Jenett led them over a low ridge and down into the valley beyond. This valley was bigger than the one they had just been in and on the far side there was a range of tall peaks, blue in the distance. Netra stared at the range, frowning. They were too big. She hadn't had time to look at ki'Loren closely when Jenett opened the side to let them look out over the ocean, but she'd seen enough to get a general feel of how large it was and there was no way it was big enough to contain such large mountains.

Jenett led them along the bottom of the valley. The plant life was quite thick with no visible trail through it. However, as they made their way through the plants – bright blue shrubs with clumps of white and orange flowers – there always seemed to be just enough room to pass through them without stepping on any of them. When she looked back the way they'd come, she saw no visible trail, no sign of their passage at all. Just another strange thing about a place that seemed to have no end to its strangeness.

In time they came to a small clearing with a pool of clear water in it. On one side of the pool there was a small hillock and in that was a cave. The floor of the cave and the area around the pool were covered with soft, white sand. Ferns and flowering plants draped the cave opening. It was tall enough even for Shorn to stand upright in. "You will be able to drink from that water," Jenett said, indicating the pool. "There is no salt in it." She reached into one of the flowering plants and picked a curved, orange fruit and gave it to Netra. "You may eat these safely. They will sustain you. However, avoid the ones which have begun to yellow as you will find them bitter."

Netra looked at the fruit. It was soft, with what looked like tiny seeds all over the outside of it. She raised it to take a bite, but Shorn stopped her.

"I do not trust them," Shorn rumbled.

"If they want to kill us, there's nothing we can do about it." She bit into it. Juice ran down her chin. It was very sweet.

"I must leave you now," Jenett said.

"Are we just supposed to sit here?" Netra asked as she started to turn away. Jenett did not answer. Though she did not seem to hurry, within a couple minutes she was out of sight.

Netra sighed and sat down. After a moment, Shorn sat as well.

FIFTY-ONE

Netra awakened the next morning to the sight of Ya'Shi standing over her, staring at her. She started at the sight of him and sat up, putting some space between them as she did so.

Shorn awakened and came to his feet in one smooth movement. He was not subtle about putting himself between Ya'Shi and Netra. Next to Ya'Shi's slim figure, Shorn looked huge, unstoppable. Like he could break Ya'Shi without even trying. Ya'Shi ignored him.

"Now perhaps you are ready for answers," he said.

Netra rubbed her eyes and got to her feet. "Are you going to help us against Melekath?"

Ya'Shi held his hands up. "I already have."

"How?" Shorn barked. "By stealing us and bringing us here?"

Ya'Shi tilted his head to one side. "That didn't help?"

"Can you take us to Golgath?" Netra asked, pushing Shorn to the side so she could see Ya'Shi better. Shorn moved grudgingly.

"We're going to get to see Golgath soon enough," Ya'Shi replied. "But I don't think he'll be a lot of help. The gods never are, you see."

Netra thought of Xochitl's silence and had to agree with him. "What about you and your people? Can you help us against Melekath?"

"Again you are fixed on Melekath. I told you, it is his Children you should concern yourself with."

"His Children then." Netra wasn't sure she agreed with him, but she didn't feel like arguing with him right then. "Can you help us against them?"

He shook his head vigorously. "No one can help you against them." He beckoned her close and lowered his voice. "They are immortal. And hungry. It's a hunger that gets only worse, never better. It is a hunger that will break the world."

"So you think it's hopeless?" Netra asked, unable to keep the bleakness out of her voice. Black despair settled closer around her. *My fault. What have I done?*

"No, it's not hopeless," he replied somewhat peevishly. "You're doing that thing again. I told you to stop. I can't stand it."

Netra stared at him, confused. He had his arms crossed and was glaring at her. "What thing?"

"The guilt thing." He threw up his hands. "It's all my fault!" he cried in a high-pitched voice. "I've gone and broken everything!"

"Stop it!" Netra cried. "I feel bad enough and that's not helping."

"No," he said, his voice once again normal. "What's not helping is you beating yourself with your guilt. You're no good to the rest of us this way."

"I can't help it," she said, her voice breaking.

"Then I can't help you," he replied, turning away. He seemed to be studying the high mountains Netra had seen the day before.

Netra looked at Shorn. The look on his face was murderous. She knew that with the merest nod of her head he would attack Ya'Shi. And he would lose. And it would do them no good.

"I'm sorry," she said. "I will try."

"Look up there," Ya'Shi said, pointing at the mountains. "There's someone up there who wants to talk to you."

"What?" Netra squinted, but could see nothing. "Who are you talking about?"

"Come on," he said, taking her arm and starting to lead her away. "We need to hurry before she changes her mind. Oh, you don't know how lucky you are to get to talk to the Ancient One."

"Wait a minute," Shorn growled, grabbing Ya'Shi's wrist. "We're not going anywhere until you – "

"*You're* not going. Just her," Ya'Shi said. He pulled back, just the merest effort, and slipped from Shorn's grasp as easily as if he was a child.

"She goes nowhere without me."

"Fine. Then no one goes." Ya'Shi sat on the ground, crossed his legs and started humming tunelessly to himself.

Shorn looked at Netra, his expression murderous. "It's okay," she said, putting her hand on his arm. "I'll be okay."

"Surely you are not going with him."

"I am. You can't protect me from everything."

"Do not do this," he said roughly. There was a pain in his eyes that he could not hide, not from her.

"We don't have any choice," she said. "We have to have any help we can get against Melekath."

"Against the Children," Ya'Shi chimed in.

"Against the Children." She looked down at Ya'Shi. He was still looking off into the distance. "Shall we go?"

He stood up slowly and stretched. His back popped audibly. When he turned to her he looked as if he'd aged decades. The contrast was astonishing. His eyes were filmy and his hands shook visibly. He sighed and peered at the mountains. "They look awfully big," he mumbled. "I'm not sure I can climb them at my age." He sighed again and began walking toward them, his head down. Every step looked like a huge effort.

Shorn gave Netra a meaningful look. "Are you sure? I still don't trust him."

"And I don't expect you to," she replied. "But I think yes, I need to go with him." She started after Ya'Shi. He had only a small head start on her and as slow as he was going, she'd have no trouble catching up to him. Once again she noticed that though the plant life was thick all across the floor of the valley, it never seemed to impede her progress. She had no trouble going where she wanted to go. It was as if the plants parted for her but, try as she might, she could never actually see them part. There just always seemed to be a way through, a way she didn't notice until she was right on it.

She looked up and was surprised to see that she hadn't caught up to Ya'Shi yet. He was just starting up the side of the steep mountain range, bent halfway over, his hand on his back as if it pained him. He was limping. She wondered if he was actually hurt or if this was just more of his foolishness. Why did everyone here put up with him? He was clearly crazy. Maybe they were just humoring him. That didn't seem likely though. She'd seen the way Kelseth and the other two Lementh'kal acted when Ya'Shi showed up. They were clearly deferential, if not downright afraid.

She pushed it out of her mind. Who knew what went on in the minds of the Lementh'kal? They were vastly different from humans. It was doubtful she would ever understand them.

There was not nearly as much vegetation on the side of the mountains and the path leading upward was clearly visible. Ya'Shi was barely a stone's throw ahead. She needed to stop looking around and taking her time and catch up to him. She wanted to ask him about whoever this was they were going to see. She hoped they were actually going to see someone and that this wouldn't turn out to be just a wild goose chase.

A short while later Netra paused and wiped the sweat from her face. That was strange. She'd been pushing hard, going as fast as she could, but she hadn't gained on Ya'Shi at all. If anything, he was getting further ahead, though now he was bent over so far he was nearly crawling up the mountainside. She called out to him to wait but he either didn't hear her or chose to ignore her.

Then he went around a fold in the mountainside and disappeared from sight. Suddenly uncomfortable about being out here alone, Netra hurried after him. Her breath was soon labored and there was a stitch in her side. Sweat coursed down her in streams. But when she came around the same fold she saw that she still wasn't any closer to him. She looked up the mountain, hoping to be able to see the top, but there was no sign of it.

She continued on. The path grew fainter. For the first time since arriving in ki'Loren she saw what appeared to be actual rocks, sticking out of the mountainside. A new kind of plant appeared as well, nearly black, with crooked limbs and long thorns. There weren't that many of them but, unlike the plants down in the valley, these did not move out of the way. In fact, it seemed to her as if they actually tried to impede her path, catching at her pants and scratching her painfully more than once.

Finally, she just stopped. She couldn't see the path anymore. Somewhere along the way it had gotten dark and a stiff wind was whipping around her. Looking back, she realized she could no longer see the floor of the valley. All of a sudden she just lost it.

"Ya'Shi! Ya'Shi!" she screamed.

He popped up almost in front of her, startling her so badly she yelped and fell backward. In one smooth motion he stepped forward and caught her arm, arresting her fall. "Are you all right?" he asked, his expression concerned.

"What's going on? Where'd you go?" she yelled.

"I've been right here all along," he said calmly. "You're taking forever, you know."

"What?" She was so upset she could hardly speak. She didn't know whether to be angry or confused or frightened.

"If you go any slower we won't make it there today," he said calmly.

"What?" she repeated, aware that she sounded like an idiot but unable to find anything else to say. It was all so bizarre.

"Here. Take my hand. I'll help you." His tone was solicitous and kind. He took her arm and began guiding her up the slope, which suddenly didn't seem so steep. "You know, if you weren't so heavy, this wouldn't be so difficult for you."

"What?" she said a third time. "Are you saying I'm fat?"

"Oh, no," he assured her earnestly. "I mean heavy with self-importance. Being the most important person in the world is a terrible burden. It's bound to drag you down."

"But I'm not…I never said I was the most important person in the world."

"Not with those words," he replied, patting her on the arm. "Look. Up ahead. I think we're almost at the top. You're going to get to meet the Ancient One. This will be a big moment for you."

Netra paused, suddenly uneasy. "Wait a minute." He paused and looked at her inquiringly. "Who is this Ancient One? What am I supposed to say to her?"

He shrugged. "Say something nice about her hair. She's very vain."

That was it. She was finding it hard to think, hard to keep up with him. Everything he said confused her and made her head hurt. She decided she was done listening to him. Nothing he said made any sense. This was a waste of time. She tried to pull her arm away from him but his grasp on her was firm. That's when she just gave up and let him pull her along, neither resisting nor helping. It was simply easier that way.

"That's it," he said encouragingly. "Now you're getting it. Stop trying so hard and you'll finally see that the answers are right in front of you."

Pulled along by him, she finally had a chance to really take in her surroundings. The day was not dark. The ground underfoot was dark, a green so dark it shaded toward black. The trail had not disappeared; it had only faded. Now that she wasn't laboring so hard, she could clearly see it and it led around the spiky bushes, staying well out of reach of their thorns.

"Let the current carry you," he said, right in her ear. "It will lift you if you let it."

322

Netra nodded without speaking. It seemed she could feel ki'Loren's strange Song passing over her skin, lifting her, energizing her. She didn't have to do this alone. All the power and strength she would ever need was right there if she would simply quit fighting and allow it to help her.

Ya'Shi let go of her arm but now she didn't need his help. Though the way was steep, she passed over it easily. She seemed to hardly try but the least effort carried her far.

All at once she was at the top. The mountain just ended. She found herself on a small, flat area, a couple dozen feet across. Sitting in the middle of it was an ancient Lementh'kal, so old that her skin had turned completely white. A sparse clump of hair grew from her head and down to the ground around her. She was sitting cross legged and her eyes were closed.

One eye opened and fixed on Ya'Shi.

"It looks as though you have made progress with her, Ya'Shi," she said.

"It won't last, though," he replied. "When she leaves here it will all come crashing back down on her again."

"But she's not hopeless."

"No. Not hopeless. Just very, very filled with herself."

The eye shifted to her. "They can't be killed, you know."

"I know," she said. "Ya'Shi told me. What I don't understand is why Xochitl imprisoned them for it."

"The Shapers tolerated Life because it died and returned what it had taken from the Spheres, thus restoring the balance. Immortality upsets that balance."

"But they were only a few, Melekath's followers. How could so few upset the balance that much?"

She shrugged. "It was long ago. Who knows?"

"The important thing is what they have become," Ya'Shi put in. "Now they truly are the abominations your holy book says they are. But it was the prison that made them that way."

"The centuries cut off from the flow of LifeSong have made them insane. They have a hunger that can never be sated." The Ancient One had closed her eye once again. "They will drain more and more of it until finally they consume the River itself. But even that won't be enough."

"Then they will turn to the Spheres and the power contained there. In their hunger they will consume them as well." Ya'Shi didn't sound as though he cared either way. He was staring at a spot on his arm. He scratched at it.

"And they can't be killed," the Ancient One repeated.

The lightness and power she had felt only moments before faded and Netra suddenly felt too heavy to stand. She felt unbearably weary. She wanted to cry. It was hopeless.

"She's doing it again," Ya'Shi said, without looking up.

"I noticed," the Ancient One said.

"You see what I've had to put up with?"

"It really is too much," she agreed. "Your patience is to be lauded."

"Stop fighting it," Ya'Shi said, turning to Netra. "Why put yourself to so much trouble? Why not just lie down and give up?"

Netra sagged to the ground. "There's no chance," she whispered. "There's nothing we can do."

"And you think she's the one?" the Ancient One asked.

"Oh, definitely," Ya'Shi replied. "She broke the prison, you know. There must be something special about her, though I can't figure what it is."

"I didn't mean to," Netra whispered.

They ignored her. "Will she stop feeling sorry for herself, do you think?" the Ancient One asked.

"Probably not. But you never can tell."

"You will have to open the way for them to return," the Ancient One said to Netra.

"I can't...I don't know what you mean." It felt difficult to get the words out. Her head felt too heavy to hold up.

"That's because you aren't listening," Ya'Shi said sharply, suddenly rising and standing over her.

"I'm sorry," she whispered.

He sighed and rubbed his forehead. "Why can't I be the one who sits up here all day doing nothing?"

"You had your chance." The Ancient One chuckled. "But you were born too late." Her tone grew serious. "Do you think we got through to her at all?"

Ya'Shi stretched. "Probably not."

"You said that already," she said sternly. "Say something new."

Ya'Shi walked to the edge of the mountain top and stared off into the distance. "We're out of time." There was doom in his voice and Netra trembled all over.

"When the time comes, Netra," the Ancient One said, sounding hurried for the first time, "you will have to be the doorway. Remember that. Stop fighting and let go. Everything you need is already within you. You just have to allow it."

"You have to understand your enemy," Ya'Shi added. "But first you have to understand who your enemy truly is."

"I don't know what you're saying," Netra said.

"Well, we tried," Ya'Shi said. "Too bad it didn't help."

Ki'Loren shook then, as if struck by an earthquake.

"His vengeance comes for Golgath," the Ancient One said. "Too bad the gods listen no better than mortals."

"Time to go," Ya'Shi said, taking hold of Netra's hand and pulling her to her feet.

"Wait! Where are we going? What's happening?" Netra could feel it too. There was electricity in the air, tremors in the ground.

"*We* are going to witness our god's death," Ya'Shi said. "*You* are leaving. But not if you don't move."

Numbly, Netra followed Ya'Shi off the mountaintop. She took one last backward glance at the Ancient One. She was once again sitting with her eyes closed, seemingly oblivious to everything that was happening. Netra wondered if she would ever make sense of what had happened here.

This time she was able to catch up to Ya'Shi as he made his way off the mountain. Far below, on the valley floor, she could see groups of Lementh'kal moving down the valley. They were not running, but they were clearly moving quickly. She grabbed Ya'Shi's shoulder and tried to pull him around to face her, but it didn't work. One moment she felt his smooth, cool skin under her hand, and the next she held nothing.

Without looking back he said, "Vengeance has come to Golgath. Our god is under attack."

Without thinking, Netra said, "He's not a god, you know. Not really." Then she frowned. Why did she say that?

"God. Shaper. Nipashanti. They are only words." Ya'Shi sounded bored by it all. "Golgath thought he was far enough away. He thought Melekath would overlook him." He shook his head. "Well, he was right about that. Melekath thinks only of his Children. But vengeance comes for Golgath all the same. The memories of the Shapers are long and their anger does not abate easily. Though they were not caught in the prison itself, still they were trapped by it and the Guardians had a long time to plan their own vengeance."

"You are going there now, aren't you? To help him?"

"We're going there. But we can't help him. Nothing can help him against the *ingerlings*."

"What are *ingerlings*?" Netra asked.

"They are creatures of the abyss. It is foolish to use them. Just as it was foolish to use the power from that place for the prison. The world may yet be destroyed by those decisions." He stopped and turned toward her. His look was grave. His shoulders sagged slightly and his eyes were half closed. "What will happen when there are no gods for them to feed on? Who will send them home? What will they devour then? Nothing we can do but attend and observe. Golgath observed our birth; we shall observe his death." He continued on, faster than before.

Netra was practically running to keep up. "Maybe we should come with you."

"No, no. That won't do at all." He started whistling. He tilted his head and shoulders back, for all the world like a man out for a casual stroll, though his deceptive speed continued unabated. "Happier places for you."

"What are you going to do with us?"

"Send you back, of course. You have to save the world. Or have you forgotten?" He turned at these last words and gave her a stern look. "That's still your plan, isn't it?"

"How am I going to save the world? You said I was too self-important and now you say I have to save the world! I can't do that!" Netra realized that she was shouting at him suddenly, and fought to get herself under control.

"There was no reason to think it would take. Not with someone as stubborn as she is," he said, seeming as if he was taking to another person who wasn't there. "Still, it was worth a try. It's quite a nice world at times."

"If you would just tell me what I need to do." She tried to make her voice calm.

"Why would I try and tell the most important person in the world what to do? What sort of fool do you take me for?"

"Please," Netra said. "You're confusing me."

"No, the best thing to do is just jump right out there and take care of things. Maybe you will even figure out what to do before it's too late."

"If you would just slow down for a minute and answer a couple of questions," Netra said desperately. She had the feeling of events rushing out of control around her. Time was running out and she knew nothing.

"No time for that." He put his hand over his brow like a man shading his eyes from the sun – though of course there was no sun – and then pointed into the distance. "There's your friend now. He's easy to see. Over here!" he yelled, waving his arms. "We're coming!" He continued on, turning his head to give Netra a big, cheerful smile. The way he turned his head was eerie, as if there were no bones in his neck at all. Suddenly he was looking backward at her, but at the same time he continued hurrying down the steep slope. "He looks happy to see me. I hope he's happy to see you too."

They reached the valley floor and Shorn was there, frowning at Ya'Shi, who gave him a huge smile, showing the odd bristles in his mouth. "Ready to go?" Ya'Shi asked him. "Have you packed your things?"

"What are you talking about?" Shorn growled. "We don't have any things."

"Sure you do. You just forgot to bring them with you."

"Are you all right?" Shorn asked Netra, ignoring Ya'Shi.

"I'm fine. Confused, but fine."

"Do you know what is happening? The fish people are upset."

"Lementh'kal," Ya'Shi corrected him. "Not fish people. They sound nothing alike."

Shorn ignored this as well, continuing to stare at Netra. "Their god is being attacked," she said. "We're leaving."

"Good," Shorn said.

"Right this way," Ya'Shi said, leading them off across the valley.

Netra looked around. He didn't seem to be leading them back the way they'd come in. She started to ask him about it, then refrained. She didn't think she could take too many more of his answers.

Ya'Shi led them to what looked like a big rock sticking out of the floor of the valley. When he got to it he stopped, squared his shoulders, and knocked, looking for all the world like a man knocking on a door. Then he waited, cracking his knuckles and whistling tunelessly. He didn't meet their eyes and seemed to have forgotten they were there or that he was in a hurry.

"What is the fool doing now?" Shorn rumbled.

"Ya'Shi is a consummate actor," Jenett said. They both started. The young female had come up to them without them noticing her. She blinked slowly. "That is the right word, is it not? Actor?" When Netra nodded she continued. "He is doing it for you."

"Why?"

She shrugged. The gesture looked almost normal now. "Perhaps to make you feel at home. We are very different from you."

"It's not working," Netra said.

"Then perhaps for his own amusement. We do not understand Ya'Shi either. But he is what we who have renounced our world strive to be. He of all of us is nearly free. He truly has no attachment to any of this. He does not care one way or another."

"Then why did he bring us here? What did all this accomplish?"

"Again, I cannot say. Perhaps there is one last thread connecting him to our world. Perhaps he sees something in you and he genuinely wants to help you. Or perhaps it is only a game to him."

"I don't think I could stand to be around him for very long," Netra said. "He makes my head hurt. I can't think when I'm around him."

Jenett laughed, a light, sparkling sound like the waterfall of a small stream. "You have much company in that, my land friend." She took both Netra's hands in hers, then bowed, touching her forehead to her hands. "May you find the answers you are looking for."

"I don't think there's much chance of that," Netra said bleakly. "I feel more lost than ever. I have no idea what to do next."

"Just because you cannot see the path anymore doesn't mean you've fallen off it. Don't give up. Simply take the next step. It will all make sense when it needs to."

"I hope you're right," Netra said. She looked around at ki'Loren's beauty. "I would like to have had more time here. This is a magical place."

"Perhaps in another turning," Jenett said.

Just then Ya'Shi began shouting obscenities at the rock face. At least, they sounded like obscenities. The actual words he used were gibberish. His face darkened and he began kicking and hitting the rock.

All at once a small opening appeared in the center of the rock, quickly spreading until it was big enough to walk through. Sunlight came in through the hole.

"Found it," Ya'Shi said, turning to them with a smile. He was completely calm. He bowed. "After you. I insist."

Netra started forward, but Shorn was quicker. He went through the opening first, looking around warily. Netra followed and found herself standing on a small beach. The outside of ki'Loren stretched upwards behind her to a series of low peaks. It really did look like an island. Ya'Shi stepped out beside her.

"There they are," he said, pointing. Their packs lay on a rock nearby. "I thought I brought them, but I wasn't sure." He shook his head. "It happens at my age."

Netra looked around. There was no land anywhere in sight. "What do we do now? We can't swim."

"No, you can't," he said sorrowfully.

Netra waited. He didn't add anything. "Well?" she asked at last.

"Oh," he said. "Your ride."

Netra turned. Something large and round was rising up out of the water. A moment later she realized it was a turtle the size of a house. It floated there, looking at them with huge, dark eyes.

"We're going on *that*?"

"Nothing could be truer," Ya'Shi said. "Well, since there's nothing else." Before they could react he had stepped back through the opening and it was closing behind him.

"Wait!" Netra called, but it was too late. She stood there for a moment. There was no sign of where the opening had been, nothing but sand and some scraggly plants. She looked at Shorn. "Am I dreaming? Did any of that just happen?"

Shorn nodded. He didn't look happy.

"What do we do now?" she asked.

"We ride the turtle," he replied. He walked over and picked up the packs. They seemed full. He didn't open them. There was no point. Either they had what the two of them needed, or they didn't. There was nothing they could do about it either way.

They climbed on the turtle's back, its thick legs moved, and they began to float west. Behind them ki'Loren slowly sank into the sea and   was   gone.

FIFTY-TWO

When Netra first got on the turtle she was agitated by all that she had been through. Her head was spinning. It felt like she'd spent her whole life running in circles. To say she was lost and confused was a massive understatement. On top of that was the fact that she was floating on the *ocean*. Other than her brief glimpse that first day in ki'Loren, she'd never even *seen* the ocean before. Now here she was in the middle of it, no land, nothing in sight in any direction. It was unheard of. People just didn't go out into the ocean. She grew up a long way from the ocean and even she knew that it was filled with monsters that wouldn't hesitate to swallow a person. The ocean was something to stay away from. Every child knew that.

But she hadn't been on the turtle long before she found herself starting to nod off. Some sort of moss or something grew thickly on its back, making it surprisingly comfortable. And there was something soothing about its slow, gentle motion. She fought it for a while. It was still afternoon. She needed to think about the things Ya'Shi had said. She needed to figure out what she was going to do next. But finally she gave up and lay down.

When she awakened it was the next morning. Shorn had taken her blanket out of her pack and laid it over her. She was shivering slightly and she wrapped the blanket around her more tightly.

Then the sun began to rise and she forgot about being cold. She forgot about being in the middle of the ocean. She forgot about everything but the wonder of that fiery red ball lifting out of the water. It was stunning, one of the most beautiful, magical things she'd ever seen in her life.

She stood up and raised her arms to it, greeting it. She'd slept soundly, more soundly than she'd slept in months. Her mind felt clear. She felt hopeful. She still had no idea what to do, but she had hope that something would come to her. And that was later anyway.

For now there was nothing she *could* do but enjoy the sunrise. Shorn sat up.

"Good morning," she told him, smiling. It felt good to smile. How long had it been?

He nodded at her.

"Not a morning person, I guess," she said lightly. Something in her tone made him look at her questioningly. She laughed at the expression on his face and walked over to him. "Ya'Shi said something about letting go. He said..." She trailed off. It didn't come to her. "I don't remember exactly. But it doesn't matter. I know what he means. I think."

Now Shorn was really giving her a strange look.

"Lighten up," she told him.

Very seriously he replied, "Okay."

That made her laugh and that felt good too. When she was done she said, "Right now there's nothing I can do about Melekath. Nothing at all." Guilt over breaking the prison tried to intrude suddenly, but she pushed it away. She wasn't going to give into that right now. "It's a kind of freedom. I have two choices, two ways I can respond. I can worry about it. Or I can just enjoy where I'm at right now." She looked at the sea, gray-green around them, tiny whitecaps breaking against the turtle's immovable shell. It was actually rather peaceful. Why did her people fear the sea so much? "And you know what? I'm just going to enjoy it." She waved at the western horizon. "When we get to land I'll worry about what to do next. For now, I'm taking a break."

Shorn frowned as he considered her words.

"This really is a pretty amazing creature," Netra continued, walking along the turtle's back towards its head. The head was the size of a boulder, covered in wrinkled, leathery green skin. Its neck was as long as she was tall. She stopped when she got close, hesitated, then reached out to touch its neck with her fingertips.

She gasped and stepped back as the turtle turned its head slowly to look at her. Its massive legs, each as big around as a large tree trunk, continued their slow, steady motion unabated. Its eyes were saucers, black and depthless. They stared at her unblinking.

"You're not a sea monster are you?" she said softly, inching her way back towards him, one hand held out.

"This is not wise," Shorn said, coming forward quickly.

"Oh, relax. If it wants to kill us all it has to do is sink underwater. I don't think we have anything to fear from it. Do we, big fella?" she said to the turtle. "You don't want to hurt us, do you?" The Song coming from the turtle was unusual, but she sensed nothing threatening there.

The huge head moved toward her outstretched hand slowly.

"I think it's sniffing me," she said, turning partly toward Shorn.

Suddenly an explosive, coughing sound came from the creature.

With a cry, Netra threw herself backwards and fell down. The turtle blinked at her. She was covered with a wet, slimy substance. Then it dawned on her. The turtle had sneezed on her. She looked up at Shorn.

Something rippled across his face and for a moment he kept his usual stern expression. Then he started to laugh. His whole body shook with it. She stared at him, realizing she'd never heard him laugh before. Finally, she said, "Are you going to help me up or not?"

That made him laugh harder.

It took several days for the turtle to get them to land. Fortunately, their packs had been adequately supplied with food and water. The food was some kind of dried plant that Shorn wrinkled his nose at, but it sustained them well enough. The extra water skins seemed to be made from a plant bladder that was surprisingly strong. The weather was mild the whole time, though once they saw a storm on the horizon.

It was Shorn who saw land first. He seemed to spend a great deal of every day staring to the west. Several times Netra tried to draw him into conversation about the things Ya'Shi had said and what he thought about them, but each time he answered the same: "Empty nonsense." Finally, she gave up and tried her best to simply push it out of her mind. The truth was that she needed a break badly. She needed time to recover, to somehow process everything that she had been through, and this time on the back of the turtle, with nothing to do and nowhere she could go, was perfect for that. She even suspected that Ya'Shi had put them on this creature for just such a reason. The slow pace gave her time to grieve for the loss of her family at Rane Haven and though it wasn't enough time to get over it, at least it was a start. She even found that she could allow her thoughts to touch on the things she had done during those desperate days that culminated with breaking the prison: the Crodin she had killed, the way she had treated Shorn. As with her grief, it wasn't enough time to fully recover from the impact of it all – sudden guilt still seized her several times a day out of the blue – but she could at least manage it somewhat. It was as though she had been severely wounded. The wound wasn't healed, but she could work the muscles around it, she could move about, even touch it somewhat, without the pain overwhelming her.

All in all those were good days spent on the back of the turtle. She slept a great deal. She watched fish swim by. There were some large fish with long dorsal fins that spent hours swimming and playing alongside the turtle. She even put her hands in the water a few times. And when Shorn announced that he saw land in the distance, she felt ready for it. There was a pang of sadness at leaving this brief interlude in her life behind, but she was ready for it now.

She walked up and stood beside Shorn. Just visible in the distance were the walls and towers of a large city, far larger than Nelton, where she encountered the Guardian Gulagh.

"Do you know what city that is?" he asked her. "Is it Qarath?"

"I don't know. I've never been to Qarath." She combed through her memories. Brelisha had spent some time going over maps with her and Cara, teaching them geography, but she'd paid no more attention to those lessons than she had to the others. But one memory did come to the surface. "I don't think it is. If I remember right, there are mountains by Qarath." The land around the city they approached was fairly flat, with only a few hills off to the south.

"What other city would it be?"

She started to say she had no idea, but then she remembered another city that sat by the ocean. "Thrikyl?"

Shorn stared at the city. "Its walls are strong." Then he turned to her. "Why did that creature send us here?"

Netra shrugged. "I was hoping to go to Qarath." She wanted badly to see if any of the others from Rane Haven were there. She would give anything to talk to Cara just for a moment.

They watched in silence as the city drew ever closer and the walls grew slowly larger. As they approached, Netra found herself growing more apprehensive. At first she just passed it off as nervousness over returning to land and all that she faced there, but as apprehension turned to dread she realized something else was going on. There was an emptiness surrounding the city. It was like a vacuum that pulled at her, like a vast coldness that drained the warmth from her.

Reluctantly, she went *beyond*. Pushing past the tattered mists she beheld the city –

And recoiled in horror at what she *saw*.

The city was empty. There were no flows of LifeSong anywhere within it. Nor were there any nearby. It was as if something had cut the entire city out of the fabric of Life, leaving only emptiness behind.

Netra withdrew from *beyond* and staggered. Shorn caught her. "What is it?" he asked.

"It's…dead," she gasped. "Everyone. Everything."

He raised his eyes to the city. There was no sign of attack or siege, but he did not question her. "Melekath?" he asked.

"The Children. It was their hunger." She leaned into him, shaking. Seeing what they had done to Ferien was bad, but this was worse. So many lives. All gone.

All because of her.

"Are they still here?" Shorn asked.

Netra shook her head.

It was nearly dark by the time they got to the shore. The turtle lumbered up onto the beach and then set itself down. Netra and Shorn slid from its back. It felt strange to be back on solid land again, and Netra's first steps were wobbly ones. The turtle lowered its head until its huge, luminous eyes were level with Netra's own.

Netra touched its beaklike mouth. She wanted to speak, but a vision of this beautiful creature floating dead in the ocean, victim to the Children's hunger, interceded and she turned away. The turtle drew itself ponderously to its feet and retreated to the ocean.

Netra turned and faced the walls of Thrikyl, silhouetted by the last light of the sun. "We'll go in in the morning."

"Why? You said they were dead."

"I owe them that much," she replied.

FIFTY-THREE

Netra didn't sleep well that night. The dead crowded her dreams and gave her no rest. She was up before the sun, the morning air crisp and breezy. Clouds were blowing in off the ocean and there was moisture in the air. She ate nothing and took only the barest sip of water. When she picked up her pack and put it on, Shorn was already standing there waiting, ready to go. He said nothing, but his presence was a rock that she could hold onto. She stood next to him for a moment, looking at the dead city, drawing what strength she could from him.

"You do not need to do this," he rumbled.

"Yes, I do," she replied, and started across the sand. She saw some dead crabs on the beach and the carcasses of several gulls. Were they her victims too? She fixed her eyes on the walls looming over her like cliffs, somehow fragile now. They had not repelled death when it came for them.

The first gates they encountered were closed tight and they continued on. After a time they saw a place where the walls had been breached, huge stones littering the opening. By one of them was the body of a boy. A club lay by his outstretched hand. His flesh was withered, his skin gray. Netra turned her face away from him and stumbled up to the opening, then paused there, momentarily unable to continue on.

Thrikyl was a void. No buzzards rode the wind down to feed. No flies swarmed the corpses hidden within. The Song which had fed the city had been devoured and no new Song flowed in to fill its place. Entering Thrikyl would be like throwing herself into a cold, black pool.

Netra put her hand on Shorn's arm, squared her shoulders, and entered.

Ice seemed to fill her being. The emptiness hit her like a physical blow. She gasped and reeled for a moment, her heart laboring in her

335

chest. She felt like she was drowning. Shorn steadied her, but she could feel the tension in his muscles, see it in the hard set of his jaw. Though not as aware as she was, still he could feel the wrongness of the place.

After several long moments she was able to continue. She raised her head and scanned the street. There were bodies – shrunken, desiccated – sprawled on the harsh cobblestones and again she stopped, hanging onto Shorn's arm, swaying slightly. A cry of pain rose inside her and she had to fight to keep it inside. She'd seen enough. She wanted nothing but to leave this place as fast as she could.

She forced herself to walk to the closest body, lying crumpled at the base of a water trough. It was a man lying on his stomach, his mouth stretched wide, his eyes shriveled to raisins. His back was arched, the long bones of his arms and legs bowed as if they'd gone through a great fire. His fingernails had broken on the cobblestones, as he tried to crawl away from his death.

Netra crumpled to her knees beside him. There was no blood. His skin and hair were leached of all color, turned a gray-white. She put a hand on him and her tears began to flow. "I'm sorry," she whispered brokenly. "So sorry."

Shorn's shadow fell over her and when she put her hand up he took it and pulled her to her feet. His eyes radiated his concern. "It is enough," he said. His words echoed hollowly across the lifeless street. "Let us go now."

Netra shook her head. "I have to witness. I owe them that much." She wasn't sure if she said the words aloud or they were only in her mind, but when she pulled away, Shorn let her go and then followed.

A doorway stood open on the street she led them down. Netra went inside and then walked up a flight of stairs to a narrow hallway. Three more doors lined the hall, one of them open. She entered and found herself in a small room with simple furnishings: a table, four chairs, some shelves with jars and cooking implements on them, a hearth. A doorway led off to another room.

Sitting in a circle in the middle of the room, huddled together, were a man, a woman and two small children. All had their throats cut. The knife lay inches from the man's dead hand. Dried blood had gathered in a large pool around them. Netra knelt beside them, hardly able to see for the tears that filled her eyes. Despite the blood and the gaping wounds in their throats, their faces were peaceful compared to the man outside. The girl, probably about five years old, gripped a doll tightly.

Netra stood over them, a black abyss opening at her feet. Her legs were straw; they wouldn't hold her. There was someone sobbing in the depths of her mind. She tried to say a prayer for them but she was choking on something too painful to be borne. She turned toward Shorn. "I don't..." she began. "They..." Then she quit trying and stumbled toward him. He opened his arms and held her tight as she sobbed. In the vast lake of grief and sorrow within her was a tentacled thing that was dragging her to the bottom.

At length she pushed him away, angry at him for reasons she could not explain. "I'm okay," she snapped. She did not meet his eyes. She left the room without looking down at the corpses again.

Everywhere in the city it was the same. Most people had killed themselves and their loved ones. She saw features contorted with poison and faces black with strangulation. Some had stabbed themselves. Quite a few had leapt to their deaths and sprawled brokenly in the streets. A few had thrown themselves in the public wells to drown and they floated in black water, hair spread out around them in a shroud.

Worst of all were those without the courage or the will to kill themselves. Hapless souls like the first one she had seen, who had thought to hide from their attackers or run from them. All those were shriveled like dead lizards, their features contorted in the terror of their last moments. Most seemed to have died fairly quickly, but others had clearly been toyed with, drained of Song slowly over time.

It was early afternoon and Netra was numb with exhaustion when she and Shorn walked into a square that was fronted on one side by an ancient temple. Netra knew she could not last in the city much longer. Her mind felt wrapped in cotton and her body was betraying her. She needed to leave, and soon. But something felt different about this square, a faint screech or a whine felt as much as heard with her inner senses.

Shorn saw it first.

There was the hiss of breath sharply taken in and he put his hand on her arm, stopping her. He pointed.

Lying on the steps of the temple, as if trying to crawl inside, was a body.

But this body was different.

It was moving.

FIFTY-FOUR

They advanced cautiously. For the first time that day Netra heard the faint rhythms of LifeSong, but it was like no Song she had ever heard before. It screeched and moaned, very faint, but definitely there. It came from the body that twitched on the steps of the temple and it hurt Netra to hear it. It was madness and pain twisted around each other. It was a wounded animal caught in a trap and dying. But she knew in the next moment that, unlike a wounded animal, this dying would go on and on forever. There was no release of death waiting for this one.

"It is one of Melekath's Children," Netra said.

The figure was lying face down. One leg was completely torn off, lying some distance away across the square. One arm still clung to the shoulder by tattered flesh. The other arm was missing at the elbow. The back of the skull was cracked open.

Netra knelt and reached.

"Don't," Shorn said.

She ignored him and took hold of a shoulder. A jolt went through her as she touched the figure and she jerked back, feeling the emptiness where Song had drained from her. Taking a deep breath, she built up her inner barriers, sealing herself. Then she gritted her teeth, took hold of the shoulder and rolled the figure over. It still hurt when she touched the figure, but her sealing worked well enough that she only lost a little bit of Song. Netra left *beyond* and returned her attention to the torn figure.

She had once been an old woman, judging by her gray hair and what remained of her face. Her belly had split open, withered organs spilling out onto the ground. One cheek was torn completely away. It looked like she had been burned badly, far in the past. The nose and ears had grown back partway, but crudely.

One eye opened. It fixed on Netra. The torn lips moved. A faint sound came out. Netra leaned closer.

"Help...help me," came the dry whisper. The faintest touch of color had returned to the shrunken face. The Song she had lost to the woman had given her new energy. It wasn't much though, and it wouldn't last long.

In that moment everything changed for Netra. The Children were monsters. She had believed this completely. She had only to look around her at the ruined city for ample proof of that truth. But this woman lying before her was also, undeniably, human. She and the rest of the Children had once been living, breathing people like Netra was. Nothing could change that fact. Out of nowhere, completely to her surprise, compassion welled up inside her. "What can I do?"

Shorn said, "Netra. Do not do this. She is your enemy." But she waved him to silence and leaned close to hear the woman's reply.

"This. A temple to Xochitl once."

Netra looked up. It was hard to tell what god the temple was made to sanctify. But the building was clearly very old. It could well date to the days of Empire. It could be a temple to Xochitl.

"The Mother...forgives. Maybe..." The woman's voice trailed off but the eye stayed fixed on her, pleading.

Netra looked up at Shorn. "We have to get her inside."

He shook his head. "She is one of them. This may be a trick to steal your Life-energy."

"I don't care." Netra began to slide into *beyond* once again. Maybe she could seal herself long enough to drag the woman inside.

Shorn made a sound in his throat and pushed her aside. At first Netra thought he was stopping her from helping the woman, but when she realized his true intentions she tried to cry out a warning.

It was too late. His hands contacted the woman's body and he grunted explosively and jerked his hands back.

"She is...cold." His eyes were wide.

"I tried to stop you. You can't touch her. Only I can."

Shorn flexed his fingers, shot a look at Netra, then slid his hands under the woman. He stood up with her in his arms.

"Shorn!" she cried. "Are you okay?"

"It is..." He hesitated, choosing his word. "Unpleasant." Netra shook her head. Somehow his alien Song was shielding him.

"I will not be able to hold her long," he said gruffly. "Open the door."

Netra hurried up the steps and took hold of the door handle. The door didn't budge. She rattled it ineffectively. Clearly it was barred on the inside.

"Move," Shorn said. When she did, he raised one booted foot and gave the door a single, mighty kick. It splintered inwards, the bar breaking in half, hinges tearing away. Shorn clumped through the sudden opening. His words drifted out to her. "Where do you want her?"

Netra hurried in after him. It was hard to see in the dim interior. A few rough pews stood in rows, an aisle between them. The ceiling soared high overhead. At the other end of the long room was a dais with what appeared to be an altar on it.

"Up there," she said, hurrying past him. There was a body lying sprawled before the altar, probably the priest of the temple. An empty cup lying by his hand indicated he had poisoned himself after barring the door. There was a small statue on the altar Netra didn't recognize, a man with four arms. "Put her down here," she said, pointing to the floor at the base of the altar. "It's as good as anywhere I guess."

He laid the woman down, none too gently, and then stepped back, rubbing his arms.

Netra crouched over the woman. "What is your name?" she asked.

At first there was no sound, then the woman whispered, "Orenthe."

Netra raised her face to the altar and spoke a prayer to Xochitl. When she was done she looked back at the woman. Something in her face had eased slightly. "What else can I do for you?"

The woman had closed her one good eye. At first Netra didn't think she would respond. Then she said, "Nothing...anyone can do. It is enough."

The trapped Song still skittered and whined within her, but it seemed to Netra that it didn't have quite the same frantic quality as it had before. She stared down at the woman's torn figure while the full horror of the woman's existence slowly dawned on her. It was the Gift, of course. The blessing that had turned out to be the worst sort of curse. She tried to imagine centuries of miserable experience, longing for death every moment and unable to find it. She wanted to hate the creatures who had destroyed this city and killed all they could lay their hands on, but she knew they were people as well and she could not help but feel a terrible empathy for them.

"I will free you," she said softly. She could not tell if the woman heard. She left the temple and Shorn followed.

FIFTY-FIVE

They left the dead city and it was like coming up for air for Netra. When they were out of the shadow of Thrikyl's walls she stopped and sat down, breathing deeply, feeling life and energy flow back into her. Shorn sat down nearby.

"This is going to sound really crazy," she said. Shorn swung his head to look at her. All at once she wondered how many things she'd said to him since she'd known him that sounded crazy. Probably a lot more than she realized. "But I think something good may come out of this."

His heavy brow drew down in puzzlement as he absorbed her words, unsure what she was talking about.

"I'm talking about the prison breaking."

Now he was looking at her as if she truly was crazy.

"I know, I never would have dreamed I'd say that either. And maybe it is crazy, but I realized something back there with that woman. With Orenthe." Somehow it seemed important to say her name, to acknowledge her as a person and not as a faceless enemy. "You didn't feel what I did or maybe you'd understand what I'm trying to say."

"Tell me," he said.

"The horror Orenthe has been through…I can't even imagine it. It's the Gift, you see? The Gift made her, made all of them, immortal. *She can't die*." She stared at him, willing him to understand.

"I see," he replied, though it was clear he did not.

"For centuries she and the rest of the Children have lived down there in the darkness of the prison. It must have been horrible. They were utterly cut off from all Song. It would be like constantly suffocating, like what we felt in Thrikyl only a hundred times worse."

He pondered this. "I would not wish to remain in that city," he said at last.

342

"Now imagine it is far worse and you're stuck there for thousands of years. That's what Orenthe and the rest of them have endured since the prison was created. No matter what happened to them – it looked to me like Orenthe had been badly burned long ago – they couldn't die. Their lives were just one long, never-ending nightmare."

Shorn nodded.

"That's what I'm getting at. It's why I'm saying that something good may come out of all this suffering. If we can find some way to release the Children from the curse of the Gift, we can end their misery. We can set them free."

Shorn didn't look completely convinced, but he nodded. Then he asked, "How?"

It was easy to see where the Children had gone when they left the city. All along on both sides of the coast road that led north there was a gray stain a hundred feet or so wide. In that swath everything was dead. The grasses had turned gray. The leaves on the trees and the bushes had turned gray and most had fallen off. Here and there were dead creatures as well, those too slow or too oblivious to escape. Birds lay on the ground. The feathers of the brightly-colored ones were dull and almost completely bleached of color. There were dead lizards on the rocks and a dead snake in the road, curiously flat.

They did not make it much further that first day after leaving Thrikyl. The time they had spent in the city had drained Netra. Every step was difficult and made harder by the fact that they couldn't take the road but had to walk through the countryside, outside the dead swath created by the Children's passage. Even though they walked outside that area, still Netra could feel it, dragging her down into coldness and emptiness.

When they stopped for the night she asked Shorn to gather a lot of wood. She wanted a large fire to combat the chill that she had not been able to shake the entire day. After the fire was built, and they had eaten, Netra said, "I can feel them up ahead of us. They're not as far ahead as I thought they were. We can catch them in a few days if we hurry."

"You want to catch them? Why?"

"I need to see. I *have* to see them. I don't know why, just that it's important. Don't worry. I won't get too close."

"They will catch you."

"No. I know how to shield myself now. I can keep my Selfsong from radiating outwards."

Shorn thought about this for a moment, then nodded. "After that?"

She shrugged. "We'll circle around them and go to Qarath, I guess."

He frowned. "Going into a siege is not wise. There will be no escape."

"I know. But I have to. You see that, don't you?"

"I do not."

"I have to be there. I have to be part of it. It's my fault and I – "

He put up his hand. "The only sensible thing that fool on the floating island said is that you are not to blame."

"How can you say that, after what I did?"

"Because it is true. You were a tool for Melekath. You thought you were doing the right thing. If he had not been able to use you, he would have found someone else."

"That doesn't excuse what I did. I should have known better. I should have seen that he was manipulating me."

Abruptly Shorn shifted his tack. "How old do you think Melekath is?"

That surprised Netra. Where was he going with this? "I don't know. Hundreds of thousands of years. More? A lot."

"How old are you?"

"I don't see – "

"Tell me."

"I'm…" She thought about it. She'd lost track of the days, but her birthday must have been in the last month or so. She'd totally forgotten about it. "I guess I'm nineteen now."

"He is hundreds of thousands of years old. He had three thousand years in prison to plan his escape. Yes, he tricked you. There is no way he would *not* have tricked you. You never had a chance. You were the tool he was looking for and he used you. That is all. You are spending too much time on blame. It clouds your thinking. Melekath chose you because there is something about you that he needed. Maybe there is also something about you that can end this. But you will not think of it until you stop the blame and begin to think."

Netra was stunned. Those were by far the most words she'd ever heard Shorn say at once. Was he right? "I have never thought of it that way," she said softly.

Shorn put his hand gently on her shoulder, then stood up. "Sleep. I will keep watch."

FIFTY-SIX

It was late in the day and the Takare were stopping for the night. They were in gentle country, the hills rolling and covered with knee-high grass. Plentiful streams wound through the gentle valleys, thick with fish, the trees bordering them home to dozens of species of birds that the Takare had never seen before. The farms were numerous in this country, the houses built of stone and timbers, but every single one of them was empty. A few had been burned and in front of most of those wooden posts were set in the ground; tied to the posts were corpses burned beyond all recognition. Strangely, the posts themselves were unburned, as were the ropes that bound the victims.

Behind them, growing smaller every day, was Landsend Plateau. Somehow the destruction of their old home was more striking from a distance. Black scars ran down its sides, rivers of lava that had not completely cooled. Gaps like broken teeth showed at its top. Smoke still rose from it and one night there was a rumble in the earth and a gout of orange fire shot into the sky, burning for several minutes before subsiding once again.

They had passed through Guardians Watch days ago, all of them, even Rehobim, silenced by the carnage that was still evident there. The dead of Qarath lay under the rubble of the old stone tower, the broken stones alive with crows, buzzards, and some kind of lizard that grew as long as a person's forearm, all feeding well. The dead from Kasai's army lay where they had fallen, rotting. The carrion eaters had not touched them. The black marks on their foreheads were still visible.

Shakre was in the rear as they passed through, helping Ekna and Lize with Intyr. She saw Jehu standing at the top of the pass, looking down over the dead. He touched his forehead, probably remembering his own mark, and she saw tears in his eyes. She squeezed his arm as she went by and he gave her a wan smile.

They went cautiously, with scouts out far ahead and off to both sides, but they saw no sign of Kasai's followers. The country seemed to have been deserted. Had the Qarathian army's victory been so complete? Shakre wondered. She remembered the city the wind had shown her, and the size of Kasai's army. Its numbers seemed far greater than the dead they had found. It was more likely that Kasai had simply withdrawn and was waiting. But that made no sense either. Now that Melekath was free, why did the Guardian not move south to meet up with him? It was possible that the Guardian had moved swiftly, and gone south before the Takare got this far, but if that was the case they would have seen the signs of the army's passing. The Takare were superb trackers. A deer couldn't cross their path without notice, much less an entire army. It worried her. It worried all of them. Was Kasai planning another trap? One night while they ate the evening meal Rehobim asked her bluntly why she had not ridden the wind to see what lay ahead. Why did she do nothing?

"Because it's gone," she told him.

Rehobim snorted. "Impossible. I can feel the wind on my skin right now. I can see it moving those bushes."

"There is movement, it is true," she replied, "but it is not the wind as I have known it. There is no intelligence there. I have not heard the wind speak since the prison was broken."

"Then call it."

"I have tried." And she had. More than once. Which seemed odd to her. How many years had she wished for the *aranti* to leave her alone? Now it was gone and she wished it would come to her. "It does not answer."

"Where did it go?"

"I don't know," she snapped, tired of his rudeness. "I am not its master."

"Increase the patrols," Youlin said, speaking for the first time that day. Rehobim twitched at her words. He hadn't heard her walk up. "Send them further out. This time we will not fall blindly into the trap."

He stiffened at her words and the barely-concealed rebuke there. He scowled, but he knew better than to challenge her, so instead he turned his anger on Shakre. "How convenient that your powers are gone when they would be of help to us," he snarled, turning and stalking away.

"Keep trying," Youlin said when he was gone. As usual she was hidden within the depths of her hood. It was warm down here, compared to the Plateau, and the Takare wore very little these days, but Youlin stayed wrapped always in her fur cloak. Her hands, slim and pale, were the only skin visible. Shakre thought she saw a shiver pass over the young woman. "Try every morning and every night. Try every time we stop. I will know what Kasai plans."

Shakre nodded. She wanted to know what Kasai was up to as well.

"I haven't – " Nilus broke off and an odd look came over his face. His eyes went flat and empty, just for a second. Then they narrowed and his features twisted. His lips stretched taut, pulling back from his teeth. The muscles of his jaw bunched. The transformation was so extreme that Shakre fell back a half step, raising one hand. It was as though a completely different person stood before her, someone she didn't know at all. The rage she saw expressed on his face was almost palpable.

A second later the rage passed, disappearing as if wiped away. Confusion appeared in Nilus' eyes and he staggered slightly. "What...?" He brought his hand up, pressed his fingertips into his temple. "I don't feel well." He started to turn away, but Shakre caught hold of his arm.

"Wait," she said. "Something just happened to you." She pressed her fingertips to his wrist. His pulse was racing. His skin felt clammy. "Sit down."

"I'll be all right," he protested.

"I'm the healer," she replied. "Let me take a look at you."

"I don't have time. Rehobim has called us for training." Every day when the Takare stopped, Rehobim took the spirit-kin – there were now about fifty of them – aside and they practiced with their weapons until after dark. "I must go." With that he pulled away and hurried off.

Shakre was left looking after him, wondering what had happened. She heard someone walking up behind her and turned. It was Werthin. Ever since the young man carried her down off the Landsend Plateau when it was destroyed, he seemed to be always nearby, always ready when she needed anything.

"This is not the first time that has happened to one of the spirit-kin. I have seen others who stopped in the middle of saying something, suddenly lost. Last night a warrior from Black Cliff

Shelter began shaking for no reason. He fell down, his whole body twitching. His eyes rolled back in his head. We had to hold him to keep him from injuring himself." Though Werthin was not yet one of the spirit-kin, he was in line to be and one of those who trained with the spirit-kin sometimes. "Rehobim forbade us to speak of it."

Shakre was not surprised at his words. In the days since beginning the journey to Ankha del'Ath she had been keeping a close eye on those who held within them the additional Takare souls. Most of them she did not know, but it seemed to her that they were not quite themselves.

"Windrider, I am afraid."

Shakre broke out of her thoughts and focused once again on Werthin. Like most of the warriors, he had begun wearing his hair in a multitude of long braids, as had once been common among their people – yet another custom laid aside when the Takare forswore violence and moved to the Plateau. He had earnest blue eyes and the slow, measured speech of one who has pondered what he says before he says it.

"Rehobim orders me to kneel to Youlin tonight, to open myself to the old spirits of our people. I am ready to fight our enemies. I will give my life without hesitation for any of my people. But my heart feels afraid when I think of doing this and I am ashamed of my fear." He looked steadily into her eyes as he spoke.

She put her hand on his shoulder. "There is no shame in fear. Fear helps us stay alive when danger threatens. I am glad you brought this to me. There may be dangers here we do not yet see." She tightened her grip on his shoulder, feeling her own fear, fear that this young man who had shown her so much kindness, as fierce a fighter as any, yet utterly gentle at heart, would yet be lost to her. "Don't do it, Werthin," she whispered fiercely, feeling a tear in her eye. "Resist him longer. Let me find out more about this."

After Werthin walked away, she went looking for Elihu. He was helping gather wood for the evening fire. He listened to what she had to say with a thoughtful look on his face. When she was done, he said, "I too have noticed that the spirit-kin do not seem themselves."

"What do you think it is?"

He shook his head. "I think two cannot ride the same horse for long. In time, the one who does not hold the reins will try to take them from the other."

"That's what I was thinking too," Shakre said glumly. "Somehow I was hoping you would say something else."

"What will you do?"

"What *can* I do?" Shakre said, frustrated. "There's nothing I can do. Youlin barely listens to me. Rehobim hates me more than ever. I don't even have the wind any more. What I want to do is give up."

Elihu smiled. "When you give up, *then* I will be concerned."

"Maybe this time I really will."

"No, you won't."

Shakre growled at him and resisted the urge to stomp off. "Youlin toys with things she does not understand."

"Youlin would see the Takare returned to their old place."

"But at what price?"

He nodded. "That is the question, isn't it? Perhaps it is the only question."

"There is a city north and somewhat west of here, called Fanethrin. I believe that is where Kasai is."

"What makes you think that? Is the wind speaking to you again?" Rehobim said with a sneer.

"No, the wind is still silent." Shakre turned away from him, directing her words to Youlin, hoping the young Walker was listening. Hidden in her hood, it was hard to tell what went on with Youlin. "It is the largest city in this area, the only one close to Guardians Watch. What I think happened is this: Kasai was sent by Melekath to build an army. For whatever reason, maybe because one of the old gods was helping Qarath, Kasai couldn't build an army there, or in any of the nearby cities, for fear of being attacked and destroyed. So the Guardian built its army in Fanethrin, drawing soldiers from all the nearby countryside, towns and smaller cities. Then, when it was ready, it tried to move that army through the pass at Guardians Watch. Somehow Qarath got word of it and got there first and defeated them. Logically, Kasai would next try to go to Melekath's aid by going down through this valley that we're in now, circling the Firkath Mountains to the west instead of to the east. But we've seen no sign of that army's passage so that must mean Kasai is still in Fanethrin. The question is why."

"To try and trap us," Rehobim said.

"But why? We're not the real threat. Qarath is. No, I think there's something else going on."

"Let us take the fight to them," Rehobim growled. "We have more spirit-kin every day. Let us show them how to fear the Takare."

"No," Youlin said. "Our purpose is not to seek revenge. Not yet, anyway. For now we go to our homeland. We reclaim that and we rebuild. That is our purpose."

FIFTY-SEVEN

It was morning and the Takare had not been walking long when Shakre sensed something wrong in the flows of LifeSong. She paused and concentrated on her inner senses, trying to pinpoint what it was. But everything seemed perfectly normal and she wondered if she'd been mistaken. She hadn't been sleeping much. Maybe she was just tired. Over the past few days she'd had a growing conviction that an attack from Kasai was imminent and it had put her on edge. She hardly saw where she was walking, so focused was she on her inner senses. She slept poorly at night, awakening again and again, straining to hear, sure the attack was about to begin.

She stilled her mind and went *beyond*, hoping to learn more. The flows of Song became visible, lines of golden light branching everywhere. She reached out and laid her awareness across them. The flows formed a vast, interconnected web. By touching the web, she would be sensitive to the minute vibrations caused by living things too far away for her to see.

Then she waited.

There it was. Something was moving. The vibrations grew stronger. Hundreds, perhaps thousands, of people were approaching. Radiating outward from them was the burned feel that came from those who carried Kasai's mark.

She opened her eyes.

The morning was clear, the hills gentle and rolling. The tattered remains of an early morning fog hung over the land, but it was burning away quickly. There were a few trees along a small stream in the distance, but that was it. There wasn't cover enough for more than a few people, certainly not an army.

But there was no denying that there were people out there, somewhere.

She ran forward along the line of Takare, looking for Youlin, and found her near the front. The young Pastwalker had her hood up as usual. She put her hand on her shoulder and pulled her around.

"They're coming!" she gasped.

"The wind tells you this?"

"No."

"Then how do you know?"

"I can *feel* them. They're coming from the north. They're close."

The hooded face turned to survey the landscape, then back to her. "I do not see them."

"I don't either," Rehobim said. The tall, young warrior had turned back and was glaring at Shakre suspiciously. "You are confused, Windrider."

"I'm telling you, they're there. Thousands of them, along with some of the blinded ones. You have to trust me," Shakre pleaded. She could feel them getting closer by the moment. "We have to run. We have to get out of here."

"We will not run," Youlin replied firmly. "Never again will we run."

"We have to do something."

"We will." The young Pastwalker turned to Rehobim. "Take the spirit-kin and array yourselves in the front line. The rest of our warriors will array themselves behind you, in case you need them." She paused. "But you will not."

Rehobim nodded. "As you command, Pastwalker, it will be."

He strode away, calling commands to the others as he went. Quickly the spirit-kin arrayed themselves in a line about a hundred feet away, about an arm's length from each other. Rehobim stood in their middle. Crossed long swords were strapped to his back, and he wore daggers on each hip, but he did not draw any of them. He crossed his arms and stood there, waiting. The rest followed his lead. Except for the hawk-like intensity of the warriors, they might have been merely waiting patiently for someone to arrive. There were about sixty of them, men and women alike. Some were barely into their teens. Others were at the far end of middle age. All wore their long hair in a multitude of thin braids. Gone were the heavy furs of the Plateau; most wore tanned leather leggings and simple leather shirts.

Thirty or so paces behind them, in a triple rank, the rest of the warriors lined up. With the elderly and the very young, Shakre waited in the rear. Elihu was on her left, Jehu on her right. She could see Werthin amongst the warriors who were not yet spirit-kin.

Shakre tried to stay calm, but her hands were shaking and it was all she could do to stay still. It was maddening, being able to sense the approach of the enemy, but not being able to see them.

In contrast to her, the Takare seemed completely calm. Even the children were silent. There was no nervous shifting of stances, no fidgeting. They simply waited. It was one of their traits she had long admired about them. Whether it came from their training in the martial arts or it came from living on the Landsend Plateau, where death came so easily, they had a way of staying calm even in the face of certain death. Was it acceptance or fatalism? she wondered. Did it matter? Elihu squeezed Shakre's arm reassuringly.

Then the tatters of fog began to fade, and as it did so massed ranks of armored soldiers were revealed. The front two rows were pike men and they crouched, setting their pikes so that the air before them bristled with hundreds of bright metal points. Behind them were a half dozen ranks carrying axes, swords and maces, many with shields. A dozen paces past them was a line of archers. All told there were probably two thousand soldiers facing the Takare.

Shakre relaxed somewhat. Though the foes facing the Takare outnumbered them greatly, she had seen the Takare train. In the time since the failed ambush the Takare had improved greatly. She did not doubt that the weakest of them could face three or four of Kasai's soldiers and prevail. And that wasn't even accounting for the spirit-kin. They were just plain frightening. Sometimes, when she watched them train, she had to rub her eyes. They seemed to blur rather than move, and the way they rained blows, it was as if each one had four arms.

This was a battle the Takare would win.

For a minute the two armies faced each other. Still the spirit-kin had not drawn their weapons. Each moment Shakre kept expecting the soldiers to charge the Takare, but they didn't. She focused on the pike men again. She knew very little about the ways of armies, but it looked like they were set in defensive formation. If this was a trap, it was a strange one. There was no reason for the Takare to charge into that bristling mass of steel. None at all.

Shakre frowned. Something was happening, though she could not figure out what it was. She could feel energy beginning to build, but could find no source for it.

Quickly she went *beyond*. Beyond the mass of *akirmas* that were the Takare and Kasai's soldiers were a score of others. They looked as if they were covered with gray cobwebs, red sparks spitting from them intermittently.

Confused, Shakre left *beyond*. Were those the *akirmas* of blinded ones? She couldn't see them, though there was still some patchy fog behind the ranks of Kasai's soldiers.

Then the attack started.

A column of gray flame burst up from under the feet of one of the warriors, completely enveloping her. She screamed and staggered to the side, colliding with the warrior next to her, who also caught on fire.

More flaming columns appeared. Screams filled the air as Takare went up in flames amid clouds of oily black smoke. The flames didn't just strike the warriors either; some appeared among the elderly and the children, where Shakre waited.

Shakre had the briefest warning of an approaching power surge, just to her right. She shoved Jehu just enough to off balance him, while she fell the other way. Jehu stumbled away, throwing out one hand to catch himself. A column of writhing gray fire roared up in the spot where the two of them had been standing.

Mere seconds after the attack had begun, the air was filled with the stink of burning flesh and acrid black smoke. Takare discipline evaporated. Those in the rear began to flee and dozens of the warriors were joining them, running south to escape.

Shakre realized all at once that they would not get away, that there was still more to this trap that had been laid for them. Off to the sides were thousands more of Kasai's soldiers, many of them mounted. They began to close in, weapons drawn. Arrows flew through the air. Kasai meant for this to be the end of her adopted people.

Shakre turned back to the north. If they were to have any chance, the burned ones had to be killed. But no one else knew where they were.

Shakre made her way through the chaos to Youlin and grabbed her shoulder. "It's the burned ones. They're the ones doing this. Tell the spirit-kin to kill them."

Youlin turned to her. "Where are they? I can't see them."

"Past the soldiers, hidden in the fog."

Youlin wasted no time questioning her. She shouted Rehobim's name. Somehow, through the din, Rehobim heard her and turned.

"Burned ones!" she shouted, and pointed.

Rehobim yelled a command and sprinted toward the massed soldiers without hesitation. The surviving spirit-kin followed him instantly. They did not draw their weapons, but charged their enemies barehanded.

The ranks of pikemen braced for the charge, while those behind them readied swords, axes and maces. This was why they had not charged. They were there only to defend. Kasai had planned the trap well. The Takare warriors would either have to mount a suicidal charge into the face of thousands of points of bristling steel, or they would have to flee and be cut down by the soldiers waiting on the flanks. Even if they charged, they would not be able to get through the soldiers fast enough to save their people.

But Kasai had not reckoned on the spirit-kin.

In moments the spirit-kin had closed the gap. The massed soldiers braced themselves for the impact. But instead of impaling themselves on the pikes, they simply *avoided* them. Moving with impossible agility, at the last moment the charging spirit-kin slipped around the waiting points, slapping the pikes aside, and slipping through their ranks like a stream passing through the rocks.

In moments they were through the pike men and charging the rest of the soldiers, who seemed bewildered to be facing them so quickly. Axes and swords swung, but they might as well have been wielded by children for all the harm they did. The spirit-kin easily avoided the blows.

And then they did something even more astonishing.

They leapt into the air. Before the startled soldiers could react the spirit-kin were running across them, stepping on shoulders and heads. A couple lost their footing and fell, but most made it through unscathed.

All that remained between them and the blinded ones were archers. The archers had time for only one volley of arrows and none of them struck the spirit-kin, who dodged or slapped down the oncoming arrows. Rehobim did neither, simply grabbing the arrow coming for him out of the air with his left hand. As he ran towards the archers he snapped the arrow in half and let it fall to the ground. The rest of the arrows struck their own soldiers, who were struggling to turn and adjust to this enemy that was now behind them.

The archers broke as one, throwing down their bows and fleeing in all directions, like chickens with a wolf in the henhouse.

The spirit-kin disappeared into the fog bank. Screams rose from its depths and there were several flashes of light. A column of flame erupted a few paces in front of Shakre and Youlin, disappearing almost as rapidly as it appeared. One or two more appeared amongst the Takare, sputtering out just as quickly.

Gradually the fog bank dissipated, revealing the spirit-kin, their weapons bloodied, gray-cloaked forms littering the ground around them. Not a single blinded one was still standing.

Kasai's soldiers began to flee the field but it was too late for most of them. The Takare were ruthless. The spirit-kin closed on their enemies from one side, while the Takare warriors closed from the other. Weapons flashed and bodies fell.

FIFTY-EIGHT

The day after the battle with Kasai's soldiers, at the evening meal, one of the spirit-kin, a young woman, Hone, suddenly rubbed her eyes and looked around like one who awakens from a long sleep. Abruptly she stood, her bowl of food falling to the ground unnoticed, and drew her sword.

"Who are you people?" Hone demanded roughly. But her voice was no longer hers. It was deep and rough and undeniably masculine.

"We are your people," Nilus, her husband, said, standing and reaching for her.

She jerked away from his touch and pressed the tip of the sword into his chest. "I have never seen you before." She looked around, taking in the rough fire circle, the other Takare who had come to their feet. "Where are we? I do not know this place. This is not Ankha del'Ath."

"We journey there now, my wife," Nilus said, his hand still raised to her. He had been one of the first to volunteer for the spirit-kin.

Hone put one hand to her temple. "What is happening to me?" She shook her head and took a step back. "Why did you call me wife?" Her gaze fell on her arm, and an oath came from her, the words of the oath unfamiliar. "What have you done to me?" she cried. "What sort of sorcery is this that you have put me in a different body?"

Nilus reached for her again. "Only let me explain…" he began.

Suddenly her sword was against Nilus' throat.

Nilus stepped back, his face ashen. His eyes roved the crowd and met Shakre's. His gaze was pleading.

Hone turned slowly, her sword at the ready. She was in a fighter's crouch, muscles tensed, moments away from bloodshed. Then she shivered, a violent wave of motion that began at her feet and passed up through her body, so strong she stumbled. She closed her eyes, and when she opened them they were once again hers. She looked down at the sword in her hand uncertainly. She raised her eyes and found Nilus. "Husband?"

Nilus came forward and took her in his arms. As the Takare watched in stunned silence, he led her away.

Afterwards, Shakre sought out Youlin. She was sitting on the ground at the edge of the Takare camp, staring out into the gathering darkness. "This must cease," Shakre said. "At least until we know more."

Youlin sat huddled in on herself and Shakre wasn't sure she had heard her. Just as she was about to repeat herself, Youlin replied.

"The horse with two masters will not know who to obey until one of the masters takes control for good."

"We're not talking about a horse here," Shakre snapped. "We're talking about people. Didn't you see what happened? Hone is my friend. We almost lost her tonight. What happens next time?"

"What happens is the spirit which is strongest will take control of the body. That is what will happen. Did you ever think it would be otherwise?"

"You knew this would happen?" Shakre asked, aghast.

"I suspected."

"Yet you went ahead anyway?"

"Kasai has made war on my people, on *our* people, Merat-reborn. Three times that thing has nearly destroyed us. What difference if a few of our weaker warriors lose themselves? If Kasai wins, we will all lose."

Once again Shakre found herself slammed into the hard wall of brutal necessity. Her heart cried out that this was wrong – as it had cried out so many times ever since the first outsiders appeared on the Plateau – but brutal necessity said that survival demanded everything the Takare had to offer. Everything and more. "So you mean to continue calling in the old souls?" she said in a low voice.

"So long as there is breath in my body."

Shakre found no words to reply. Strangely, her attention was drawn to one of Youlin's hands. Hand and wrist had slipped free of the cloak she wore at all times. She had always been a slight woman, but now her hand looked almost skeletal. The veins stood out thick and blue against her white skin. Shakre's healing instincts came to the fore, pushing past her other concerns. "Pastwalker, are you okay?"

Youlin jerked as if struck, and pulled her hand back into the depths of her sleeve. "It is of no matter."

"But that's not true." Shakre hurried on, before Youlin could interject. "I am a healer. Whatever else my failings, you know I am to be trusted on this."

Youlin hesitated.

"Let me have a look at you."

Youlin shook her head. "No."

"Now who is failing her people? You are our leader. We count on you. If you fall, then we do too. You told me that nothing mattered but that our people are safe, yet you risk us all if you push yourself beyond your limits."

Youlin seemed to recoil. "I know my limits, Windrider."

"Then you shouldn't mind me looking you over."

The hooded head turned toward her. At length Youlin nodded.

Shakre set her hand on the young woman's shoulder, letting their Songs touch, then drawing forth a whisper of Youlin's Song and letting it play over her, feeling her way through its subtleties, looking, probing. After a minute she pulled back and straightened.

"You are dangerously weak. You push yourself too far."

"Respectfully, Windrider, only I can be the judge of that."

"If you go too far – "

"Did you find sickness or taint?"

Shakre hesitated. "No."

"Then you have done your duty. Leave me now." Shakre thought she saw a grim smile accompany the next words. "As you said, I need my rest."

"I cannot say no any longer. I must accept the old spirit." It was the end of the day. Werthin's voice was low and calm, but he could not hide the anguish he felt from Shakre. She could feel what this struggle was costing him and her heart ached with her desire to help him. She did not need to ask him what he referred to; she knew all too well. "It is my duty to my people. To refuse again will be to fail them."

Three days had passed since Shakre checked Youlin's health. Not only had Youlin not slowed in her efforts to call in more old spirits, but she had actually increased, calling in several new ones each night. The pressure on those warriors who were reluctant to be vessels for the old spirits was increasing. Nor was Werthin the only one who had resisted. None could deny that the spirit-kin were changed; they camped apart from the rest of the Takare at night. They ate apart. They trained apart. They slept apart. They behaved strangely, often talking to themselves. Fights broke out among them regularly. Only the day before one spirit-kin had killed another. The cracks were showing, and they were getting larger.

Shakre did not try to argue with Werthin. She understood the demands of family, of people. Always strong, they were even greater now that the Takare were so close to utter destruction. Much as she hated what he was going to do, she even agreed with him. What would she not be willing to sacrifice for these people she loved?

"I understand," Shakre replied, putting her hand on Werthin's shoulder. "Know that whatever you do, I will be here for you."

Wordlessly, Werthin gripped her hand for a moment, before turning away. Shakre followed at a distance as he walked a short distance from camp. Several warriors were waiting there already, a loose group standing behind Youlin, who was staring off into the darkness. Tension poured off the warriors in cold waves; they knew all too well the risks they were taking.

A score of Takare – family and friends of those about to undergo the hosting – waited at the edge of the clearing, and Shakre took her place among them. She found herself standing beside an old woman who had her eyes fixed on one of the waiting warriors. He was a man in his late middle age, stockier than was common among the Takare, most of the black in his hair replaced by gray. The old woman was biting her lower lip. Her tresses were entwined in her fingers. Shakre wanted to speak to the elderly woman, to reassure her, but no words would come to her. What would she say anyway? That everything would be all right? Such reassurances meant nothing in this new and frightening world they all found themselves in. If she still had her faith she would have offered up a prayer, but that fire had long since grown cold. She wrapped her arms around herself and tried to be strong for Werthin. She would be strong for him if she could not be strong for herself. She found herself wishing for Elihu's reassuring presence, but she did not know where he was right then.

Werthin moved forward and knelt next to Youlin. She slashed the back of his neck with her knife and then called out to the old spirits. An answering cry came in from the darkness.

A wraithlike, glowing mass appeared, twin burning coals within its depths. The wraith circled the two of them, faster and faster. As it did so, its wail grew louder.

Shakre frowned. Something was wrong. The spirit's wailing was too loud. People were pressing their hands over their ears. She thought someone cried out, but it was too loud to be sure. The sound grew louder and the pain in her skull increased. Shakre looked back at the wraith and what she saw there caused her heart to pound wildly.

Now there were two sets of glowing coals within that amorphous mass.

Shakre screamed a warning to Youlin, to Werthin, but her words were lost in the cacophony. She could only watch in horror as the wraith settled around Werthin, coalesced, and began to pass into his wound.

In seconds it was over. The wailing died away and silence descended over the clearing. Shakre ran forward, but before she could get to him, Werthin's knees buckled and he toppled over. A moment later, Youlin did as well.

Shakre ran over to them. She laid a hand on Youlin and it took only a moment to ascertain what she already suspected: the young woman had collapsed from exhaustion, nothing more.

"Make her comfortable," she told the people standing there, then turned her attention to Werthin. He was burning up, the heat radiating off him like a bed of coals.

Rehobim came up. "See to the Pastwalker first," he ordered her. "She is more vital to us."

"Shut up, Rehobim," she snapped without looking at him. She heard the sharp intake of his breath. "She'll be fine, but if I don't do something for Werthin soon, he'll die."

"If he is too weak to handle an old spirit, he is of no use to us."

She turned on him then, her temper blazing. "Get out of here, you idiot! I'm done with you. You have no idea what you're talking about."

There were shocked looks on the faces of those standing around and Rehobim's fists clenched. She realized he might kill her right then and there, but she simply didn't care anymore. She was done tolerating him.

She turned back to Werthin and went *beyond*. As she'd suspected, there were two Heartglows inside his *akirma* beside his own. He had received two of the old spirits. Both of them were larger and brighter than his and they were pressed close to his, as if trying to envelop it.

She had to get them out of there, and quickly. But how?

Elihu came running up and she turned to him gratefully. She told him what had happened. When she was done, he said, "So cut open his *akirma* and remove the other spirits."

Shakre stared at him, disbelieving. "I don't know how to do that. Who do you think I am, anyway? Xochitl?"

"I think you are the Windrider. I think you are the one who saved me from the poisonwood. The one who found us and led us out of the destruction of our home. The one who cleansed Jehu of his mark. That's who I think you are."

Shakre bit her lip. "I might be able to do it, if I'm really, really careful and very lucky. But if I make the smallest error…"

"If you do nothing, he will die."

It was possible. In the days of the Empire the Tenders had been able to perform such surgery. At its root it simply required a very fine control of one's Selfsong, extending the boundaries of her *akirma* and using that energy to form a sort of ethereal hand.

Werthin moaned and his Heartglow flickered. That decided her.

She went *beyond* and concentrated on her right hand. After a moment it began to glow more brightly, as Selfsong gathered there. She focused her will and gradually a glowing protuberance extended from her hand. She shaped it into a sharp edge and placed it against Werthin's *akirma*. With a quick swipe she made an incision in his *akirma* about six inches long. Werthin's *akirma* split open suddenly and Selfsong began shooting out of the cut in a spray of white light. She would have to work quickly.

She reached into his *akirma*, caught hold of one of the other spirits and pulled it out, then released it. It tried to go back into the opening in Werthin's *akirma*, but she slapped it away and it sped off into the darkness.

She reached back inside. This one was harder to get hold of as it seemed to actively avoid her grasp. All the time she was conscious of how much Selfsong Werthin was losing. His *akirma* was sagging.

Precious seconds ticked by before she could get hold of the other outside glow, pull it out and toss it aside. Quickly she laid her hand against the cut in Werthin's *akirma*, releasing some of her Selfsong into it and sealing it shut.

She pulled back, hoping she had been fast enough. Werthin might still die from the loss of Song.

"You sent them away."

Shakre looked up. Supported by a young Takare warrior, Youlin was looking down on her, frowning.

Shakre nodded.

"You denied two of the old spirits the chance to fight for their people."

"He was dying. I had no choice."

"You shame him. You shame my people. We are stronger than you know."

"You don't know what you're talking about. If I'd done nothing, he'd already be dead. He was burning up."

"He was the first," Youlin continued, as if Shakre hadn't spoken at all. "The first to be chosen by two of our ancestors. Who knows what he might have become?"

"He would have become dead."

Youlin stared down at her for a long moment, then gestured to the one who was helping her and they moved away.

Shakre touched Werthin's forehead. Already he was cooler. "I think he's going to make it," she said.

"I never doubted you," Elihu replied.

"I'm glad one of us was so confident."

With the help of some others, they got Werthin back to the camp and laid out on his blanket.

When they were alone later, Elihu said, "I have good news. I was able to touch one of the plants today."

"That's wonderful," she said. Since leaving the Plateau, Elihu had not been able to commune with any of the plants that lived down here.

"I do not know this plant. I only saw one for the first time yesterday. It is a tree with hooked yellow thorns."

"It's called a haldane."

"The connection was not good, but I was able to draw it out of itself somewhat. It is quite a strong plant."

"It's a vicious plant, that's for sure." The thorns on the haldane were more than an inch long and very sharp. Shakre had had several losing run-ins with haldanes when she was a child.

"I do not know that there is much need for my Plantwalking skills down here," Elihu said, "but it is nice to know I have not completely lost my skills."

X X X

"I called and two answered instead of one. It may happen again." It was the next day, the Takare were taking a break, and Youlin was

365

lying on a litter that the Takare had made for her. She had tried to walk that morning but only made it a short distance before collapsing.

Youlin looked small and frail lying there. She really was little more than a girl, Shakre realized, terribly thin and hollow-eyed. She wondered what she was like before she shouldered the terrible burden of saving her people. Was she always so serious and solitary? Was there a time when she smiled and laughed?

"So you are going to continue calling the old spirits in," Shakre said.

"Yes."

"Even after what happened?"

"Did Kasai perish when it happened? Did any of our enemies perish?"

"Maybe this is a sign that we intrude in things we have no understanding of."

"No. I have thought on this. The old spirits of our people see the terrible dangers that face us. They see us returning to reclaim our ancestral home. They are eager to join the fight and that is why two came this time. Now is not the time for weakness." She looked down at herself and her nose wrinkled in disgust. "I have to be stronger. I *will* be stronger."

"You push yourself too far."

"It doesn't matter. *I* don't matter."

Sadness washed over Shakre at her words. "Why, Youlin?"

Youlin's dark eyes flicked back to her. "Have you not been listening? I do this for my people. For *our* people."

"That's not what I meant. Why must it be you who carries this burden, and why must you carry it alone?"

Youlin went very still. Her eyes grew bright and she blinked several times. She turned her face away while she struggled to master herself and Shakre thought she would not answer, but then she began to speak.

"I have always heard spirits," she said in a low voice. "Since I was a child they were my companions. I spent my time with them instead of the other children and they told me things, things no one else knew. I thought it made me special. But as I grew older I got tired of being different, of never being included by the others. And there was this boy with beautiful yellow hair. I wanted him to like me. I wanted to be normal. So I told the spirits to leave me alone. I refused to listen to them anymore." A tear slid down her cheek and she had to swallow hard to continue. "On the day the outsiders came the spirits tried to warn me, but I yelled at them to go away. I thought that finally the boy was starting to notice me and they would only ruin everything."

She wiped the tear away and turned her head to face Shakre again. "That boy is dead now. Everyone from my village is dead, because I refused to accept my fate." Her expression grew fierce. "I will never make that mistake again. The spirits have chosen me to be the bridge that lets them return to this world and help our people. I don't know why they have chosen me, only that I will not shirk my duty again."

She closed her eyes and called out to the two who carried her, waiting nearby. "Come. It is time to go."

FIFTY-NINE

"I thought more of them would stay," Rome said glumly.

He and Quyloc were standing on top of the wall near the main gates of the city, watching people leave, some on foot, some in wagons or on horseback, carrying those possessions deemed too necessary or valuable to leave behind. It had been several days since he'd spoken at the morning services and told the people of Qarath what was coming for them. So many people fled the first couple of days afterwards that there were times he wondered if he'd end up defending a ghost town.

Rome came down here every day and spent a couple of hours watching them go. He thought it was probably the most depressing thing he'd ever seen. Every person who went through those gates was an accusation, a finger pointed at him, condemning him for failing to protect his city.

"At least there's not as many today," Quyloc replied.

"I guess that's something," Rome said morosely. He had a flask of rum in his hand and he tried to take a drink off it, only to discover that it was empty. He squinted at it, wondering if he'd forgotten to fill it before leaving the palace. It was only mid-morning, kind of early to already be out.

Rome noticed the scowl on Quyloc's face as he watched him and he said, "I know, I know. I'm drinking too much. Bonnie already yelled at me once today. But what else is there for me to do?" If a normal army was approaching there would be a thousand details to see to, defenses to shore up, weapons and food to stockpile. But there was none of that this time. No normal defenses would hold back the Children. No normal weapons would hurt them. And there was no need to worry about food; easily half the population had already left. They were probably going to die, but they wouldn't die hungry.

"You won't help your people much if the Children show up and you're drunk."

"Don't worry about it," Rome growled. "I'll be ready when they get here. Ricarn said they are at least two days out. It could even be longer." The Children's pace was slowing as they burned through the Song they'd stolen. Rome threw the flask down. "I wish they would just get here right now. I can't stand this waiting. I've never been good at it."

"Be glad for every minute they are delayed," Quyloc replied. "The longer it takes them, the weaker they'll be." Other than the wildlife they were able to snare, the Children wouldn't be feeding again before they reached Qarath. Every town and village between Qarath and Thrikyl had been evacuated – forcefully when necessary – to deny the Children access to more Song.

"You're right, of course, but the waiting is killing me." He clenched his fists. "I feel so helpless."

"Stop thinking about it," Quyloc said. "Go spend some time with Bonnie."

"I already did. She told me I was making her crazy and I should go find something to do." The truth was that being around her just made it all harder for him. Every time he thought about the child he had coming he felt a surge of love and a desire to protect his child that was so strong it made him feel weak. Mixed with that was a terrible despair, the knowledge that there was nothing he could really do, that both Bonnie and the child were most likely going to die.

Rome had faced his own death many times and it didn't particularly bother him. But the knowledge that those he loved were also going to die, mixed with the sense of responsibility he felt toward the whole city of Qarath, was almost more than he could bear.

SIXTY

Darkness was falling fast, the moon just rising out over the ocean, fighting its way through a growing bank of dark clouds. The road the Children were following had looped out of the rolling hills and down to the coast, where a small village stood. The village was empty, as had been both the other villages they had encountered in the past few days as they traveled toward Qarath. In their frustration, the Children had knocked down a few buildings and one of them had lit a fire that had raced through the village, reducing it to smoking ashes. Melekath was not surprised that the villages were empty. Qarath knew they were coming and no doubt they had sent men to make sure the villagers were evacuated, thus making sure the Children would not grow stronger as they traveled. It was a sensible strategy.

The Children were scattered along the beach near the village, clustered in small groups. One group was gathered around Reyna, who was on her knees in the sand, feeding on one of the young women she had brought from Thrikyl. The young woman twitched and writhed weakly. She was nearly dead. Her twin was already dead, her body lying in the dirt a day behind them.

The Children gathered around Reyna moaned and shivered with hunger and desire, but they stayed back out of her reach. At the edge of the waves knelt Karrl, holding the torn pieces of his face, whimpering. He'd made the mistake of trying to feed from Reyna's prize; he was lucky she had not hurt him worse.

Melekath watched from a distance, his expression bleak. He hoped the woman died soon. Watching her suffer bothered him more than he cared to admit. He could no longer delude himself that Reyna would change. There was a hunger within her that went beyond her need for Song. If he was honest, he had to admit to himself that it had always been there, even before the prison.

He should never have given her the Gift.

He shifted his gaze to Heram, down the beach from Reyna, several of his followers clustered around him. He was staring at Reyna fiercely. Melekath could feel the depth of his hatred for her from this distance. Heram was another one he shouldn't have given the Gift to. He should have been more selective.

Melekath turned away. Nearby, two of the Children, an older couple, had tied three planks into a tripod and were struggling to attach to it a piece of canvas they had salvaged somewhere. Now and then they cast anxious glances at the thick bank of clouds building out over the ocean.

Melekath's mood lifted somewhat. He walked over to them. "If you attach the rope here – "

He got no further.

"We don't need your help," the woman said stiffly.

"Had enough of that for this lifetime," the man added, giving him a dark look.

"But you…"

"Go on with you," the man said gruffly.

Melekath stepped back, surprised at the depth of the pain he felt in his chest. He stood there for a moment longer, then turned away.

It was the same everywhere in the camp. Most simply avoided looking at him, finding something else to do, somewhere else to turn, when he drew near. A few glared at him and he heard muttered curses, each one stabbing deeper than he would have thought possible.

He left them and walked to the brow of a low hill, where he stopped and looked back down at them. He had lost them. He had lost his Children. Thrikyl had been the last straw.

He should leave. They didn't want him here. He should just walk away.

And yet, he knew he could never do that. However angry they were with him, however they treated him, they were still, and always would be, his Children. He would do anything, sacrifice anything, for them.

He feared for them. They thought their newfound power made them invincible, and nothing he said could convince them otherwise. But he knew differently; Durag'otal had taught him the foolishness of arrogant power. His Children faced a foe with unknown abilities and they made no effort to learn what those abilities were. They had no plan of attack. They made no preparations for retreat in the event the defenders of Qarath had a surprise weapon to strike them with. They sent no scouts forward to look for traps. Which meant they had only him. This was why he would not abandon them. They were his Children, his responsibility.

The defenders of Qarath were not idiots. Of that Melekath was sure. There still was no sign of the Guardians and he could only assume that they, and the army he had sent them to raise, had been defeated. There was no other explanation as to why they were not here. The defenders of Qarath no doubt had Lowellin working with them, and who knew how many of the Eight as well. If they had put together an army only a fraction of the size that had besieged Durag'otal, they would finish the Children off in minutes.

Melekath took some solace from the fact that they had not been attacked yet. That could indicate that the Qarathians were not as powerful as he feared. But it might also be that the Qarathians had prepared a trap, and were merely waiting for the Children to stumble blindly into it. That was one of the things that Melekath feared most. He needed more allies. He needed eyes out in front of them, feeding him information. But there was only him and he was painfully weak.

Melekath realized then that he could wait no longer. He had to know more, whatever the risk. He had hoped to wait until he had had more time to rebuild his strength. But his strength was maddeningly slow in returning and Qarath drew closer every day.

He was going to have to travel through the Stone. Like so much else, it had once been easy for him. It involved entering the Stone, not plain rock, but the essence of Stone itself. Traveling through Stone required that he dissolve this form that he held, letting its component parts merge with the Stone. He would then pass through the Stone as pure consciousness, devoid of form, and rebuild his form at the point where he wished to exit.

But it was risky. It meant submerging himself in the raw energy of Stone power. If he wasn't strong enough, his essence would be torn apart and scattered like dust in the wind. His awareness would remain – at least he thought it would – but he might never regain himself in any form.

Melekath walked into the gathering darkness, heading for a stone quarry he had seen from the road as they approached the village. He did not hesitate or worry over his decision. He would take twice the risk for his Children. He could do nothing else.

The question he wrestled with was where to go. Should he go to Qarath, and see what he could learn of its defenders? Or should he try to find the Guardians? He was reasonably certain he did not have the strength to do both at this time. One trip was all he would get. He had to make it count.

In the end he decided to try and find the Guardians, Kasai specifically. He had given Kasai authority over Tharn and Gulagh. From Kasai he could learn what had happened to his army. Together he and the Guardian could prepare for the protection of the Children.

Melekath was almost at the quarry when he stopped, noticing something wrong. A simple hut stood on the lip of the quarry, its windows dark. A feel of corruption came from it. Frowning, Melekath walked closer, then stopped abruptly.

The man who had lived in the hut lay dead inside, his dog lying beside him. But that was not what made Melekath stop. It was how they had died. The traces of Song that lingered around the hut were tainted with some poison he could not at first identify. There was no sign of it anywhere else; it was all concentrated in the hut, as if whatever it was had bubbled up from below and taken the man while he was asleep.

All at once Melekath knew what it was and his alarm increased. The poison was chaos power. There was no mistaking it.

But how could this be? He knew that some chaos power had leaked through into this world during the raising of the prison wall by the Eight. But they had sealed that leak. They were not such fools as to leave something so dangerous leaking into this world. Chaos power was anathema to everything, Shapers and humans alike. Besides, had it been leaking all this time, this world would already be destroyed.

Then where had it come from? What had caused this new rupture in the barrier between their two worlds? How widespread was it?

Finally, he backed away and walked down into the quarry. There was nothing he could do about it now. Maybe Kasai would have some answers.

Melekath walked up to the bare rock and put his hands on it. He was surprised to realize that he was nervous. This would not be like calling up the power that lay within the stone wall that had enclosed Ferien. Loose stone, the rocks and boulders that littered the world, held only trace amounts of power. The power within Ferien's wall was no more than a faint ember compared to the raging bonfire that waited within this stone, still connected as it was to the source of Stone power.

Nor would he be merely dipping into Stone power, as he had done the night before entering Thrikyl, when he was trying to learn more of the Guardians' whereabouts.

To travel through the Stone, he would have to enter its power completely, immersing himself in it. It would take all this strength, all his control. And still it might not be enough.

Melekath steeled himself and pushed into the rock face. Under his touch the stone softened and his hands sank into it. He continued pushing and when he was up to his shoulders he contacted Stone power directly.

His body jerked and he bit back a cry, surprised at how much it hurt. It burned with a heat greater than any fire. It gnawed at him greedily, as if millions of ants tore at him with their jaws. Unlike Song, the power of Life, which was gentle and nurturing in its touch, Stone power was wild and vicious, with the inexorable weight and brutality of a rockslide.

When he had first set out to create new beings, all those millennia ago, he had tried at first to work solely with Stone power, but he had failed miserably. He had failed because Stone power allowed for nothing less than the elemental strength of the Shapers. It was a cruel and demanding power. It was only when he had finally thought to mix the brute force of Stone power with the power of Sea and Sky that he had succeeded. Sea power was cruel and terrible as well, but different in its energy than Stone, and the two opposing forces had evened and calmed each other in some way he had never understood. The final touch was the power of the Sky, light and airy and energetic, solidifying the balance and giving rise to the gentle Circle that he had come to name Life.

Melekath gritted his teeth and fought against the Stone power. He was drawn deeper into its grasp. It was all he could do to hang on. Twice he felt himself being sucked in and he had to fight wildly to regain his balance. It was like putting into a stormy sea in a flimsy boat. He had to enter at the right spot, the right moment, the trough between the waves. Otherwise the boat would capsize and he would be pulled under, never to resurface.

Then, all at once, the opening was there, the tiny eye of calm in the center of the maelstrom. Melekath seized the opportunity and threw himself in.

Reyna stood on the lip of the quarry and watched as Melekath put his hands on the stone face, wondering what he was doing. She'd seen him walk away into the hills and she'd followed, hoping to learn something that would give her an edge. She longed to depose Melekath and be rid of his meddling forever, but before she acted against him she had to be sure. If she wasn't, and he defeated her, she would likely be weakened so much that Heram would be able to destroy her.

A strange, reddish glow began to emanate from the rock. First Melekath's hands, then his arms, sank into the rock. The glow grew brighter and brighter until she had to squint against its glow.

Then there was a flash, something not really visible, more felt than seen, and painful, so that she fell back and threw up her arms to shield her face.

When she could see once again, Melekath was gone. The reddish glow faded and disappeared.

SIXTY-ONE

The power at the heart of the Stone was brutal, crushing. Vast and impersonal, it pressed on him from all sides. At first he could do nothing against it. The weight of it was overwhelming. He was flickering out. He had been a fool to enter here. He was too weak, too far gone, to survive. It would be a relief to let go, to let it crush him to nothing.

He had not felt this weak and helpless since he first fell to this world. The memory of that day came to him, falling and falling, then slamming into the world's surface, lying there stunned and broken, dimly aware of others falling around him. How long he lay there he didn't know, aware of his surroundings, but completely unable to do a thing, his body shattered and useless. Why did he not die? Where had he fallen from? Who was he? There were no memories, nothing to mark his past at all.

He remembered willing his shattered form to move over and over. Then, the first twitches. Elation, but mixed with fear. Something was different about his body. Something was wrong.

More struggling. He heard a grating sound, harsh and heavy. Finally, he was able to sit up, to look down at himself and what he saw stunned him.

He had no body. There was only a rough pile of stones. He moved, and some of the stones moved. He felt terribly heavy and clumsy. Again the stones moved when he tried to.

Looking around, seeing a harsh landscape, wild, foaming seas pounding against a shore of jagged black stone. Howling winds, lightning stabbing at the ground, the ceaseless roar of thunder.

Around him were other piles of stones, some of them moving, twitching. There were shapes within the sea as well, crude and helpless. Figures dimly glimpsed in the clouds, thrown this way and that by the storm. And he knew that these were his brethren, fallen here with him, just as lost and helpless.

Melekath – that was not his name then; the name came later – was the first to stand, the first to fully realize that his body *was* the stone, that he could exert his will and control the stone as part of him. He could shape the stone, he could shape himself, all by exerting his will.

Melekath pushed the ancient memories away. He could not let himself get caught in the past. He had to fight back. Not for himself, but for his Children. They needed him. He would not fail them. Not again. No matter what it cost him.

With every ounce of his will he pushed back and created the tiniest space for himself. The weight of the world still lay on him, but he had an opening.

He paused there for a moment, feeling for the unique vibration that was Kasai.

There.

He could not move. The Stone was too heavy. He had become too weak. He was trapped here, in the heart of the Stone, and here he would stay.

But he did not quit and in time he was able to move closer to his destination. He rested, then fought his way forward once again. Over and over he did this and slowly he felt himself draw closer to Kasai.

He could not stay within the Stone any longer. Though he was not completely to Kasai, he had to leave now, or he would never have the strength to do so.

He fought his way up and out of the Stone. Then he was at the surface and his greatest challenge still awaited. He would have to rebuild his body, Shape himself from raw Stone.

Grimly he drew together the pieces needed, forming a hand, a wrist, an arm, and pushing it out of the Stone and back into the world. He Shaped another hand, then the arm, and pushed them forth as well.

He gathered his will, forming his head, his torso, legs and feet. When the idea of them was solid enough, he tried to step free the rest of the way.

And couldn't.

The Stone would not let go. It was pulling him back. He flailed wildly for his arms.

Something caught hold of his hands. He felt a mighty tug and he was jerked free of the Stone. He fell out, into air once again, losing his balance and falling on his face.

He groaned and rolled over onto his back. He felt fragile, poorly put together. He lifted one hand and looked at it. It was a hand, but it was not his hand. The fingers were different thicknesses, the joints in the wrong places. His skin was streaked with black and red. It was very stiff.

Then a face filled the sky above him. Something resembling a face anyway.

It was cracked, reddish stone, the features blunt and vague, two indentations for eyes, a rough hole where the mouth should be. There was a diagonal slash across the face, a deep, reddish glow emanating from it.

"Tharn," Melekath said through lips that seemed not to belong to him.

A massive, boulder-sized hand came into view, encircled his chest and lifted him to his feet. Melekath staggered when Tharn let go, but managed to keep his balance with difficulty. It was cooler here than where he had come from. Patchy forest, mostly pine and fir, but mixed liberally with massive oaks and other hardwoods, surrounded him. The moon was fat in the sky, casting a generous light.

Tharn stood staring down at him, a small mountain given life. Melekath barely came up to its waist. There was a deep gash in the junction of its neck and shoulder, two more on the side of its face. Reddish light leaked from them. Something had badly injured the Guardian. Melekath's concern grew. Somehow, probably with the help of chaos power, Lowellin had defeated the Guardians and the army they had gathered.

"What happened?" Melekath asked.

Tharn stared at him without replying. Melekath started to repeat the question. Then Tharn spoke.

"Kasai waits."

Without another word, Tharn turned and rumbled away.

They walked through the forest for a time. Then the trees cleared away and they stood on the lip of a long descent. In the distance, set in a fold between two hills, was a walled city.

"What city is that?" Melekath asked.

"Fanethrin."

Melekath remembered a city with that name, though it had been much smaller than this. Most troubling, Fanethrin was nowhere near Qarath, days and days at a hard march. Was Kasai injured as well? He wanted to hurry on ahead and cursed the weakness that limited him. One leg seemed to be shorter than the other and though he put some effort into fixing it he couldn't seem to do anything. He felt like he was made out of mismatched parts.

They made their way onto a road that led toward the city. There were no other travelers on it. As they drew closer to the city, Melekath saw something unusual up ahead, dark shapes lining the road on both sides. It wasn't until they got closer that he could figure out what they were and when he did, he recoiled.

They were wooden posts, set into the ground, five or six paces apart. From each one hung the gnarled, burned shape of a person. Men, women, and children. Their mouths were stretched wide in silent agony. Most of the flesh was gone, little more than bones and sinew remaining.

Melekath stopped at the first one. It was small, probably a child of six or seven.

"What is the meaning of this?" he demanded. "What happened to these people? Why are they here?"

"An example. A warning. To those who break their vows," Tharn replied without turning.

"What vows? What are you talking about?"

Tharn stumped onward without slowing.

The gates of the city were open. The city was eerily silent, with none of the normal sounds that occur wherever people gather and live in close proximity: no laughing or cursing, no crying, no background hum of conversation. There was a group of people standing silently in the open gates, watching them as they drew close. They drew aside as he and Tharn approached, their faces shadowy in the uncertain light of the torches mounted in iron sconces on the walls.

Melekath followed Tharn through the gates. Beyond was a street leading to the center of the city. It was lined with soldiers clad all in gray, men and women alike. They stood like a silent gray wall, their ranks six or seven deep, every eye fixed on Melekath, every face expressionless. On every forehead was a black smudge, like a thumbprint burned into their skin. Melekath could *see* that the burns went beyond the surface, with black tendrils that branched throughout their *akirmas* like spider webs.

What had Kasai done to them and why? In their eyes was a reflected anger too deep and too old to be theirs. Did Kasai look through those eyes?

Melekath followed Tharn through their ranks, keenly aware of the eyes on him. The accusation in their gazes was stronger than words. He felt old and awkward and guilty.

The street led to the remains of a massive stone building, probably the palace. It had been completely destroyed, every wall and tower thrown down. The stone lay in great piles. In the center was open ground. Hundreds of gray-cloaked figures stood on the open ground, facing toward the center, where lay a massive block of stone. On top of the stone was the white-skinned figure of Kasai.

Kasai was tall and lean as a skeleton, its skin a dirty white shading toward ivory. Its limbs were too long, its joints in the wrong places. Its mouth was a harsh, vertical slash and there was a single, red-rimmed eye in the center of its forehead. It was staring at Melekath.

Tharn stood aside and motioned Melekath forward. For a long moment he couldn't move. The gray-cloaked figures turned towards him at some unheard signal and parted, clearing his way to Kasai. In the light of the torches ringing the area he saw suddenly and with horror that their eyes had all been burned away, leaving only gaping, blackened sockets. Tharn shoved him so that he stumbled forward.

The stone was broken on one corner, so that there were crude steps of a sort that Melekath was able to use to climb on top. When he got there he looked out over the gathered figures, a pang of regret and sadness passing through him. Then he turned to Kasai.

"You did not come," he said. "The Children are free, but you are not there."

The lipless mouth opened. The voice that issued forth was thin, piercing, like the wind through high, cold mountain crags.

"Nor will I."

"I tasked you – all of you – with raising an army."

In answer, Kasai gestured at the city around them.

"Why are you here?" Melekath asked.

"We were defeated." Kasai gestured at two wounds in its lower torso. Something clear leaked from them slowly.

"What did that?"

"Lowellin. He sent one of his to the shadow world, *Pente Akka*. The man carries a *rendspear*."

That shook Melekath. "He is a fool. His hatred for me has blinded him. The power from that realm cannot be used here."

Kasai shook its head and its eye narrowed. "This was always your flaw. You fear the weapons that would save you and those you claim to love." Its mouth twisted as it said the last word, as if it tasted bad.

"It is not fear – " Melekath began, but Kasai cut him off.

"Lowellin is not the only one to use such power. Look, and see its uses."

Kasai reached down, picked up a stone the size of a man's head with one long-fingered hand. The stone was flat on one side. Kasai rubbed its free hand across the flat side and it turned silver. It shimmered, then a vision appeared. Melekath moved closer to see.

The scene was underwater, deep in the ocean. Small, dark, ravenous things swarmed around a squat, powerful being. It roared soundlessly at them, swatting at them with its clawed hands. Around it swirled finned creatures, their mouths filled with rows of sharp teeth. The finned things darted at the dark shapes plaguing their master.

But none of it did any good. The squat, powerful being howled with pain each time it struck one of the things, and the finned creatures died whenever they bit down on one of the ravenous things.

They settled about their prey in a thick cloud, landing on him and burrowing into him. His struggles became frenzied and the water about him churned wildly.

Kasai dropped the stone. Melekath rubbed his eyes. His voice, when he spoke, came out shaken. "That was Golgath."

Kasai nodded. "Because of the *ingerlings*, Golgath will not trouble you. Neither will Tu Sinar. This much help I have given you, using what you fear to use."

"And what of the *ingerlings* when Golgath is dead? What will they feed on next?"

Kasai shrugged. "There are still Khanewal, Xochitl, Protaxes, the others."

"And then?"

"I will send them home. Unless another of the First Ring troubles me and I must remove him as well."

Melekath did not miss the veiled threat. He took a step back. "Why?" he asked, aware his voice sounded weak and thin. "Why have you turned your back on those you vowed to protect? Why have you done this to them?" He gestured at the gray-cloaked figures, pressed close to the stone, noticing as he did so that gray fire now burned around their hands, filled their empty eye sockets, danced in gray crowns around their heads.

"Three thousand years. That is a reason. Trapped in that desert, unable to flee." Its fingers looked like claws; its hairless skin seemed to glow with its anger. "But most of all because you are a fool. *You* refused to take the fight to the Eight. *You* used the power from the Heart of the Stone to build a shield, when it could have destroyed them as soon as they came against us. Even when you saw what they meant to do, the power they meant to unleash, *you* still refused to act." Its voice had become an angry hiss. "My vows are no more. Never again will I raise a hand to serve your pathetic humans. Never again will I be a servant to anyone. Now the humans serve me, as it should be, for I am of the Nipashanti, ancient before the first of them were born."

"You do not speak to one of the First Ring that way," Melekath barked, his anger roused to sudden wakefulness. He drew himself up even as he reached down into the stone, summoning power to himself. "You have forgotten your place." He began to Shape his power.

"No," Kasai said. "Never again."

It gestured. Stone leapt up around Melekath, encasing him tightly up to his neck. The gray-cloaked figures let out a harsh, victorious shout and the flames around them grew higher.

"You cannot hold me with mere stone," Melekath said. He flexed the power he had summoned, meaning to shatter the stone that held him.

It was gone.

He reached again, but there was nothing. Some barrier had come between him and the power.

"There is nothing there for you," Kasai said. "You have weakened yourself too far. And for what? For the stupid creatures that follow you?" A harsh sound that might have been a laugh passed through its lipless mouth. "They hate you. They turn their backs on you. You have lost them and you are nothing."

The words hammered Melekath, so painful because they were true. "I don't care," he insisted. "I owe them."

"Still you prove your stupidity." Kasai gestured again and the stone encasing Melekath sloughed away, was reabsorbed back into the stone they stood on.

"Go," Kasai said, turning away. "Leave now and I will not harm you."

SIXTY-TWO

Melekath emerged from the Stone with barely the strength left to crawl. Traveling through the Stone had been worse this time and he'd thought he would not get free of its grasp. Probably he would not have, had Kasai not opened the Stone power for him and nearly flung him through. It was yet another ignominy, that one who had for so long been his inferior should be the only reason he had survived the Stone which had been his home since his memories began.

Melekath leaned up against the rock face in the quarry and looked up at the sky. He would just sit here while he gathered his strength. The sun was close to rising. He could hear the surf in the distance. Kasai's words bit deep, echoing what he had told himself many times during the years in the prison. The mistakes were his and his alone, but so many had suffered for them. Nothing he did would ever change that. How could he have been so wrong?

"Where did you go?"

Melekath started and raised his head. Reyna was standing there, arms crossed, looking down at him. The dress she had left Thrikyl in had become stained and torn. Her red hair was no longer as glossy and it was unwashed and tangled. Yet still she was the picture of strength and power, taller than him by a head, her limbs straight, her skin flawless. Melekath suddenly felt very small and shabby.

"To find the Guardians."

Reyna stared down at him, waiting. When he didn't add any more she said, "And?"

"They...they aren't coming."

"Why?"

Melekath looked away. It was too hard to look into that ferocious, hungry gaze. He had made a mistake with this one. "They serve no more."

"Well, we don't need them anyway, do we, *Father*?" As always, she put a mocking emphasis on the last word. "If we're not more powerful than they are now, we will be after we take Qarath."

Melekath considered this, then nodded. "You're probably right."

"You look worse than usual."

Melekath looked down at himself. His skin was the color of old granite, streaked here and there with red and black. His hands were lumpy and misshapen, his legs different sizes. He concentrated for a moment, trying to reshape the smaller one. There was a swirling of the skin and nothing else. "It is not easy…traveling through the Stone."

"Probably not," she replied, bending and grabbing one arm just below the shoulder. She lifted him to his feet with ease. He staggered when she let go, but managed to remain standing by leaning against the rock face. She took his face in one hand and turned it up to her.

"You're not going to give me any more trouble, are you?"

He met her eyes then and what he saw there hurt more than he would have thought. "It was a mistake," he said. "I should have refused you the Gift. All you ever cared about was power."

She laughed. "The lowest street urchin in Qarath knew that, all those years ago. And here we have the greatest of the Shapers, just figuring it out."

SIXTY-THREE

Netra stopped and doubled over suddenly. A wave of nausea washed over her, spiked with pain that stabbed deep into her gut.

"What is it?" Shorn asked, alarmed.

"I can't…" she gasped. "Give me a moment." She fought back, pushing it away from her, building her inner walls up bit by bit. Gradually, the nausea and pain began to recede. Gripping Shorn's arm, she straightened and wiped away her involuntary tears. She swallowed. "We're close," she said. "They're just a mile or so away."

"Are you going to be okay?"

"Yeah." Strangely, she really thought so. "I just need to be careful, keep my walls up."

They continued on, Shorn sticking close, ready to catch her if she stumbled.

"Still you mean to see them," Shorn said.

"Yes, Shorn," Netra replied wearily. Walking in the wake of the Children was like slogging through deep sand. Every step was difficult. The air felt thick and sluggish. Worst of all, though, was the emptiness. Seek as she might, Netra sensed no Song anywhere around them, other than the flows that sustained her and Shorn, and those were weak and fitful. Shorn seemed mostly unperturbed by it – many times she had envied his alien stamina and make up – but she felt it more keenly every day. Often it was all she could do to put one foot in front of the other. When she went to sleep at night it was like falling into a black, bottomless well. Sleep did not replenish her. The food she ate seemed made of sand. Water burned her throat.

"I do not understand."

She gave him a wan smile. "Neither do I. Not exactly. It is only a feeling. It's something Ya'Shi said, something about understanding my enemy, who my enemy really is. Maybe it's because of the woman we found in Thrikyl, Orenthe. They're not just a faceless enemy anymore. They're *people*. I have to see them. I have to try to understand." This was not the first time she had explained this to him and she knew he would be no closer to understanding than before. How could he be, when she herself didn't really understand? But what else did she have to go on?

"I could carry you."

Netra gave a half smile and put her hand on his arm. "Not yet, my friend."

The road wound up the side of a hill, doubling back near the top to circle around a stand of tall trees. The trees were dead, of course, as was everything else in the Children's wake, turned gray and brittle, all the leaves gone. No insects whined in the late afternoon warmth. No birds flitted in the trees.

"There's another one up ahead," Netra said when they were near the top of the hill. "In the trees."

Several times they had encountered broken ones in the days they had been following the Children. The first was a man. His arms and legs had been torn off, his neck broken. When they approached him his eyes lit up with a fierce desire and his mouth opened and closed in a biting motion. Netra had not tried to touch him, but even without doing so it seemed she could feel his desperate hunger as if it were her own, and it hurt to leave him there without being able to help him. The other two they'd found had been no better off.

This one was a child. At least, he was the size of a child. He was as wrinkled as an eighty-year-old man. One side of his head was simply gone. There was still some dried-out brain matter left in the skull cavity and a broken jaw hanging from one joint only. His legs had been torn off. They lay nearby, broken in numerous places. One arm was gone at the elbow. With the remaining arm he reached for them, his sole eye rolling in his head.

"They are turning on themselves," Shorn said, studying the child dispassionately. "If they can be slowed enough, there will be far fewer of them to fight."

"Qarath is only a couple days away now," Netra said, staring at the boy. Some of his hair had grown back in, fine and straight and so pale it was nearly white. Even from this distance she could feel his hunger pulling at her, surprisingly strong. If she was not shielded against him she felt certain he would be draining her LifeSong now. What would happen to him then? Would he simply regrow his lost limbs? "I can hear Qarath in the distance, like a humming in the background. I imagine they can hear it too. They're going to push harder now. We're going to have to hurry if we want to catch up."

SIXTY-FOUR

The Takare were about a day out of Ankha del'Ath. The Truebane Mountains filled the horizon to the southwest of them, stark granite peaks capped with snow. They were not an especially big mountain range, but they were tall and they looked to Shakre to be unclimbable. Which, she supposed, was what made Wreckers Gate effective. Once closed it effectively sealed off the interior of the mountains from the outside world.

It was early afternoon and the Takare had stopped to take a break beside a robust stream that flowed outward from the looming mountains. The countryside had flattened somewhat and become dryer, though not nearly as dry as the desert Shakre had grown up in. There were still streams, but they crossed only one or two a day instead of every hour or so.

Four children ran by, laughing, heading for the stream. A young woman snatched a young man's water skin from him before he could take a drink from it, playfully slapping at his hand when he tried to get it back. Two old ladies watched them. One whispered something to the other and both smiled.

It had been this way over the past couple of days. Shakre heard laughing and singing regularly now. For the first time since the destruction of the Plateau the Takare seemed to have recovered their natural cheerfulness. Youlin had even pulled her hood back to let sun fall on her face. She had regained her strength enough that the litter was no longer needed. Shakre accepted some food Elihu dug out of his pouch and sat there in the fall sun trying to savor these moments of peace as much as she could. She knew it would not last, but for now the cloud had lifted and what else could she do but rejoice in it? Who knew what tomorrow might bring?

Her eyes fell on Pinlir, sitting with his mate. There was no smile touching his face. He watched his brethren with his perpetual scowl. His mate held out some food to him, but he shook his head without looking at her. He had been the first to become a spirit-kin after Rehobim, the intensity of his need such that the other two warriors who had vied to be next had both stepped back. Even the other spirit-kin left him alone. He seemed to have descended into his own private world and slammed the door shut behind him.

Shakre caught a sense of unease stirring through her people and forgot about Pinlir, looking to see what was happening. Heads were turning toward the mountains. She stood up. One of the scouts was returning at a hard run. She didn't need her inner senses to know he was driven by something. By the time the scout stopped before Youlin and Rehobim the entire body of Takare had gone silent.

"The gate is closed." The scout was panting from his run.

The Takare looked at each other, each trying to understand what this meant. Youlin had once again retreated to the depths of her hood and seemed to be staring at the ground.

"How can that be?" Rehobim demanded. "Who closed it?"

"I don't know. I saw no one."

"Were there tracks? How long has it been closed?"

"I saw no tracks," the scout said, "but I did not go clear to the gate so I don't know if it is recently closed. I thought you would want to know as soon as possible."

Rehobim didn't answer him. He was looking at Youlin. She did not return his look, but instead started walking, her pace fast. Wordlessly the rest of the Takare gathered up their possessions and fell in behind her.

They pushed on hard after that, not stopping for the night until several hours after dark and then starting before daylight the next day. It was late morning when they had their first look at Wreckers Gate. At the top of a long, steady rise they broke out of a small forest of hardwood trees and there it was. The hard, sharp peaks of the mountains crowded in from both sides, only grudgingly allowing this one small entrance into their domain.

Even though Shakre had seen Wreckers Gate numerous times in the communal journeys with the Pastwalker, she was still stunned by its sheer size. It was a massive affair, far taller than any castle wall, two or three hundred feet tall at least and spanning about the same distance. It appeared to be formed of a single, seamless block of obsidian, volcanic glass. There were no battlements at the top, no towers. No indication of how it was attached to the cliffs on either side of it. Those cliffs were of a reddish-brown stone, taller than the Gate, and nearly as sheer.

Shakre could see why the Empire's siege of Ankha del'Ath had failed so miserably. How does one besiege a mountain? Climbing the Gate would be impossible. A good bowman could shoot an arrow with a line attached over the top, but then what would it hook onto? No catapult could throw a stone over it, and any stones lobbed at it would simply shatter. Other cities, such as Thrikyl, had mighty walls that could hold out any invaders, but in that case the invaders need only to wait them out. Even the best-supplied fortress ran out of food eventually. But that wouldn't happen here. Within the protective embrace of the Truebane Mountains was a long, fertile valley. The Takare needed nothing from the outside world. They could not be starved out.

Undoubtedly there were ways through the sharp peaks that loomed all around, but they would be poor, narrow ways, easily defended.

Even more humiliating for the Empire's forces was the fact that the Takare didn't even bother to respond to them when they arrived. They simply closed Wreckers Gate. They put no warriors on top of the gate. They sent no one out to speak to the invaders. They simply ignored them. The siege could have gone on for a thousand years and it wouldn't have mattered to the Takare.

And now that same Gate was closed against them.

Ahead Shakre could see Rehobim standing close to Youlin's slim frame. He seemed to be talking urgently, his face dark, his hands gesturing sharply. It didn't look like Youlin was listening to him. While he was still talking she resumed walking and after a moment he followed her, then the rest of the Takare as well.

Every eye was on the Gate as they approached. Had it been recently closed when whoever was within saw them coming? Or had it been closed for many years, perhaps since shortly after the Takare left? The Takare had left it open when they went. The Empire could have sent someone to close it

The Takare reached the Gate and spilled out along its length. Up close Shakre could see that there were veins of red within the obsidian, so dark they were nearly invisible. She knew it opened in the middle, the two halves swinging out to the sides, but she could not see the line where the two halves met, so perfectly was it formed. She looked around. Though the Takare came close to the Gate, none of them touched it, as if it were a holy relic and to touch it would be to profane it. Even Elihu seemed to be in awe of it.

Shakre laid her hand on it and was struck by how cool the stone was. A moment later she felt something else and pulled her hand away. She looked around. No one seemed to have noticed. She put her hand back and waited. There it was again. Something, almost like a heartbeat, thudded from within its depths. Was it power? An awareness?

She pulled away and craned her head back, trying to find the top, and wondered – not for the first time – how the Takare had built it. By their own admission they were not stone workers. They had no true city hidden within the mountains. Even at the height of their power they had preferred simple wooden homes. She had asked Rekus, the Pastwalker for Bent Tree Shelter, about it once.

"No one knows," was his terse reply.

"Is there nothing in the past then?"

He shrugged. "What difference does it make? It is there and we are not."

Shakre touched the cold stone once more. It seemed impossible that something so big could ever be moved, but she knew that it had been built with such perfect balance that a single person could swing it open without straining. It was truly a marvel.

She heard a gasp from the Takare. People were staring and pointing at the top of the Gate. Shakre stepped back, trying to get a better look.

A lone figure had appeared at the top, looking down at them. It was tall and gaunt, the bones standing out sharply under the skin. Its skin was blackened. Its eyes were empty holes, its mouth toothless. Weeping sores covered much of its body.

A sick coldness gripped Shakre.

The figure that looked down at them was Gulagh, the Guardian known as the Voice.

SIXTY-FIVE

Quyloc sat up suddenly out of a deep sleep, aware that someone was sneaking up on him. He was in his secret room underneath the tower. A glance at the tiny window told him it was still dark outside, though he had a sense that morning was not far off. He sat up on the cot and reached for the spear. Whoever was approaching was just outside the door. Noiselessly, he slipped out of bed and padded across the room, raising the spear as he went.

The door swung open, Quyloc had a dim impression of a hulking figure in the darkness, he pulled back the spear to strike –

"Quyloc! It's me, Rome!"

Quyloc lowered the spear, his heart pounding. Of course it was Rome. If his head hadn't been so addled with sleep still, he would have known that. Especially once he picked up the spear. Rome's Song was as distinctive as his voice.

"What are you doing here?"

"I came to talk to you. I couldn't sleep."

Quyloc walked to the room's lone table, found the lamp and lit it. "I couldn't sleep either. At least, until about an hour ago."

"Sorry about that," Rome said.

He seemed to fill the small room with his presence, crowding Quyloc so that there was no longer any place for him. He felt a surge of anger at Rome. This was his place; Rome had no right to be here.

Rome started pacing the room and Quyloc sighed and sat down. Rome had something on his mind, and when he got like this the only thing to do was hear him out. "What is it?" he asked wearily, rubbing his eyes.

"I've been thinking."

Quyloc smelled rum on his breath and knew that wasn't all he'd been doing.

"We have to *do* something, something bold."

392

Here it comes, Quyloc thought, knowing he probably wouldn't be able to talk Rome out of whatever idea he'd had, that he had the bit in his teeth now and he was going to run with it and damn the consequences.

"It's time to attack."

Quyloc blinked, surprised. "What? You mean march out against them?"

"No. That would be suicide. I'm talking about just you and me."

"You want the two of us to attack Melekath and his Children by *ourselves*?" Had Rome lost it? How much rum had he drunk? Was the pressure getting to him finally?

"Don't be stupid. I'm talking about just attacking Melekath. You with your spear, me with the axe. We could bring him down. Sure, he'll be more dangerous than Tharn or Kasai were, but we'll be working together. Just you and me, like it's always been. We can do it. I know we can."

Quyloc shook his head. "Even if that could somehow work, didn't you hear what Ricarn said? It's not Melekath we have to worry about; it's the Children. They're the real danger."

Rome brushed off his concern. "I heard her, all right. I'm sure she's right. But something else occurred to me. Remember what the FirstMother said when you asked her if she could put up a shield to protect the city like the Tenders did to protect Kaetria in the final days?"

"Yes. She said she'd need hundreds more Tenders and about a year to prepare such a thing."

"Then she said the biggest shield they could possibly put up would only be large enough to cover the main gates."

"So? What are you getting at? What good would that do us?"

"After she said that, Ricarn said a shield that small wouldn't do any good because Melekath would just melt a hole in our walls to let the Children in." Rome grinned at him like a kid who's just found a way to sneak in and steal food from the kitchen.

Quyloc stared at him and it took a minute before he figured out where Rome was going with this. "You think if we take down Melekath then we won't need a shield larger than the gates."

"Exactly," Rome said, his head bobbing. "It doesn't matter how strong they are, how deadly, if they can't get through our walls. Without Melekath, they won't be able to do that."

Quyloc considered this. As implausible as it was, there was some merit to the plan. If it worked, it would at least buy them some time. "We should call a meeting and get some input from the others."

"No. We should just do it. Now."

"Are you crazy?"

"Maybe. But last night Ricarn said the Children would probably arrive in two days. We're running out of time. Besides, I want to attack him while it's still dark. Catch him off guard." Through Quyloc's surprise he noted that Rome had the black axe strapped to his back.

"Even if we decided to do this, they're still miles away. There's no way we could get there before the sun comes up."

Rome grinned and it was feral in the lamplight. "We could if you took us through the borderland. Like you did when you crossed the battlefield and attacked Kasai."

"What? I don't even know if I can travel that far, much less take you with me."

"But you could at least try. If it doesn't work, well, no harm done."

"It's a terrible idea. At the very least we should tell the others what we're doing so they know if something goes wrong."

Rome's grin faded. "This isn't a request, Quyloc. It's an order. We're going and we're going now."

"You don't know what you're saying, Rome," Quyloc protested. "To go in there and travel for miles? I doubt if I could even lead us to the right spot."

"How did you find the right spot with Kasai?"

"I don't know. I could just *feel* that thing's presence." Quyloc's words trailed off. Maybe he *could* find Melekath in there.

"Surely Melekath would be even easier to find. We can do this, Quyloc. Let's go right now, hit him before he's awake. We strike fast, we strike hard, and then we get out. He won't be expecting it. If we wait until he's here, we'll lose the surprise. We have to hit him now while he's unprepared."

Quyloc tried one last gasp. "You have no idea how dangerous that place is. We could both be killed and what will happen to the city then?"

Rome shrugged. "It's a gamble. It's betting on throwing hooded eyes on the last toss of stinger, down three games to one. But dammit, we have to do something! Our deaths, everyone's deaths, are staring us right in the face. What do we really have to lose?"

As much as he hated to admit it, Quyloc knew that Rome was right. What did they have left to lose? "Okay," he said softly. "I'm in."

Rome clapped him on the shoulder. "I knew you'd see it my way in the end. Just the two of us, the way it's always been. One more time for all the coins."

SIXTY-SIX

When it came right down to it, taking Rome into the borderland was easier than Quyloc thought it would be. He told Rome to hold the black axe in one hand and sit down on the cot, then pulled his chair close enough that he could put his hand on Rome's arm. He told Rome to close his eyes and sit still. That was actually the hard part. The big man had worked himself up to this and sitting still was almost impossible for him. He kept shifting and muttering under his breath until finally Quyloc cursed at him, told him to knock it off or get out of his room.

Once Rome finally subsided, Quyloc was able to draw the Veil in his mind easily. There was the inner lurch and when he opened his eyes he and Rome were there. Yellow sand stretched forever under a purple-black sky. Slicing the world in half was the Veil, fragile barrier between two worlds. Nalene had told him what Velma learned from Perganon about the nature of the *Pente Akka*, how it was a leak, a bubble that oozed through from the abyss when the prison was formed. At the heart of the *Pente Akka* loomed the *gromdin*, the massive creature Quyloc had glimpsed that time when he killed Rome's would-be assassins. That thing sought to tear open the Veil and let his world pour into their own; that was why it was so drawn to Song. Quyloc wondered then if every time he passed through the Veil if he weakened it slightly. He shook the thought away. One problem at a time.

Rome was staring around, openmouthed. *It's real*, he said.

Something caught Quyloc's attention. *What's happening to the axe?*

Rome looked down. Black powder, as fine and dark as coal dust, was blowing off the axe and dissipating. It was as if the axe was slowly dissolving in his hands. Rome turned the axe over in his hands. *I think we should get out of here as fast as we can.* He looked up. *Which way do we go?*

Quyloc slowly turned around. Except where the world was bisected by the Veil, the horizon was the same featureless sand in every direction. He started to say he had no idea when, surprisingly, he did. He could feel a presence in the distance, a powerful one. It had to be Melekath.

That way.

How long they walked was impossible to say. Time just didn't mean anything in this place. What was unusual was that, although the direction Quyloc chose appeared to lead away from the Veil at a sharp angle, after they had been walking for a while, he looked to his left and saw that the Veil was still there.

After a time, Quyloc felt the presence grow stronger and ahead in the strange darkness he glimpsed a faint, fuzzy glow. He pointed.

I think that's him.

Rome nodded and switched the axe to a two-handed grip. There was no need to talk tactics. They'd fought together too many times in the past. Spread out. Come at their opponent from two directions. Hit him fast, hit him hard and, above all else, hit him at the same time. No one could defend two directions at the same time.

Quyloc held up his hand and they came to a stop. Holding his spear in his right hand, he placed his left on Rome's shoulder. He took a deep breath and then they ran forward.

They emerged into the gray light of predawn. There was the smell of salt in the air, blown on a strong breeze. Nearby was the shattered remains of a town, still smoking in places. They were on the road leading into the town, the ocean just visible through a break in the line of dead trees standing between them and the beach. A figure in tattered clothing was on the road, half turned away from them. He had his arms wrapped around himself as if in pain. Quyloc knew instantly that this was Melekath. There was no one else nearby, though from the direction of the beach came the sound of voices raised in argument.

Instantly they ran at him. Quyloc was quicker, the spear giving him a longer reach. Melekath turned just as he reached him, surprise on his face, and Quyloc stabbed him twice in the chest. Melekath fell back with a cry and then Rome hit him, the axe whining through the air, the whine turning to a discordant screech when it bit deep into his shoulder and cut down into his chest.

Melekath staggered backwards. Rome and Quyloc split up and continued to rain attacks on him from both sides. Melekath defended himself only feebly. More wounds appeared. There was no blood, only a darkness inside the wounds that snapped and popped with energy.

There was the sound of breaking wood and from the line of newly-dead trees burst half a dozen apparitions from a nightmare, bent, twisted things that had once been human. At their head was a thick, hulking brute with a square head and burned-red skin.

Quyloc called a warning but Rome was already reacting. The red-skinned brute swung a fist like a small barrel at Rome's head. Rome ducked and swung the axe, cutting halfway through the man's leg and drawing a grunt of pain.

"Don't let them touch you!" Quyloc yelled. Then he could spare no more attention for Rome as three ran at him. Despite how misshapen the Children were, they moved with unnatural speed and hunger glittered in their eyes. One misstep, Quyloc thought. One mistake. That would be all he'd get.

The first one ran at him with his arms spread wide. Quyloc sidestepped him easily and stabbed him in the side of the neck as he went by. As the spear pierced his flesh there was a sizzling sound and the man screamed.

He spun and used the butt of the spear to thrust away the next one, knocking her off balance, her arms pinwheeling. The third one slowed and came in more cautiously. Quyloc stabbed him twice in the chest, shallow jabs, careful not to get his weapon stuck. The man's flesh sizzled like the first, he screamed and fell back, clutching his chest. There was no blood, but the flesh around the wounds turned black.

Quyloc heard a bellow from Rome and looked up to see that two more of the Children had converged on the big man. The black axe was a deadly blur and every swing left severed limbs and cries of pain in its wake, but their hunger was the greater force and nothing Rome did to them slowed them for long.

Two more ran at Quyloc, converging from the left and the right. Before they could close on him he darted between them, stabbing one through the cheek and hitting the other in the side of the head with the butt of the spear.

It was time to leave.

The problem was that in the fighting, whether by chance or by design, Quyloc and Rome had been driven further and further apart, and there were at least four of the Children between them. He needed to be touching Rome in order to get them out of there and he couldn't even get to him.

All at once Quyloc knew that things had just gotten a lot worse. He felt a new presence arrive on the scene, someone more powerful than the rest, from whom power radiated like heat off a furnace. He started to turn to confront this new threat when a hand as cold as death latched onto his shoulder.

Instantly, his strength failed him. He gasped and staggered sideways, turning his head to look as he did so. He saw a tall woman with flaming red hair, dressed in a scarlet dress. Her face was stretched in a cruel smile.

Somehow, with a strength he didn't know he still had, Quyloc managed to bring the spear around and swing it clumsily. The blade bit deep into her forearm, the weapon sizzled, she cursed and let him go. Energy returned to his limbs and he spun away, feinting with the spear to drive her back.

Definitely time to go. Quyloc turned to Rome.

Attackers surrounded his old friend in an ever-tightening knot. Somehow Rome found an instant to meet Quyloc's eye.

"Get out of here!" he yelled. "Just go!" He hacked at another one of the Children and fell back another step. He stumbled slightly as he did so and an attacker slipped past his defenses and got a hand on his right elbow.

His arm dropped and Quyloc thought Rome was dead for sure. But somehow he caught hold of the axe with his left hand as it fell from the nerveless fingers of his right. He brought the weapon up in a back swing and the blade bit deep into the attacker's side, just below his ribcage. The man howled and fell back, losing his hold on Rome's elbow.

Rome jerked the axe free and used the blade to shove the man backwards into two more who were rushing forward, which bought him a little breathing space, but it wouldn't last long and neither would he, not with his right arm dangling uselessly.

"Oh, no," Quyloc said under his breath. "You're not doing this to me."

He took off running. How he got through them he would never know. He fought like a madman, the spear an extension of his will, too fast even for thoughts. As if it had a mind of its own the spear flashed this way and that, stabbing and cutting. He ducked and dodged flailing limbs, aware that he was yelling incoherently.

He saw one woman rise up in front of him and stabbed her through the throat. There was no room to dodge and no time to slow so as she went down he simply leapt over her.

Only two more stood between him and Rome. He slammed one on the side of the head with the butt of the spear just as Rome hit the other on the hip with his axe.

Quyloc took another step, reaching for Rome –

A hand grabbed his heel.

His leg went dead and Quyloc pitched face first onto the ground.

The Children howled and surged forward.

Quyloc rolled, saw Rome step forward to meet the new attack, and desperately grabbed onto Rome's leg.

He drew the Veil in his mind even as he cringed inwardly, waiting for the coldness as his life was stolen from him…

Rome swung his axe, knowing there were too many of them, that they were coming too fast, and all at once the world changed and he was standing on the sand under a purple-black sky.

We made it.

He tried to reach down with his right hand to help Quyloc up but his right arm was like a block of ice, completely numb and useless. Quyloc rolled away and made it to his knees, where he paused, trying to breathe.

We did it, Rome said. *You did it. I don't know how, you crazy bastard, but you did. Once again I owe you my life.* He reached down with his left hand – still keeping his grip on the black axe – and Quyloc took hold of his forearm and Rome pulled him to his feet. Quyloc tried to stand on his own, but one of his legs was as useless as Rome's right arm and he had to settle for leaning on Rome for support.

I just want to say, Quyloc gasped, *that was a terrible idea.*

But we did it! We hurt him, Quyloc. I know we did. We hurt him bad. And we proved that his Children can be hurt as well.

Quyloc seemed to be considering this. Then he nodded. *Maybe it wasn't total idiocy.* He met Rome's eyes for the first time and smiled slightly. *You idiot. When will you learn to listen to your chief adviser?*

Rome grinned broadly. He felt good. The doom had lifted. Battle had a way of doing that for him, clarifying things, making everything fall into perspective. *Wait till we tell Tairus about this*, he said. *Let's get out of here, go back home.*

Rome turned, trying to get his bearings, although it was hopeless because everything looked the same. *Which way do –*

Four black lines shot out of the Veil with the speed of striking snakes. In the split second before they hit, Quyloc instinctively raised the spear. The black lines wrapped around him, pinning his arms, and the spear, to his sides. The lines tightened and Quyloc was jerked toward the Veil.

On the other side of the Veil stood the hunter, hauling in its prey.

Instinctively, Rome dropped the black axe and grabbed onto Quyloc's arm, trying to drag him back. For a second he slowed Quyloc down but, though he dug his heels in and fought as hard as he could, he had no purchase under his feet. Quyloc was dragged closer to the Veil. One step. Then another. They were only about three steps away now.

Rome's eyes went to the axe, lying on the sand. Would it cut through the black lines and free his friend? It was their only chance. But to grab it he would have to let go of Quyloc and hope he was fast enough.

Before he could act, there was another, harder jerk. Rome lost his balance and then it was too late.

They struck the Veil and were dragged through.

SIXTY-SEVEN

"Something is happening over there," Shorn said.

Netra straightened from where she'd been getting a rock out of her shoe and hurried up to stand beside Shorn. Down in the bottom of the small valley she could see that most of the Children were clustered together around something. "I wonder what it is." She shaded her eyes against the rising sun. "It looks like there's someone on the ground. Can you see who it is?"

A moment later Shorn said, "I believe it is Melekath."

"Really? Your eyes must be better than mine."

"He is injured."

"How could that happen?"

"There are others who are injured as well." Shorn pointed.

The sun was starting to break over the horizon and the light was getting better. Squinting, Netra could see that there were a half dozen figures on the ground. A couple didn't seem to be moving. "Have they been fighting among themselves, do you think?" A stranger thought occurred to her. "Were they attacked?" Shorn didn't answer. Netra turned to him. "I have to get closer. I have to know what happened."

"You said they would be able to sense us if we got too close."

"You, yes, but I think I can do it if I go alone."

Shorn shook his head. "It is too risky. I can't help you if we don't stay together."

"I can do this," Netra said, getting excited now. "You forget. I can seal off my Song. And I can pull away the flow that is attached to me as well. They won't be able to sense me."

"It is too dangerous," Shorn stubbornly insisted.

"I can't pass up this chance. If that really is Melekath down on the ground, we have to know more. How badly injured is he? How about the others? Don't you see? This could be the chance we've been hoping for. If someone or something managed to attack and hurt them like this we have to know who it was and how they did it. Of course it's dangerous. But any chance, however slim, is worth any risk. Don't try to stop me, Shorn. This is my chance to right some of what I've done. I have to take it."

Shorn took a deep breath, then nodded grudgingly.

"I need to hurry, while they're distracted." She moved away from Shorn and laid her pack on the ground. Closing her eyes, she slowed her breathing, her thoughts, and then took hold of an outgoing breath and let it pull her *beyond*. This close to the Children and the wake of their devastation *beyond* appeared much different. Gone were the familiar mists, leaving that once-familiar landscape stark and cold. Gone were the branching flows of Song; the only ones that remained were the ones connected to her and Shorn. Without Song, *beyond* was stark and cold and empty. Though it was not a physical cold, Netra shivered. There was something utterly bleak and even frightening about that ethereal landscape. She almost left then, thinking she should take Shorn's advice and let him lead her far away from here. What could she really learn after all? She was no doubt taking a needless risk. Shorn had been right before and she'd ignored him.

But she fought down that impulse and instead summoned her will, focusing it on her hands. Steeling herself, she plucked away the flow that was attached to her *akirma*.

Bitter, suffocating cold descended on her. Strength drained from her limbs and she staggered slightly. The colors of the morning went flat, so that what she saw of the ordinary world looked devoid of all color. She would not be able to survive this way for long. In a short time the Selfsong which was held within her *akirma* would fade and die away. When that happened, she would die as well. She needed to hurry.

After making sure that Shorn didn't look like he was going to follow her, she started down the gentle slope, walking as quietly as she knew how, staying to the cover of brush and trees as much as she could. It was eerie within that dead swath of land, almost like she was in a dream. There were no bird calls, no insect noises. Her steps sounded muffled and dead. Puffs of gray dust arose with each step. A bush she brushed against practically disintegrated – the leaves crumbled to ash and drifted to the ground – so that only the thicker limbs and the trunk remained standing.

It didn't take long to cover the distance down to where the Children were huddled. Out of necessity, Netra had to sacrifice some stealth for speed, but it didn't seem to make any difference. Whatever was happening up ahead seemed to have completely engrossed the Children. She could hear alarm in their voices, as well as conflict. Whatever had happened hadn't been something they'd expected, which made it more likely that Melekath's and the others' injuries were the result of some attack, rather than inner conflict.

She aimed for a small copse of dead trees that was near enough to the Children that she should be able to overhear them, yet far enough away that if she was discovered she should be able to stay out of their reach.

She made it to the trees and snuck into them. Her heart pounding – partly from fear, partly from the strain caused by the loss of Song – she crept through the trees until she could catch glimpses of the Children up ahead. Then she slowed even more, exercising the utmost caution to avoid brushing against a tree limb or stepping on any twigs or limbs on the ground. She made it to a tree that was larger than the others and ducked behind it, carefully peering around.

Her first thought was that the Children looked awful. They were bent, misshapen parodies of people, not people at all. Many had mismatched limbs. Their faces were deformed, missing teeth, misshapen skulls. Right in the middle was one with red skin, as if he'd suffered a severe sunburn. He was huge, with thick, trunk like legs, arms bulging with muscle. He was nearly as tall as Shorn and even broader. The others were clearly afraid of him.

Then she realized he was injured. One leg had been cut nearly through so that he had to lean on a tree limb to stay upright. Several others were injured as well, with puncture wounds or with deep cuts in limbs or torsos. The ones scattered about on the ground had been hit the worst. One was missing both legs. Another had been nearly decapitated. They cried out in feeble voices and tried to drag themselves toward the others, but none of the rest paid them any attention.

The group shifted and Netra saw Melekath for the first time. He didn't look like the fearsome monster she'd imagined her entire life. He looked, in fact, more like someone's grandfather, a slightly built, aging man with wispy hair and a tired face, though his skin was oddly streaked with black and red and there was something wrong with his proportions. There were stab wounds in his torso and a deep cut at the juncture of his neck and shoulder. There was no blood, nor could she see any organs visible in his chest, though the cut was deep enough.

As bad as the neck wound was, he seemed to pay it no attention, focusing instead on the stab wounds. From her state of heightened perception, Netra could *see* some sort of reddish energy spilling from him, energy that was nothing like Life Song. His face had gone pale and he was trying to staunch the wound, without much apparent success.

Most interesting of all was the fact that the Children gathered around him did not seem concerned about him at all. They looked interested, and some looked darkly happy, but not concerned. From the babble of voices she gleaned that they had been attacked by two men, one wielding a spear and the other an axe. They seemed to be arguing and there were two distinct camps.

One group was frightened by what had happened. These were the ones standing closest to Melekath. They claimed that the attack proved they were not ready to attack Qarath just yet, that they weren't strong enough. They wanted to turn off, find other towns or small cities and feed on them until they could take on Qarath.

The other group, the loudest one, led by the huge, red-skinned brute, was claiming that this meant the defenders of Qarath were desperate. Their best hope was to proceed as fast as they could and take the city. As Netra watched, the red-skinned brute lashed out with his massive fists and laid two members of the first group out flat, bellowing as he did so. That seemed to scare a number of those who opposed him into silence. Many stopped talking and began to edge away.

What did this mean? Netra wondered. Who had attacked them and how? Clearly they had not used ordinary weapons. The fact that they'd so grievously injured Melekath was proof of that. The Musician she and Shorn had encountered out in the desert had said the Protector was helping the Tenders. Had he given them those weapons?

Whatever was going on, this was great news. It meant that the defenders of Qarath were stronger than she'd thought. It meant they had a chance after all.

It was time to leave now. She couldn't hold out much longer cut off from Song like this and she and Shorn needed to get moving. She wanted to reach the city ahead of the Children. Maybe what she'd learned here would help. Maybe it wouldn't. But she would be there and she would throw herself heart and soul into the defense of the city.

Then a cold, powerful hand closed on the back of her neck and a woman's voice said:

"Look what I found."

Adrenalin coursed through her and Netra twisted and threw herself to the side, trying to get away. But it was to no avail. The hand held her as if she were no more than a puppy. The hand shook her.

"Stop that. It won't do you any good."

She was lifted into the air and turned, getting her first look at her captor. The hand belonged to a tall, red-haired woman. She was a regal woman, beautiful even, but it was a cold, emotionless beauty. The woman held her up and eyed her critically.

"I smelled you back there, you know," she said with a hint of a humorless smile. "Following us. You're not as clever as you think. I knew if I just waited, you'd come in on your own accord. I had a feeling that the attack on our dear father might just be the lure that would bring you in. So I waited, and watched, and sure enough, here you are."

The whole time she spoke Netra was fighting her, which only made the woman smile more broadly.

"It won't help. There's no way you can get away."

"We'll see about that," Netra gasped. A thought had occurred to her. She could sense the Song that swirled within the woman, a frightening amount of it, but not as much as had been in the trunk line she'd used to crack open the prison. She'd survived that; she could survive this. All she had to do was give into the hunger that waited inside her always. The Song within this woman was tainted, maybe even poisoned; it might kill her, but what other choice did she have?

Netra thrust the palm of her hand against the woman's heart, and let the desperate strength of her hunger free, throwing everything she had into a hammer blow at the woman's *akirma*…

And broke through.

Cold, oily Song spouted out and Netra grabbed onto it, sucking it greedily into her.

The red-haired woman's eyes went wide and with an oath she flung Netra away from her. Netra hit hard, hard enough that she thought she might have cracked a rib, but the need to escape outweighed the pain and almost instantly she leapt to her feet to flee.

She made it only one step when something struck her low down on the side of her rib cage, the impact great enough that she was thrown down again. She rolled and came to her knees and what she saw when she looked down at her side shocked her.

There was something attached to her, something that looked like a gauzy, grey-white tether. It felt like it had punched a hole in her, but there was no visible wound.

Instinctively, she grabbed at the thing and tried to rip it off, but it burned her hands when she touched it and she wasn't able to dislodge it. The pain in her hands grew too great and she had to let it go.

She looked up. The red-haired woman was standing there with her mouth open. She looked at the gauzy tether sprouting from her palm closer, her expression puzzled. She tugged on the tether experimentally, the action drawing a whimper from Netra.

"Well," she said, "I didn't expect that." She moved closer. "I guess you didn't either, did you?"

"What...what did you do?" Netra gasped. She could feel something inside her, branching out, spreading throughout her body.

"I don't exactly know. It seems I am acquiring new powers." She cocked her head to the side. "Oh, this is good. Can you feel that?"

Netra could. Song was beginning to drain from her body, trickling down the tether into the red-haired woman.

"I think this will prove useful," the woman said. "Don't you?" She shook her head when Netra didn't reply. "You surprised me, you know, attacking me like that. I didn't know there was anybody who could do that. I should be angry. I should kill you right now for daring to attack me, but I think I won't. I think I'll keep you alive. You taste good, and there is a great deal of Song within you, much more so than anyone else I've encountered." She gave Netra a piercing look. "It's almost as if you've been taking Song that didn't belong to you. Could that be it?"

Netra saw Shorn an instant before he charged the red-haired woman. She started to cry out, to warn him off, but it was too late.

Shorn hit the woman from behind and she flew forward and landed on her face. Before she could recover, he jumped and drove his feet into her back.

"Run!" he snarled at Netra.

"I can't!" she cried, gesturing at the tether.

Shorn grabbed at the tether, then jerked his hand back as it burned him.

In that instant when he was distracted, the red-haired woman reacted. With surprising strength, she rolled and threw Shorn off her back. Before he could recover, she latched onto his wrist with one hand. Netra felt the surge as she sought to drain his Song from him.

But Shorn's alien constitution saved him. Whether it was the unusual nature of his *akirma,* or the difference in his Song, she got enough to weaken him, but not enough to stop him.

With his other hand he punched her in the face, the blow hard enough to crack stone. Her head snapped back and she flew backwards. The movement caused the tether to jerk at Netra and she cried out.

Shorn leapt after her, hammering her with his powerful fists as she sought to rise. Netra heard his grunts as he landed each blow and she felt the pain that it was causing him.

Netra felt a jolt as the woman suddenly drew hard on Netra's Song, and she knew the woman was strengthening herself for a counterattack.

"Look out!" she yelled, but it was too late.

With a snarl of rage, the woman jumped to her feet and backhanded Shorn, knocking him sprawling. She threw out a hand and one of the grey-white tethers shot out and struck Shorn in the chest as he climbed to his feet.

Shorn was knocked down once again, but when the woman pulled on the tether it came free.

Surprise on the woman's face, turning quickly to new rage. "What are you?" she howled.

Netra felt the other Children approaching at a run. She saw the unusual clumsiness in Shorn's movements and knew that he had been badly weakened. He turned his head slightly, saw the other Children coming, then looked at Netra. As closely attuned as she and Shorn were, she knew instantly that he had decided to change tactics. He was going to try to snatch her and run.

But it wouldn't work. The tether was too strong. It had dug too deep. He wouldn't be able to break it, and if he ripped it free, it might kill her in the process.

"Get out of here!" Netra yelled. "Go! You can't save me!"

The red-haired woman hit Shorn with another tether, knocking him down yet again. This time he was slower to get up. His eyes darted around. Netra could feel his pure anguish.

"Run," she said again, her voice little more than a whisper this time. "Run."

Shorn turned and ran, leaving Netra to her captors.

The story concludes in *Oblivion's Grasp*.

Before you go!

I'd like to thank you for reading *Hunger's Reach*. As much as I love writing, it takes readers to make the experience complete. A journey shared is a much more powerful experience.

You may not be aware of this, but reviews are vitally important to unknown authors like me. They give other potential readers an idea of what to expect. So, if you have the time to leave one, I'd very much appreciate it. If you're busy (and who isn't?) leave a short one. Even one sentence is enough!

Glossary

abyss – place deep in the earth that is filled with unknown entities. It is the home of chaos power. Gulagh drew chaos power from the abyss and released it into the River, which is what is causing the strange diseases and mutations plaguing the land.

akirma – the luminous glow that surrounds every living thing. Contained within it is Selfsong. When it is torn, Selfsong escapes. It also acts as a sort of transformative filter, changing raw LifeSong, which is actually unusable by living things, into Selfsong.

Ankha del'Ath – ancestral home of the Takare. Empty since the slaughter at Wreckers Gate.

aranti – Shapers of the Sphere of Sky that dwell within the wind. They are the only Shapers never to war against the others.

Atria – (AY-tree-uh) name commonly used to refer to the landmass where the story takes place. It is a derivation of the name Kaetria, which was the name of the old Empire.

Banishment – when the Eight created Melekath's prison and sank the city of Durag'otal underground.

Bereth – a Shaper of the Sphere of Stone, one of the Eight, who together with Xochitl laid siege to the city of Durag'otal. Along with the Shaper Larkind, he discovered the abyss and tried to enter it. Larkin was destroyed and Bereth was permanently damaged. He is the primary god in Thrikyl.

beyond – also known as "in the mists," the inner place where Tenders can *see* Song.

Bonnie – Rome's girlfriend, pregnant with his child.

Book of Xochitl – the Tenders' sacred book.

Brelisha – old Tender at Rane Haven who taught the young Tenders.

blinded ones – those people who have had their eyes burned out by Kasai. They gain the ability to use Kasai's gray fire and are in direct contact with the Guardian.

chaos power – The power that comes from the abyss. It is completely inimical to all power in the normal world, including LifeSong, Stone force, Sky force, and Sea force. Chaos power was drawn from the abyss by the Eight to form Melekath's prison. When they did so, they did not seal the opening completely and chaos power has been leaking into the world ever since, forming the shadow world of the *Pente Akka*. The sand dunes of the Gur al Krin are a physical manifestation of chaos power that has contacted the normal world.

Children – people who received Melekath's Gift of immortality.

Crodin – nomadic people who live along the edge of the Gur al Krin desert.

Dorn – Windcaller that Shakre had an affair with as a young woman. Netra's father.

Dreamwalker – the Dreamwalkers are those who are responsible for guiding the Takare in spiritual and supernatural matters.

Dubron – one of the Children.

Durag'otal – (DER-awg OH-tal) city founded by Melekath as a haven for his Children. It was sunk underground in the Banishment.

Eight — eight Shapers of the First Ring who besieged the city of Durag'otal, formed a prison of chaos power around it, and sank it underground.

Elihu – (eh-LIE-who) the Plantwalker for Bent Tree Shelter and Shakre's closest friend.

Fanethrin – (FAIN-thrin) city to the northwest that Kasai controls. Part of the old Empire.

feeder lines – the intermediate sized current of LifeSong, between the trunk lines, which come off the River directly, and the flows, which sustain individual creatures.

Ferien – town that the Children feed on on their way to Thrikyl.

Firkath Mountains – mountains just to the north of Rane Haven.

FirstMother – title of the leader of the Tenders.

First Ring – the oldest and most powerful of the Shapers, the first to arrive on the world. They refer to themselves as the Nipashanti

flows – the smallest currents of LifeSong. One of these is attached to each living thing and acts as a conduit to constantly replenish the energy that radiates outward from the *akirma* and dissipates. If the flow attached to a living thing is severed, it will only live for at most a few hours longer.

Gift – immortality. Melekath, seeing that the *akirmas* of living creatures eventually grow brittle and crack open, thus leading to death, came up with a way to make *akirmas* unbreakable. Essentially, he siphoned off from his immortal essence and infused it into the *akirmas* of those who chose to accept the Gift, permanently altering them.

Golgath – one of the Shapers that stood with Xochitl at the siege of Durag'otal. He was the only one of the Eight who was a Sea Shaper.

Gorim – one of the Shapers that stood with Xochitl at the siege of Durag'otal. Worshipped in Veragin, the dead city Rome found at the end of the summer campaign, where T'sim was found.

Gomen nai – Crodin name for Melekath.

gromdin – the leader of the *Pente Akka*. It seeks to steal enough Song to shred the Veil, thus allowing the *Pente Akka* to spill freely into the world.

Gulagh – one of the three Guardians of the Children, also known as the Voice, in control of the city of Nelton. It has discovered a way

412

to make a small opening into the abyss and when chaos power leaks out, use a living person to feed that power back up the flow of LifeSong sustaining that person and ultimately into the River itself. It is this poison in the River which is causing the strange diseases and mutations plaguing the land.

Gur al Krin – desert that formed over the spot where Durag'otal was sunk underground. The dunes are formed by power leaking from the *Pente Akka* and contacting the normal world.

Heartglow – the brighter glow in the center of a person's *akirma*. Like concentrated Selfsong. When it goes out, the person is dead.

Heram – one of the two leaders of the Children, a blocky, muscular man who was a blacksmith in his former life.

Ilsith – Lowellin's staff. Nothing is known of this creature or why it obeys Lowellin.

ingerlings – ravenous creatures Kasai took from the abyss.

Intyr – Dreamwalker for Bent Tree Shelter.

Jenett – young Lementh'kal who helps Shorn and Netra.

Kaetria – (KAY-tree-uh) capital city of the Old Empire.

Karthije – (CAR-thidge) kingdom neighboring Qarath to the northwest.

Karrl & Linde – husband and wife of the Children.

Karyn – (CARE-in) Tender from Rane Haven.

Kasai — one of the three Guardians of Melekath, also known as the Eye. Kasai discovered a way to take the *ingerlings* from the abyss and use them against Tu Sinar. It was badly injured by Quyloc with the *rendspear* at the battle of Guardians Watch.

Khanewal – one of the Eight, the hooded figure Quyloc sometimes encountered at the entrance to the *Pente Akka*.

ki'Loren – sentient, floating island that is home to some of the Lementh'kal.

Larkind — a Shaper of the Sphere of Stone. He was destroyed eons before when he and Bereth tried to Shape chaos power from the abyss.

Lementh'kal – beings who live on the ocean. Followers of Golgath.

Lenda – simpleminded Tender who accidentally received two *sulbits* and lost control of them.

LifeSong – energy that flows from the River and to all living things. It turns into Selfsong after it passes through the *akirma*, which acts as a sort of filter to turn the raw energy of LifeSong into something usable by the living thing.

Lowellin – (low-EL-in) Shaper of the Second Ring who turned the humans against Melekath while he was away creating the Gift. He also created a rift between humans and Xochitl.

macht – title from the old Empire meaning supreme military leader of all the phalanxes. Adopted by Rome for himself instead of king.

melding — when a Tender allows her *sulbit* to join with her on a deep level. In order for a Tender to meld with her *sulbit* she has to lower her inner defenses and allow the creature into the deepest recesses of her being. Her will must be strong to keep it from taking over.

Melekath – powerful Shaper of the Sphere of Stone, one of the First Ring. After eons of existence, he became bored with Shaping and created Life by taking energy from the three Spheres of Stone, Sea, and Sky. Still this was not enough. He desired living things who were free-willed, that he could talk to, and so created people. However, then he could not bear to see them die, so went away for hundreds of years and created the Gift of immortality. It was during this absence that Lowellin turned people against him and caused them to forget he was their creator.

Musician – one of a highly secretive brotherhood who can manipulate LifeSong to create Music that transports the listener. One saves Bonnie and the others when the Grinning Pig tavern is attacked.

Naills – castellan of Qarath.

Nalene – FirstMother of the Tenders.

Nelton – small city where Netra and Siena encountered the Guardian Gulagh.

Nicandro – aide to Wulf Rome.

Nipashanti – what the Shapers of the First Ring call themselves.

Ominati – secret organization in Kaetria that was studying the power within the Spheres in an attempt to harness that power to defend Kaetria against the encroaching sands of the Gur al Krin. It was their headquarters where Netra and Shorn took refuge in *Hunger's Reach*. They were all killed when they began to meddle with Sea force, the power within the Sphere of Sea. Golgath sent the *zhoulin* to slaughter them all.

Orenthe – Tender who received the Gift. Filled with horror over those she has killed, she tries not to join in the slaughter at Thrikyl. When she does anyway, she takes hold of a trunk line so that she is torn to pieces and can never hurt another person again.

Owina – one of the Tenders from Rane Haven.

Pastwalker – the Pastwalkers are entrusted with remembering the past. They can take others to actually relive past events from the history of the Takare.

pelti – Shapers from the Sphere of Stone.

Pente Akka – the shadow world that Lowellin showed Quyloc how to access. It is formed of chaos energy leaking from the abyss.

Perganon – palace historian/librarian.

Perthen – king of Karthije.

Pinlir – Takare man who was opposed to the use of violence until his father was killed by the outsiders. He is Rehobim's right-hand man and is later inhabited by the spirit of Kirtet.

Plains of Dem – where the Takare defeated the Sertithians, thus saving the Empire from being conquered.

Plantwalker – the Plantwalkers are Takare who are sensitive to plants and can even communicate with them in a fashion.

Protaxes – one of the Eight, who together with Xochitl laid siege to the city of Durag'otal. Worshipped in Qarath by the nobility.

Qarath – (kuh-RATH) city ruled by Rome.

Quyloc – (KWY-lock) Rome's chief adviser and oldest friend.

Radagon – man who went away with Melekath when he left to create the Gift.

Rane Haven – where Netra grew up.

Rehobim – (reh-HOE-bim) Takare who is first to receive one of the old spirits, that of Tarnin, former leader of the Takare.

Rekus – (REE-kus) Pastwalker for Bent Tree Shelter.

relif crystal – type of crystal that can serve as a focal point for Stone power.

Reminder – a many-pointed star enclosed in a circle, the holy symbol of the Tenders.

rendspear — weapon Quyloc made in the *Pente Akka* from a tooth of the *rend,* lashed to a tree limb from the jungle, then doused in the River. It is capable of slicing through the flows of the three Spheres, as well as those of Life.

Reyna – one of two leaders of the Children, she was a powerful noblewoman in old Qarath.

Ricarn – Tender of the Arc of Insects.

River – the fundamental source of all LifeSong, deep in the mists of *beyond.*

ronhym – race of ancient shapeshifting beings that are able to merge with the stone, manipulate it and move around in it at will.

seeing – the act of perceiving with inner, extrasensory perception. It has nothing to do with the eyes yet what the mind perceives while *seeing* is interpreted by the brain as visual imagery.

Selfsong – when LifeSong passes through a person's *akirma* it becomes Selfsong, which is the energy of Life in a form that can be utilized by the body. It dissipates at death. It is continually replenished, yet retains a pattern that is unique to each individual.

Sententu – a *pelti*, Shaper of the Sphere of Stone, one of the Eight who joined with Xochitl to besiege Durag'otal. He sacrificed himself to fill in the crack in the prison.

Sertith – high grassland area to the north of Qarath. Nomadic horse warriors live there. It is believed they toppled the old Empire after it grew weak.

Shakre – Netra's mother. She lives with the Takare, having been driven to the Plateau by the wind after being exiled from the Tenders.

Shapers – powerful beings inhabiting the world long before life. Each belongs to one of the three Spheres, Stone, Sea or Sky, though some left to be part of the Circle of Life.

shlikti – Shapers of the Sphere of Sea.

Shorn – powerful humanoid from Themor who was exiled and crashed to earth near the Godstooth.

sonkrill – talismans that the Tenders receive/discover at the end of their Songquest. The use of *sonkrill* came about after the fall of the Empire, as the Tenders sought to recover their lost power.

Sounder – one who has an affinity for the Sea and its denizens. Due to the ancient wars between the Shapers of the Sea and those of the Stone, in which many people died and the seas and coastal areas abandoned, the people of Atria have a long history of fearing the Sea. As a result Sounders risk injury and death if they are found out.

Spheres – Stone, Sea and Sky.

spirit-kin – Takare who have received the spirit of a Takare ancestor. The spirits are those who did not follow the Takare into exile, believing it to be a mistake.

spirit-walking — an ability that the Tenders of old had, a way of separating the spirit from the body, the spirit then leaving the body behind to travel on without it. A thin silver thread connects the spirit to the body. If the thread is broken, there is no way for the spirit to find its way back to the body.

sulbit – creatures that dwell in the River, living on pure LifeSong. In an effort to gain allies in the fight against Melekath, Lowellin gives them to the Tenders. When a Tender melds with her *sulbit*, she gains the creature's natural affinity for Song. As the *sulbit* becomes larger and stronger, the Tender can use its ability to touch and manipulate Song.

T'sim – (TUH-sim) *aranti* Rome meets in the dead city of Veragin.

Tairus – (TEAR-us) General of the army.

Takare – (tuh-KAR-ee) the greatest warriors of the old Empire. After the slaughter at Wreckers Gate they renounced violence and migrated to the Landsend Plateau.

Tel'al – Tender who first discovered the *Pente Akka.*

tenken ya – Themorian life debt.

terin'ai – the Themorian warrior's search for the hidden self. To face it is to face one's self honestly, without excuses or regrets. It is the greatest battle a Themorian can fight.

Tharn — one of the three Guardians charged with protecting Melekath's Children, also known as the Fist. Rome badly wounded it with the black axe in the battle at Guardians Watch.

Themor – Shorn's home planet.

Thrikyl – coastal city, most of whose inhabitants killed themselves to avoid being killed by the Children.

Trakar Kurnash – leader of the band of Crodin killed by the Children.

Truebane Mountains – home to Ankha del'Ath, ancestral home of the Takare.

trunk lines – the huge flows of LifeSong that branch directly off the River. From the trunk lines the feeder lines branch off, and off the feeder lines come the individual flows that directly sustain every living thing.

Tu Sinar – one of the Eight, who hid under the Landsend Plateau and was the first Shaper destroyed by the *ingerlings*.

velen'aa – Themorian term. "*Velen'aa* is not just war. It is any fight which fills a warrior's life. To embrace it is the beginning of *unserti* (wisdom)."

Velma – Tender that Nalene leaves in charge when she leaves with the army.

Werthin – young Takare man who carries Shakre off the Plateau and keeps an eye on her.

Windcaller – men reputed to be able to call the wind and make it serve them. They are considered blasphemers by the Tenders.

Windrider – name given by the Takare to Shakre after she rides the wind to save the people of Bent Tree Shelter when the Plateau is tearing itself apart.

Wreckers Gate – the name of the main gate protecting Ankha del'Ath, ancestral home of the Takare. According to the Takare, the wealth and acclaim they received as the Empire's greatest heroes blinded them. Eventually a rogue Takare led the Takare still living at Ankha del'Ath to rebel and the great gate was shut. The Takare legions returned home and slaughtered their kinsmen. When they realized what they had done, they threw down their weapons,

419

forswore violence, and moved to the Landsend Plateau, where the affairs of the world could no longer tempt them.

Wulf Rome – leader of Qarath.

Xochitl (so-SHEEL) – the deity worshipped by the Tenders. She is a Nipashanti of the First Ring and was a Shaper of the Sphere of Stone before moving to Life.

Ya'Shi – Lementh'kal who abducted Netra and Shorn to save them from the *zhoulin.*

Yelvin – name of the two Insect Tenders who accompany Ricarn.

Youlin – (YOU-lin) young Pastwalker from Mad River Shelter. She awakens the Takare warriors to their past lives and calls in the old spirits.

zhoulin – powerful, deadly creature that Golgath sent to kill the Ominati when they began to meddle with Sea force.

ABOUT THE AUTHOR

Born in 1965, I grew up on a working cattle ranch in the desert thirty miles from Wickenburg, Arizona, which at that time was exactly the middle of nowhere. Work, cactus and heat were plentiful, forms of recreation were not. The TV got two channels when it wanted to, and only in the evening after someone hand cranked the balky diesel generator to life. All of which meant that my primary form of escape was reading.

At 18 I escaped to Tucson where I attended the University of Arizona. A number of fruitless attempts at productive majors followed, none of which stuck. Discovering I liked writing, I tried journalism two separate times, but had to drop it when I realized that I had no intention of conducting interviews with actual people but preferred simply making them up.

After graduating with a degree in Creative Writing in 1989, I backpacked Europe with a friend and caught the travel bug. With no meaningful job prospects, I hitchhiked around the U.S. for a while then went back to school to learn to be a high school English teacher. I got a teaching job right out of school in the middle of the year. The job lasted exactly one semester, or until I received my summer pay and realized I actually had money to continue backpacking.

The next stop was Australia, where I hoped to spend six months, working wherever I could, then a few months in New Zealand and the South Pacific Islands. However, my plans changed irrevocably when I met a lovely Swiss woman, Claudia, in Alice Springs. Undoubtedly swept away by my lack of a job or real future, she agreed to allow me to follow her back to Switzerland where, a few months later, she gave up her job to continue traveling with me. Over the next couple years we backpacked the U.S., Eastern Europe and Australia/New Zealand, before marrying and settling in the mountains of Colorado, in a small town called Salida.

In Colorado we started our own electronics business (because, you know, my Creative Writing background totally prepared me for installing home theater systems), and had a couple of sons, Dylan and Daniel. In 2005 we shut the business down and moved back to Tucson where we currently live.